Four Contemporary Romance Novellas

Romancing the Elements

Ellen E. Withers

Delores Topliff

Tonya B. Ashley

Jenny Carlisle

Scrivenings
PRESS
Quench your thirst for story.
www.ScriveningsPress.com

Ellen E. Withers

Scrivenings
PRESS
Quench your thirst for story.
www.ScriveningsPress.com

For my grandsons. Ben, Wyatt, Dylan, Liam, Jack, Dax, and Maverick.

One

Amelia Kincaid wanted to scream.

Instead, she turned her attention away from the frustrating meeting and gazed out the conference room windows. Her office building bordered downtown Chicago's Grant Park, which resembled a winter wonderland with snow-covered grass and shrubs. Bare tree branches whipped back and forth in the fierce wind. Arctic temperatures had arrived.

Even a walk in this frigid weather would be an improvement over this torturous meeting. As a girl, she'd always run from boredom to seek something fascinating.

"Windy Jack" droned on and on about his team. In his recent management evaluation, she'd cautioned him about his proclivity for rambling during meetings. It wasted everyone's time and made him seem pompous. Now here he was, at it again. He'd failed to take her admonition to heart.

She gritted her teeth and fought to keep her facial expressions neutral. "Windy Jack" appeared to be blowing inside as much as Mother Nature blew outside. Time to intervene.

Before she could say anything, a knock sounded on the conference room door.

Heads turned toward the noise.

Heather, Amelia's administrative assistant, peeked in. "Sorry to disturb. There is an important call for Ms. Kincaid. An emergency."

Amelia leaped to her feet, delighted for the excuse to end the meeting. "Jack, hold the rest of your thoughts until next week. Everyone, thank you for all your hard work. Now, please excuse me."

Once in the hall, Heather passed Amelia her cell phone. In a whisper, she added, "It's your sister."

"Thanks, Heather." Amelia took the phone. "Bells. What's wrong?"

Belinda sobbed at the other end of the worldwide cellular network.

Amelia rushed to her office and closed the door.

"I can't ... I can't handle it anymore. The dogs, the kids, Dan's needs ... everyone looks to me to be the problem-solver. I'm toast."

"It must be hard to handle everything your family throws at you," Amelia said. "You have a multitude of responsibilities. Wife, mother, homeschool teacher, housekeeper, animal wrangler, and seamstress."

Guilt stabbed Amelia's heart. She'd been so busy working, she failed to notice the pressure on her sister. She should have scheduled a fun weekend together or invited her to Chicago for a visit. Either of these options would have given her a break from her family.

Belinda was her favorite sister. That she was also her only sister didn't diminish her affection. Although opposite in personality and interests, sisterhood drew them together.

Amelia murmured inadequate words of apology. "We're long overdue for a sisters' weekend. It's been nearly a year since I've seen you, and that's my fault."

Belinda sniffed. "I'm losing my mind, Melly. Between

homeschooling the kids, Dan's work hours, taking care of the house and the animals, I've become ... like a machine. A machine that's breaking down and crumbling."

"You're a wonderful mother and wife. I don't understand what prompted this. Is your health okay?"

Belinda blew her nose. "I guess so. I feel overwhelmed. Like I can't handle one more thing. Not one."

"So, what pushed you over the edge?"

"It's only a few weeks until Hope's birthday, and two days ago, she decided the Suzy Lou doll was the only thing she wanted."

Amelia wasn't familiar with Suzy Lou dolls. "Is that a bad thing?"

"It is when none are available. She's sold out at local stores, and the online shops list her as unavailable. If Hope wanted other things, this wouldn't be a big deal. But all she wants is this doll."

"Any chance you can teach her about supply and demand?"

Crickets.

"Okay, I'm sorry. I merely thought I'd try humor to cheer you."

"When you find some, point it out to me."

With a dramatic voice, Amelia said, "You wound me with sarcasm."

"Sorry." Belinda sighed. "She's a sweet girl, and I can't allow her to think we don't care about her birthday wishes."

Amelia cleared her throat and took a stab at the root of the problem. "Although the search for the doll is frustrating, you need a break. A vacation."

"Yes, I do." Belinda broke into more wailing. "But we can't afford a vacation. I'm stuck here, losing my mind."

While Amelia could not guarantee locating the doll, she could provide Belinda with some time away. Far from the children, animals, and everything else associated with the other household duties crushing the soul of her sister.

With Belinda "ugly crying" in her ear, Amelia cooed soothing words while she outlined a plan in her head. She'd accumulated a million vacation days because she always worked. Even though her teams were in the middle of developing an important marketing campaign right now, her sister's needs trumped work needs.

"Bells, let me help."

"Be my guest. You're always a miracle worker."

"Well, I wouldn't go that far, but I can be the voice of reason in a crisis. I'll find a Suzy Lou doll in this city somewhere."

"That would be fantastic." Belinda burst into tears again.

When the crying morphed into hiccupy noises, Amelia interrupted. "I also have an idea. A surprise for you. I need to talk to Dan about it. Is he available?"

"He's working from home today."

"Please put him on the phone."

"I'll see if he can take a call. Why?"

"Indulge me."

With one more hiccup, Belinda said, "I love you. Thanks for letting me dump on you."

"Love you too. Now let me talk to Dan."

While Belinda walked the phone to Dan, Amelia ruminated on the situation. Money was always tight with Belinda and Dan. Squeaky tight. They were a one-income family. Her brother-in-law worked hard to provide for his family and cover all expenses. This left no extra money for luxuries.

Amelia's percolating idea would be a tremendous gift to two over-worked, under-rested parents. A four- or five-night stay at a fabulous hotel in a city would be perfect. An adventure for only the two of them. They'd converse with no child interrupting them, eat adult food at an upscale restaurant, get a massage, and enjoy being adults who loved each other.

This gift was an act of love for her sister. The girl who'd thrown rocks at her when they were kids.

Guilt was a powerful motivator. Amelia had been too busy to join Bells and Dan for Christmas. Same for New Year's.

Now, nearly Valentine's Day, she still hadn't taken time to visit them.

To Belinda, Amelia said, "Don't think I was ignoring you and your family this past Christmas. An enormous work project was due at the end of the year."

A sigh crossed their connection. "You've ignored us for too long."

"That's not fair."

"I agree. It's not fair because we're your family. We'd like you to be present in our lives, not someone who only sends presents. Come and make memories with us. Burn food for us."

Amelia stiffened. "Hey. I've improved my cooking skills."

"Prove it. Come here and cook for us."

Amelia harrumphed. Her sister's insults proved this gift must be a surprise. Belinda wouldn't believe she could handle everything at the house. Dan must embrace this plan to make it a reality. His chances of selling this idea to Belinda exceeded hers. He'd be more persuasive.

When he took the phone, Amelia launched her plan. "Dan, I want to surprise my sister in the nicest of ways."

"Fantastic. She needs something special."

"You will also benefit from this gift."

Dan chuckled. "Even better. What do you have in mind?"

"I'm giving you both a long weekend. What do you think about a four- or five-night stay in Hot Springs, Arkansas, at the Arlington Hotel? It's a swanky, historic hotel."

"That would be fantastic!"

"You'll have fabulous meals. Belinda receives an all-day spa treatment, and you receive a round of golf if the weather cooperates. If it doesn't, we'll think of something else for you."

"We can't afford that."

"You won't be spending a dime. No money required. It's my present to the two of you. Totally my treat."

"A break would be wonderful. What a fantastic gift. But what about the kids?"

"I have a plan for them too. I'm going to stay with your children, and your dogs, your cat, and your ferret."

"No more ferret. We rehomed him."

Amelia knew better than to cheer. "Any other creatures living at your house right now?"

"Fish."

She sighed with relief. They often fostered animals for the local animal shelter. "Could you hold off taking in more of God's creatures until this getaway is over?"

"For this? You bet."

"Thank you. What about the fish?"

"We only have two tanks, and I can buy special food to feed them while we're gone. All you have to do is admire them."

"Perfect."

He cleared his throat. "You think you can handle all the humans and animals at our house? They aren't your thing."

"Well, not for everyday use, but I'll rise to the occasion to care for my beautiful nieces and handsome nephews—and your animals—for a few days. Scout's honor."

"Okay."

"Your job, should you choose to accept it, is to convince your wife this is an opportunity of a lifetime. Go to that enormous calendar-planner thing in your kitchen. Find some days that seem relatively free of activities. Then text me those dates, and I'll make the arrangements."

"Bless you, Amelia. You're going to make me cry if you keep talking about this."

Amelia laughed. "Call me back to confirm. It needs to be soon, considering your wife's tenuous mental status."

"I promise."

After the call, Amelia felt like a superhero. She enjoyed problem-solving. It's what made her a terrific upper-level manager. This surprise gave her the opportunity to solve her sister's problem and spend quality time with her nieces and nephews.

She'd take care of the kids, the dogs, the cat, and the fish. No problem.

That's a lot of living creatures, but I can do this, can't I?

As much as she loved these kids, and they loved her in return, she'd only been around them in small doses.

Did she even know what to do with them?

No matter. She'd figure that out later.

Two

In less than a week, Amelia pointed her sporty automobile toward Arkansas. The distance between Illinois and Arkansas was one reason she didn't return home as often as she liked.

Belinda and Amelia grew up in Fountain Hill, a tiny community in southern Arkansas. Dan and Belinda lived in Morrilton, Arkansas, a larger town more centrally located, but still filled with charm.

During her ten-hour road trip, she listened to an audiobook. The popular title detailed how successful managers prioritize the needs of their teams above their own.

Ironic, wasn't it? She had time to listen to this audiobook because she'd taken off from work to focus on a task benefiting her family.

As soon as Amelia arrived, Belinda ran out of her eighty-year-old, two-story Craftsman-style home. Although something always needed updating, the house was cozy and welcoming. The wide wooden staircase led visitors to a covered front porch decorated with wicker chairs, a table, and a porch swing.

Belinda greeted her with a genuine smile. Her blonde hair, cut in a flattering pixie style, made her large blue eyes seem enormous, emphasizing the bags under them.

Amelia jumped out of the car, and they threw their arms around each other. Belinda's embrace was more like a stranglehold from a drowning woman than her usual hug.

Amelia peeled Belinda off and laughed. "Super Sister has arrived. Too bad I'm not *Super Nanny*."

"Dan convinced me that you can handle everyone for a few days." Her eyes sparkled with delight. "You might regret this."

"I'm a capable professional who manages a staff of three and a team of twenty-two employees. What's the challenge of four children, three dogs, a cat, and a few fish for four days? Do the math. It will be a piece of cake."

Belinda raised her eyebrows and stared her down.

"Okay. A challenge. But I will prevail."

"That's more realistic, sister. So, tell me where you're sending us."

"Absolutely not. Dan is aware of your destination, and he's told you what to pack. That's all you need. You can pretend you're having a second honeymoon."

Belinda wrapped her in another hug. "You're the best sister ever."

"Without a doubt."

They shared a smile.

Dan appeared in sweats and a T-shirt, his short brown hair falling into his line of sight. He gave Amelia a quick hug and walked to the trunk of her car to grab her bag. He was a dear man of medium height, leaning further into portly every time Amelia visited, yet intelligent, kind, and thoughtful. Everything she could want in a life partner for her cherished sister.

The children rolled, skipped, and sauntered out of the house, with smiles of welcome for her.

Grace, the oldest, had grown several inches since Amelia's last visit more than a year ago. She was now ten, going on twenty. Her blue jeans emphasized her long legs, comparable to those of a filly racehorse. Although blonde like her mother, Grace had inherited her father's chocolate-brown eyes and long eyelashes. A beauty inside and out.

Trailing Grace was Caleb, the three-year-old, who rushed past his sister to greet Amelia. His dark hair had thickened, and his round face lengthened. He now sported the lanky arms and legs of a boy.

A pang of sadness washed over Amelia. She'd missed this stage of his life and would never have another opportunity to enjoy it.

In a whirlwind of shouts and windmilling arms, the two middle children bounded down the porch steps and ran to hug her. Hope, the youngest girl at six, sported dark hair like Caleb. She wore a sparkling blue gown that Amelia recognized as the Cinderella costume she'd sent for Christmas.

James, the oldest boy and second-oldest child, was eight. His auburn hair was identical to hers, and she delighted in this shared genetic trait. His brief public hug, though short, thrilled Amelia. She worried this soon would end.

"I have missed you all so much." Amelia blinked back tears. Remorse for failing to visit sooner bubbled to the surface. She vowed to make the most of her time with the kids. Her greatest aspiration was to be their favorite aunt, and she could only accomplish that by hours spent together, not by mailing gifts.

When Dan returned from taking her suitcase inside, he gathered the kids. "Today is the last day of sunshine and warm weather for at least a week. Let's go to the park."

They shouted their agreement.

Dan winked at Amelia and then turned to the children. "I'm going to wear you all out on the playground equipment while your mother and aunt have a moment to talk."

When the loud group ambled away, Amelia and Belinda turned to each other and smiled.

"Alone at last." Belinda gestured toward the front porch. "Let's sit out here. I made sweet tea. Care for a glass?"

"You better believe it. It's a treat not found in Chicago."

Belinda pointed to a rotten area on several of their steps. "Be careful to walk on this side of the tread. The boards have almost rotted through. Dan is going to fix that side when we return."

Amelia perused the dilapidated set of stairs. Perhaps she'd arrange for the whole set to be replaced before Dan and Belinda returned.

"Come in. We'll grab our tea and a plate of oatmeal cookies. The kids will appreciate any leftovers when they return."

"I'll appreciate them right now. I haven't had a homemade cookie since my last visit."

Amelia followed her sister inside. The three family dogs greeted her. Sarge, the Mastiff, was the size of a pony. He must have remembered her as an easy touch for petting because he walked over and nuzzled his gigantic head under her hand. She rewarded him with pats while she bent over to greet the Mexican jumping bean dog.

Taco was a tiny Chihuahua mix, but her heart and bravery were unsurpassed in the house. Taco dominated the humans, the Mastiff, and the other dog, a hound mix named Snoopy.

"Where's Cow?"

Cow was the black and white cat named by Grace, who'd been a toddler when they added him to the menagerie. She thought he resembled a Holstein and refused to call him anything but "cow," so the name stuck.

"He'll appear the minute he realizes you're visiting. He hides from strangers, but he has a soft spot for you."

Amelia didn't share that she'd slipped cat treats to him at the beginning of their relationship. It was their secret, which continued with every visit.

In the living room, Amelia admired the multitude of decorations on the fireplace mantel. Paper hearts, snowflake cutouts, crude cupid drawings, and red-and-white twinkle lights covered the space. "How festive."

"Oh, it's the kids."

Amelia rolled her eyes as she gestured. "I didn't think you'd cut out that cupid."

"Every time we go to a craft store, the kids talk me into buying things to make decorations for the upcoming holiday. Wait until you see their rooms."

Amelia's eyebrows shot to the top of her head. How could they be more jubilant? "I'm out of touch. I didn't realize how important Valentine's Day is to them."

"This year is a little different. They're all involved in a play at church for Valentine's Day. It's a celebration of three love relationships from the Bible."

"Really? Which relationships?"

They made their way to the kitchen, where Belinda pulled glasses from the cabinet. "Ruth and Boaz, Abraham and Sarah, and Jacob and Rachel."

Amelia opened the refrigerator and grabbed the pitcher of tea. "That's interesting. The kids learn about the Bible while doing something fun, like acting."

"The children are excited. Mostly because of their costumes."

Amelia chuckled. "Any chance James is playing Boaz? I'm still waiting to find my Boaz."

Belinda harrumphed as she led the way back to the front porch, a plate of cookies in her hand. "James is a shepherd. As far as your Boaz, you've left behind a lot of worthy contenders over the years."

"I disagree. No one met all my expectations. He must be a Christian, an intelligent man, have a fantastic sense of humor, and be capable of winning an occasional argument with me."

Belinda shook her head. "You're too picky to fall in love."

They settled into chairs on the porch.

With a frown, Amelia poured the tea. "I've considered it. Falling in love, I mean."

Belinda pushed the cookies toward Amelia. "You don't *consider* falling in love. Your heart is filled by a person."

"After my dating experience with Doug, otherwise known as

Captain Control Panel, I want nothing to do with anyone who is controlling or demanding. He insisted I change everything for him, but would never change anything to suit me. I'd rather be single than experience another situation like that."

Belinda nodded. "You were right to end it with Boyfriend Bossy Boots."

Amelia chuckled.

"However, that doesn't mean your Boaz doesn't exist out there somewhere. You need to keep looking for him, even if he has been elusive."

"I agree with the elusive part." Amelia bit into a cookie and moaned with delight. "Oh, these are divine. I miss these cookies almost as much as I miss all of you. My compliments to the chef."

"Noted. But I don't have time to make any more before I leave in the morning."

Amelia shrugged. "My loss. So when is this play?"

"If you can stay a few extra days, they're performing it next Friday."

"Not tomorrow night, but a week from tomorrow?"

"Exactly. We wouldn't be gone with the kids performing."

Amelia nodded. "You wouldn't miss it. It's comparable to my missing a project deadline."

Belinda studied her with serious blue eyes for a moment. "Any chance of becoming a consultant or doing long-distance work? I miss you. I'd like you to be around here more often."

"Bells, to be honest, I've been exploring that idea. I should have enough experience to start my own marketing consultancy business. It would give me so much more freedom. Live wherever I want to live—"

"Like Arkansas."

Amelia pierced her sister with a stare. "As I was saying ... I'd have flexibility with the projects I take on and could mentor some amazing people as they begin their careers. That part of my job is most rewarding." She thought of "Windy Jack." "Well, when they listen and take my advice, it's rewarding."

"Please think about it. You've been a full-blown career woman for over ten years. Why don't you consider a career side-step that allows you to work fewer hours and enjoy a more rewarding life?"

"I like my job. I'm not cut out to be an Earth Mother like you. I can't imagine living your life with all the kids, animals, and craziness around the house."

Belinda nodded. "For sure, but I'm not saying give up your career. I'm suggesting you restructure. Live life your way. Your current career path is leading you up the corporate ladder, but I don't think it fulfills you."

"Says the sister who needs a break because she's losing her mind."

"Hey. It takes one to know one."

"Point taken."

That evening, Amelia watched Belinda and Dan as they juggled, cajoled, and pleaded with the children and animals to settle down for sleep. She also received a quick course on the locations of the thermometers, first-aid kit, bandages, children's fever reducers, and other medications in the primary bedroom.

With a frown, Amelia asked, "Why is everything here instead of in the kids' bathroom? Not yet trustworthy with medication?"

Belinda rolled her eyes. "You're kidding, right?" She waved for Amelia to follow. "Let's go put the children to bed."

When they entered the fairy-princess room the girls shared, it felt as if they had stepped into the Kingdom of Girly-Girls. The walls were the color of a pink bubblegum explosion. There was a twin bed and a dresser for each girl. Everything in the room either glittered or shone.

The boys slept in the adjacent room. A pistachio green covered their walls, one dotted with multicolored climbing spikes. The remaining surface featured various movie and superhero posters. The theme was a combination of Middle Earth, jungle, and speedway. Caleb's bed sported a bedspread with racecars, while James's twin bed appeared to be made from actual trees.

Amelia examined the construction and turned to James. "Did your dad make this bed?"

He nodded. "I helped him. We found this driftwood along Beaver Lake. It's where we go canoeing."

She ran her hand along the branches. "This is beautiful."

Caleb piped up from his bed. "Daddy's going to make me a race car bed next."

Amelia smiled. "That will be amazing."

A rug on the floor resembled a roadway for cars. Prior to Belinda suggesting this as a Christmas present for Caleb, Amelia was unaware a rug could multitask as a highway map.

While Belinda gave kisses to the boys, Amelia thought about her title as Queen of Christmas Gifts. She loved being the aunt who fulfilled their greatest desires. It was an enviable position to hold. However, the gift of her time was also valuable. Now she could spend time with all of them. If only she could handle it.

Before she slept, Amelia received the final briefing, which detailed several things about the children.

"Grace is the mature one."

Amelia nodded. No surprise there.

"Yet her siblings consider her bossy. I felt the same when you tried to tell me what to do when we were kids."

Amelia kept her lips zipped. Any defensive comments might ignite her sister's fire of resentment.

"As a result, the rest of the kids do their best not to follow any of her orders, much to Grace's frustration. However, in an emergency, they fall in line and obey her commands like she's their drill sergeant."

"Good to know."

"Hope needs peace and quiet for part of the day. She used to disappear, but now she announces when she is doing art or retreating to her room for silence."

Amelia nodded. "I can relate to that. I may have to do the same thing."

"Never interfere with Hope's art desk." Belinda pointed to a card table and chair tucked into the corner of the living room.

Amelia studied the art sanctuary. "Duly noted. What about the boys?"

"Think of the boys as monkeys. They need activities and to be fed. Constantly. Oranges, apples, and bananas are acceptable. No chips."

"Exactly what I would feed monkeys." With a wink, she added, "I'd better hide my chips."

Belinda gave her the stink eye. "If you bring a bag of chips into this house, I will find them and destroy them. If I can't find them, Sarge will."

Amelia let out a nervous laugh. "Chips? I meant carrot chips, not potato chips."

Belinda rolled her eyes. "*Sure, you did.* You'd best leave any chips in your car. It's the only place safe from the animals."

"Got it."

"The boys will swing from the chandeliers if they're stuck indoors all day. They need regular exercise."

"That sounds doable."

"Don't let Caleb run away from you. Hold his wrist in a tight grip. You can't merely hold his hand. That boy is a Houdini. He can slip his hand out of yours as if it's greased."

With trepidation in her tone, Amelia said, "Houdini. Got it."

"As loud and busy as they can be, they're also loving and need snuggle time. Sometimes you must entice them with popcorn and a movie to garner snuggle time. I have organic popcorn in the upper cabinet by the fridge."

"Do I have to share?"

"You do."

Belinda pulled her into the kitchen and gave a quick rundown on sustenance for the children and the animals.

On the refrigerator, a chart outlined everyone's daily duties, and Amelia was to verify the proper completion of the duties and mark each task with a star. This was how they earned their weekly allowance.

Her sister also included a safety briefing. "No grapes or hotdogs, as they're a choking hazard. Same with small lollipops and hard candy."

Belinda led Amelia to the freezer.

"You mean even while you're having a meltdown, you keep yourself together enough to pre-prepare meals acceptable for the kids?"

Belinda straightened with pride. "Yes."

"Are you afraid I will poison your children?"

"No. I didn't want you to go to any trouble."

"I can cook."

Belinda frowned. "Since when?"

"Well ... I can microwave. That's cooking, isn't it?"

Belinda's peals of laughter echoed around them.

"Glad I still make you laugh."

Three

"Y̶ou should go." Amelia waved Belinda off as she served breakfast to the kids. "I can feed them."

Amelia turned to Dan, who rose from his chair and gulped his coffee. "You can drive by a coffee place along the way for your second cup. Go on. Go."

Dan strode to Belinda and swept her into a hug. "Time to run away, my love. The suitcases are already in the car."

The children responded to their parents' antics with a mix of groans from the boys and cheers from the girls.

Amelia shooed Dan and Belinda out of the kitchen and turned to her charges. "If everyone does their morning chores right now, that leaves us the rest of this beautiful morning to play in the park."

"Aren't we going to wave goodbye to Mommy and Daddy?" Hope asked.

"Of course. However, immediately after that, all of you back here. If everyone focuses on their duties, we can move fast and spend more time at the playground."

When Belinda stepped out the front door, she stopped. "Maybe this isn't the best plan. How can you handle all the children, not to mention the animals?"

Amelia sighed. "I won't tolerate that defeatist attitude, Bells. 'Superwoman' Aunt Melly is in charge, and we are going to be fine."

A stuffed bunny flew between Amelia and Belinda and landed on the porch. A high-pitched wail reached their ears.

Belinda pointed to the bunny. "See what I mean?"

"Simply kids being kids." Amelia grabbed the bunny and hurled it through the threshold, back into the living room. She leaned into the house. "If anyone else takes something from Caleb, they're going to be the sole chore worker in this house with no allowance. Understood?"

Silence.

Amelia turned to her sister. "See? Nothing like a threat to set things straight."

Dan walked onto the porch with car keys in one hand and a small bag in the other. His offspring rolled out behind him.

Amelia jerked her head toward the car. "Go. Go." To the children gathered on the porch, she gave each of them a withering look. "No more misbehavior until your parents have left. Do you understand?"

They nodded.

It took several tries before the ten-year-old Honda Civic eventually roared to life. They owned an even older van, left for Amelia to haul the children.

Belinda's eyes filled with tears, and she blew kisses at her brood as the car made it to the street. The rear bumper bottomed out, grinding on the road. Two pairs of hands covered ears at the high-pitched squeal of metal scraping asphalt.

They all shared a laugh about the car, which lightened the mood. Dan and Belinda drove away with shining faces. The children shouted, "Goodbye" and "Have fun."

Once the car rounded the corner and disappeared, fear stabbed Amelia. She was now the only adult on the property. The parents, who knew everything, had left her in charge of the household. Her. The woman with no children or pets. Have they lost their minds?

She prayed for their safe travels and added a sincere request for God to keep her and the children in His hands. She also prayed that their days luxuriating at the beautiful vintage hotel in Hot Springs would lift both Dan's and Belinda's spirits.

With a sigh, Amelia gathered her "Superwoman" cloak around her. If she could manage people at work, she could handle a small household full of miniature humans, one enormous dog, two normal-sized dogs, a cat, and two fish tanks.

Amelia herded the children back inside to finish breakfast and do their chores. Their previous rebellion remained squelched for now.

A half hour of effort put paid to the morning chores. Armed with proper outdoor clothing, which included mittens and scarves plus the two larger dogs on leashes, she and the kids made their way to the playground. Amelia kept a firm hold on Caleb's wrist because he insisted he walk to the park rather than ride in the stroller.

As they walked, the children's chatter surrounded her. She thought of Julie Andrews in *The Sound of Music*. Maria was a governess with no previous training. Like Maria, Amelia was untrained and in charge of multiple children. Although she only had four charges instead of Maria's seven, didn't the dogs count to fill the missing slots?

Last night, Dan gave her a childcare tip. "If all else fails, put them in the van and take them for a ride. No matter who has a meltdown. No matter what time, day or night, they settle down after riding in the car for fifteen minutes."

At the park, Caleb crowned himself the slide king. She expected he'd tire of it after a few slides, but he enjoyed the trip about a thousand times before he finally took a break. Amelia found a bench, and they snuggled while watching the older kids.

Her thoughts drifted to Belinda, who would love discovering

their surprise destination was Hot Springs, also known as Spa City. Amelia's assistant found the Arlington Hotel, a beautiful, newly remodeled historic hotel. Amelia splurged on a suite for them.

Bathhouse Row was steps from their lodgings. Those facilities featured thermal water piped in from the downtown Hot Springs National Park, as did their hotel. There were fine restaurants within walking distance.

Belinda and Dan could relax, eat wonderful meals, and receive massages and spa treatments. She imagined they'd stroll along, holding hands and enjoy being a couple. A revitalization for them was her wish. How happy it made her to have the funds to spoil them occasionally. It was rewarding to help someone, especially people she loved.

An exhausted and red-nosed Hope interrupted her daydreaming. The girl joined her and Caleb on the bench. Eventually, Amelia decided the Von Trapp family should head home. Within ten minutes, the brood retraced their steps. This time Grace held Caleb, Amelia clutched the leash of Sarge the pony dog, and James grasped Hope's hand and Snoopy's leash.

Amelia shared with the kids how hard it had been to hold their mother's hand when she and Belinda were young. The kids laughed. Delighted with this reception, Amelia relayed more antics involving their mother. They loved hearing about her mischievous side.

Three blocks from the house, James said, "Let's race home."

Grace shook her head. "I can't, silly. I've got Caleb."

Amelia suggested a solution. "If you'll hold off racing until we reach your block, I'll trade with Grace. She can have Sarge, and I'll take Caleb. Sound fair?"

The older three cheered, but Caleb wasn't happy. "I wanna race."

She smiled at him. "No racing by yourself, but how about we run with them?"

Caleb nodded, pleased with the plan.

Amelia added a stipulation. "To make it a fair race, James must keep Snoopy. Sarge hinders Grace, so it's only fair you have the hound."

Grace giggled. "Snoopy only runs after rabbits. I'm going to win this race."

When they reached their block, they traded leashes and a toddler. While the older kids ran ahead, Amelia maintained a trot, bouncing Caleb on her hip as he squealed with delight.

James and Grace's race was a tie until they reached the porch. Sarge and Grace conquered the steps with uncommon gracefulness while James did his best to cajole the hound to ascend the stairs. He failed.

Grace shouted from the top of the porch, "We won! We won!" She opened the door and Sarge raced inside, his leash trailing behind him.

"Ah, you wouldn't have if you'd had Snoopy." Frustration peppered James's tone. "I want a rematch."

Snoopy strained against the leash at the bottom of the steps.

Amelia called out, "We'll have a rematch tomorrow with no dogs in tow."

James smiled. "That means I'll win."

Amelia slowed when she reached the house, her breath labored. She possessed no energy to run up the stairs with the weight of a three-year-old added to hers.

Caleb squalled his disappointment, so she loped up the steps in imitation of Sarge. With a sense of horror, she realized she was on the decayed side of the steps. Before she shifted off the dangerous part, the board under her right foot splintered with a loud crack.

Her foot sank into the void, followed by her entire leg. Instinct caused her to toss Caleb onto the porch with quarterback skills akin to Patrick Mahomes. Caleb landed on his side, bounced about a foot before he skidded to a stop, and emitted a paint-peeling wail.

Pain shot through her hands when they smacked the top of the crumbling boards as she instinctively tried to stop her fall. The leg that crashed through the board hovered, useless, above the ground. Her other leg bent awkwardly behind her.

Grace rushed to Caleb and scooped him into her arms.

Amelia called out, "Is he okay?"

"I think so. He's upset, but I can't find any blood. Why'd you toss him?"

"I threw him to keep from falling on him."

"Well, it scared him."

To Caleb, Amelia said, "I'm so sorry I threw you, buddy. I was afraid I'd break your arm or leg if I fell on you."

Caleb turned his head away.

Grace shrugged. "Give him a minute. He'll calm down."

While Grace worked to comfort Caleb, Amelia struggled to gain enough leverage to push herself out of the hole. No luck after repeated tries. Not enough arm strength. She blamed her failure to make workouts a priority.

She glanced around for help. Hope stood in front of the door, staring at her, brow furrowed. James remained on the sidewalk, still urging Snoopy to climb the stairs.

"James, can you come grab my arm? I need help. Seems I can't manage this alone."

The boy frowned. "What do I do with Snoopy? He won't budge."

She turned to Hope. "Can you come down and stay with Snoopy while James tries to help me?"

Hope nodded and ran down the safe side of the stairs to James. In a flash, he handed the leash to his sister and ran to Amelia.

In her predicament, James stood above her. He bent over and tilted his head. "Are you hurt?"

She tried to make light of the problem. "I don't think so. Some help in escaping this silly hole would be appreciated."

He tugged on her arm several times, but to no avail. "Aunt Melly, this isn't working."

Grace flapped a hand in excitement. "Hope? I'll bring Caleb to you, and you give me Snoopy. I'll run Snoopy up the stairs and then help pull on Aunt Melly."

Everyone adopted Grace's suggestion willingly and without complaint. In a flash, Grace convinced Snoopy to climb the stairs and enter the house.

Belinda is right. The kids do what Grace tells them in an emergency.

Even with Grace's extra muscle, Amelia remained stuck, a cork in a bottle, her muscles burning, the rough wood biting into her skin. A frustrated groan escaped her lips.

Grace sighed. "We need Mr. Shorty. He'll help."

"I'll go." James sprinted down the stable side of the steps.

"Wait," Amelia called. "Where are you going?"

James hesitated. "Mr. Shorty lives a few houses down. At least for now."

"Do you have to cross the street?"

He pointed to a two-story Colonial. "No. He's right there."

Amelia nodded. "Okay. Go, but be careful."

She turned to Grace. "I'm so sorry about all this. Thanks for your help."

"I'm sorry about this too." Grace pointed to Hope and Caleb. "But Caleb is smiling now."

This brought Amelia comfort. At least he felt better. But how could a man named Shorty help her?

With such a name, she was probably three times his weight and twice as tall. People called Shorty were usually the size of a jockey or a hobbit. Perhaps old and bent over.

Even with the best intentions, would he have the physical strength to handle her? She'd die of embarrassment if the fire department needed to rescue her.

Bells might not forgive her for throwing Caleb. Add in a call to the fire department and gossip by the neighbors, Bells would never, *ever*, let Amelia be alone with the children again. Even for five minutes.

Quick footsteps on the stairs filled her chest with hope. Although the situation robbed her of the ability to turn toward the sound, help had arrived. When an imposing figure the size of Dwayne Johnson moved into her line of sight and blocked the sun, she flinched.

Four

W ho was this lumberjack? Mr. Shorty? Sporting a plaid flannel shirt and khaki shorts, this giant of a man gave Paul Bunyan a run for his money.

Upon closer inspection, she spotted tiny shavings of sawdust on him. "Man glitter" dotted his wavy strawberry-blond hair, eyebrows, eyelashes, and stuck to the mustache that matched his hair.

He smiled, displaying even white teeth. "Sorry to surprise you. I'm Shorty. I knew Belinda and Dan planned to go on R&R. I didn't know about you."

She gave him a half-smile. "Amelia. Thanks for coming. I'm in a pickle."

His dark blue eyes twinkled. "James said you fell. Your 'pickle situation' is more in line with skewering the disintegrating step. Need a hand?"

"I do. But first, check on Caleb and make sure he's okay? I tossed him onto the porch when I fell."

The man walked over to Grace and gave Caleb a quick once-over. "He seems fine. You're the one needing help."

When he returned, Amelia asked, "Did you bring Babe, your blue ox? It might take both of you to extract me from this mess."

A deep rumbling chuckle filled the air as he leaned near her. "I can handle it."

He stomped his sandal-and-white-sock-encased foot near the hole that trapped her leg. This further splintered the board, widening the gap and relieving the pressure on her dangling leg.

"Ah," she said. "That helped."

"Let's finish this." He leaned over. His giant hands gripped her upper arms. With surprising strength, he pulled her straight up, freeing her from the hole.

Setting her gently on her feet, he remained holding her arms. "Do you have feeling in both legs?"

"My right leg is tingling. Its circulation must have been compromised. My left leg is sore from being twisted behind me."

"Understandable. I'm going to hold you upright for a minute. We need to ensure proper circulation, and that you have enough strength to stand."

"Thanks for the rescue." This close to him, she inhaled the scent of his cologne mixed with the tang of freshly cut wood. So manly.

"Glad to help. When your right leg stops tingling, we'll go inside. You can make sure you don't have any concerning cuts or bruises anywhere under your jeans."

His voice resonated. A man of his size should have a deep voice. Big man, big voice. If he could sing, she imagined the sound would be heavenly.

Without thinking, she brushed some stray wood curls from his shoulder. Her cheeks heated.

He wiped his hands down his sawdust-covered shirt. "James found me doing a little woodwork in the garage. I was turning a table leg, which showered me in particles."

"Do you make furniture for a living?"

"No, I'm a civil engineer for the state. I'm on medical leave, but I can't stand not being busy, so I was making a replacement for a burned table leg."

When he didn't explain further, she changed the subject.

"You're not what I expected. When Grace suggested getting Mr. Shorty, I imagined a septuagenarian about the size of a fireplug or a stepladder. Never figured a man named Shorty could repair a roof without a ladder."

He chuckled. "Never heard that one before. It's usually, 'How's the weather up there?' or 'Are you a Viking?' But never 'Ladder-free roof repair.' Not a bad marketing slogan for a home repair service."

She delighted in his sense of humor. "I shouldn't have teased you."

"Throughout my life, my height has been the fuel for teasing. My buddies in the Army gave me the ridiculous nickname."

"I like the juxtaposition of the nickname compared to reality. What's your real name?"

"Ian."

"That's a fantastic name."

"When my buddies started calling me Shorty, I couldn't see the humor, but it's grown on me. What about you? You're not too short yourself."

"True. I enjoy my height. It helps spread my weight around."

His eyes ran from the top of her head to her toes. "Looks perfectly placed to me." He grinned. "Just saying."

She narrowed her eyes at him.

His grin faded. "I've offended you in some way."

"If I weighed six hundred pounds and were wide instead of tall, most people wouldn't dare comment on my size."

He ducked his head. "Sorry. Didn't mean to be rude."

"Didn't anyone tell you it's dangerous to comment on a lady's weight?"

"Wasn't that a complimentary comment?"

"I suppose." She shrugged. "Back to the height discussion. My height is an advantage in the business world. It's hard for a man to dismiss you when you're towering over him."

He grinned again. "I've never met a woman taller than me."

It was her turn to smile. "Ever been to Amsterdam?"

"Not yet."

"Those women are proud of their height. They wear four-inch heels even when they're well over six feet tall."

"I'll move that destination to the top of my travel wish list."

She placed more weight on her right leg. "I think I'm more stable now."

He removed his hands from her arms. "Go inside and check your leg for any bad scratches, bleeding, or bruising. You might need a doctor."

"I think I'm fine."

He cocked his head at her and raised a sawdust-dotted eyebrow. "No argument will be tolerated. Doing so is a tactical error on your part."

James rushed up to her, tears in his eyes. "When you fell, it scared me."

She reached her arms around him and gathered him into a hug. "It scared me, too, James. Accidents happen sometimes. You helped me by running for Mr. Shorty. That was brave. Thank you."

She spotted Grace holding Caleb again, much to his delight. "Let me examine Caleb. I threw him like a javelin."

Ian followed her. "I credit you with fast thinking. Toddlers bounce. Falling on him might have hurt him."

"Is that another remark about my weight?"

He grinned. "I'm not that brave. Go see about your leg, and I'll check out Caleb. I received medical training in the Army."

"Okay."

"We'll be in the kitchen. I want enough light to scrutinize Caleb." He stepped back and shook like a dog, sending sawdust in every direction. The children laughed.

Amelia made her way to the bathroom. The soreness in both legs hit her as she pulled off her tennis shoes, socks, and jeans. Under the glow of the lights, she inspected her injuries.

Her right leg, which skewered the porch, as Ian aptly described, sported several long scratches running from calf to upper thigh. Her socks had protected her ankle, but she had wounds above that. None seemed to be actively bleeding. Bruises would appear soon enough.

The leg that had twisted behind her showed some swelling and a developing bruise on her knee. Nothing worthy of medical care. She prayed the same for Caleb, the toddler cannonball.

* * *

Ian carried Caleb to the kitchen with his thoughts running wild. What a blessing this day was turning out to be. How often did he have the chance to rescue a beautiful damsel in distress? And this one was tall and full of fire.

Surrounded by chattering children, Ian half-listened to them as he examined a wiggling Caleb. While he stripped clothes off Caleb to check for any bruises or other injuries, Ian asked James to bring him a small flashlight.

In a moment, James returned. "Will this work, Mr. Shorty?"

James handed him a thin silver flashlight attached to a set of car keys. "Mama uses this light all the time."

"Perfect, James. Thank you."

When he focused on a bruise on Caleb's shoulder, Grace explained it was an old injury.

After finding no signs of concussion or new bruising, Ian freed Caleb and searched for a way to silence the masses. If he filled their mouths with some lunch, perhaps that would give him a chance to figure out how to spend more time with the gorgeous woman in charge here.

Within seconds, he located a loaf of bread, a jar of peanut butter, and a half-jar of strawberry jelly. While assembling sandwiches, the children warned him about their Aunt Melly's cooking.

He mentally shrugged as they described her propensity for oven fires. So she didn't cook. He didn't care.

When he heard Amelia's footsteps, he stopped the lunch assembly and grinned at her. "What's the diagnosis?"

She smiled in return. "Scratches and bruising. Nothing serious."

"Great news." He gestured toward the open jam jar with the peanut-butter-covered knife in his hand. "Jump in and help feed the starving crowd. I'm outmanned here in the mess hall."

He noted her genuine delight at seeing him. Was she excited that he started feeding the kids, or was she showing interest in him? He hoped it was the second option.

She moved behind the kitchen island. "I'm sure they're starving. It's been a long time since breakfast."

"Knives are in this drawer." He pointed with a movement of his head.

"What's the diagnosis for the other patient?"

"I checked him for any signs of concussion. All negative. I stripped him down to skin and Mickey Mouse underwear to check for bruises or scratches. Nurse Grace here"—he smiled at Grace—"insisted the only bruise he had came from an unfortunate confrontation with the living room table a couple of days ago."

"That's a relief. He could have been hurt."

He raised his eyebrows. "More like you could have been." After a pause, he had an idea. "That's why, as soon as we feed these animals, I'm coming back to fix the porch steps. This will never happen again."

"That would be fantastic, but you're on medical leave. Don't you need to take it easy?"

"I'm careful with my feet, which is where I'm healing." He glanced at the two oldest children. "If you'll lend me Grace and James to be my assistants this afternoon, we'll have the steps repaired before dinner."

"Don't you need supplies?"

"I do. Once we take measurements, I'll run to the store to buy them."

"We'll all go because I insist on paying for the materials. And what about your labor costs?"

He hesitated. "Can't we barter the labor costs? I'll be starving once we finish the work on the porch. You could order pizza."

"I've got a better idea. There's a lasagna Belinda made for us, tucked in the freezer. How about that lasagna and a salad for dinner tonight?"

"I accept as long as you're not making the lasagna. I've been warned about your cooking."

"What?" Amelia glanced at the children in the room. "Who's the traitor in this bunch?"

Three pairs of eyes looked away. One pair was too young to understand the conversation, but he smiled, which caused his half-chewed organic animal cracker to fall from his mouth. Amelia laughed.

Ian said, "Don't be mad at them. They've told me how much they love their Aunt Melly. They also warned me not to eat your food."

While Amelia pinned the oldest three to their chairs with daggers from her eyes, Ian smiled. He'd have the afternoon and the evening meal to impress her in some way. Now he just had to hurry up and figure out how.

Five

W hile Ian ran home to grab his jacket, Amelia resisted the urge to call her sister. She'd promised Belinda peace, not calls quizzing her about gossip related to a neighbor.

On the emergency number list Belinda left, there was no Mr. Shorty listed, but Ian McIntosh was there. How many Ians would be in a town this size?

For answers, Amelia tracked down the most observant and talkative child. Grace was in the living room reading a book to Caleb. When Grace finished, and Caleb ran off to play, Amelia shamelessly pumped her for details about their neighbor.

"I like him. He's friends with Dad. They do lots together."

"What things? Golf?"

Dan played when he could afford it.

"No. I don't think Mr. Shorty plays golf. He helped Dad fix the gate on the fence. They planned to fix the porch steps once the weather is better."

"What's Mr. Shorty's last name?"

Grace shrugged.

"He said his first name is Ian. An Ian McIntosh is on your mom's emergency call list. Do you know a Mr. McIntosh?"

Grace danced around the living room, incapable of staying still for more than a few minutes. "It could be his real name, but everybody calls him Shorty. Mom and Dad make us call him Mr. Shorty because it's not polite for us to call an adult by their first name."

"I'm sure that's Mr. Shorty. Whoever started that nickname must have been going for irony. I think Fezzik from *The Princess Bride* would be a better fit for a giant's name."

Grace pondered this for a moment. "Do you think he's dreamy?"

"Dreamy?" Amelia blinked at the ballerina. "I wouldn't go that far. He certainly is a pleasant man, and a large one. Cute, perhaps. But a man who wears socks with sandals can't be dreamy."

Grace stopped dancing, her forehead furrowed. "He has medicine on his feet. He's supposed to wear socks until his feet heal."

"Oh." Amelia pondered this for a moment. "What's wrong with his feet? Some kind of fungus?"

"Burns. He burned his feet rescuing someone from a fire."

"Doesn't he have fire boots?"

James popped his head up from the small table where he worked on a colored-pencil masterpiece. "Mr. Shorty isn't a fireman. His apartment building burned. He ran downstairs to help a neighbor in a wheelchair. He was only wearing a robe and slippers. His slippers melted onto his feet."

"Oh my. That is brave."

Grace nodded. "Mom said God protected him. Dad said he's a hero."

"So he moved in nearby?"

James stood up and walked to Amelia. "For a bit. Our real neighbors found out Mr. Shorty's apartment caught fire. They spend the winter in Florida and gave Mr. Shorty permission to live in their house while they're gone. He was already renting space in their garage to do his woodworking before the fire."

The children's knowledge of Ian's situation amazed her. They were little sponges, soaking up all the details. When she needed gossip in the future, she would start with the Munchkin Information Brigade.

"Let's get ready for Mr. Shorty's return," Amelia announced as she shooed away the older children to grab their jackets.

Within minutes, she'd retrieved soft woolen jackets for the younger two. The struggle to dress the squirming, giggling little people involved a flurry of tiny limbs and muffled protests. "Me do it" and "I want to do it myself" accompanied her efforts. It was a symphony of rustling fabric and childish shrieks.

In the main bedroom, which was hers until these moppets' parents returned, she located her coat and purse. Rounding the corner from the hall to the living room, she realized the dogs needed to go out for a quick break. More time and effort to leave the house.

With kissy-noise coaxing, she motivated the furry tribe, minus the cat, to follow her to the back door, where brown grass inside the fenced yard awaited them. Taking care of a household made her appreciate everything her sister had to accomplish to go anywhere. Was this something she wanted? Her life was a breeze by comparison.

She stood on the back porch a few minutes later when the door opened.

James announced, "Mr. Shorty's here."

"Thank you, James."

"Don't worry about this deck." He gestured toward the new boards at her feet. "You're safe here. Dad and Mr. Shorty replaced it this summer. It was worse than the front steps."

"Good thing they fixed it." Before he disappeared, she asked, "Is there a magic word to entice the dogs inside?"

He grinned. "Yes, it's a treat. I'll show you where Mom hides them."

When she entered the house, a trail of dogs behind her, Ian leaned against the counter, grinning.

"Hello, Red."

"Red, huh?"

"It fits you. You have a problem with it?"

"You're not far from being a 'Red' yourself."

"But I already have a nickname."

"You can call me anything you'd like as long as you don't call me late for dinner." She smiled. "Ready for an adventure?"

James, always helpful, pointed to an upper cabinet. "The dog treats are inside that one."

This action resulted in a symphony of eager yelps and barks from the furry menagerie.

She waved in Ian's direction. "Almost ready. But first, I must deliver on my promise to these wild beasts."

He chuckled. "Look at you. They're eating out of your hands."

"Literally." She held up a wet palm. "Let me wash off Sarge's slobber."

Amelia had never driven a van. She hadn't shared this with her sister or brother-in-law because they might not have left her with the children. How hard could it be?

She approached the monstrosity full of car seats with trepidation but comforted her nerves with one fact—when transporting children, they were strapped in. The children could still make a lot of noise, but they couldn't move out of their assigned seats.

She and Ian shared a chuckle when the children loaded into the van with enthusiasm. Grace and James gave her play-by-play instructions on strapping Caleb into his car seat and Hope into her booster seat. Ian reached around and verified all seat belts were secure.

Upon entering the driver's seat, she discovered space was limited. She tossed her purse at Ian and wedged herself into the tiny space the giant in the passenger seat had left her. His physique required all the capacity on the right side. Broad shoulders, long legs, enormous paws. Like taking a bear for a ride.

Even strapped in, the children bounced around like bumper cars when she hit the first curb. Everyone laughed about it, but she felt humiliated. This vehicle was enormous compared to hers.

Ian winked at her. "You'll get used to this in no time."

"I certainly hope so, or else I'll be permanently embarrassed about driving anywhere in this tank."

After that, their trip to the local lumberyard was fun, if she laughed about people staring at the show they presented. Amelia muffled her laughter as the bear of a man made his way up and down aisles surrounded by talkative cubs. Some cubs pushed carts, others touched things they shouldn't. She maintained a sharp eye for rule enforcement from the rear.

When she helped load the treated lumber and other supplies into the van, Ian teased her.

"You'll mess up those nails of yours."

"It gives me an excuse to go to the nail salon."

That twinkle in his eyes sent a thrill through her. If he'd moved to Chicago, he would be a fun person to date, so different from all the "suits" that filled her dating pool.

Once back home, supplies unloaded, the children watched Ian's every move. He worked hard but made time to encourage Grace and James to take part in measuring and watching him cut the lumber.

After a few minutes, Amelia dragged Caleb away for a much-needed nap. It was hard to settle him with the noisy repairs outside his window. He fell asleep, but not before he declared his desire to be "just like Mr. Shorty" when he grew up.

While Caleb napped, she busied herself making the salad and preparing the garlic bread to accompany tonight's feast of lasagna. It lay thawing, covered, on top of the refrigerator. Grace warned her that the Mastiff could reach the counter and would gobble the frozen lasagna if given the opportunity. *Note to self: Never own a dog large enough to reach the kitchen counter.*

With her early dinner preparations complete, Amelia grabbed a coat and ventured outside to help Ian.

He smiled. "You mean it? You're willing to join in?"

"Jesus was a carpenter. I can be one too." She pulled knitted mittens from her pocket. "Let's do this."

"I'm going to show you how to run the saw, but first you need real work gloves." He dug around in his toolbox until he pulled out a pair of leather gloves. "These will be large, so don't catch them on something that will pull your hand into the teeth of the saw."

She blinked at him, nodded, and took the gloves. "I've done this before."

"When?" Excitement painted his tone.

"Years ago. My dad was always fixing something. As the oldest, it fell to me to help him."

He smiled. "This is great. We'll finish in no time."

They walked over to a large table saw, where he relayed detailed instructions about its safe use. When he encouraged her to cut a few sample pieces, his dark blue eyes flashed with satisfaction.

With her proven ability to cut, James and Grace acted as runners. One of them would relay to her the measurement taken by Ian. She'd cut to that length, and they'd run the board back to be nailed in place.

She observed him while he worked. How precisely he measured. How his tongue found the corner of his mouth as he wedged in a new board and worked it into place. This man was patient.

He let James measure and praised him for watching Amelia as she measured the board and marked the proper length before she cut. Ian also encouraged Grace to participate, letting her cut with safety glasses while Amelia supervised all safety precautions.

Ian's openness to Grace's interest delighted Amelia. Having lived alone for so many years, she knew firsthand that a girl should know a few things about small home repairs.

After a few minutes of begging, Ian taught James how to use his nail gun. Although James struggled to keep the enormous safety glasses in place, his eventual shouts of glee relayed his nailing skills improved as time passed.

Soon all workers sported sawdust sprinkles. Before they finished, Amelia stripped off her coat to go inside and put the lasagna in the oven.

Ian inadvertently threw sawdust on her as he removed his own gloves and safety glasses.

"Hey." She stepped back. "I have plenty of 'man glitter' on me already. I don't need yours."

"My apologies, Red. I'm going to have to go home and shower before dinner."

"What?" James piped in with disgust in his tone. "Another one?"

She and Ian shared a laugh at James's repulsion of a two-shower day.

Later that evening, she succeeded in keeping the children from all talking at once during dinner. As they took turns, she smiled often at Ian. The children's stories were hilarious if you forgave them for repetitiveness.

Ian insisted on cleaning up the dishes while she supervised bath time and read several bedtime stories until everyone's eyes drooped. After overseeing prayers, she returned to their guest.

In the kitchen, Ian hand-dried the pans.

She rushed to him. "You don't have to do that."

He laughed as he held the pan and towel aloft, far from her reaching hands. "I'm finished. You cooked, I cleaned. The perfect combination."

"I didn't cook. I assembled and heated things."

"Works for me." He eyed her for a second longer than comfortable. "I put the leftover lasagna in a plastic container. You might have enough to feed it to the kids for lunch."

She nodded. "Thank you for everything you've done today. It's been jam-packed with excitement."

"And on that note, I'm going to head back to my house. You

need some sleep. Those kids will be up and at it by the break of dawn."

She glanced at the spotless countertop. "How does my sister do this? Day in and day out? I'm exhausted."

"She's used to it. But you've done a fabulous job today." He walked into the mudroom and grabbed his coat.

When he returned, he added, "I didn't want to say anything in front of the kids, but there's a possibility we're going to have an ice storm in a few days."

"Oh, no. I remember those storms when I was a kid. It's part of growing up in this state."

"It will be fine. I wanted you to know that a cold front is moving in. Depending on the temperature, it could be rain or snow. But if it's cold enough to bring freezing rain but not cold enough for snow, then we'll get ice. Right now, it's a guessing game."

He mentioned several more scientific explanations about possible ice, but she didn't listen. What would she and the kids do if trapped by ice, perhaps without power?

Ian must have spotted her panic. He walked over and patted her shoulder with one of his paws.

"Don't worry. Tomorrow I'll come over, and we'll make a list of all the food and other supplies you might need. We'll go shopping together."

She inwardly sighed with relief. "That would be fabulous, Ian. Thank you."

Once he left, she let the dogs out for the last time and checked on the cat. Cow had hidden on shelves in the living room or the mudroom area since she arrived. He was easier to find when she offered a treat. After a few minutes of petting him and being paid with purrs, she turned off the lights and headed to bed.

Her thoughts returned to the giant man residing down the street. She'd only known him for one day. And what a day it had been.

In twelve hours, he'd rescued her, accompanied her and the

children to buy supplies, repaired the steps, and shared dinner with them.

She'd enjoyed every moment. He was fine company, remarkable with the kids, and an industrious worker.

She'd resisted men for years, decades even. What particular things about this guy caught and held her interest? His height? His sense of humor? His ability to fix almost anything? *All of them.*

Why did You put this one in my path, God?

Six

Amelia stood in the kitchen wearing her pajamas and robe, doing her best to warm frozen blueberry pancakes in the toaster oven while scrambling a half-dozen eggs. Four hungry-eyed children watched her every move.

When the eggs were cooked, she turned off the burner. Before she'd allow them to eat, they had business to discuss.

Turning to the assembled crowd, a wooden spoon in her hand for emphasis, she eyed Caleb and Hope. "Why did I wake up with two of you in my bed this morning?"

Hope scrunched in her chair, eyes darting from side to side. "Caleb woke me up because he was crying."

Amelia frowned. "Caleb is in a different room. He should have awakened James."

When Amelia glanced toward James, he shrugged. "He might have cried. I could have slept through it."

Turning back to Hope, she said, "Try again."

Hope's face colored. "I missed my mommy and daddy. When I crawled into bed with Caleb, he woke up and cried. I stopped him by taking him into your room."

Amelia stared at both children. "Your mother warned me that

Taco might join me in bed, but imagine my surprise to find two children. Children. Two. Instead of one small dog."

Hope shrugged. "You're the substitute for our mommy and daddy. Where else were we supposed to go?"

Amelia turned and ladled eggs onto plastic plates. "Excellent point. Tonight, let's stay in our own beds and give Taco a chance to snuggle up with me instead. Okay?"

Reluctant murmurs occurred behind her, but she'd made her point. She didn't want them to see her smiling. She was proud they'd wandered to her for safety. She hadn't heard them come in.

Her first awareness that they were in her bed occurred when Caleb smacked her in the face with his arm. She'd screeched at the nocturnal affront until realizing what had happened. He'd been rolling over in his sleep.

While they were cleaning up breakfast, her cell phone rang.

"Oh, no. I left my phone in the bedroom."

"I'll get it." Hope raced off and returned a minute later. "... Yes. We've been very good—" When she reached Amelia, she held the phone aloft. "It's Mama."

For about ten minutes, Belinda chatted with Amelia. She seemed relaxed and happy, giggling in a way Amelia hadn't heard in a long time.

She confessed her accident on the porch but downplayed it as much as possible so Belinda and Dan wouldn't worry. Immediately, Belinda pounced on the fact that Ian had rescued her.

"So, what do you think about Ian?"

"He certainly is friendly. An enormous guy."

"Isn't he the cutest?" Her sister gushed. "I'm glad you met him, as long as you weren't seriously hurt."

"Nothing but bruises and a few scrapes." She didn't mention she'd thrown Caleb like a football. Bells would take issue with that. "Actually, Ian is coming over later today to go shopping with us." She slapped a hand over her mouth. Was her sister aware of the potential ice storm? She didn't want her to rush back home.

47

"That's awfully nice of him, Amelia, but didn't I leave enough food already prepared for you guys?"

"Of course you did. The temperature is supposed to drop. Today might be our last chance to take the kids out to enjoy shopping and a stop at a park."

"Please thank Ian for us. He's wonderful with the kids."

Amelia breathed a sigh of relief as the conversation veered from dangerous subjects. "Yes, he is. That's interesting. Does he come from a large family or something?"

"You'll have to ask him."

Her sister's response was cagey, but she let it slide. "Will do."

They switched to a face-to-face call, so all the children could see and talk to their parents. Then Amelia used the excuse of children arguing in the living room to end the phone call.

She broke up the disagreement by assigning each child a task to accomplish while she took a shower. With Ian expected at any moment, she needed to be dressed. *How does Belinda do this every day of her life and add homeschooling to all her other duties?*

* * *

Ian admired their handiwork as he climbed the new porch steps. They'd accomplished some excellent work yesterday, and he'd seen a carpentry side to Amelia that was unexpected but admirable. He liked how she could flip from career woman to tomboy and maintain her charm throughout.

At his knock, Amelia opened the door, and Caleb slipped between her legs and ran outside like a prisoner escaping through an open gate of a prison. Amelia gave chase, but with two or three giant steps, Ian passed her, caught up to the escapee, and scooped him into his arms.

"We will have no AWOL soldiers on my watch, young man," he said.

Amelia caught up to them and huffed. "Thank you." Then

she turned to Caleb, still captured and wiggling in Ian's arms. "Don't you ever do that again, young man. You hear me?"

Caleb's lip quivered as he nodded.

Ian bounced him in the air a few times. "Running is not safe, Caleb. You understand Aunt Melly is trying to keep you from getting hurt, right?"

Caleb nodded again, his face brighter.

Ian grinned at Amelia over Caleb's head. "Hopefully, he's learned his lesson."

When they entered the house and securely closed the door, Ian put Caleb down. "Now, be free. But do it safely."

Caleb hightailed it out of the room, giving Ian and Amelia an opportunity to share a smile.

"You are one fast man, Mr. Shorty."

He took delight in her compliment. "That's my Army training kicking in. You ought to see me run when food is involved."

She nodded. "I bet that's a sight."

Together, they made a list of food items that were more "ready to eat" in nature. Toaster pastries that could be consumed without being toasted, gallons of water, iced tea, juice, and flavored drinks.

Amelia added pre-made iced coffee drinks to the list. "If hot coffee's not an option, I'll have to make do."

He stared at their tabulations. "You can tell a lot about a person by how they make a grocery list."

"Considering I'm doing all the writing and you're merely the idea man, it's obvious who's practical."

He pressed his hand against his chest. "I'm cut to the quick by your remark."

Amelia laughed.

She didn't mind being teased, which was another point in her favor.

They debated other things they might need. He campaigned

for plenty of ready-to-eat chow. Amelia added dog food, dog treats, and a new game for kids who might be trapped inside.

"How about hot dogs?" he asked. "I have some long skewers I can bring over. The kids could cook them over a fire, if necessary."

"Belinda warned me off them. Dangerous somehow."

He nodded. "You have to cut them lengthwise to prevent the kids from choking. We can do that."

She stared at him in amazement. "How do you know that?"

He shot her a grin. "My sister's kids. I'm around them all the time since I moved here."

"What about Caleb getting too close to the fire when he tries to cook?"

"I volunteer to be his fire monitor."

"Great." Amelia smiled. "I understand you're a hero when it comes to fires."

He didn't like talking about what happened because people made his actions out to be more than what they were. He shrugged. "I did what needed to be done."

She eyed him for a moment.

He braced himself for more questions.

"What about marshmallows?" Her pen hovered over the page. "We could make s'mores."

Relief lifted his shoulders. "My skewers should work for the gigantic marshmallows they sell now. Let's see if we can find them."

"Plus graham crackers and bars of chocolate."

"Exactly."

"Give me a moment. I want to look for some indoor entertainment ideas for children." She searched her phone.

He watched her profile as she worked. She might not be able to cook, but she was fun-loving, smart, and organized. All qualities he admired.

She added several items to the list. "If we're stuck inside for hours, the kids need fun things to do that are easy to clean up.

Bells would be furious with me over any misuse of permanent markers or industrial glue."

He nodded. "My sister would be exactly the same."

When satisfied the list was complete, they gathered the children and loaded them into the van.

Ian said, "We are officially Oscar Mike."

"What?"

"Army speak for on the move."

At the end of the driveway, he turned and grinned. "Are you game for a quick detour?"

Squeals of delight erupted from the back of the vehicle.

"Any army term for detour?"

He pursed his lips. "Let me think. Circumvent?"

"If this detour involves food, count me in."

He deflated. "No food, but I hope it's interesting."

"What is it?"

"A surprise."

From the car seat in the second row of the van, Caleb shouted, "A prize? I want a prize!"

Everyone laughed at Caleb's declaration before Grace explained the difference between a prize and a surprise.

"I'd rather have a prize than a surprise," Caleb said.

"Well, the rest of us are happy to have a surprise," Amelia said.

Ian twisted to see the passengers in the back seats. "How about we play twenty questions, and you try to figure it out?"

"Is it an animal?" James asked.

"No," Ian said.

"Is it a vegetable?" James tried for a second time.

Hope stated with an exasperated tone, "If it was vegetable, it's food, and Mr. Shorty already said it wasn't food."

Ian held up a hand. "Very logical, Hope. James, those are good questions." To Amelia, he said, "Turn left at this intersection and slow down."

She did as he requested. "We're only three blocks from the house, and we're stopping already?"

Ian gestured toward a massive three-story Victorian to their left. A dilapidated porch wrapped around the front and side of the house, which sat on the corner lot.

Amelia's gaze traveled across the missing shingles, peeling exterior paint, and overgrown landscaping, He prayed she spotted things of beauty, too, such as the old oak trees that stood sentry in the yard.

"What's this?" Amelia put the van in park.

"Go ahead and pull into the driveway." Ian pointed to the gravel area ahead. "There. I want to give you a tour of the house."

She did as he asked and turned off the car. The click of seatbelts unbuckling snapped behind them.

With a smile, Amelia turned to him. "This is some surprise, all right."

"I hope you like it." He wasn't ready to tell her her how much he hoped she'd love it. "I bought this last week. Isn't it amazing?"

Enthusiasm flowed from her as she said, "She's a beautiful old lady who needs some loving care. She has excellent bones. You're going to fix it up and sell it?"

He watched her reaction to his answer. "Not quite. I'm going to fix it up and keep it."

"Oh, how wonderful!"

Her eyes sparkled, and genuine passion colored her voice. It gave him hope. Could she fall for a former soldier who found happiness and purpose in a project such as this?

"I'd been eyeing this place for months. When my apartment burned, it forced me to find a new place to live. I chose her. Would you like a tour of the interior? She's packed with character."

Please, God, let her see the potential in this home. Let her see the potential for us.

Seven

She had to admit, Ian's house surprised her.

When she admired it from the van, her stomach flipped. She adored old homes like this one. A perfect example of a neglected house begging to have life and love breathed back into it.

She studied the elaborate asymmetrical design, the decorative Queen Anne gables and bays, and the wraparound porch. The right side of the house featured a three-story turret. "This is a fantastic place, Ian. An amazing house."

"I'm so pleased you like it."

"Can we get out?" and "I wanna see! I wanna see!" came from the rear of the vehicle.

Amelia and Ian shared a glance. "Well, then,"—Amelia unbuckled her seat belt—"I guess we'd better take a tour."

With enthusiasm in his step, Ian led the group to the front door and pulled a keyring from his pocket. "The first thing I want to do is replace this modern door with a refurbished one from the time."

Amelia nodded and glanced around. "Yes, perfect. But this porch needs even more love than Dan and Belinda's did. Stay close, kids. No one needs to fall through like I did."

"I'll need to pull this down and rebuild it." He pointed to a broken corbel. "I can take these broken ones and make new ones in the same design. Same for the damaged spindles along the railing. I'll have to make sure it meets code, but that shouldn't be a problem."

"You're going to do all of this yourself?"

"I have a contractor who specializes in older homes. I'll do what I can and leave the rest to him and his crew." He grinned at her. "Unless you want to help."

"My expertise would be more along the lines of refinishing furniture and choosing paint colors, but I live hundreds of miles away."

"Relocate here. Then you could help."

She stiffened. Was that a demand?

Ian tilted his head. "Something wrong?"

Should she tell him about Captain Control Panel?

At that moment, Caleb tugged on Ian's leg. "Let's go in!"

He opened the door, and they stepped onto the parquet floor in the front entry and hallway. This area featured wooden wainscoting in the hallway, a staircase swirling to the second floor, and ornate trim work around the doors and the floors.

Amelia danced through the rooms. Such a beautiful place. She didn't focus on the peeling paint, shedding wallpaper, or spotty damage to the wainscoting. All of that could be repaired or replaced. When finished, this place would be spectacular.

The children ran ahead.

"Hey, guys," Ian called. "Stay inside the house."

His tone reminded her of her childcare duties, and she added, "Someone needs to hang on to Caleb or else he has to stay with us."

Grace took Caleb's wrist. "I've got him. We'll behave."

"Thank you. Don't break anything."

Ian spun to face her. "So you think she has potential?"

She emitted a happy sigh. "I adore her."

"Come see the dining room."

Ian led her through the threshold of the dining room, pulling out the massive pocket doors for her to admire.

She spotted an antique gilded mirror on a wall nearby and walked to it. "This is lovely."

"It came with the house."

She glanced at Ian with a grin. "Did you hang this, by chance?"

"Yes. Something wrong?"

"Let me show you." She stood in front of the large piece. "I see my face, but that's all. I can't use this mirror to check my outfit because you've hung it so high."

Ian laughed. "I take full responsibility. I forget I'm so much taller than everyone else. Especially when I'm by myself. I wanted it on the wall instead of on the floor, leaning against it."

She patted his arm. "No problem. It's nothing that can't be fixed. Like this house. A lot to repair, but oh, so worth it."

They went from one room to another as Ian gave her a grand tour with pride in his voice as he shared his vision for transformation. The children's running footsteps and laughter echoed around them.

When they entered the old kitchen, Ian launched into vivid details about his renovation plans. "I'm going to remove the wall between the kitchen and the butler's pantry, which will open more area for the kitchen. I'll take half the dining room and transform it into a mudroom and laundry room that connects to a new back porch. That mudroom will have a door leading to the detached two-car garage."

She walked over to the formerly white enamel sink, now scratched and rusted. She ran her hand across the enamel wings on either side, used as drying racks during its heyday. "You're keeping this, right?"

Ian frowned. "You think I should, Red?"

"I know a firm in Chicago that refurbishes these. You'd think it was new when they're finished. I'll bet a place in central Arkansas can do the same."

He tilted his head and studied the sink. "I hadn't thought of that. Perhaps I will."

"You must. This can be a showstopper. You need to leave some original pieces in this house for charm. Like that too-high mirror in the dining room."

They shared a laugh.

Her phone rang in her pocket. When she pulled it out and recognized her work number, she silenced the ring and set the phone on vibrate. She'd deal with work later.

Ian smiled. "You're a fan of historic houses?"

"I love them as much as my sister does, but I've never found the time to buy and refurbish one in Chicago."

"This could be your chance." He reddened. "I mean, your chance to help me make this a 'showstopper.' Would you ever consider moving here?"

Ian's question surprised her. She stepped away to think about what he'd said and reached out to open one of the cabinet doors in the kitchen. It came off in her hand. She stared at it, dangling from her fingers, for a moment.

With a smile, she turned to Ian. "Here. This needs some repair."

"What did you do that for?"

Her smile deepened. "I didn't do it on purpose. When I do something on purpose, you can count on it being a disaster."

His eyes twinkled. "Like falling through steps?"

"Nope. That was another accident."

"Like agreeing to take care of four children and various-sized animals for several days?"

She grinned. "Exactly like that. But it's turned out to be a great decision."

He straightened. "Really?"

"All in all, it's been wonderful. Belinda and Dan are enjoying a much-needed break, and I've fallen in love with these children in a deeper way. I've gotten to know them better. Of course, you've come to the rescue several times."

"My pleasure. It's allowed me to become acquainted with one amazing redhead."

With the tour finished, they spent the afternoon purchasing food and supplies. A stop at a park gave the children some much-needed playtime. When they returned home, unpacked, and stowed their purchases, Ian announced it was time for him to go.

Amelia followed him through the living room. "Thank you so much for all the help you've been today."

He hesitated before opening the door. "Are you going to church tomorrow?"

She nodded. "I'd like to. The problem is gathering everyone, then getting them fed and dressed in time."

"May I take you and the kids to brunch afterward?"

She smiled. "That would be great if we go to a place that isn't fancy. I have no idea how the children will behave."

"You pick the place."

"Hang on." Amelia strode to the kitchen and grabbed the list of restaurant recommendations her sister left. She returned and perused the list, then pulled out her phone and tapped the screen. "I can't find the brunch place Belinda recommended."

"What did she suggest?"

"The Star Diner."

"Oh. It changed its name to Eggsactly about a year ago. E-G-G-S-A-C-T-L-Y."

After tapping that into the search engine, Amelia said, "Well, here it is. Finally. Why did she give me the wrong name?"

"A lot of people still call it The Star Diner."

"How silly."

Ian smiled. "Not silly. Human. Have you ever called your married friends by their maiden names?"

"All the time."

"This is similar. It's all in what you're used to."

She nodded. "Eggsactly."

They chuckled until his smile faded. "There is one other thing I'd like to suggest." He glanced toward the children in the living room, then smoothed his mustache in a nervous gesture. "I don't want them to worry, but predictions are still being made for an ice storm. Starting late tomorrow night or early Monday morning."

"Oh, no. I haven't looked at the weather for fear it would upset them."

He nodded. "I have an idea. It's unconventional, but I think it's the best option for the safety of you and the kids."

"What?"

"How about we have everyone in this house, animals included, camp out in the living room?"

"You mean overnight?"

"It might be several days. Since you're a native Arkansan, you know how brutal these ice storms can be. If I'm here and you lose power, I can start a fire in the fireplace to keep us warm and give us a heat source for cooking."

"You think it will come to that?"

He shrugged. "I have no idea. But being prepared is half the battle." He gestured toward the fireplace. "Can you light a fire?"

"Not a real one. I have a gas fireplace in Chicago with a remote start."

He chuckled. "Of course you do. But I'm an old Army guy and a Boy Scout. I know my way around fire-starting."

With a grin, she echoed him. "Of course you do." She realized the only safe option was to accept his offer. "Bring your camping gear tomorrow night and plan to stay for the duration. Thank you. I feel better."

"It will be fine. I promise."

"Do you think us sleeping in the same room is questionable or a bad example for the children? Even if it is the living room?"

He frowned. "It's a weather emergency. If we explain that we're safer together with ice outside, they'll understand. Don't you think?"

"I have no experience with this. I'll pray they understand."

She glanced at his sandals and white socks. "It's smart to have you here. You've been so helpful to the kids and me. I wouldn't want to have to call you for help, forcing you to slide around outside in those sandals."

"Let's explain that to the kids. They'll understand the logic."

That night, while getting ready for bed, she reached for her phone to charge it overnight. That's when she spotted the missed call from work. They'd left a voice message.

For the first time in a very long while, she'd put her life before her work.

Was God giving her a sign that she needed to adjust her priorities? And that question from Ian about moving back to Arkansas. Could she consider it?

All her life, she said she'd never give up her career for a man. However, moving here wouldn't mean retirement. She had several options to explore to become a consultant and choose her hours.

This would let her live near her sister, brother-in-law, and these darling children. It made her smile to consider living near a bear of a man who was a gentle giant. A godly man.

Were all men demanding like her old boyfriend? Or was Ian as wonderful as she imagined?

She'd amassed a small fortune and respect from her colleagues. But was that all she wanted from life?

Eight

S unday morning was hectic. She'd dealt with the crisis at work, which caused her to lose time getting ready for church.

If her sister went through what Amelia'd been through to rush everyone out of the house, no wonder she needed time away. Taking care of the animals and getting the children fed, dressed, and loaded in the van was more time-consuming than she'd imagined. Adding the work issue, what time she had left was barely enough to dress, throw her hair into a messy bun, and add a dash of makeup.

They made it to church with a few minutes to spare. When she entered the sanctuary, gripping Caleb's wrist, three more children trailed after her like ducklings, and she spotted Ian immediately near the front. His height caused him to sit taller than everyone else—an obvious objective.

Ian turned in his nearly empty pew and waved them his way. He stood and helped pull off the children's coats. She and Ian naturally bookended the children without discussion, which kept them corralled and quiet.

Before Pastor Dave began the Call to Worship, Ian leaned across the children and whispered, "You look nice, Red."

"Thank you," she whispered in return. "A miracle considering the battle I've been through this morning."

"Well, that outfit is pretty, and it's not a BDU."

"BDU?"

"Battle dress uniform."

She adjusted her jacket. "It might not be BDU, but it's the uniform for female soldiers of God. A dress made of no-wrinkle material and a jean jacket to cover it."

He grinned, then turned his attention to James, encouraging him to stop swinging his legs.

The sermon featured Isaiah and emphasized the transformative power of faith and God's ongoing work in their lives. How had she not realized all the messages God had recently placed before her about her choices? God's handiwork appeared all over her current situation.

She needed to step back and think. Did she want to continue her career without changes? No, some things had to be purged. Her career consumed too much of her. Could she figure out a way to modify her career to be less demanding but more rewarding?

Was it time to move closer to her sister and family? With the speed her nieces and nephews were growing, if she didn't do something different, she'd completely miss their childhood.

Her time here showed her a different life she could lead if she made different choices. A life with family at the forefront. Perhaps one including a bear of a man with a kind heart. Was this man her Boaz?

Once the church service concluded, Ian helped her round up the brood. Together they loaded everyone into the van, and he followed them to the restaurant in his pickup truck.

Eggsactly turned out to be a darling diner, a perfect family place for after-church eating. Amelia sat across from Ian in a large booth, both of them surrounded by children.

He entertained the children with stories and knock-knock jokes until their food arrived. Amelia caught herself staring at him as he kept the kids interested. Was it ridiculous for her to want to stare at him for hours? To memorize his face, his smile, his hilarious expressions?

Although she hadn't come here to fall for someone, it seemed to be turning out that way. Ian appeared right for her in so many ways. The thought equally scared and pleased her.

Ian put away pancakes, several pieces of bacon, biscuits and gravy, and hash browns. The surprise was James, who polished off a similar plate of food. Who knew these guys could eat so much?

After pondering the price of groceries, Amelia said, "As much as I try to help, I don't understand how Dan and Belinda can afford to feed and clothe these kids on one salary."

Ian's blue eyes warmed. "It's a labor of love for them, even though they're basically broke. Dan takes side jobs when he can to buy supplies for fixing up the house. That's why I help him. He can't afford to hire anyone."

In a whisper when James was distracted, Amelia asked Ian, "That boy eats so much you'd think he has a tapeworm. Is that normal?"

"He's a growing boy like me." Ian patted his belly.

Amelia eyed Ian's flat stomach. "So far you have your weight under control. I can't imagine how you can eat what you just did and remain in shape."

Ian leaned across the table. "One word. Workout."

"So you hang out at a gym?"

"Only three days a week. With my feet messed up, I'm forced to cut back on things. But in a few more weeks, I should be released to go back to my normal routine."

After Ian insisted upon picking up the tab, Amelia carried two containers of leftover food to the van. Either the dogs would have a feast, or the children would have a second chance with their meal choices.

Ian opened the car door for her and took the containers from her hands. "I'll hold this precious cargo while the rest of the precious cargo gets in place."

She appreciated his manners. His offers of help made her feel feminine, not incompetent.

Because the temperature in the car was frigid, she started the engine and cranked up the heat. Once she and the children were belted in, he walked around the van, placed the food on the floorboard of the passenger side, and returned to her side.

When he did, she lowered the window. "Where did you learn your manners?"

"First, from my mother. She was a stickler about insisting I become a gentleman. The Army also teaches you respect and manners, both for your fellow soldiers and your commanders. Regardless of gender."

"What made you leave the military?"

"In college, I joined ROTC to help pay for my college expenses. I went into the Army after graduation and did my required service for the ROTC commitment. There was an option for a military career, but moving from place to place didn't suit me."

"Because you like old houses?"

He grinned. "Because I like small towns. The Army doesn't generally assign you to those."

"Where did you grow up?"

"In the big village of Siloam Springs, Arkansas."

"What brought you here?"

"My sister and her husband moved here several years back. When my father passed away, my mother packed everything and moved here to be near my sister while I was in the Army, seeing the world. When I got out, I wanted to live close to my remaining family."

She thanked him again for picking up the tab for brunch. "We'll see you later tonight, right?"

He nodded. "That will be soon enough to explain our plans."

"How about you come for dinner? I'm sure my sister has something marvelous in the freezer."

He flashed his white teeth as he smoothed his mustache.

"As long as you're not cooking, Red, you've got a deal."

She pouted. "You'll like what you get, regardless of who cooked it, and that's an order."

He saluted her. Equally unexpected, he leaned inside the window and kissed her cheek.

The children oohed and aahed from the back of the van.

She and Ian laughed, and she drove away, feeling all the feels. This man was her kryptonite, and he appeared to like her too. His appeal forced her to further consider the decisions about her future.

She hadn't experienced sensations like this since high school.

Was it silly to want to talk to him about everything? Or that she wanted him to tell her everything about himself?

After only a few days, she was smitten. Hook, line, and sinker. Or should she say salutes, BDUs, and army boots?

Nine

Late Sunday afternoon, while Caleb was still napping, her phone rang. Amelia smiled when she saw her sister's name and swiped to answer.

"Why didn't you tell me an ice storm is headed our way?" Belinda screeched across the connection.

Amelia's smile disappeared. "Well, hello to you too."

"Don't play funny with me. I'm angry."

Amelia gritted her teeth and prayed for patience. "Obviously."

"We could be halfway home by now." Belinda's words were clipped.

"And that's the reason I didn't tell you. There's no need for you guys to shorten your vacation."

"Of course that's what we would do. We're responsible parents. The question is, what are you going to do?"

"Have a little faith in me, please." Amelia sighed. "So far, this has been a fantastic visit. We're getting along very well."

"I'm not worried about what's already happened. I'm worried about when the storm starts. It's almost upon us. We can't risk trying to drive home now. How can you feed the kids and handle the animals, potentially without power?"

"A plan is in place. An excellent one. I admitted I would need help. Ian and I have put together options for the worst-case scenario."

"Ian?" After a pause, her sister asked, "How is Shorty helping you?"

"We've made lists of everything essential, stocked up on supplies, and even purchased extra games and entertainment for the kids."

"That's a relief. He can do almost anything you need. Cooking, carpentry work, electrical stuff, and plumbing. You name it, and he can do it."

"That's why he's coming over this evening and planning to stay."

Belinda gasped. "What? You two alone in the house with the children? What about appearances?"

Amelia inhaled a slow breath and tried to remain calm. "It will look like two adults, four children, three dogs, and a cat camping out in the living room. We're trying to make the situation fun, not scary."

"It's not right for Ian to sleep over."

"I agree ... under normal circumstances, but that's not what we have here. He's offered to help me manage the kids and the animals. I'm grateful for the offer. I'm not worried about appearances. We're putting the children's safety first."

"What if you lose power?"

"I can't start a fire in the fireplace, but Ian can. That's one of the reasons he's staying."

After a pause, Belinda said, "I guess that's reasonable."

"If we lose power, and Ian's here, he can start a fire. We'll roast hot dogs and make s'mores. I've got all the supplies."

"The kids would enjoy that. But cut those hot dogs lengthwise."

Amelia chuckled. "Ian already told me about that." With another sigh, she added, "If Ian isn't already here and the power goes out, he might not be able to return. He can't walk on ice with those sandals he has to wear. He'd fall and hurt himself."

"Okay, okay. You're right. It's a reasonable thing to do. But you should have told me."

Amelia gathered her verbal ammunition. "If I'd told you about the possibility of the storm, you and Dan would've raced home. You'd forget about yourselves and the break you need."

Belinda's voice was calmer but remained firm. "You should have respected me enough to keep me informed of the situation. It was my decision to make. They're my children."

Amelia deflated like a pierced balloon falling from the sky. She hadn't thought from the perspective of a parent.

"You're right. I'm so sorry, Bells." Regret colored her tone. "Truly, I'm sorry. I should have told you. My only motivation was how much you needed this time away."

Silence.

"What can I do to make it up to you? I've admitted I was wrong. You know that's not easy for me."

"No, it's not. I'm relishing the moment. It's rare to hear you admit being wrong."

"Extremely rare."

"Rare that you're wrong or rare that you admit you're wrong?"

"Both."

They chuckled.

"Bells, I am sincerely sorry. And ashamed I didn't tell you."

Her sister's tone lightened. "I believe you."

"Thank you for understanding."

"It's not that I understand. It's that I can't do anything about it now."

"Again. My bad."

Silence stretched between them. "You're going to have to keep me updated on the weather and how everyone is handling the situation."

"Okay."

"I mean, every few hours."

"Done. I appreciate you giving me some grace in this mess."

"Your heart's in the right place." After a pause, she added, "I have two auxiliary phone chargers in my bedroom. In the top drawer of my dresser. Plug those in and charge them while you can. They'll fully charge your phone if you lose power."

"Thanks." Amelia made her way to the bedroom and located them while Belinda continued with instructions for handling an icy situation.

After Amelia promised to do everything Belinda told her to do, she began a rotation of children for each to have a quick conversation with their parents. She promised to call back once Caleb awakened so they could talk to him.

"Thank you for forgiving me, Bells."

"I haven't forgiven you. I'm merely not as mad."

"Maybe the storm won't be too bad," Amelia offered. "The way the weather is around here, nothing is certain."

"Dan had planned for us to go to a museum tomorrow. The Gangster Museum of America is right across the street from our hotel."

"How fun for Dan."

"If I see a cute T-shirt, would you like one?"

"I'd better pass on that. I'm not sure I can wear it in Chicago. They're a bit sensitive about their gangsters."

"Why?"

"Al Capone was one of many mobsters who operated in Chicago during Prohibition. He visited Hot Springs for vacation or to leave town when the law chased him."

"See? Another reason for you to leave Chicago. You don't need to live somewhere sensitive to its mobster history."

"Are you keeping a list of why I need to move?"

"Yes, and proximity to Shorty is going on that list."

"Well, I can't argue about that line item. He is a great guy. He took us to brunch after church today, and we took a tour of his new old home yesterday."

"He did? Isn't that house beautiful, even with all the repairs it needs?"

"It is."

"And close to our house. If the stars align, perhaps you could live there one day?"

"Now you're playing matchmaker?"

"You'd be hard-pressed to find a better guy than Shorty."

"Or a taller one, for that matter."

After they hung up, Amelia thanked God for her forgiving sister. A blessing that she ought to live closer to. Perhaps in the beautiful old lady down the street?

She needed to get through this possible storm and save decisions about her future for a calmer time. Maybe exposure to Ian during a potential storm would give her more insight.

Ten

Amelia pulled a tuna casserole from the freezer. Any leftovers would be easy to heat in the microwave or near the fireplace. She prayed for an absence of fireplace cooking, but best to be prepared.

As a special treat, she called the older children into the kitchen, and they prepared two types of brownies from box mixes. If she expected the kids to forget her burned brownies in the past, she was mistaken. Grace supervised the oven temperature and the cook time so these wouldn't char. Because Amelia used a mix, the children helped her follow the directions on the box.

Amelia turned to her management and organizational skills to lighten the burdens of their current situation. If they lost power, everyone needed to start this adventure clean. Ian mentioned the house had electric water heaters. Without electricity, they'd have to heat their water over a fire.

After Caleb woke from his nap and enjoyed the promised conversation with his parents, Amelia filled the children's tub with bubbles. She enticed Caleb into the water with a flotilla of plastic boats. Once his bathwater cooled and the bubbles faded, she pulled him from the tub and wrapped him in a towel. The second she released her hold, the imp scampered off naked, his towel puddled at her feet.

"Help! Please. Naked boy on the loose."

Grace, James, and Hope scrambled into service, all the while giggling at the situation.

Amelia rounded a corner, headed into the kitchen, and slipped on a wet spot formed by the absconder's dripping hair. She slid across the floor like a crazed ice skater, her arms pinwheeling. She skidded into the island and stopped herself before gravity took over.

The children's laughter reverberated off the walls as she continued her chase of the escapee. Catching the runaway in his room, she returned him to the bathroom and dressed him, admonishing him every step for being naughty.

The rest of the children took turns bathing without incident. Only Hope needed help with hair washing.

As rain began to fall, Ian drove over and unloaded a multitude of camping supplies. She ran out to help him after James volunteered to entertain Caleb. In addition to the grate and racks brought for fireplace cooking, Ian packed cast iron skillets and a muffin pan, two coolers filled with ice, and several sleeping bags.

With this inventory, they'd weather this weather with no problem.

"I think you've got us covered, Ian."

He grinned. "I'd rather bring too much than not enough. We won't have the option of picking up anything else if Mother Nature unleashes her fury."

The equipment unleashed curiosity in the children.

Grace asked, "What's Mr. Shorty going to do with all of this cool camping stuff?"

With a quick glance at Ian, Amelia replied, "We'll explain as soon as we gather everyone in the living room. I'll grab the boys."

Finding James and Caleb playing well together, Amelia announced the family meeting.

Caleb asked, "Can I bring my boats?"

"Sure." Amelia eyed the boats lined up on the floor. "They're not wet, are they?"

James said, "No, Aunt Melly. I made sure all the water was out of them when we got them out of the bathroom."

"Thank you."

When they entered the living room with Caleb's flotilla, Amelia asked the children to line up on the couch. Ian, who'd been leaning against the doorjamb between the living room and the kitchen, walked over to a recliner and sat.

Taco, seeing an opportunity for petting, jumped onto the couch and settled in Grace's lap.

Amelia gave an encouraging smile. "We may have some ice soon."

This news caused James to frown and squirm on the couch. Grace's petting hand moved faster than before, much to Taco's delight. Caleb and Hope didn't register any surprise or concern.

Amelia held up a hand. "Before you worry too much about this, understand that Mr. Shorty is going to stay here and make sure we're safe."

Hope smiled. "He's staying here?"

"Yes. He has many skills I don't have. For example, he can build a fire in the fireplace to keep us warm if the power goes out."

With a fading smile, Grace asked, "Why would the power go out?"

"I'm not saying it will, but if we receive freezing rain and the ice builds up on our power lines, those lines can break. If we lose power, we lose our heat."

Caleb glanced up at her. His brow furrowed. "No heat?"

"Perhaps. It may never happen. Or it could be cold enough outside to give us snow instead of ice."

Hope smiled. "I love snow."

Grace turned to Hope. "It's rare. Don't be too excited."

Amelia walked in front of the couch, stepping carefully over the prone bodies of Sarge and Snoopy. "The people who predict the weather aren't exactly sure what will happen, which is why we must be prepared. If it snows, we'll have fun. No worries about power. If it ices and the power fails, Mr. Shorty will build a fire in the fireplace. We'll all camp out here in the living room."

James asked, "When?"

"The rain has started. Whether it will freeze—who knows?" After checking for any further questions, Amelia sat in the other recliner.

Grace walked over and perched on the arm of Amelia's recliner. "When will we know for sure?"

Amelia patted Grace's back. "It was colder after church, right?"

Several heads nodded.

James added, "It's even colder now. Sarge and Taco didn't want to go outside when we got home from brunch. Snoopy won't care. He loves the outdoors, no matter the temperature."

Amelia smiled at James. "The weather is changing. I doubt any of the dogs will like that. But Mr. Shorty has a plan to keep them from slipping down the stairs to the yard."

Ian turned toward the anxious faces. "I've brought a lot of the tarps I use for painting and woodworking. The plan is to spread them on the back deck and stairs. If we get ice, your aunt and I will shake them now and again to break up any ice and keep the steps from getting slick."

"May I help?" James sat on the other arm of her recliner.

"Thank you, James, but I need to help Mr. Shorty do this," Amelia said. "We don't want any of you getting wet or falling out there."

James frowned but made no further appeal.

Grace joined him in a frown. "What about the fish? Will they freeze or suffocate if there's no power to make their bubbles run?"

Amelia glanced at Ian.

He nodded. "If the power does go out, it won't be for long. But we can warm up water on the fireplace, treat it with chemicals, and pour it in with them. They won't freeze."

"What about the bubbles?"

"They should be fine for a few days without bubbles."

Hope asked, "Are Mom and Dad coming home?"

"No, sweetie, they're going to stay in Hot Springs, where they may have decent weather. Please don't worry about them. They'll come home when the ice or snow has melted or when the storm passes without causing a problem."

Hope burst into tears, wailing that she wanted her parents to come home.

Amelia was unprepared for this turn of events. She blinked at Hope's despair for a moment, then rushed over to reassure her. She scooped her up, and they sat on the couch together.

Grace sat stiffly with a furrowed brow. Caleb appeared content playing with his boats.

Amelia waved Grace to join them, and reached over and gathered Hope, James, and Grace into her arms. "I promise you we are going to be fine. God, Mr. Shorty, and I will see us through whatever happens with the weather."

The children glanced at her, skepticism painting their faces.

"We have hot dogs, s'mores, the brownies we made, and lots of games. It's going to be fun. I promise."

The mention of food brightened James's face. She turned to the girls. "Want to play with my makeup? We can do that too."

This transformed the girls' sad faces. She peered over their heads at Ian.

He nodded.

She tightened her arms around the kids. "Let's all kneel and ask the Lord to watch out for us."

It surprised her when Ian got on his knees and joined them in prayer.

When they finished, everyone rose in a brighter mood. She found a cute children's movie and started it on the big television, then excused herself to prepare dinner.

Amelia made a huge salad to accompany the tuna casserole, placing half of it back in the refrigerator for a future meal. No power was required for salad. Instead of calling the children to help her set the table, she left them in the living room, hoping the television would keep them distracted.

When dinner was ready, she found Ian on the couch with two children on each side. "Your aunt loves you very much. You know that, right?"

Four heads nodded.

"She's an untrained soldier facing an unfamiliar group of people in unfamiliar territory. She's not used to having children and animals around her all the time."

Grace piped in, "She lives alone in a fancy apartment."

"Yes. You guys realize I was a soldier once, don't you?"

Three heads nodded. Caleb was back to playing with his boats.

"As a soldier, one of the worst situations you can face is being in unfamiliar territory with unfamiliar people. Because she loves you, she's doing the best job she can to take care of you. She wants to keep you fed and happy. She's doing all these things with bravery, fairness, and kindness."

The older three stared at him, hanging on every word.

"We're trying to be good," Grace said.

"And you are doing a great job. However, you also need to understand that your aunt needs your support. She needs you to tell her she's doing things right. She came here to give your mother and father a much-needed vacation. How about we try our best to keep a cheerful outlook about circumstances she can't control? Like the weather."

"We can do that." James nodded.

"Yeah. We can," Grace added.

"Excellent," Ian said. "You're the best."

Amelia retreated to the kitchen and wiped away the tears in her eyes. *This man. Thank you, Lord, for putting him in my path.*

Eleven

6〜9

D inner turned out to be a light-hearted event. Whether the credit was due to Ian's pep talk or they were calmer after accepting the situation, she wasn't sure. For now, they were happy because Mr. Shorty regaled them with some fishing and hunting adventures he'd experienced while growing up in Northwest Arkansas.

James piped in about his excitement over the upcoming Valentine's play. "I get to wear a costume. A real costume."

The others chimed in with chatter about their costumes and the lines they needed to memorize. While Amelia and Grace cleared dishes, Grace turned to Amelia. "Did Mommy tell you all the things that happened during our Christmas pageant?"

Amelia furrowed her brow. "I don't think so."

"Aw, Grace," James protested. "You're going to get me in trouble with Aunt Melly."

Amelia patted his shoulder and grinned at him, then spun around to Grace. "Spill every detail."

James hung his head. "I got carried away."

Grace returned a bowl to the table, devoting her attention to the story. "James was one of the three wise men. During the reenactment, a shepherd, who is younger than James, stole baby Jesus from the girl playing Mary."

Amelia gasped. "Stole him right out of the manger?"

"He stole him right out of Mary's arms."

"Oh, my."

Ian spun in his chair until his broad back faced her. Waves of silent laughter convulsed his shoulders.

"Can you believe it?" Grace put a hand on her hip for emphasis. "James and the shepherd got into a tug of war, which ended with baby Jesus's leg coming off in the other boy's hand."

"Oh, no."

"The girl playing Mary screamed and started to cry. Her mother ran up to comfort her, and Pastor Dave jumped between the two boys."

James shrugged. "Pastor Dave fixed baby Jesus's leg and wrapped him again. Then he handed him back to Mary."

Amelia held in her laughter as she replied, "Amen."

Ian turned. "The congregation went crazy with applause when Pastor Dave returned Jesus to Mary."

Grace rolled her eyes. "The naughty boys bowed, like the applause was for them."

"Wasn't it?" James asked.

"No. It was for Pastor Dave fixing Jesus."

Ian lost his battle with silent laughter. Deep, reverberating guffaws filled the room.

Amelia joined in the hilarity.

Hope added, "I was proud of Sarge. He did a great job."

Amelia blinked. "Sarge? Your dog?"

With a vast smile lighting her face, Hope nodded.

"What did he play?" Amelia eyed the Mastiff, who snored under the dinner table. "One of the camels?"

"No, silly." Hope giggled. "He was a donkey."

Grace added, "Training him to tolerate the long ears on his head and the stuffed bags across his back took time."

With a pucker of her lips, Amelia tried to envision Sarge as a donkey. About the size of a small pony, a donkey wasn't much of a stretch. "I'm sorry I missed this."

Ian turned to her, still sporting a grin. "It was three times as funny in person. I promise you."

Inspired by their conversation, Amelia suggested, "What do you think about practicing your upcoming Valentine's Day play? It's only a few days away."

Grace asked, "Can we wear our costumes?"

"It's not a real rehearsal without them."

Cries of joy rang out.

Amelia turned to the girls. "A little practice with my makeup would also be necessary for a full-dress rehearsal."

Hope clapped, and Grace jumped up and down in excitement.

"Not too much, you understand. A little color is required when you're on a stage and have stage lights pointed at you."

The girls nodded and joined their brothers in running to their rooms to find their costumes.

To Amelia's dismay, the boys showed no interest in stage makeup. She didn't push the matter. Their mother would return in time to address this issue.

Once the girls were dressed, and she'd instructed them on the proper application of stage makeup, they returned to the living room. James paced while he studied a paper in his hand.

Amelia asked, "What's this?"

Grace frowned. "It's his script, of course."

"Silly me." Amelia smacked her forehead with her palm.

The children laughed, which calmed the tension in the room.

They decided the stage would be the hearth and the audience would gather on the couch. Amelia couldn't help but smile as she snuggled into the sofa with Sarge, Taco, and Snoopy.

James was a shepherd, looking darling in his robe and sandals. His prop, a large shepherd's staff, took her by surprise.

She sucked in a breath when he held it aloft. "You are the best shepherd I've ever seen."

"This staff of mine is a symbol of protection and love. Notice the curve at the top." James made a sweeping gesture to the crook of the staff.

Caleb watched the performance from the floor. James and his staff clearly captivated him.

"This allows shepherds to rescue sheep from dangerous situations and to pull them back into my flock," James continued. "These are things God does for us as He is our shepherd."

Although Grace was one of the major characters, she didn't have many lines. She portrayed Rachel. Her lines explained how Jacob worked seven years for her hand in marriage and was tricked into marrying her older sister, Leah. Grace then stepped out of character to discuss her friend who was playing Leah.

Amelia and Ian shared a grin.

With a sweeping return to seriousness, Grace continued her lines about Jacob working seven more years to pay for marrying Rachel.

Amelia struggled to keep a straight face at Grace's theatrics. This girl was a natural actress. She didn't merely speak her lines, she became Rachel, who married the man she loved and who loved her in return.

Hope did a fantastic job with her lines, only needing two small prompts from Ian. Her theatrical duty was to explain the domestic jobs that female servants in biblical times performed. She added explanations about how some servants held significant roles within the household.

Although Caleb was too young to have any lines, he did have a costume comparable to his older brother's. When Amelia remarked on the similarity, James insisted Caleb was not a shepherd but a child playing a game with other children to the stage's side.

Caleb ran out of the living room in a huff. He returned with a small plastic baseball bat. Before either of the adults could react, Caleb swung the bat at the staff James held.

Amelia leaped to break up the fight before it became a proper brawl.

James swung his staff, which caused Caleb's bat to go flying, arching across the room and smacking Hope on the arm. She howled in pain. Ian rushed to her.

The towel wrapped around James's head blocked his vision, and he fell off the stage, stepping on Cow in the process. With a screech, the cat dashed to a safer place.

During this melee, James trod on Grace's gown.

The terrible rip of material filled the room, followed by an outcry of grief from Grace. Tears poured down Grace's cheeks when Amelia rushed to console her.

Once Hope had calmed, Ian moved over and kneeled to examine the edge of Grace's gown. After a moment of study, he proclaimed, "This is not a problem. I can repair this as if nothing ever happened."

Both Grace and Amelia stared at him.

Amelia gathered her wits. "You can sew?"

"Of course." His eyes twinkled. "The Army makes you put patches on your uniforms. Until you can afford to have them professionally sewn on, you sew them on yourself."

She stared. *Was he joking?*

Grace believed him. She pulled from Amelia's arms and announced, "I'll change and bring my costume back here along with mother's sewing kit."

Of course my sister would have a sewing kit. It must be required when you have children.

Amelia's stomach lurched. This would have been a disaster if Ian hadn't been here. She had no sewing skills and paid other people to make any alterations.

After Amelia shooed the children off to change into pajamas and hang up their costumes, Ian asked, "Something wrong?"

Amelia sank onto the couch, blowing out air in frustration. "I'm a capable manager, but I can't properly care for these children. Your sewing skills are the only thing that prevented tonight's events from becoming a huge crisis."

He rose from the fireplace stoop and joined her on the couch, wrapping an arm around her shoulders. "We all have our skills. I have sewing ability. That doesn't make you a lesser human being. I know nothing about makeup—the stage kind or the stuff you women wear."

Amelia sighed. "There are so many things I can't do or don't know how to do that are necessary for raising children."

He studied her. "And why does that bother you?"

"Because I'd like to have them someday." She fiddled with her fingernails. "At least I think I would. All these thoughts of motherhood have taken me by surprise. I've been so focused on my career that I've rarely thought about children."

He patted her arm. "It's understandable. I was the same. I spent my time in service and didn't get serious about anyone. Now that I'm in a friendly town and recently bought a fantastic house to refurbish, it makes me think about sharing my life with someone."

"Do those thoughts of yours include rug rats too?"

"You better believe it."

She tipped her head toward him.

His deep blue eyes locked on hers. "You need the right man. One who can appreciate your career and your capabilities."

She reached for his hand and threaded their fingers together. "Know anyone like that available?"

He leaned toward her. "Absolutely."

Just as she moved in to accept his kiss, a small pajama-clad girl, holding a costume and a sewing basket, interrupted them.

Twelve

Around ten o'clock, the distinct ping of frozen precipitation pelting the roof, the deck, and the trees began.

Ian and Amelia traded a look of concern. They rose from the couch and stepped past various sleeping children and animals to converge in the kitchen.

Trepidation laced Amelia's voice when she asked, "How bad is it?"

He took his time to answer. No need to scare her. He studied the precipitation from the window an extra minute. "I'd feel better if this were more like sleet. It's freezing rain right now. Perhaps even freezing fog." He glanced at his watch. "Is there a piece of paper and a pen handy?"

"Sure." Amelia rifled through her sister's catch-all drawer and found both. "What's this for?"

"I'm keeping track of the storm details." Ian wrote the time and the type of precipitation. "It's not practical to keep an electronic diary if we're out of power for hours, or days."

Amelia shuddered. "We're going to freeze to death."

Ian grinned at her. "Oh, ye of little faith. I won't let that happen. You're lucky I've trained in cold environment survival skills."

"During your time in the military?"

"Yes, but I also grew up in the Fayetteville area. Snow and ice are regular occurrences in that neck of the woods."

"I didn't think. Belinda and I grew up in southern Arkansas."

Ian glanced out the window again. "Let's see if we can sweep the water off the deck and break up any ice. Also, we need to make the dogs go outside one more time. Then we'll get the tarps down and grab some shuteye. We're going to be fine."

Amelia fidgeted with the edge of the countertop. "I'm concerned about this. I should have told Belinda and Dan to come home when I first heard about the storm."

"I disagree. You're tired. A good night's sleep is what you need. We can handle this. Let's 'embrace the fight,' as the military teaches us. Trust me."

"I trust you. The problem is me."

He waved her toward the mudroom. She followed, and they attired themselves in hooded coats, boots, and gloves. Ian didn't like to complain, but putting boots over his wounded feet caused him to wince in pain. He tied them loosely, but tight enough to stay on his feet.

Outside, the deck was icy, so they formed a plan of attack against the thin layer of frozen precipitation collected there. Ian broke the thin sheet into pieces with a shovel, while Amelia swept them off the surfaces.

The dogs appeared tortured by the idea of going outside. They balked at the slick surface, but the promise of treats finally coaxed them to quickly do their business and race inside.

Ian and Amelia relaid the tarps on the deck and stairs and returned inside.

Amelia pulled off her gloves. "How are we going to encourage them to go out if there's an enormous layer of ice tomorrow?"

"When we pull up the tarp, it should break any accumulated

ice. It might be hard to raise, but I have no other ideas to make the steps safe for them."

Amelia held up crossed fingers. "It's an interesting plan. Hope it works."

Back in the living room, he was glad Amelia settled on the couch. Ian had previously insisted she sleep there by claiming, "No man worth his salt would let a woman sleep on the floor or a chair with a perfectly comfortable couch available."

That left him to sleep on Dan's recliner. Amelia'd argued with him, but he'd won the skirmish.

"I'm a former soldier. A recliner is a luxury compared to sleeping on the ground."

Once he was comfortable, Ian prayed that God would help him keep the living creatures in this home safe and sound.

If he was going into battle with this storm, he was glad to have Amelia by his side. So she couldn't cook or sew. No big deal. He could do both.

But she wasn't afraid to work hard and get her hands dirty. How many women could do carpentry work? And how many could take his teasing and throw it right back? He preferred those qualities.

* * *

The next day, a faint early-morning light filtering through the living room windows woke Amelia. Ian had beaten her to sleep last night, and she'd been left debating who snored louder—him or Sarge. It was a toss-up.

It took her three seconds to realize Caleb wasn't anywhere on the living room floor.

She sprang from the couch and ran from one lumpy area to another. No Caleb.

Ian stirred in the recliner. "What's wrong?"

"I can't find Caleb."

Ian rose and checked the front door, then walked into the

kitchen. When he returned, he said, "All the doors are bolted. There's no way he got out."

The lumps revealed all the sleeping dogs and children, except for Caleb. Panic caused her stomach to clench. She glanced at Ian and whispered, "Where is he?"

"In a bathroom. Or his bedroom."

They checked both bathrooms to no avail. At the door of the room Caleb and James shared, Ian stopped and turned to her.

"I'd be more comfortable if I knew whether we faced a bed full of stuffies or a floor full of army men."

She glanced at his socked feet. "My money is on the army men."

Ian opened the door. Caleb snoozed in his bed, surrounded by all his stuffies. Toy soldiers lay scattered across the floor.

Amelia smiled. "I was right. You stay here." She tiptoed to the window, closed the blinds, and reversed out of the room.

They headed to the kitchen, where the anxious faces and wagging tails of three dogs awaited them. Amelia giggled. "Put your boots on, pal. These soldiers are ready for action."

Ian petted the two large dogs. "Roger that." He glanced out the window and scribbled some notes in his weather notebook.

They outfitted themselves for the Arctic. Leaving the dogs inside, they braved the backyard. Outside, a colorless but sparkling ice fairyland awaited them. The weight of ice and sleet accumulation made the surrounding tree branches droop. Some branches and bushes littered the ground, while others merely hung near it in a graceful bow.

"It's like the branches are touching their toes."

"Careful, Amelia. Watch where you're stepping. It's slippery."

Ian held her arm as she gingerly made her way across the deck. They worked as a team to pull up the tarps, breaking off a quarter inch of ice. Ian used a snow shovel to clear ice mixed with sleet from the deck and stairs.

Amelia's talent with a broom was improving. Practice made perfect. As she swept, she asked, "Any chance this stops soon?"

Ian glanced at the clouds, still dripping with moisture. "Possibly."

"What other frozen state of precipitation remains?" She gestured toward the contents of the tarps. "We've had freezing rain, sleet, a little snow, freezing fog, and perhaps some hail."

He shrugged. "I'm enjoying being trapped inside with you, the kids, and the animals. I don't care what happens out here if the power stays on."

She smiled. "Honestly?"

After a quick nod and an elusive grin, Ian pointed to the other end of the tarp he held. "Hurry. Freezing rain is pouring down my neck."

Amelia giggled. "A hat will fix that, but I doubt pink is your color."

"You think not? Depends on how much freezing rain cascades down the back of my neck."

Back inside, she cooked breakfast. Please, *Lord, let me keep these guys warm, fed, and happy until this storm is over.*

The day passed quickly. Amelia sent detailed reports to Belinda, who appeared pleased all was going well.

It stayed fine until four o'clock in the afternoon, when a thunderous boom jerked their attention from the family movie they'd gathered around.

The screen went blank, and the lights went dark.

They'd lost power.

* * *

The children and dogs loved cooking their evening meal over the fireplace. To appease both her and Belinda, supervision was extreme, and no injuries occurred.

The s'mores were a hit with everyone but the animals. Ian reminded the children that dogs are deathly allergic to chocolate, so they went without.

Thanks to Ian's amazing battery-powered lanterns, they were

able to play numerous board games after dinner. When the children grew restless, Amelia suggested a game of hide and seek.

James jumped up from the table. "Can we use the whole house?"

Amelia exchanged glances with Ian. "No basement and no attic. Everywhere else is within bounds."

Caleb was unable to count to fifty, so an adult supervised his counting and peeking.

Laughter and good-natured screams ensued.

It didn't take the adults long to observe the dogs giving away the location of the children. They would stand in front of closet doors or cabinets, waiting for their people to come out. The children believed the adults were the best trackers in the world.

Much later in the evening, when Sarge snored, and the children slept soundlessly, she and Ian sat on the couch.

Amelia patted Ian's knee. "Today was a success, even with the lack of power. That wouldn't have happened without you. I'm very grateful."

He reached an arm around her and drew her into a soft kiss.

Any hesitation on Amelia's part melted away as an electric current passed between them. *This man. He is unplanned and irresistible.*

Slowly pulling away, Ian brushed a lock of hair behind her ear and smiled down at her. "This may be too sudden, but is there any chance for me in your life?"

Amelia nodded. "I'd like that, but I've never been able to make a long-distance relationship work."

He shrugged. "Although I've never done it, I'd like the opportunity to try one with you."

She ran a finger across the back of his hand. "Would you consider moving to Chicago?"

With knitted brows, Ian blinked at her. "But your family is here, and so is mine. I recently closed on the beautiful lady down the street. We both have roots here. Would you consider relocating?"

Amelia's face flamed. "Roots? You're talking about roots here without considering the career I'd have to throw away to move to this town."

Ian stiffened.

She jerked away. "Are all men alike? Do you teach each other how to be demanding? Why is it that a man always expects a woman to ditch her career?"

His face scrunched up in anger. "I'm not asking you to ditch your career. You've mentioned a change in your career path. I assumed such a change would make your sister and these children a priority, which logically includes proximity to them."

"I haven't decided. But it's my decision to make."

Ian threw up his hands in a surrender gesture. "Of course it is. My mistake."

Light from the kitchen blinked and then glowed with brilliance when the power returned. The television blared back to life.

Amelia grabbed the remote to silence the movie before it woke the children.

Ian shuffled to the kitchen, turned off the lights, and adjusted the blankets in the recliner. He flopped down and said nothing else.

Later, the dueling snores of Sarge and Ian were but one of many things that kept her awake throughout the night.

She'd overreacted to Ian's suggestion of her relocating and was ashamed of her temper. Why had she frozen him out?

Ian was a fine man. A Christian who made her laugh and appreciated her mind.

Her family was here. This wonderful man was here.

Even in an ice storm, the weather in Arkansas was much better than Chicago. Why didn't she start a new career here? Where all the people she cared about surrounded her and supported her.

Thirteen

Three days later, Amelia helped load everything in the car, laughing at the children's excitement about their upcoming performance. Although nervous, the children radiated positive attitudes.

Belinda left the house with her van stuffed full of actors, scripts, and costumes. Dan and Amelia followed them to the church.

Dan took Amelia's arm as they ascended the stairs to the vestibule. "I'm so glad you stayed for this performance."

"I've seen a preview," Amelia said. "The kids ran their lines in full costume during the storm." She shrugged off her coat. "You have a family of natural thespians, Dan. Every one of them gave us a solid performance."

They hung up their coats, a man handed them a program, and they made their way down the church aisle. Clusters of people crowded into the front pews. A children's play filled the front better than any other service.

Dan waved her into a pew. "Amelia." Halfway down, he gestured to two ladies in the row behind them. "This is Mrs. McIntosh, Shorty's mother. And his sister, Maisie White."

A beaming septuagenarian and a redheaded woman, who

appeared a few years younger than Ian, said, "Hello" and "How do you do?"

Their presence here surprised Amelia, but she gathered her manners. "Pleased to meet you both."

Mrs. McIntosh sported twinkling dark blue eyes like her son. "Same here."

Maisie shared Ian's strawberry-blond hair and appeared above average in height. "Delighted to meet you, Amelia. Ian has regaled us with tales of his time helping you with your nieces and nephews."

Amelia glanced around. "Speaking of Ian, is he going to be here?"

Mrs. McIntosh nodded toward the front of the church. "He's helping herd the children."

Maisie said, "My husband, Alan, roped him into assisting. They'll be out soon."

After another smile at Ian's mother and sister, Amelia took a seat. Did Maisie have children in this production too? Likely. Ian mentioned she had lots of kids. Any redheaded child might belong to her.

Sadness overtook her. Her relationship with Ian was blown before it even started. Would she ever have a chance of having redheaded children of her own?

After a few minutes, Belinda joined her and Dan on the pew. "The kids are so excited. I pray there's no altercation with this production like the Christmas Nativity play."

Amelia stifled a laugh behind her hand. "They told me about that one."

Belinda rolled her eyes. "I kept that from you because of my embarrassment over James being involved."

Amelia whispered, "It sounded hilarious. Is there a video?"

"Partially. I was taping the performance, but the tug-of-war distracted me. I have footage of the aisle carpet through part of the skirmish."

"Whatever you have, I want to see it. Ian said no one who witnessed it will ever forget."

Belinda covered her face. "That's what I'm afraid of."

Amelia glanced around again. "Why is Ian still back there?"

"He's helping them."

She turned to her sister and whispered in a quivering voice. "Is he still mad at me?"

Belinda hesitated, then whispered, "He was deeply hurt when you blew up at him."

Amelia whispered in reply, "I overreacted to what he said and blame most of it on my experience with Captain Control Panel."

"I explained to Shorty about your over-controlling, demanding ex-boyfriend." Belinda narrowed her eyes. "You should have told him about Doug. Your history with Boyfriend Bossy Boots caused you to make a big deal out of Shorty's innocent remark. You owe him an apology, but at least he understands why you did it."

Amelia squirmed. "You're right. I owe him a sincere apology. I'm glad you explained it to him. At least now I hope there's a chance he'll forgive me."

Belinda patted her leg. "He's fine. He'll be out in a moment."

The more time ticked along with no sighting of Ian, the tighter Amelia's belly grew.

Pastor Dave came down the aisle from the rear and made his way to the pulpit. After greeting everyone and asking the congregation to join him in prayer, he took a seat.

Ian exited the right-side choir door. Amelia nearly gasped. He wore a choir robe over a shirt and slacks, but the robe was too short for him. The white socks and sandals needed for his injuries contrasted sharply against the formality of the robe.

When he halted in front of the right side microphone, she frowned. *What is he doing?*

* * *

Ian pulled the microphone as high as possible but still had to lean down to it. "Welcome, ladies and gentlemen, to the First Annual Biblical Valentine Celebration."

The tension he felt faded as he spotted Amelia in the audience. Belinda had told him backstage that Amelia was here, but seeing her caused him to grin directly at her.

"Please turn your attention to the program you received as you entered. In it are the names of tonight's performers. Thank you for coming. The children of this church, their parents, and the youth pastor, my brother-in-law, Alan White, take pride in bringing you this celebration."

Ian remained at his podium while Alan escorted the first group of children. They performed the Boaz and Ruth segment. Family members resembled paparazzi as they recorded the presentation. When the performance concluded, clapping and cheers erupted.

Ian introduced a new segment as Alan led the first group out and returned with a new group who performed the Abraham and Sarah story. This was again repeated during the last act, which depicted the story of Jacob and Rachel.

Throughout the entire production, Ian remained at the podium, smiling encouragement and providing reminders of forgotten lines in whispers so audience members would not overhear.

At the end, Ian announced the acts, and the children rotated in to take a bow for their scenes. When finished, he encouraged them to take a seat in the choir pews.

As the children settled in, Ian thanked the adults involved in bringing the production to life. "The scriptwriters are Youth Pastor White and his lovely wife, Mrs. White." He joked his sister wouldn't forgive him if he didn't compliment her beauty, causing a ripple of laughter to flow through the crowd.

Ian leaned over the microphone again and added, "A special thank you to the talented seamstress who designed and made the costumes—my mother, Mrs. June McIntosh."

The audience and the performers joined in applause for her.

He took in a breath and prayed the next act would receive rave reviews. With a smile, he said, "I also want to take this opportunity to show my appreciation for one other important person."

Ian glanced at Pastor Dave, who nodded.

"I've been given permission to go off script tonight, but the theme about love and relationships remains." Ian focused on Amelia. "This entire production is about love. Yet every biblical story reenacted tonight reflected the trials and tribulations of a romance. Love is hard work, but it is rewarding."

Amelia's head cocked sideways, and her brows knitted as he continued.

"Earlier this week, someone I care about asked me some tough questions. I wasn't prepared to give her my best answers. But tonight, I have the answers she needs to hear, thanks to these biblical relationships."

Amelia squirmed in her seat.

"Like Isaac when he spotted Rebekah, when I first met Amelia, it was love at first sight. Like Ruth and Boaz, when I experienced the love and care she showed toward her sister, her brother-in-law, and her nieces and nephews, I admired her dedication to family. Just as Jacob worked for Rachel's hand, I pledge to work for her as long as it takes to earn her hand in marriage."

The congregation applauded.

He held up a hand. "To make this happen, she must understand that I'll find a new job in Chicago, that together we can purchase a beautiful old lady of a house and remodel it, and that we can start a family whenever it suits her and her career."

Belinda nudged Amelia, who inched down the pew as the occupants shifted to let her pass.

Ian raced to meet her at the end of the pew. He wrapped her in a hug and lifted her off the ground.

Amelia smiled at him. "I owe you a huge apology. I let

circumstances from my past color my reaction. I overreacted, and I'm sorry."

"Apology accepted. Your sister explained what happened. I promise to always be mindful of your needs."

It worked. They'd somehow forgiven each other.

Amelia squealed. "I guess I needed to know you'd relocate for me. But I don't want you to do that. Let's make a life together. Here."

"Roger that, Red. I love you." He drew her to him and kissed her.

And they received a standing ovation.

About Ellen E. Withers

Ellen is an award-winning fiction writer, freelance writer, and retired insurance fraud investigator. Her professional writing career began in 2003, as a freelance contributor to the *Arkansas Democrat Gazette*. Ellen has written for *Life in Chenal* Magazine since 2006. Her non-fiction articles have been featured in international, national, and regional magazines. She's a contributing columnist to *Writers Monthly Magazine*, an online guide for professional writers, about Writing for Contests.

Her publishing credits include short stories in over twenty anthologies and two creative non-fiction stories featured on KUAR's radio show *Tales from the South*. One of her short stories garnered a nomination for the prestigious Pushcart Prize in the published short story category.

She is a member of ACFW, White County Creative Writers, OWFI, Sisters in Crime, and Tornado Alley, a local chapter of SIC. Prior associations include Pioneer Branch of the National League of American Pen Women and board member of the Arkansas Writers Conference.

Enduring Stones

Delores Topliff

Scrivenings
PRESS
Quench your thirst for story.
www.ScriveningsPress.com

To family and neighbors in places we've lived, (or who have lived with us), who have become family.
We are rich indeed!

One

C had Kinkaid's phone jangled with the ringtone reserved for his Afghanistan combat buddies, a tune he hadn't heard in five years. He grabbed his phone, glanced at the Caller ID, and hit connect. "Ted? Ted Weldon? Is it really you?"

"Sure is." Ted's voice boomed across the airwaves with a half snort.

"How on earth are you?"

"Better, now that I hear you on the line."

Chad fished the antique Afghan coin he'd smuggled out as a souvenir from his desk and gripped it.

"I'm ready and able to accept your Montana tour."

"No kidding? Took you long enough."

"My bad," the voice on the other end sputtered. "But don't they say better late than never?"

"They do." But why now? Chad glanced at the mound of paperwork on his desk and his appointment book, every day filled. As much as he wanted to see Ted, how much juggling would it take to make it happen? He stood the coin on its edge and spun it. Would it be heads? Or tails? It slowed, stopped, and stood on its edge. Chad stared. That didn't happen often.

"We were a pair, weren't we?" Ted said. "Me Lightning and you Thunder."

"Those were the days." They fell silent, Afghanistan intruding on Chad's thoughts. "In some ways, it's sad those days are over."

"They're not completely. I'm still lightning fast."

"And some things make me thunder. When are you thinking timewise?"

"Mid-to-late August. Three to five days? Plus, I'm bringing someone."

Chad's head jerked. "You got married?"

"No, nothing that drastic."

"Who are you bringing?'

"Glen Jr. You know, my brother Glen's kid. I showed you photos way back."

Ted had shared many photos years ago, but all the faces had blurred. Tall? Short? He couldn't recall. "Remind me."

"You remember my older brother?"

"Right. The hero who died saving his men in that rogue forest fire."

"His wife died a year later, and Glen Jr. joined my folks and me."

"Tough." Age? Interests? Chad rose and stepped to the window where glittering mountain ranges defined the horizon. That view always gave him peace. But before Ted could answer, a call squawked through the inter-office field phone.

"Emergency to headquarters—marauding bear at Three Forks Camp."

Chad groaned. "Sorry, Ted. A crisis got called in that I have to manage. Text me your arrival details. I'll make it work."

"Thanks. Can't wait."

"Same here." He'd make this a good trip for Ted's sake. He owed him that.

* * *

Chad paced back and forth across the airport waiting room in his creaking leather boots—they needed oiling again. He glanced at the wall clock. It was past the time Ted had texted, but the arrivals board showed no incoming planes. He checked his messages again. Had Ted sent the wrong date? Chad headed to the smaller desk past the main counter as a young man put on ear protectors and rushed outside. He marked off a section of black tarmac and rolled orange traffic cones into place.

Was this a one-man airline? When the young man looked into the sky, Chad did, too, and spotted a silver dot approaching, buzzing like a diving mosquito. A passenger plane? Or a crop duster blown off course?

Shielding his eyes, Chad observed the silver dot drop lower to line up with the runway. Had Ted trusted his and his relatives' lives to a one-engine flying eggbeater?

Flaps down, the toy plane bounced and rolled to a stop beyond the airport's plateglass windows. When the attendant opened the outside door, Chad hurried through to get closer. Two passengers descended the folding stairs. As the man crossed the tarmac, his gait revealed him as the comrade Chad had shared so much blood, sweat, laughter, and tears with during their two duty tours. He appeared little changed except for one silver streak crossing his crew cut like a lightning bolt.

Chad's throat tightened. "Ted Weldon. Man, it's good to see you in the flesh."

Ted guffawed as they threw well-muscled arms around each other and thumped each other's backs. "You, too, big guy. I'd recognize you in any police lineup."

An attractive young woman emerged from behind Ted. She had his striking blue eyes and copper highlights in her dark hair.

Chad blinked. "Who's this?"

Ted pulled her forward. "My niece, Glen Jr. I told you I'd bring her."

"You did, but I didn't—" Now the pieces fell into place. He'd forgotten the details, but during Afghanistan, Ted's brother's only kid had been a teenager. Chad leaned back, taking a second look. "There's a strong resemblance, but you're prettier than this guy."

Glen chuckled. "I'm glad to hear it."

When she linked her arm through her uncle's, Chad blinked. "Wow, when you stand side by side, you're two peas in a pod."

They laughed.

"That's what folks tell us," Ted said. "Strong genetics."

"I'll say." Chad stuck out a meaty paw. "Welcome to Montana's Big Sky Country."

"Thanks." Glen accepted his hand. "You're the Thunder Kinkaid I've heard about."

"That's me, but I guess it depends on what he said. My real name's Chad."

"All good. I can't wait to see if Montana lives up to its hype. And if you do."

Her voice carried the music of mountain streams bubbling over boulders. How did Ted have such a knockout niece? How come Chad hadn't heard more about her? He would have remembered, wouldn't he?

"You two were always 'Thunder and Lightning' over there?"

"That's what they called us. As solid as your uncle is, he could outrun us all."

She nodded. "Uncle Teddy's still fast."

Ted slapped Chad's back. "My buddy here's almost my equal, but he's 'Thunder' because when he gets riled, he builds up steam and rumbles like a thunderstorm. Believe me, he was good to have around."

"It sounds like you two were a great pair."

"We were." Chad released her hand. "And still might be—we should test it. But I can't believe he lets you call him Teddy. He's flattened guys for less."

She laughed. "Those near and dear to him have privileges."

"Apparently."

She was giving him the once-over too. "How tall are you? I'm tall for a girl, but you've got me beat."

"About six foot three. Six foot four on a good day."

"In all of Uncle Teddy's stories, I never pictured you this tall or this civilized."

"Wow. What did Ted say? Should I defend myself?"

"No. Most of it was good." Her smile revealed perfect white teeth. "But I'll try not to cross you."

"That won't be hard. I don't rile as easily as I used to." Was that true? Chad grabbed both duffel bags as the pilot unloaded them from the plane's belly. He lugged them into the building and glanced back through the airport's plateglass windows. "What do you call that bird you flew in on? Is it a wind-up toy? Or a real plane?"

"It's genuine, all right. A single-engine Pratt & Whitney Cessna Caravan turboprop. It reminds me of some of our rides in Afghanistan."

"The ones with bullet holes for air conditioning?"

"Yes, those."

Chad blinked as the pilot turned the prop until it caught before he climbed into the cockpit and taxied down the runway. "That's not a commercial plane. How did you work that?"

"He's a friend who flies up for guided whitewater rafting and fishing. He says the trout dance on top of the water here."

"It's true. I'll show you that Montana's wonderful." He rubbed his day-old stubble. He should have taken the time to shave this morning, but he'd had so much to do. He didn't know he would be meeting an attractive young lady. "How long can you stay?"

"Five days if you can handle us that long."

"No problem. Stay longer if you can. Will you two fly back with your friend?"

"Not sure yet. Glen won't. She's here for her new job."

Chad faced Ted's niece again. Reconnecting with Ted was proving interesting. "I guess I missed that part. Doing what?"

"Didn't I tell you?" Ted leaned forward. "She followed her dad and me into forestry. She's been Arkansas's best lady forest ranger for the past three years, and now she's hired on in your neck of the woods to bless Montana."

"Uncle Teddy." The young woman's face reddened. "Don't praise me so much. Let people draw their own conclusions."

"They will soon enough." Ted patted her shoulder. "I can't help being proud, and this guy's like a brother."

Chad nodded. "For better or for worse. Where will you be based?"

"In Kalispell for Flathead National Forest. I'll mainly teach forestry and outdoor programs in schools and community centers."

"Awesome. I do some of that myself." He took a longer look. A bright smile framed Glen's sky-blue eyes. Freckles sprinkled her nose. "Are you old enough to be a real ranger? Maybe you're a junior level."

"No, I'm the real thing."

He couldn't get enough of her laugh.

"I didn't find my degree in a Corn Flakes box. I earned it at the University of Arkansas. Trust me, my male classmates have put me through my paces since I was a girl."

"I'm sure."

"What's more"—Ted elbowed Chad's ribs—"she's younger than the rest by a year, but she still won the senior prize."

"Outstanding." Chad beamed his admiration.

Glen's head tipped in her uncle's direction. "Uncle Teddy, stop."

"Why? It's true." He waved a hand. "Chad should know."

"I think I want your autograph." Chad smiled. "I can tell you're not someone to mess with."

She shook her head. "Don't worry, you're fine. Any friend of Uncle Teddy is a friend of mine."

Ted's niece—all grown up? Chad needed to readjust every picture in his mind. She must be twenty-four or twenty-five now. He'd just turned thirty-two. He tried to swallow, but his throat had gone dry. This might be tricky. He wasn't shopping, but if he did find someone, he wouldn't rob the cradle. He had no room in his life for complications.

Chad gripped Ted's arm. "We've cheated death together. Nothing joins men more."

"Agreed." Chad reached for both duffel bags, but Glen grabbed hers.

"I'll carry mine."

"Nope." Chad already had it. "Not today. You're my guest." He held tight while Glen tugged once and let go.

"You win this time, but I'm Kalispell's newest resident, not a guest." She nursed her hand.

Chad laughed. "Humor me." He led them through the small airport to the street exit on the other side. He put down the luggage and spread his arms. "Welcome to Kalispell. Breathe in that high-mountain, clean-forest air."

Ted spread his arms too. "Magnificent. I'm impressed."

Glen snapped several pictures. "I can tell I'll be doing a lot of this."

"I'm sure you will." Chad loaded their things into the back of his Jeep. "Tell me if you need anything before we leave town and head to Glacier National Park."

"We're going there right away?" Glen practically stood on tiptoe. "I can't think of anything except seeing more mountains. We glimpsed some from the plane, but we're closer, and these are majestic."

"You'll see plenty. We'll head out as soon as we grab some gear from my folks' place. Have you guys eaten?"

"Sort of." Ted patted his flat stomach. "Ate a sandwich in Little Rock before we flew."

"Fine. We'll gather gear and groceries at my folks' and head north."

Glen kicked something hard and shiny on the ground near his Jeep. She bent, picked it up, and slid it into her pocket.

"Did you lose something?" Chad asked.

"No. I found something." She smiled and followed Chad to the Jeep doors.

Two

Afer Chad cooked a campfire dinner, Glen got busy clearing all food from their site.

Uncle Teddy groaned and sprawled across his sleeping bag. "Chad, you stuffed us full, plus I'm stiff and sore from so much hiking. You really keep your word. A full fishing creel in minutes. Giant bear prints and scat on the trails. Phenomenal."

Glen sighed. "Even better than that—a shining wall of mountains frames every scene. And canoeing on a crystal-clear lake with mossy blue flowers blooming at the bottom." She raised her arms. "I've never seen anything this grand, but I'd hate to swim in that water."

"I'm glad you're pleased." Chad gave a thumbs-up. "I'm succeeding then?"

"You're knocking it out of the park." Glen's fingers sifted the dirt next to her sleeping bag and held up a rock that gleamed in the firelight. "We have mica schist in Arkansas too. This is a perfect souvenir." She dropped the stone into a pocket of her backpack.

Chad laughed. "I'll tell you a secret. Swimming in glacier water is a required initiation here, but few of us repeat it. I had to do it again when I rescued a stranded fisherman and once more when a moose broke through lake ice and needed help, but you're a great sport." He beamed like a lighthouse.

"Thanks, but when that icy water topped my boots, I shrieked like a baby." She poked the bulging bicep straining his shirt sleeve. "Please overlook that."

"Done. That's also part of the initiation ... to connect and share experiences together so people survive and thrive in this north country."

"No kidding." Uncle Teddy sprawled on his sleeping bag.

She tossed a pine cone into the fire and watched it blaze. "No wonder Montana grows on people."

"Like moss?" Chad quipped.

"Not quite." She tossed another pine cone. "So tell me, you and Uncle Ted actually saved each other's lives overseas?"

"That's right. Once each in combat." Her uncle's dimple flashed. "And again, if you count me rescuing him from some cranky Afghan elders."

"That sounds like a story." Glen leaned closer.

"I never told you?" Her uncle loosened his belt.

"No, but I'm listening now."

Chad's eyes narrowed. "Ted, don't be a blabbermouth. I try to keep that story quiet, but you were a lifesaver."

"Don't ever forget it." Ted locked eyes with Chad.

"You might as well tell her." Chad flexed his fingers on both hands. "It's been ten years, but I'm not over it. I still have nightmares."

"No wonder." Ted's laugh rumbled. "I picture a wife in hijab, with a string of little kids in Middle Eastern garb running after you—fast."

"Close." Chad sputtered. "Don't make it worse than it was."

"I'm not, and you know it. There are stories like that on reality TV all the time. It's a wonder that girl's male relatives didn't kill you."

"I thought they might." Chad stared at the ground. "Thanks for getting me out of there."

"Hurry up and tell me. This sounds crazy." Glen sat up on her sleeping bag and wrapped her arms around her knees. The fire had died down until it grew so dark she could barely see. *How old is this guy? Uncle Ted's friend is pretty neat. He can't possibly be my uncle's age. He'd be good husband material for someone.*

Chad narrowed his eyes at her. "You have to promise you won't pass it on."

"I do. Scouts honor." She placed her hand over her heart.

Chad cracked his knuckles. "All right, that should do it. As our combat tour wound down, our commander sent us into the countryside to deliver emergency supplies to civilians. He wanted our last contacts to be excellent PR and build goodwill."

"Most units try to do that." Uncle Teddy cleared his throat. "It was the northern villages where they still live by ancient laws."

"They do." Chad nodded. "Like the Dark Ages. We went house to house, bringing food and gifts to hungry people. A girl around fourteen in full hijab ran toward me from one house. She reminded me of a neighbor kid from home. When I handed her bags of flour and powdered milk, her eyes gleamed through the holes in her head covering. She got so excited, she flashed a hand sign and jabbered a string of gibberish with a big smile. I didn't understand what it meant, but the next thing I knew, her large family surrounded me, and her dad shook my hand. When I tried to go on to the next place, he held my arm tight and wouldn't let me go."

"Scary." Glen frowned. "Didn't he understand you were taking food to everyone?"

"I don't know what he understood, but he acted like my actions meant much more. Later, our interpreter told me that in their culture, when a man looks directly into a woman's eyes, it's a marriage proposal. Her return gaze means she accepts. That's what the girl's gibberish meant, but I didn't understand." He shook his head. "It gets worse."

"How could it?" Glen gripped her knees tighter. "What did you do?"

"What could I do? I was surrounded—but your uncle rescued me."

"Terrific, but how?"

Uncle Ted puffed his chest like a strutting rooster. "Chad's lucky I was there, or my best buddy here would head up a large family in the Hindu Kush. The girl's parents said he had gazed too long at their daughter, so they were claiming him as a son-in-law. They viewed the food gifts as a dowry payment and told the village elders to write up a marriage contract."

"Terrifying." Glen's eyes widened. "I'll bet you died on the spot."

"I wanted to." Chad wiped his brow. "My whole life passed before me. I thought I was done for—that I might never see the U.S. again."

"I can imagine."

Uncle Teddy cleared his throat. "I found an interpreter who told them that Chad didn't understand their ways. Plus, he'd suffered a head injury that basically turned him into an idiot. I even showed them the shrapnel scar on his head to prove it."

Chad patted his scalp. "I do have one. It came in handy and is still there."

"I told them he didn't mean to stare too long at their daughter, and though she was lovely, he couldn't sign a marriage contract." Her uncle's laughter exploded again. "It's funny now, but not so much then."

"I'll bet."

Chad tapped his shoulder. "Stop any time, bro. You're enjoying this too much."

"Can you blame me?" Her uncle snorted. "It's hilarious. At least I got you out of there."

"But how? What did you do?" Glen twisted her hands. "Don't leave me hanging. I can't believe I haven't heard this story before."

"I told them Chad was engaged to my sister back home. That I'd pledged my life to keep him safe in the war zone and bring him home for the wedding, sorry specimen that he was."

Chad clenched a fist. "Don't make me hurt you, bro."

"I laid it on thick. We gave them more bags of food and bowed and scraped as we backed up to our Humvee, saying 'sorry, sorry' over and over in their language. Once we got in, I hit the gas, and we took off like a July Fourth rocket."

"Though I wanted to go faster." Chad brushed a mosquito away.

Glen's eyes widened. "I wish I'd been there."

"No, you don't. It was a wild ride, but worth it to get out in one piece." Chad rolled up his camo hat and shoved it in his pocket. "I didn't feel safe until our transport plane left Afghan airspace. But your uncle never lets me forget." Chad tapped his friend's shoulder. "Do you, buddy?"

"Nope. Why should I?"

"I don't blame him." Glen stifled a laugh. "Sorry, but that's scary funny. You owe Uncle Teddy big time."

"Don't I know it. We're friends forever."

Ted and Chad high-fived each other. "I promised then I'd repay him with anything he ever asked for, but that it should be something huge."

Ted rubbed his hands together. "This trip for you and me, Glen, is what I want. Get you up to speed on northern terms and plants, I'll be repaid well."

"No problem, and I'm paying up with a smile." Chad grinned. "Let's seal it with our unit's secret handshake." Their hands flew through the air in movements too fast for Glen's eyes to follow until they shouted, "Huzzah," and their arms shot in the air to close the deal.

"Wow, Uncle Teddy. I've never seen you do that before."

"I haven't been with my best buddy. That makes the difference." Ted stretched out farther and heaved a sigh. "It's great to reconnect—been way too long."

"Roger that," Chad said into the darkness. "Glen, when do you start your new job?"

"In two weeks, at the first of the month. Why?"

"I've been thinking ... Are your days full? What do you have going on?"

"Not much. Once Uncle Teddy goes back, I'll set up my apartment and open a bank account. Get to know Kalispell a little —things like that."

"None of that takes very long, so consider this. After Ted leaves, I need to drive around the western half of Montana on day trips, visiting district offices and updating field programs. I'll check wildlife projects the public seldom sees and return to Kalispell each night to write up notes and prepare for the next day. I'm inviting you. Can you picture yourself coming along for any part of that?"

"Definitely." Glen widened her eyes. "It sounds great, but what if—"

"What?" Her uncle nudged her. "Girl, just agree. It's fabulous."

She tilted her head to study Chad. "You're sure you don't mind a green-as-grass tag-along?"

"Not a bit. And you're talented. It would almost be like having Ted along." He chuckled. "But I confess to an ulterior motive."

"Oops." Glen's voice rose. "What's that?"

"I've seen you jotting down facts, temperatures, and doing sketches. You use some kind of condensed code, too, right?"

"Ye-es." She tucked a strand of hair behind her ear. "I devised a shortcut code to speed up my university classes and everyday life."

"Excellent. I'm great at photos and mapping, but I'm weak in other parts. For me, compiling reports is like pulling teeth without a painkiller, but you make it look easy."

"It's not exactly easy, but I manage."

Ted chuckled. "Don't let her kid you. She was on the honor roll every semester since high school."

"I'm not surprised. If you come with me and help me pull my trip notes together, I'll write the best reports of my life, and I can give you northern facts, flora, and fauna so you'll be the best forestry education officer Montana has ever had. What do you say?"

Glen gazed into the dying fire. "That's amazing, but don't rank me too high. Check my notes over the next few days to see what you think. I wouldn't want to disappoint you."

"There's no chance. I wouldn't ask if I didn't already see you'd be great. Plus, I'll add in northern woodcraft skills and anything else you need."

"What a deal."

He stretched out a hand. "Can we shake on it?"

"Yes. But I can't shake as fancy as you and Uncle Teddy."

"No problem."

They laughed.

Three

Sometime in the night, Chad rose to feed the fire. Glen heard Ted stir nearby and then speak softly. "You've never been serious about anyone since Sandra?"

"Nope. How could I? That mess gutted me. I may never try a relationship again."

"Don't say that. I hope you're not that burned."

Glen didn't intend to eavesdrop, but she couldn't help overhearing. She listened without making a sound.

Her uncle continued, "The picture you showed me of Sandra and the ways you described her before the *Dear John* letter made her sound like a keeper. Do you know what happened that changed her?"

"Not a clue. Friends said different things, but nothing made sense. After we got shipped north to Baghlan Province, she wrote one last letter that missed me. It didn't catch me until we were back in the States, and by then I'd heard she was married and pregnant, so I didn't even read it. Her daughter was born seven months after their wedding. We had been junior youth leaders at church and exchanged promise rings to wait for each other."

He knuckled his cheekbone. "I guess that meant nothing to

her. I tossed my promise ring to a hungry kid in Kabul to trade for food, but I don't know where God was. There were times in 'Stan when God could have shown up, but He didn't. Senseless killings. Women and kids mutilated ... You saw it too." Chad's voice broke. "How do you stand it? I can't understand."

"I hear you, and yes, I was there." Ted's breath rattled. "I also have nightmares like rolling movies I can't shut off. But God showed up plenty of times, and things did turn out—or you and I wouldn't be here. There must be more to Sandra's story. Some key fact you don't know. Aren't you curious?"

Chad's Adam's apple bobbed. "Nope. Even if there is, it doesn't change anything. I figure I didn't really know her. Perhaps she didn't actually know herself."

"Could be. Or something terrible may have happened to her."

"Who knows? I've stayed busy, trying to build a normal life. At least after Sandra married the guy, they moved out of state. I haven't had to see her. That helps."

"For sure." Ted coughed. "But just because she slipped up doesn't mean all women do."

"So they say. But you're still single."

"For now, yes. That doesn't mean I will be forever. I'm not quite forty-two. There's still time."

"What do you have going on?"

Just then a pine knot on a log in the fire popped and shot sparks into the darkness, lighting both men's grim faces. "I haven't met the right gal, but that may be changing. I help a Big Brother organization—kids without dads. We take them fishing, camping, support school projects, and show up for them." Her uncle swept a hand through the air. "They'd love locations like this. One boy's dad died in a car wreck, but his mom is special. She took EMT training and works on an ambulance now. I'm taking it slow, but I like what I see. If things go well, I'd gain a great wife and a bonus son."

"Sounds interesting. Keep me posted. Believe me, I'll be

happy if you are." Chad's sleeping bag rustled as he changed positions. "Aargh. There are rocks in this sand."

"A few, but you're tough. Pretend we're back in the desert."

"I don't even want to think about it. There. That's better. Listen, Ted, I'm not against marriage ... If I found the right gal—and she could tolerate me."

"You're not so bad." Ted gave a gentle laugh. "A little rough around the edges, but a great catch."

"You think so? Like a northern pike or a dogfish on the line?"

"I didn't say that. Your words, not mine. You're a man of good character."

"I'm a character at least." Chad gave a bitter laugh. "Can I list you as a reference?"

"Any time. Always."

Their words slowed until silence reclaimed the camp.

Hours later, Glen was not sure whether birdsong or the nearby rushing stream woke her. It was too dark to read her watch, but dawn's fingers shot pink into the sky. She lifted her arms to praise the beauty and breathed in the fresh scents of towering spruce and pine. "Lord, You're here. This is a cathedral. There's lots more going on in this trip than me learning about Montana. Show me."

Glen rose and renewed the fire. She measured water and coffee grounds into the dented percolator and put it on to boil. She didn't hear Chad leave, but the next time she glanced his direction, his sleeping bag was empty. Soon the coffee's rich aroma brought her uncle to his feet. He stretched and yawned. "Where's the beast?"

"What?"

"Chad. Where is he?"

"I'm not sure. Scouting around. Or visiting Mother Nature."

"I'll do the same." Uncle Teddy shuffled into the trees. A holy hush hung over the campsite except for the sizzle of breakfast bacon in the pan.

Chad returned with handfuls of earthy-smelling mushrooms. "Can you use these? They're some of the best."

"Yes, I'm glad to have them." Glen accepted them. "I'll wash them in this pail of water."

"Don't bother. I rinsed them in the lake."

"Even better." She cracked eggs and sliced the mushrooms into the pan. The complex aroma became tantalizing. "Thanks, Chad. This is now a feast." She stopped stirring. "Do you teach mushroom identification too?"

"I teach a little bit of everything."

"Wow, Uncle Teddy asked the right man to train me."

The flames jumped higher and revealed Chad's flushed face. "My watch is in my duffel. What time is it?"

"Coffee time." She handed him a cup of dark brew rich with cream.

He drank several swallows. "This is exactly how I like it. You paid attention."

"I try. This place is heaven." She lifted her arms to the sky. "The kind of place where I could stay forever."

Chad chuckled. "I know what you mean. That's why I do this line of work. Except for government red tape, it's worth it." He noticed her uncle's empty bag. "Where's my friend?"

"Off somewhere. He wandered away before you came back, but he's been gone quite a while."

"That's strange. There aren't many places to go." Chad walked to the edge of the trees and called, "Ted." And then louder. "Ted?"

At first, they heard only silence and then a strangled cry.

"Help. Out here!"

Chad paled. "He's in trouble."

He and Glen took off running along the barely discernible trail. The sun hadn't fully risen, but they dodged the dark shapes of large trees and jumped ditches and a creek that cut the trail. "Ted, call again."

"Over here." His cries came louder and slightly ahead.

Finally, Chad pointed.

Above them, Ted dangled at a crazy angle in a tall tree.

Chad stared in disbelief, then dashed forward with Glen right behind him. "Hang on, buddy. What on earth happened?"

Uncle Ted looked green, almost corpse-like. "Some fool set a steel snare and caught me in it. Help me down."

"Working on it." Chad fanned his arms through underbrush and branches to find the hidden vertical wire. "I've got the trip wire but—"

"Hurry. I grabbed a horizontal branch instead of dangling, but I can't hold on much longer. One boot is cinched tight. I'm stuck."

Chad brushed through more foliage. "I see it. Cutting you free now." He whipped the Leatherman tool from his belt and used the wire cutter. "There. That should do it."

"Except now my boot's wedged in the tree fork. Can't budge." Ted struggled and groaned.

Chad climbed several branches. "Can you climb lower so I can reach you?"

"I'll try. Maybe if I loosen the cinched wire and wiggle my boot off. There. Here I come."

"Careful, Uncle Teddy. Don't fall." Glen clasped her hands as Ted descended, and branches shook and rattled.

At last he hit the earth and collapsed to his knees. "Thank God for solid ground."

Glen grabbed him. "I'm thankful you're all right."

"It's good my boot went in the snare instead of my head, or I'd be a goner."

"Don't even say that." Glen's stomach lurched in sympathy.

"I'm not leaving your boot up there." Chad turned his Leatherman to another feature. "If I stretch high and use the saw blade—" He sawed through the imprisoning limb and brought Ted's boot down. "Here you go."

Ted sat. "I'm shaking like a leaf."

"You had a close call. Give yourself time. How did it happen?"

"I visited Mrs. Murphy in the woods and lost the trail. When I ducked under low branches, the snare caught me, and up I went." He shuddered again.

Glen clung to him. "The Lord saved you, Uncle Ted."

"Don't I know it." He wiped perspiration from his face. "Who would set a snare in a national park that could snag and kill a man or large animal?"

"Someone careless or crazy." Chad pulled in the heavy steel wire. "We'll save all this for evidence. It's 9-gauge, strong enough for a deer or larger animal. I'm glad you weren't alone."

"That's scary." He stretched his boot until he finally worked his foot back in. "Is it hunting season yet?"

"No. This guy's in serious trouble. When we catch him, I've got him dead to rights on major charges. He set the thing near the main path but covered it with bent saplings, so anything passing by had to bend low to pass through, and bingo."

Ted shook his head. "It works. The noose sideswiped my head and caught my foot. If it had been the other way, I would have swung until I was dead."

Glen gave him another quick hug and wept.

"It's all right, girl. That's my closest call since Afghanistan. We'll write that on the list of ways God has kept us."

Chad shook his head. "That was too much like combat days."

"I'm grateful you were here to save me. I didn't know Montana was a danger zone."

Chad set his jaw. "It isn't normally. We'll find him, I promise. I'm sorry this happened."

Glen kept her arm threaded through her uncle's. "Why would anyone do that in this gorgeous place?"

"Greed or stupidity," her uncle answered. "What's your guess, Chad?"

"It could be a poacher wanting black bear organs for high prices in the Chinese medicine market. But he's dumb. If he poaches an animal, he'll face maximum poaching charges. If he kills a person, it's homicide."

Glen trembled. "You'd think he'd stick around to check what he caught."

Chad's eyes narrowed. "Are you sure he didn't?"

* * *

When they reentered camp, Glen hurried to the fire pit to check her frying pan. She could smell the scorch before they were close enough to see the charcoal mess. "Well, that's my first try at breakfast ruined," she said. "But at least we're all okay."

"Exactly. I brought enough extra food for you to start over if you like. Or I could drive us out of the park to a diner."

She dropped her hands to her hips. "And leave this scenery and atmosphere? No, siree. I'm staying here. Give me more groceries. I'll scour this pan and start over."

"I'm surprised we didn't hear someone that close by," her uncle said. "Any idea when it happened?"

Chad jotted in his pocket notebook. "No, but I don't think it's been long."

Glen made a mewing noise in her throat. "I hate thinking that criminals free walk in this paradise."

"That can happen anywhere." Chad clamped his jaw. "But don't worry, we'll catch him. It was too dark earlier to find tracks, but we'll go back and take photos."

"Chad's good at tracking," Ted said.

Glen started a new pot of coffee. "Gracious, is there anything he can't do?"

"I'm sure there is." Chad's face blazed.

Ted rested a hand on Chad's shoulder. "He was our best-trained tracker in Afghanistan."

Chad walked past the fire pit and lifted his cell phone. "If I can catch a signal, I think two animal rescue guys are doing a sweep near here this morning. If we connect, they can bring tracking kits."

"Great. I'll work on breakfast." Glen scrubbed the frying pan and started over.

"Thanks for fixing breakfast." Ted sat by the fire and rubbed his hands. "After all that, I'm hungry enough to eat a bear."

"Don't say that too loudly," Chad quipped. "We have them around here."

Four

C had shared fascinating hunting stories that kept his guests amazed or laughing while they ate. Afterward, they scrubbed everything with sand and rinsed their plates in the lake. Then they rolled up their bags, doused the fire, and were tidying camp when two men advanced through the trees.

"Halloo," the taller one called while entering the clearing.

A barking, black dog accompanying them lowered its head and charged. It knocked Chad flat and landed on top of him.

Ted dove toward Chad but wasn't fast enough. The dog bathed Chad's face with its tongue.

"What?" Ted backed up as Chad hugged the animal. "That thing is yours?"

"Sure is," Chad said. "She's a rescue. A Doberman-Shepherd mix, as far as we can tell. Mom volunteers at a shelter. When this one showed up all cut and burned, Mom adopted her." He tussled with his dog again. "I'm glad to see you, too, Peaches."

"Peaches?" Ted echoed. "Shouldn't a brute like that be named Killer or Fang?"

"Mom is convinced a gentle name will keep her sweet-tempered, and so far, it works. Don't let her fierce looks fool you.

She's a sweetheart." He cradled the dog's face in his hands. "You can't help what some bad person did to you, can you, girl?" Chad tugged her ears and patted her head and neck with long, smooth strokes.

"She was an absolute angel on our ride out here," the taller man who delivered her said. "She's practically a lap dog."

"That's right," Chad said. "And you healed up well from that attack, didn't you, Peaches?"

"What attack?" Ted squatted and leaned back on his haunches.

"Three weeks back, I brought her along to check campsites when I found a guy dealing drugs. When I arrested him, he pulled a knife. Peaches lunged in to save me and got slashed from eye to mouth. Her lip bulges, and her mouth won't shut now. The vet saved her eye, but she looks scarier and drools." He petted the animal again. "But you're beautiful, aren't you, girl?" She nuzzled his neck. "You stopped that bad guy from hurting me."

"She's a guard dog too?" Ted lifted his phone to click a picture.

"Absolutely. She's good at everything."

Glen squinted. "She reminds me of that dog in Greek mythology that guards the underworld."

"You mean Cerberus?" Chad gasped. "You know that story?"

"Yes. My mind retains unusual facts."

He laughed. "Mine too. Cerberus describes Peaches all right. Her fierce looks alone keep bad guys away. I wanted to name her that, but Mom won't."

"That's funny." When Ted held out his hand, the dog snapped so fast, he jerked back. "Holy Toledo. She's no lap dog— she's an attack animal. Is she safe to have around? You need a muzzle for her. She could kill in a nano-second."

"No, she won't. I don't know why she reacted like that with you. Maybe she thought you were big enough to hurt me. I have a muzzle but haven't had to use it. She obeys my ground rules." Peaches shuddered ecstatically as Chad placed his large hands around the tops of her legs and massaged each one down to her paws.

"She's an angel," Glen's voice grew silky. "Tell us your ground rules."

"They're simple." Chad counted on his fingers. "Move slowly around her. Let her set the pace to invite you into her space, or not. So far, Mom and I are the humans she trusts most—except it looks like she's fine with these guys. Ted and Glen, meet Reilly and Pete." He waved over the two Animal Rescue men. "Thanks for bringing the kits and Peaches."

"It's a pleasure. No problem." The shorter, stocky man had *Pete* embroidered over his shirt pocket. "Since your folks are away, when the vet released her, he suggested we bring Peaches to you. We would have kept her 'til you got back, but it worked to meet up now."

"It's perfect." Chad rubbed her ears. "I'm grateful."

Both men wore the same olive-drab pants and tan shirts, with Fish, Wildlife & Parks Animal Rescue shoulder patches. They scanned the camp.

"Nice setup here," Reilly said. "And it's a great location."

"Except for this." Ted pulled out the deadly snare wire.

"Holy Cannoli," the tall one said. "Someone was poaching?"

"It was intentional, so that's our conclusion." Chad waved to Ted. "The steel wire caught my friend's foot instead of his neck, but even that was serious."

"I guess so." Pete released his breath in a slow whistle.

"It's light enough now to take photos," Ted said. "And your kits will help us collect evidence. Chad promises we'll catch the guy."

"I will." Chad's jaw clamped like a Channel Lock Wrench.

"What are the penalties for poaching these days?" Glen asked.

"Stiff." Chad closed his notebook. "We levy maximum fines plus confiscate weapons and give jail time. We make it steep enough to discourage folks. But if they kill someone? That's way more serious."

* * *

"Show us where it happened," one of the Animal Rescue men said.

Glen stuck close. "I want to see it again. I have so much to learn."

"Over this way." Ted led them to the scuffed-up area under a towering spruce tree and pointed to its base. "Here's where I found the snare. He looped the wire over that high limb and covered his trigger with brush and grass. After getting jerked up short by it, I don't consider it humane for animals either."

"I can imagine." Reilly tugged the collar of his shirt. "I can almost feel that around my neck."

"I know." Chad angled his camera to take photos with Peaches at his heels. "Help me find clear prints?"

"Here's one." Ted kneeled. "It's a distinctive ridged pattern of a full Vibram sole."

"I see it." Chad slid his boot next to the clear impression. "It's smaller than mine but wider. Around a size eleven. I'll grab those Plaster of Paris kits to make casts for evidence."

"Fascinating." Glen sketched the print. "I've read about that but haven't seen it done."

"If you'd like to help, hold the mold steady while I add water to the dry powder. That's right. Just a little more."

"How's this?" Glen gripped the mold where Chad positioned it.

"Just fine."

She studied the ground. "It looks like the outside edge of the left foot sinks in deeper. Does the poacher have a limp?"

Chad squatted. "Possibly. Good catch. If something unusual is going on, these casts are even more important." He stood again. "If you're ready, I'll pour."

"Yes, go ahead."

The whitish-gray gypsum material flowed like thick gravy and filled the mold. "There, that's enough. It will harden fast and be ready in minutes. Every clue will help us catch the guy."

"Excellent." Glen straightened as Chad lifted two solid plaster casts and secured them in evidence bags in his backpack.

"Those are fine prints," Pete said. "Good job."

Ted moved past the tree and found more faint disturbances in the earth. Pete and Reilly advanced with him. "From the direction of these footprints, I'd say the person hiked in from there. He must have used a headlamp to come during darkness."

Chad nodded. "I agree. Makes sense. There's a public boat access dock about a mile that way. If we search there, we might find signs of a truck or all-terrain vehicle, but it's strange." He stared at the trees. "We were both awake at times last night. Why didn't we hear something?"

"These days many machines have super quiet engines. If we find activity at the dock, we'll know more."

"We're parked near there," Reilly said. "We'll be on our way but wish you luck in capturing the guy." They both lifted their fingers to their hats in a salute and followed the path.

"That parking lot is where we'll leave from later anyway for going to one of my favorite spots, Bird Woman Falls," Chad said. "We'll check for signs and tire tracks when we get there."

"I love waterfalls." Glen eased her shoulders. "We had them at the Christian camp I loved every summer as a kid. Arkansas has over two hundred waterfalls. Some are big. I imagine Montana's are also big."

"You're right about that." Chad grinned. "We may have fewer, but with our high altitude and snow, ours are giant-economy-sized." When they returned to their campsite, he swept his arm in a circle to include the surrounding mountains. "In fact, *Montana* means 'mountain.'"

"I guessed that." Ted snapped more photos.

Glen turned to a fresh page in her notebook. "*Arkansas* means 'South Wind.'"

"A south wind would be fantastic during our cold Montana

winters." Chad lifted his camera. "I want a shot of you two against this backdrop. Glen, please stand next to your uncle." When Ted slipped his arm around her, Chad quipped, "Show this shot to your Arkansas buddies and see which background scenery they prefer, Arkansas or here. The waterfall at Bird Woman Falls drops six hundred feet."

"That's major." Glen craned her neck to see the surrounding panorama. "How will we get there?"

"In my Jeep, with a detour to check the boat launch on our way."

Glen sketched their current scene in her notebook. "How did your falls get their name?"

"Have you read about Sacagawea? The Native American gal who guided Lewis and Clark west? Her name means *Bird Woman*. Without her, their expedition would've failed."

"I've heard that." Glen finished her sketch. "Did she travel through here?"

"That's debatable. Local legends say she did. Historians claim she was fifty miles south, but they named the falls after her anyway. Tourists can spot them from two miles away on the Going-to-the-Sun Road, but no official park trails reach the falls."

"So we can't get there?" Ted stroked his chin. "That's too bad."

"I didn't say that. I know the unofficial trails." Chad grinned. "You have to be half mountain goat, but we'll get there. That's why I carry rappel ropes in my pack."

"You're kidding." Glen blinked rapidly. "You promised us an unforgettable Montana tour. You're keeping your word."

"Always." His eyes met hers.

She pointed to Peaches at Chad's heels. "Can she keep up with us?"

"Just watch her. She goes everywhere with me."

Peaches wagged her tail.

They climbed into the Jeep and drove to the boat launch

parking area. Chad parked at the entrance so his tire tracks wouldn't destroy evidence.

"It's deserted," Ted said. "Let's search."

They examined the paved turnaround and the ramp that guided boat trailers into the water. Next, they checked the gravel area edging the pavement where brush and undergrowth met. In one narrow strip between the gravel and the forest, Glen spotted a muddy four-by-four tire print and marked it with her toe.

"Chad? Look at this. Is this something?"

"Show me."

Ted followed.

"It's a small, block-like pattern with larger gaps and deeper tread than car tires. It has *siping*—those thin cut marks that four-by-fours use to increase traction on wet surfaces."

"Right. This appears recent. It could be our guy." Chad angled his camera and clicked several shots.

"So four-by-fours are used by hunters and poachers?" Glen asked.

"Primarily. Also by trappers and summer tourists. Prospectors too. We have lots of those in Montana."

"By comparison, Arkansas is short on those." Ted bent down. "What do your prospectors hunt for?"

"Mostly gold."

Ted turned his head until he and Glen locked eyes.

"Nice. Will we find gold on this trip?" she asked.

Ted beamed. "If you do, make it a bonanza."

"No promises, but if you do the state inspection day trips with me, I'll show you Montana mining, both underground shafts and placer panning. We'll collect samples too."

"That's exciting." She tilted her head. "I'm not sure I know the difference, but I'd love to learn."

Chad removed his sunglasses to look closer at the ground. "Years back, I helped my uncle on his placer claim one summer. We only found enough flakes to catch gold fever, but I'd love to do it again."

"I don't blame you." Glen nodded. "I'd sign on for that. It sounds like an *Indiana Jones* movie."

Chad met her gaze. "If some local stories are true, they make *Indiana Jones* sound ordinary."

Ted whistled. "Whoa. Don't hold out on us, buddy. We need maps, title deeds—the works." He slapped the billfold in his pocket. "If you find a promising claim, I'll invest—if you want a partner."

"It's possible." Chad chuckled. "I'm not that far yet, but I'll keep you in mind."

"Don't forget me." Glen waved a hand. "I'll be a laborer, laundress, cook—you name it—and get paid in gold."

"Ha ha." Chad slapped his thigh. "You're an optimist. There's nothing to tell yet, but there is potential for sure. Meanwhile—" He pointed to the boat ramp entrance. "Once we're on a decent road with a strong signal, I'll fire these photos to our criminal lab to analyze. As we drive to the falls, I'll let you decide which of two amazing campsites we'll choose for tonight."

"That's hard." Ted walked forward. "We'll love both."

Chad's eyes focused on him. "Are you limping, buddy?"

"A little. The snare didn't do me any good, and in my full-time forestry job, I haven't done this much hiking for a while. It's okay. I'll live." Ted stretched his arms to ease the crick in his back. "But remember, Chad, you're eight years younger. Practically a baby. That gives you an advantage."

"So that's why you teamed up with me in Afghanistan? You were babysitting?"

"At first, yeah, but you proved yourself fast."

Chad's voice deepened. "I'll never forget the hero you were. You'll never be old in my book. But my pack carries Vaseline for your boots and liniment for your muscles if you want it."

Ted grunted. "That makes me sound ancient. Plus, I'd smell like a horse."

"An achy one." Glen giggled. "You should give it a try."

Ted opened the bottle and inhaled. "That stuff smells amazing. I'm tempted to drink it."

Chad slapped his leg. "You'd be sorry, buddy. It's good for muscles but not more. You're always good for a laugh. I've missed having you around."

Glen stepped to the water's edge. She bent, chose a striped agate, and lifted it to the sun before smiling and dropping it into her backpack pocket where it clinked against the other stones.

Chad watched. "What have you got there?"

"Nothing really. Just making memories."

"Make sure they're good ones."

Five

"So, where do you two want to camp tonight?" Chad repeated as they rounded the next curve, revealing scenes that stole Glen's breath. "High glaciers? River rapids with the canyons they've carved? Alpine meadows? Or across the Canadian border into Waterton Lakes?"

"It's impossible to choose," Ted protested. His cell phone rang as they reentered signal range, and he swiped it open. "Weldon here. Yeah, Sullivan, great time." His face froze. "Ouachita Forest blew up with lightning strikes? When?"

Glen gripped his arm. "Uncle Teddy, what's wrong?"

He covered his phone to tell her. "An out-of-control blaze with high winds near Hot Springs. Crossed the highway. Threatening summer cabins and that forestry campground and lodge."

Glen's hands flew to her face. "I spent a summer there and love that place. Are lives at risk?"

Ted uncovered his phone. "Are there injuries? People in danger?"

He listened and told Glen, "Not yet. They're hitting it hard."

He returned to his phone. "Sure, I'm onboard, Sullivan. Early tomorrow? Which airport?"

Ted caught Chad's eyes and mouthed, "Kalispell? Ten a.m.?" Chad nodded. "Doable."

"Can do. My buddy will get me there. See ya then."

While Chad drove the sharp turn that led to the next scenic showstopper view, Glen's eyes bored into her uncle. "What else did he say?"

"There's no threat to life yet, but it's racing towards that pristine forest beyond the lodge. If that candles, it will be hard to stop because of dry trees and high winds."

"You have to go," Glen said. "I'm tempted to go with you, except I'm signed on here."

"Right. I'll fight for both of us."

"Give me details," Chad said.

Ted took a deep breath and leaned against his seat. "An out-of-control blaze in Arkansas's largest national forest. They're flying a Montana hotshot crew out of Kalispell early tomorrow and want me to lead it."

"Wow. Sorry to lose you, buddy, but I'll get you there."

Glen reached over the back seat and gripped her uncle's sleeve. "That area is truly special. Thanks for saving it."

"I'll do my best. Pray for us."

Chad drummed the fingers of one hand on the dashboard. "Okay. Since plans have changed, I'll make an executive decision. I'm taking you to a destination I was saving for later." He poked Ted's shoulder. "Except promise one thing. You'll come back someday, and we'll do the rest of this trip."

"I want to. Guaranteed. Besides, I'm leaving my favorite niece behind." He turned from the front seat to squeeze Glen's hand. "Well, look at that," he said. "Peaches is sprawled over you with her head in your lap." He nudged Chad. "She's letting Glen pet her."

Chad checked his rearview mirror. "Wow. So far she only lets Mom and me do that, but you can't fool dogs. Glen is obviously special."

Ted jabbed Chad again. "See? I told you."

As soon as Chad parked at the next overlook with commanding views, all three rushed to the valley's rim for panorama shots. Ted sidled next to Glen and spoke in a low voice. "Are you comfortable with me leaving early and you being alone here?"

She sighed. "You don't have a choice. Besides, I'm a big girl and need to establish my life here. It's not like I'll bug Chad much —even if I help with a few district day trips."

"He has rough edges, but as fierce as he was in 'Stan, I love seeing him so gentle with Peaches. I'm impressed all over again."

"Rough edges? Where?" Glen looked all around. "I don't see them. You two should have stayed in touch more."

"She's right, Ted." Chad couldn't quit looking at Glen's hair. "Copper," he said.

"Excuse me?" Glen's eyebrows quirked.

"Montana is a world copper producer. I'll take you to Butte and show you their mining history. Prospectors found fabulous copper veins while prospecting for gold in the fifties."

"That's impressive. Is Butte on your list of regional office visits?"

"Not yet, but it could be." He pointed to the sky. "When the sun shines on your hair, it turns it to copper."

Glen reached up and finger-combed a strand. "Thanks—I guess."

"Definitely." He nodded. "It does the same to your uncle's hair, but he has less of it, plus it looks nicer on you."

Ted brushed his fingers through his crew cut. "My silver streak makes me look like a skunk."

"Nah." Chad laughed. "I don't think so. It marks you as a man of action, like always." He swiped a hand through his dark waves. "Mine's ordinary. I'm envious."

"Yours isn't a bit ordinary." Glen's hand moved. "It's nice. I'd like to get my hands in it."

"Really?" Chad's eyes widened and blinked. "There's a place near Butte with amethyst and smoky quartz deposits. Lots of gem-quality crystals too. I wish every Montana school kid could see those."

"Maybe I'll mention those in my education classes." Glen scribbled in her notebook.

After all three climbed back into the Jeep, its chassis rattled and washboarded while Chad bounced up the narrow mountain road. He suddenly spun his steering wheel into a sharp left to climb a rutted gravel side road that disappeared into the clouds.

"Whoa, Nelly." Ted braced himself against the dash. "Where are you taking us?"

"Somewhere unforgettable. We're almost there."

Glen worked her jaw. "My ears just popped. We're gaining altitude."

"That's right." Chad rounded the next dizzying curve and braked where the gravel stopped. His front Jeep tires rested against white, glistening ice. "We're here. Grab your mitts, and be ready for the best view of your lives. But be careful—it's slippery."

The wide vista of Glacier National Park spread before them like a large bowl surrounded by high peaks. An aquamarine lake shimmered jewel-like in the center. To the north, a plunging valley and its watersheds stretched across Canada's border to connect with Waterton Lakes Provincial Park. Glen crossed her arms and shivered as her boots crunched on glacial ice. "This is impressive. I've only seen scenes this gorgeous on calendars."

"You're right." Ted slapped Chad's back. "Remember that time they sent us on maneuvers in the Hindu Kush, and we had a snowball fight?" He scooped up snow and pasted his friend, but Chad pivoted and pushed a handful down Ted's neck.

"Hey," Ted yelled. "You're killing me. Southern boys aren't made for this."

Chad laughed. "Welcome to the north." He chased Glen with another snowball, but she ducked behind the Jeep.

"You heard Uncle Teddy. Southern folks aren't made for snow. Besides, I'm a lady." She jumped up and plastered Chad with a good one.

He swiped snow off of his face. "Hey, girl. You can't play both sides of the game. You need to take as much as you give." He dodged left and hurled a snowball straight at her, but she ducked as it whizzed past.

Peaches ran between them barking, her toenails sliding on ice. "Come here, Peaches," Chad called. "Don't switch loyalties on me. Remember, you're a *northern* dog."

Soon, all three clambered partway up the glacier, slipping and sliding back almost as much as they climbed.

"Okay, this is far enough. Follow my example." Chad dropped to the seat of his pants and shoved off the ice, whooping and hollering as he hurtled down the slope. Ted and Glen followed, managing turnaround spins like an amusement park cup-and-saucer ride. Peaches did rollovers and yowled.

Chad found his feet and brushed ice crystals from his clothes. "How was that?" He eyed his friends. "Had enough?"

"Not yet." Glen turned and struggled up the slope again.

Ted followed with a full smile.

After two more runs, they brushed snow and ice from their clothes.

"How about now?" Chad checked the position of the sun. "Shall we get back in the Jeep? There's more I want to show you before dark."

Glen rolled her shoulders. "I hate to leave here, but I'll never forget this. Most fun ever. Montana is impressive."

Chad pumped a fist in the air. "Yes. That's what I wanted to hear. I live in Montana because I was born here, but I think it's great."

Ted peered into the distance. "It's fabulous, all right. What's our elevation?"

"Let me see." Chad checked his iPhone. "The Flathead River down there is at 3,100 feet. Montana's highest point, Mount Cleveland, is 10,000 feet. This spot is halfway between the two."

Ted threw both hands in the air. "The highest elevation in Arkansas isn't even twenty-seven hundred feet. Nothing like here." He inhaled. "In fact, the air's thin, but a man breathes in clean scents of spruce, pine, and granite."

"That's what I'm telling you. I love this place. Climb in my Jeep, and I'll turn the heater on high blast for you Southerners."

"I'll let you." Glen hugged herself tight.

The instant Chad opened the Jeep doors, Peaches dove in and curled up on the floor.

Glen laughed and petted her. "What a smart dog."

Peaches cocked her head.

"Have you noticed the way her mouth doesn't quite close makes her look like she's smiling?"

"It does." Chad chuckled. "That's because she is."

Ted shuddered. "My clothes are soaked, bro." He turned up his coat collar and huddled into it. "Where will we camp tonight?"

"That's a surprise." Chad turned from the gravel road onto Going-to-the-Sun Road. "My friend Everest runs a ski lodge. His place is full all winter but stays close to empty in the summer. He invited us to stop by, and he'll comp us rooms since I take him elk hunting every fall."

"Warm rooms?" Glen asked. "With roaring fireplaces? Our hero."

Chad smiled. "And great steaks."

Ted gusted a happy sigh. "Is Everest his real name?"

"I've wondered. He calls his place Mt. Everest Lodge."

"That's fitting." Ted leaned back. "I hate to admit it, but Montana is heaven."

Chad slapped his steering wheel. "I knew you would see it my way."

* * *

Everest was exactly as Chad remembered him, as hulking as the mountain he was named for. His beard had grown and rivaled the

Duck Dynasty characters' beards. And the same bright red tasseled snow cap rode his head.

He welcomed them into his lodge. "You had a poacher in Many Glacier Valley?"

"We did." Chad opened his photos. "This is the snare and footprints. He was likely going after black bear since their paws and gallbladders bring high prices for Chinese medicine."

Everest shook his wooly head. "I know. It's criminal. My guests talk about it."

Chad closed his camera. "The worst part is the guy snared Ted here. It caught his foot and jerked him upside down. We found him and cut him free, but someone alone in the woods caught in high gauge wire couldn't free themselves. They would die."

Everest gripped Ted's shoulder. "That's rough. It's good you escaped. We don't have much poaching here, but it makes me want to catch whoever it was."

"You and me both." Ted opened more photos. "Look at this four-by-four tire print from near the boat ramp. We think it could be his rig."

Everest squinted. "That's a four-by-four all right. One dude who comes through here brags about Chinese medicine sales. I don't know if he's for real or pranking me since it's illegal." He pulled his beard. "Actually, a few guys talk it up. It's big money, but there's something odd about this guy."

"Like what?" Chad leaned in. "Can you tell me his name? Anything more about him?"

"Not much. He's a little off." Everest pushed his ski hat farther back on his head. "He does a little trapping and prospecting. Hangs out somewhere northwest of here where the best claims are. He wears a pistol on his hip since trappers and prospectors are allowed to. He boasts about what a fine shot he is and how much gold he gets—makes himself sound like the best at everything, but I figure he's mostly talk."

"He sounds interesting." After Chad caught Glen's eye and

gestured, she pulled out her notebook and pen. "Can you tell us if he's tall? Short? Any identifying characteristics?"

"Umm. In between. Red hair. Nothing else stands out except a slight limp. He says he caught his foot in his own bear trap once."

Ted whipped around and met Chad's eyes.

His lips tightened. "Noted."

Glen stopped writing. "How much of a limp?"

"Not bad, but noticeable." Everest's gaze rested on her. "It's worse when he's tired or if he walks any distance. Sometimes he hauls an old four-by-four in his truck. I don't know the tire tread."

"This helps." Chad palmed his phone and slipped it into his pocket. "Thanks, Everest, for good food and for letting us stay."

"You're doing me the favor. There's not much for tourists to do on a ski hill during summertime. A man gets lonesome." He studied Glen. "Lady rangers are always welcome—with or without these bozos." He narrowed his gaze. "If anyone in Montana doesn't treat you right, young lady, just tell me. I'll straighten them out."

Glen smiled. "Thanks, but I prefer to take care of myself."

Ted chuckled. "She sure does. My folks and I overdid it when raising little Miss Independent. We don't worry about her. She's even studied martial arts."

"I hear you." Everest backed up two steps and removed his cook's apron. "Sleep well, you guys."

Ted stopped halfway up the rustic log stairs. "Chad? How far is it to Kalispell? How long will it take to reach the airport?"

"Under an hour." He tapped his chin. "Glacier Park has an international airport used primarily for tourists. You'll use Kalispell City Airport, ten miles farther south. That's where I picked you up the other day."

"That's right. I want to keep those straight. So, it's Kalispell? Not Hungry Horse, where I'll join the hotshot crew?" Ted leaned against the stair rail.

"I'll double-check, but I think that's right. I'll phone to confirm the departure plans. I'll bet your director doesn't know we have two airports. If we have time, I might show you both. We'll see how it goes. I often work with those guys—great staff."

"I won't officially meet them tomorrow then," Glen said. "But it'll be fun to glimpse some Montanans I'll work with."

"They'll be eager to meet you." Chad grinned. "By the way, tomorrow or anytime you enter any local ranger station, don't accept their coffee unless you have dental insurance. They make the world's worst. It won't even pour. It dents your teeth when it hits them, and then you chisel the stuff out of your cup and chew."

"That sounds ghastly." Glen giggled. "I'll avoid it and hope the Kalispell office makes better stuff."

"They don't. You've been warned." Chad hiked one eyebrow.

"Then I'll make it part of my job responsibilities to brew good coffee and teach them how."

"She's a master," Ted confided. "Spoils me rotten."

Chad laughed. "Pull that off, Glen, and you'll have so many marriage proposals, you'll have to fight men off with a stick." But he wasn't laughing inside. Oh, how he didn't want that to happen.

"For real?" Glen cocked her head. "I can't tell if you're teasing or not. That hasn't happened, even in a Leap Year."

"Don't let her kid you." Ted shook his head. "She broke several hearts by telling guys she wasn't interested."

"Uncle Teddy." She punched his shoulder, and Peaches growled. "Stay out of my business."

"You're right. I get carried away."

"Having the locals chasing you is *not* a problem you want." Chad's mouth quirked. "They say word is out about a new ranger joining the district. People are curious. They welcome new blood like hungry mosquitoes. I doubt they realize you're a woman. Your name may have confused them."

"It's rare but legal. I'm named after my dad. Does it matter? I was hoping the office wouldn't share my personal information before I arrived."

"You know how it is. They have to set up your computer, workspace, internet addresses, phone extensions—the works."

"I guess." Glen's chin dropped. "There aren't many lady rangers in Arkansas. I hope to meet and work with folks here on my terms without trying to live up to Dad's and my uncle's legacies."

Ted jerked. "Has it been that bad?"

"Not always. But there are too many comparisons." She climbed the stairs alongside him. "Dad was a hero. You're a legend. That carries expectations."

"I'm sorry, I didn't realize." He placed a hand on her shoulder. "You're made of good stuff. You'll forge your own path fine."

She sighed. "That's the biggest reason I came to Montana—for a fresh start."

"I've taught you well. You'll do great." Ted swung open the door to Glen's room and placed her duffel inside. Next, he yawned and glanced down the hall. "Chad? You wore me out. Thanks for checking with Hungry Horse about departure times."

"You're welcome. If anything changes, I'll let you know. Sleep well."

"You too." Ted entered his room.

Glen stood in her doorway and called down the hall. "Chad? Will the Forest Service staff be there tomorrow?"

"In Hungry Horse? I doubt it. They'll be swamped sending off their hotshot crew." His eyes narrowed. "Don't tell me a few hayseed guys in a small district scare you?"

"No. And I need to remember that Hungry Horse and Kalispell are different places. Kalispell is my base."

"That's right, but they team up often."

She lowered her voice. "It has been hard living in my dad's and uncle's shadows."

"I can imagine," Chad answered. "Tomorrow should just be a

quick introduction. There's never a perfect time or way to meet new people."

"I know." She glanced down. "I'd at least like to be in a fresh uniform."

"I understand, but they'll be wearing firefighting duds." He surveyed her from head to toe. "Trust them to see who you really are. Do the same for them and be kinder to yourself. You're quite acceptable."

"Well, thank you." Her nose wrinkled. "At least I can shower. I'll bet I smell."

"Like evergreen trees and wild roses. Kinda nice. See you in the morning."

As he sauntered away, Peaches at his heels, tail wagging, he saw Glen watching him go. What was she thinking? Could she ever be interested in a guy like him? Probably not. Besides, he was too smart to take risks.

Six

When Glen's alarm shrilled, it was still dark. She took a second shower and spruced herself up the best she could with the few toiletries she had. She pinched her cheeks to brighten them as someone knocked on her door.

"Good morning." Chad was all smiles. "Is your bag ready?" He looked her over. "Don't spruce up too much. We don't want the fire crew distracted by an attractive lady ranger."

He thought she was attractive? Her cheeks burned. "Thanks, but there's small chance in these clothes."

"Don't be too sure. And under their firefighting garb, you'll find heroes in disguise—truly dedicated to what they do."

"That's nice to hear. Like Dad and Ted."

"Exactly. The Montana squad does well in emergencies."

She paused. "I'll be glad to meet them. I'm sorry I made a big deal of it."

"It's no problem. We all have weak spots. You don't have to come inside the Hungry Horse station or the airport if you'd rather not. I could even drop you at the local McDonald's and come back for you later if you like." He grabbed her duffel. "It's your call."

"Thanks." She patted her hair. "I'm not that paranoid."

"Good."

Ted arrived with his gear. "Did I hear you're getting cold feet? You don't have to meet any top officials today. And you and I can say our goodbyes beforehand. It's not like I'll never see you again."

"Don't even say that. You'd *better* see me again." She blinked away something in her eye.

"Of course I will." He slipped his arm around her as they descended the stairs.

* * *

After polishing off their Mountain Man breakfasts, the three tucked money under their plates for the generous meals Everest had served. As Chad drove down the mountains, he checked his rearview mirror. Peaches had crowded onto Glen's lap and was snoring.

"Look at that. You really have made a friend for life. You can put her down if you like."

"No, it's all right." Glen petted Peaches's scarred head. "You're such a nice girl."

Peaches woke up and slobbered noisily.

"I know that sound." Chad chuckled. "You'll find napkins in the console."

"Thanks." Glen grabbed several and mopped up.

Chad swept his hand across the windshield to point out the surrounding scenery. "This is all part of Flathead National Forest —largest in our state. It includes your Kalispell base, Glacier National Park, and lots more. Our Big Sky country offers mountains, forests, and grasslands you can't beat anywhere else."

"You're right," Ted agreed. "And terrific people."

Glen took another photo through the window. "It's fabulous. Better than the brochures. I'm going to like living here."

"Glad to hear it." Chad gave a thumbs-up.

Ted massaged his neck. "It's years off, but someday I'll retire and spend time here. Build a mountain cabin. Go fishing. Anything I want."

"Great, Uncle Teddy." Glen patted his shoulder. "By then I'll have lots of ideas for you."

He laughed. "As usual."

"Plus, let's talk after you're home." Chad tapped Ted's knee. "Now that we've reconnected, I'll get back to you on those prospector claims and other things."

"Can't wait."

After they fist bumped, Chad kept both hands on the wheel to round the hairpin turns. White foaming streams rushed from high elevations and filled jeweled lakes.

"Wow." Glen shielded her eyes. "I can't find words to describe this."

Chad checked his rearview mirror again. "What are you holding now?"

"Something I saved from outside Everest's lodge with white crystal patterns on it."

"It sounds like you're collecting memories. I know a little about stones. If you like, I'd be glad to help you find good ones."

Their eyes met in the mirror as she slipped the stone into her pocket. "I might take you up on that one day, but I'm fine for now."

Chad turned from Going-to-the-Sun Road onto a larger highway. "Hungry Horse is our next town. Ted, I'll stop at the ranger station to pick up the instructions your office faxed. I'll just be a minute. You're both welcome to come inside, wait in my Jeep, or whatever you like."

"I'll come in," Ted said.

Glen shrugged. "I probably worried about nothing. This ranger station is in my National Forest. I'll come too. They won't know me from Adam."

"Or Eve." Chad's lips curved as he parked near the front door. They exited the Jeep but left Peaches inside. As soon as they entered, the receptionist offered them cups of thick black coffee.

"No, thanks." Ted patted his stomach. "I drank a quart at Mt. Everest Lodge. That's today's quota for me."

The burned smell pinched Glen's nose. "Thanks. Maybe next time."

"I'm fine," Chad said. "We'll grab Ted's fax and get him on his plane."

The receptionist and others shook their hands. "You're from Arkansas?" the receptionist asked. "I love your accent. Kalispell's new ranger is from somewhere down there. We hear he's a great guy."

Glen's head jerked.

Ted opened his mouth, but Chad handed him his fax.

"Sorry, we've got to go." He headed for the door. "Those folks are confused," he said, once they climbed back into his Jeep and headed down U.S. Highway 93. "It's like that childhood game of Gossip where people hear facts, add what they think they hear, and end up with a whole new story."

"Yep, it's crazy how that works." Ted checked his watch. "Thanks for getting us here and for this incredible time."

"My pleasure." Chad bypassed most of Kalispell before reaching the city airport and its charter flight compound.

"There's the plane." He pulled up near the high-wire fence separating the parking lot from the planes and runway areas. "It's smaller than a C-130, but a transport—bigger than that puddle jumper you flew up on."

"Most anything would be." They laughed.

"I recognize the guys loading cargo. They're almost through."

"I need a pit stop inside," Glen said.

"No problem." Chad pointed to a long, low building. "It's the first door on the right once you're inside."

"Thanks."

The moment she left, Ted poked Chad's arm. "Let's talk."

"Sure. And once you're home, tell me how it turns out with your lady friend. I want you happy."

"That's what I want to tell you. We haven't discussed faith, but I'm closer to the Lord now than in 'Stan.'"

"It shows."

Ted lowered his head. "Losing my brother hit hard. It made me dig deeper for my sake and Glen's. She's close to the Lord and won't let me get by with lukewarmness either."

Chad studied Ted. "It's good to have anchors."

"It is." Ted huffed out a breath. "My point is, I want you happy too. I'm praying for you."

"Don't pray too hard." Chad stared through the windshield. "I keep telling myself it's best to stay a bachelor at this point."

"I hear you. I thought so, too, but I was full of bologna. Sometimes we don't know what we need 'til we find it. I pray you find what you need." He slapped Chad's knee. "Take care of my girl."

"Will do. I'll show her more of Montana, and she'll help me write my best surveys yet." He jabbed Ted's arm. "Don't forget— you promised to come back so we can do more of this."

"Will do. We're still Thunder and Lightning. I've never had a better buddy."

"Same here." They left the Jeep and pumped their joined hands like a water pump.

When Glen returned, Ted hugged her. "I'll miss having you around, kiddo. Knock their socks off."

"I will. Thanks for everything, Uncle Teddy. You're the best."

He pulled her closer and kissed her cheek.

She stood on tiptoe and threw her arms around him. "I don't want to cry."

"Me either."

Chad pulled Ted's gear from the trunk. "There's the team leader you'll work with. I'll introduce you."

"Thanks. First, let's get one last picture together." Ted swung his arm around Chad's shoulder.

Chad threw his arm around Ted too. "Who's the big guy now? We've both bulked up. Glen? Will you snap our picture?"

"Sure thing." She captured them in the frame and clicked. "For posterity."

Ted slapped Chad's back. "And to remind us to get together."

Both men passed through the gate to meet the team leader. All three shook hands and chatted before two turned and climbed the plane's steps. Other crewmen boarded the transport. Soon, the outside door closed, and the turboprops roared to life, revving for takeoff. The engines screamed to maximum pitch, and the plane raced down the runway. Chad found Glen covering her ears.

"Pretty noisy," he said.

"What?" She cupped her ear.

He laughed. "It's super noisy."

The plane shuddered and lifted into the blue Montana sky. They waved until they couldn't see the plane.

"That's the end of that chapter," Glen said.

"It is." Chad noted activity near the hangar. "There's Kalispell's assistant supervisor—that small, thin man in Forest Service green with the agency's patch on his uniform."

"Wearing the Smoky the Bear hat?" Glen shaded her eyes. "He seems pretty busy writing on that clipboard."

"He's probably finishing inventory. I think it's okay. Cal?" Chad waved. "Cal Higgins. Hello." Chad crossed the tarmac and extended a hand.

The man glanced up but continued writing. When he eventually lowered his clipboard, he made no move to accept Chad's hand. "Kinkaid? What's up?"

"I just put my friend Ted Weldon on the hotshot plane to Arkansas."

"That was Weldon?" Cal's eyes moved past Glen without interest. "I've heard of him—wish I'd met him."

"You could have. If I'd spotted you sooner, I would have introduced you." Chad squared his shoulders. "Ted and I were combat buddies in Afghanistan. I was showing him and his niece around Montana when he got the emergency call."

"Yeah. That lightning strike blew into a firestorm fast. You mentioned his niece?"

"She's right here." Chad motioned Glen forward. "You know Glen is joining your office soon."

"Joining what?"

"Your office."

Higgins's eyes rested on Glen now. "Explain that."

She stepped closer. "I'm Glen Weldon, Ted's niece and your new district education officer. I start in twelve days."

"Say again?" Higgins jerked as if slapped. "Something's wrong. Our new hire is Glen Weldon Jr., named after a Forest Service hero."

"That's me. It's unusual—a family preference. When my folks learned they could only have one child, they gave me Dad's name." She scrutinized Cal. "Is that a problem?"

"I'll say. Quite a mix-up." His eyes shrank to black stones as he lowered his head into his jacket collar like a turtle withdrawing into its shell. "Didn't Supervisor Johnson manage your hire himself?"

"That's right. He'd met Dad."

"He should have told us more. He should have told me. I'm his assistant. The buck stops with me when he's gone. He hired you by phone?"

"Yes. And electronic messages."

"So he heard your voice and knew you were a woman?"

"He surely did. He welcomed me as a woman ranger. Said it would be good for your office programs."

"I don't understand. We had a problem with a woman employee before. What was he thinking?" Higgins barricaded his arms. "He told us you were Glen A. Weldon Jr., that your dad was a famous Arkansas ranger he admired. He didn't show us photos —just said he'd met your dad at a national conference before he died and was glad to scoop you up for our office."

"That's what he told me too." Glen stood straight.

"She is a great scoop, Ranger Higgins." Chad's voice hardened. "I don't know why you're concerned. Any misunderstanding isn't Glen's fault. She's bright and has impressive credentials and abilities. She'll be an outstanding education officer. You're lucky to have her."

"That's your opinion." Higgins raised his neck an inch. "A woman won't fit our personnel mix."

"Why on earth not?" Chad stared. "Would you care to explain?"

"No." Higgins jerked back as if expecting to be struck. "I don't need to answer to anyone outside our agency."

"I'm in a partnering federal agency, Higgins. What's your problem?"

"I told you, no comment."

When Chad noticed Glen shaking, he patted her arm. "Don't worry. We'll straighten this out."

"I don't see how." She lifted her eyes. "Ranger Higgins? You're clearly disappointed. Today's Saturday. I don't suppose your office opens again until Monday."

"You're correct."

"I'll come in Monday morning to meet with you and Supervisor Johnson to clarify things."

"That can't happen. He's in Sweden studying seedling production and won't return until September fifteenth. I can try to reach him, but I doubt it's possible when he's in the field. What is your starting date again?"

"September first, twelve days from now."

"With Johnson gone, you'll deal with me. I'm in charge."

"I understand." Glen squared her shoulders.

"I'll be involved too." Chad clamped his jaw tight. "I'll be there when you meet on Monday, and your human resources representative better be involved. This is no way to greet a new employee. I don't know what's so special about your station, but this is clearly gender discrimination."

"You don't understand." Higgins's mouth puckered. "It's

complicated. Things are good in our office now. We don't want change."

Chad sighed. "Supervisor Johnson seemed to think differently. Come on, Glen. There's no point in talking. We'll try again Monday." He slid his arm around her. "Let's go."

She didn't cry until they reached the Jeep. Then she wept into the tissue Chad handed her. "That couldn't have gone worse," she stuttered through her tears.

"It's sure not what I expected, and I don't understand it." Chad gave her another tissue. "I've heard good comments about him. He's a high-performance professional who wins efficiency awards. Either he's having a terrible day or didn't take his meds." Chad gave a small laugh.

Glen didn't. "If you're trying to make me laugh, it's not working."

"I'll try harder."

"It's hard to judge his age. He might be overworked or have a health issue."

"You're very kind." Chad wiped his forehead. "I haven't heard anything, but even if he has a medical problem, it doesn't justify his conduct."

"No, it doesn't." Glen dried her eyes. "College psych class taught us the Napoleonic complex—little men who need large importance. He might fit that category."

"Could be. Something is off. Gender discrimination can end any supervisor's career. Even make them lose their pension, which is harsh."

"Let's not go there." She tugged at a button on her sleeve. "I hope he reaches Supervisor Johnson and is reassured. Or by Monday morning, he's past the shock and willing to work with me."

"Fine, but until then, we need to plan wisely. When you were finalizing this job, did you speak by phone to anyone in the office besides Johnson?"

"No. He said he works in the field more than most S.O.s. We sent emails and some scans."

"Sounds good." Chad shook his head. "I'm sure you filled in the job application correctly, completed the gender box, and sent the required photo."

"I ticked the right box, but my photo was a grainy black and white. Our forest ranger hats shade our faces. There wasn't much I could do about that."

"Still, anyone viewing it or reading your records should realize you're a woman—and a capable one. What difference does it make?"

"None that I can tell." Glen gazed into the distance where her uncle's plane had taken off.

After a pause, Chad asked, "Remind me of your age?"

"Almost twenty-six."

"That's young, but you look younger for someone who's already accomplished so much."

"I've worked hard for the things I wanted. How old are you?"

"Thirty-two. Your uncle still calls me a baby, but I'm old in many ways."

"He's nine years older. And you're an amazing baby if the stories he tells are true."

"He should keep his mouth shut."

"That's not likely."

They both laughed.

"I could give you information to blackmail him."

"Would you?" Chad's eyebrows shot up as he grinned like a Cheshire cat. "That would be solid gold. I'd pay money."

"None needed." Glen smoothed her pant leg to remove its wrinkles. "Higgins seemed preoccupied. What do you think he was writing on his clipboard?"

"Who knows? Probably inventorying the crew and air- and ground-support materials he sent south. He's likely worried about sending off so much in case there's an emergency here while he's in charge." Chad pointed to her. "Frankly, by the way he responded to you, one just happened."

Glen sighed. "It's weird. I almost feel sorry for him. He looked miserable."

"Save your sympathy. I wanted to knock his block off."

She smiled. "Before you think I'm saintly, I pictured my hands around his neck."

"That's nice to hear. So not all Southern girls are sweet and syrupy?"

"Not this one."

"You feel emotions?" He snapped his fingers. "Get stirred up?"

Her cheeks reddened. "You bet. Don't test me, buster. You don't want to see me blow steam. I've lived long enough to figure out that the bottom line of most strong reactions is the other person's problem." She twisted the tissue in her hands. "But opposing him head-on would be wrong. Then I'd be like him, and I won't pay that price."

"Don't worry, Glen. You're nothing like him."

"Thanks." She shredded the tissue into small bits and then gathered them together. "He'll be a nightmare to work with."

"Impossible. But if anyone could, it's you. At least he's not the only boss in the place. The supervisor is above him."

"I could phone my supervisor back home. He hasn't filled my job there yet. He would take me back in a heartbeat. If I call now, he'd fly me home. I'd be back in our house before Uncle Ted finishes fighting his fire. I'd lose my apartment lease deposit here, but there are worse—"

"No." Chad brushed her hand. "Don't go there. I'm not a counselor, but when things go this haywire, good usually comes from it. Don't you think?"

She studied his green eyes and remembered overhearing his talk with Ted—that his fiancée's betrayal had shut his heart. "I hope so. After time goes by."

"Um—I'm sure it does. And prayer. So good eventually comes." He searched her face again. "Doesn't it?"

She paused. "I think so."

"If you don't mind me asking, why haven't you married?"

"Well, that came out of left field." She gazed through the windshield. "That's personal, but after several important people in my family died close together, I was afraid to open my heart lest I be hurt more. I filled my empty places by staying busy and doing what I wanted. I'm possibly moving past that now. What about you?"

"I've stayed busy, too, after a bad experience—I'm almost there." His arm moved around the car seat to rest on her shoulder. He pulled her closer until his head rested against hers. "You're special. Someone I could—" He stiffened and jerked away.

"Chad?"

"I'm sorry. I shouldn't—"

"Shouldn't what?"

"Follow feelings. Ted left you in my care. I should treat you like my niece or—but that's not how I—"

"I'm a grown woman—not a child."

"I see that, but I took advantage—"

"You did not. But I need to know what I'm doing. To show Higgins he's wrong."

"You will."

"We're a mess." Glen shifted back to her door. "Well, at least you didn't marry the Afghan girl. You have time to figure out what's right for you."

Chad swallowed. "Thanks to your uncle. You almost made me laugh." He checked his wristwatch. "It's nearly lunchtime. How about I show you Whitefish since we're close? It's a great town with amazing scenery. We'll find something to eat and plan a battle strategy. What do you say?"

Glen paused. "I don't have anything planned. Lunch and more amazing scenery sound perfect."

He fist bumped her hand. "This story isn't over."

Seven

~~~

O nce the hostess seated them, Glen looked around. The Montana Grill had cowhide upholstered booths. Cowboy hats, steer and buffalo heads, and lariats decorated the walls. The waitresses wore fringed shirts, bright skirts, and boots with spurs. Western songs pulsed from a loudspeaker.

"Wow." Glen sank into their booth and continued taking in more details.

Chad's eyes crinkled. "What do you think?"

"It's like a western movie set. If they charge for the atmosphere, I'll pay."

His teeth gleamed in a broad smile. "I thought you'd like it."

"Is the food as great as the décor?"

"I've never been disappointed. This place is a Whitefish icon."

She scanned the menu. "I'll try something local, but I'm surprised they offer seafood since we're inland."

"Seafood? Where do you see that?" He leaned forward.

"Here." Her finger highlighted the entrée list. "Rocky Mountain Oysters."

His face flamed. "They're not what you—"

"Welcome to The Montana Grill." The waitress smiled big. "Ready to order?"

"Almost." Glen raised a finger. "But I have a question."

"Shoot."

Glen tapped the menu. "Are your Rocky Mountain Oysters fried or grilled?"

"Fried." The waitress poised her pencil above her order pad. "You know what they are, right?"

"Oysters you've flown in, I'd guess." Glen waited.

"Not exactly." She hemmed and hawed. "You know, they're parts left over after cattle roundups that are skinned, sliced, deep-fried, and taste like oysters. We also call 'em cowboy caviar. Would you like some?"

Glen's eyes widened and her nose wrinkled. "Oh, eww." She tried to catch Chad's eye, but he seemed buried in his menu. "Uh—not today. What do you recommend that's more … ordinary."

The waitress turned the menu page. "Our high-protein Montana Bison Burgers are popular."

"That sounds better." Glen handed her menu to the waitress. "I'll have that."

"Great choice. With or without dipping or barbecue sauce?"

Now Chad's eyes met hers. "Why don't you start with it plain? You can always add a sauce later if you think it needs it."

"That's smart. That's what I'll do."

"I'll take my usual." Chad tapped the next column. "The Big Sky Steak Sandwich platter, medium rare, with fries and coleslaw on the side."

"Perfect." The server dropped her pencil into her apron pocket. "Nice to have you back again. I'll place your orders right away."

Glen scooted closer to the table. "I need to you ask you something."

"Uh-oh." Chad leaned against the back of the booth. "That's the tone Mom used when I was in trouble."

"You're not, but did you get in trouble much?"

He laughed. "I plead the fifth. You?"

"Not too bad. I was an only child and a girl." She added a grin. "That tells you something."

"It says you should be more spoiled than you seem."

"You don't know me yet. Hardships have a way of straightening people out."

"So I've learned. What do you want to ask?"

She sighed. "My talk with Higgins will be hard, but I need to fight my battles. I appreciate your offer to help, but I need to face him alone. I'm praying hard for his fears to be put to rest. Just him and me with no HR person." She spread empty hands. "If this meeting fails, then I'll call in the troops."

"You're not scared?" Chad studied her. "Your eyes are like a sunny Montana sky without clouds."

"Wow, I think that's a compliment." She closed those eyes a moment. "Scared? No. Nervous? Yes."

"I'm impressed." Chad chugged several swallows of ice water. "Ted said you were gutsy. Is that from your Dad?"

"And Uncle Teddy. He's a better role model than he thinks."

"I believe it. He also said as soon as you earned your forestry degree, you started night classes for your master's. Why was that?"

"Why not?" She unwrapped her silverware from its red-and-black gingham napkin. "I love studying all kinds of things. It all helps an education officer."

"True. So it's not some burning motivational drive to surpass others, especially men?"

"Not at all. I love researching facts and exploring terrain. I didn't care if I got a degree."

"But you did."

"Yes. The shingle's on my wall, and there are more letters after my name."

"That's rare in forestry. I'm a district manager with Fish, Wildlife & Parks now. I'm considering going for a master's but haven't decided."

"You'll know, but it's not essential." She paused and studied him. "Hands-on knowledge is worth just as much. Degrees don't always have useful content." She giggled. "I always say even thermometers have degrees."

Chad sputtered. "That's funny. You could be a stand-up comedian."

"But it's true. What matters is how people use knowledge. Learning is meant to be useful—not intellectual keep-away. These days people can earn credits and degrees for basic life and work experience. I'm sure Higgins has bushels of that."

"I imagine. I don't know his age, but he's been around a while." Chad tilted his head sidewise like a thoughtful owl. "I probably reacted too strong and fast back there. I should have given him time to cool off—not made him defensive."

"You did the best you could. It was a pop quiz situation."

"Worse." Chad's eyes held hers. "Bottom line? I don't want you hurt."

"Thanks. But don't worry about me. I usually manage what comes down the pike."

"I'll bet." Chad's gaze deepened. "At least keep me informed. Tell me when you're meeting."

"I will because—"

Their server came. "Here you go, folks. Hot off the grill. One sizzling Big Sky Steak Sandwich platter with slaw and fries, and our best Montana Bison Burger." She brought a smaller plate with four golden bumps on it. "I brought a few deep-fried Rocky Mountain Oysters with dipping sauce for you to try." She arranged the dishes and refilled their water glasses. "Tell me if you need anything."

"Will do, but this looks fine." Chad spread his napkin.

The waitress turned to seat a young family at the next table.

Chad lifted his fork. "Shall we dig in?" He took his first bite as Glen bowed her head. He cleared his throat. "Oops—shall I bless our food?"

"Would you?" She eyed the small plate of golden bumps.

"Especially that dish. Plus, that I have the Lord's help for each upcoming step."

"I'm glad to." After Chad's simple prayer, she toyed with the delicacies.

"Will you indulge?" His eyes glinted.

"Yes. I like making myself try new experiences." She speared one golden morsel with her fork and dragged it through sauce. She bit and chewed slowly and eventually swallowed a small amount.

"You should see your face," Chad said. "What do you think?"

"It's better than I thought, but one's enough. At least I tried them."

"Sort of." He laughed again.

She pushed the plate Chad's way. "I don't want to be selfish. I'll let you enjoy the rest."

"Oh, no. Don't be generous." He slid the plate to the far end of the table. "That acquired taste isn't in my gene pool, but you're a good sport."

They burst out laughing and picked up their entrees. Chad doused his fries with ketchup and chewed thoughtfully. "I figure Cal read your résumé once he realized you're a woman, and now he's intimidated."

"He shouldn't be." She stopped with the salt shaker midair. "I value his field experience. He can teach me a lot if he's willing."

"You'll have to persuade him." Chad's eyes lidded. "You are impressive. You intimidate me a bit."

"Oh, for heaven's sake." She dropped her fork onto her plate with a clatter. "Don't be silly."

"It's true. Think about it from his angle. But whatever is going on, his reaction was seriously inappropriate."

"Almost like a breakdown. I'm glad Uncle Teddy wasn't there."

"He would have decked him—like I wanted to do. The best solution would be if your supervisor returns early—before your starting date."

"That's unlikely. I need to face whatever happens." She ate half of her bison burger, wiped her hands on her napkin, and steepled her fingers. "Here's what I think. I'll meet him alone and hope we make progress. What I'd appreciate is if you'd be outside praying during our meeting." Her eyes met Chad's. "Ranger Higgins won't see you, but it will set the right atmosphere. Will you do that for me?"

The waitress interrupted them to ask about dessert.

"Thanks, but we're both full to the brim." As Chad paid the bill and they crossed the street to the Jeep, Glen laid a hand on his arm. "I am asking you to pray during our meeting."

"Do you consider me capable of that?"

"Yes, or I wouldn't ask."

He jammed one hand into his jeans pocket. "I'm more of a hands-on, confrontational guy, but I'll do my best."

"That's all I ask." Glen poked his shirt. "Besides, you don't fool me—you have deep waters in there."

"In me?" Chad's face flushed fire-engine red. "I'm not trying to fool anyone. Even myself. It's been years since anyone's taken a close look."

"That's a shame. It's about time then." When she didn't look away, he dropped his gaze.

"Ted said you're a straight shooter."

"I am." She faced him, still smiling. "Is there any other way to be?"

"Maybe not." As soon as he unlocked the Jeep's passenger door, Peaches jumped all over them. Chad gripped her shoulders to calm her down. "I'm sorry, girl. This is no fun for you."

"Here. I saved her some bison burger."

Peaches accepted it from Glen's fingers and snapped it down.

Chad shook his head. "No wonder you're her friend for life. How do you feel about driving up to the top of Montana's biggest ski resort? I'll drop Peaches at my neighbor's on our way. The view's fabulous at seven thousand feet. We can see forever—a whole new world."

"If you don't mind and have the time, that sounds incredible."

As Chad settled Peaches and drove up steep, winding curves, Glen scrolled through her phone. "I have some winning pictures to show you later, but honestly, besides being great for teaching and photo boards, you've helped me get shots I'll cherish forever."

"I'm glad to hear that. But there's even better stuff ahead."

His Jeep chugged high above Whitefish. The trees grew smaller the higher they climbed, shrinking to low brush and then no trees at all. Even through the closed windows, the air became noticeably cooler. The mountaintop world lay wrapped in stillness except for the Jeep's whining engine changing gears.

Glen breathed deep. "This is incredible."

"There's lots more." Chad pointed his rig up a steeper stretch of road and hit the gas. "Once we reach the last turnout near the top, we'll park and continue on foot."

"Neat." She opened her window. "The air's so thin, I don't hear a thing—not even birds."

"There aren't many this high, but it's a million-dollar view." He parked in the graveled turnout and left his vehicle. "This is the top of the world, matching alpine peaks on other continents."

"Like the Matterhorn or Annapurna. Even Mt. Everest?"

"Exactly."

Glen pulled her sweater tighter around her neck. "Up here, problems like Ranger Higgins don't matter."

"Not much. I would do him a favor by kidnapping him and bringing him here. Then even he should see a larger view."

She laughed. "What a great idea. Probably some rotten experience made him that way."

"Or several. You're kind to give him an excuse."

"Everyone needs a break." She craned her head to absorb the entire vista. "Just breathe this air. Everyone should see this view. Any time I have a bad day, I should come here, but for now, I'll carry it in my heart."

"Same here." Chad nodded. "It works every time."

Immediately beyond the dwarf trees and brush, bare scoured rock held tiny patches of hardy plants until a solid carpet of brilliant miniature wildflowers spread and filled every space.

"These are so lovely." Glen fell to her knees to study the perfect floral carpet. She lowered her head and breathed in the fragrance. "Teach me the names of these. This is heaven."

"Yes. I think the King of heaven planted these." He joined her on his knees. "This one is miniature rose saxifrage. Then come bright yellow buttercups, sky-blue forget-me-nots, and dwarf purple lupine—a fragrant blanket covering this peak as far as we can see."

She lifted her hands. "I have no words."

"It has that effect on me too." He extended his hand. Will you come to the far side, where the mountain plunges into the valley?"

"Absolutely. But first, I'm thanking God for such beauty. He's lavished all these shapes and colors, even if no eyes see them. My heart bursts with such abundance." She bowed her head.

* * *

Chad could barely hear the words Glen murmured, but they sounded like what his mom spoke over him from the Song of Solomon. "For, lo, the winter is past, the rain is over and gone; the flowers appear on the earth; the time of the singing of birds is come, and the voice of the turtle is heard in our land."

Was Glen saying the same thing? He bent closer.

"Lo, the winter is past ... the flowers appear on the earth ..." Her hand reached out and picked up a small glittering rock.

He leaned against her. "What did you say?"

"A Bible verse that sings in my heart."

"Those are the words my mom said I would understand when God brought me through the hard place I've been stuck in."

"Then she's a wise woman. It was a relationship, right?"

"Right. And the Bible word should be turtledove, not turtle."

Glen laughed. "I know, but turtles make noise. I've heard them."

"That's neat." It seemed natural to hold her hand. It fit just right. To his joy, Glen left her hand in his.

"Those verses matter to me too," she said. "Since Mom died when I was in junior high, and when we lost Dad in that explosive forest fire, someone sang them at his memorial. I've held onto them as God's promise that he'd give me happiness again one day."

Chad squeezed her hand. "He will. I'm sorry for the loss you've gone through.

As they slowly walked forward, they both tried to step without destroying the carpet of flowers.

Glen stood still. "I hate crushing these."

"Me too." Chad spread his hands. "But there's nowhere to walk without stepping on them. Still, breathe in that perfume."

She took a deep breath. "It's magical."

He picked and placed several flowers in her hand.

She buried her nose in them. "These are wonderful."

"Good. I'm adding this miniature blue forget-me-not so you'll remember."

"I will." She tucked it into her sweater's top buttonhole. "I'll breathe that with every breath I take." She gazed into his eyes.

He swallowed and finally broke his gaze to scan the horizon. "There's more I want to show you. Are you ready to reach the second summit?"

"Yes. Show me."

"It's not far, but the next ridge is steeper. I should keep holding your hand so you don't slip."

She grinned. "That's true. These boots aren't made for loose rocks."

"Exactly." As he gave her hand another squeeze, she bent to collect another bright stone.

He stopped. "What did you choose this time?"

"This." She displayed a small, sparkly, sharp-edged piece of granite—part of the mountain's very core. She picked up a second one. "These are the heart and strength of this place. You're meant to have one too." She placed the nearly identical stone in his hand.

"Thanks."

A moment later, Chad paused, again gazing across the valley to the next range of peaks. "Do you hear the wind singing?" He still gripped her hand. "Step this way and kneel. See this miniature world."

"It's magic. I didn't know the world held such perfect places. I cherish this. Thank you." Her eyes brimmed.

"I love sharing it with you. Look over there. See that waterfall far below?"

"I do. What is it?"

His voice gentled. "Bird Woman Falls. I want to take you there."

"I'd like that." She freed her hand to raise her phone. "Using the close-up lens, it's fantastic even from here."

"But not as nice as seeing it in person."

When she finished taking photos, he took her hand again.

"The trail's almost non-existent," Chad said, "but I'll guide you."

She laughed. "That's fine. You lead, and I'll follow."

He risked a quick glance. "I hope you mean that. Over there, a narrow basalt ledge extends behind the actual falls. It shields people from the pounding wall of water shooting from the mountain above. It's like being enclosed in the very center of God's beauty and all that's important in this world."

"I can't even imagine. Sometimes you're poetic."

"Wow." He ducked his head. "I've never been accused of that, but this is a place for special things—" He glanced at her lips. "For something I've longed to do." He closed the distance and pressed his lips against hers.

As his kiss deepened, Glen's arms encircled his neck.

"This might be heaven," he murmured into her hair.

She leaned against him. "It is. Can we stay here?"

"No, but we'll carry this in our hearts." He kissed her more deeply, cupping her head and bringing her closer until their foreheads met. "I'd like to keep you right here, tucked into my side," he whispered. "This is where you belong."

They held each other as floral fragrances swirled and fresh mountain winds sang joyful songs.

And then, without warning, Glen trembled. And teared up. "I'm sorry ..."

Chad dropped his arms. "Glen, what is it? I wouldn't hurt you for the world."

"I know. It's just that I don't know what I'm doing—going or staying. If the job will turn out or ... As wonderful as you are—"

"I get it." His voice pinched. "I had no right. It was too fast. I shouldn't—"

"Stop. You're a gift, but I'm—"

"Not ready? I understand. Forgive me." He gulped a breath. "Let me help you down this steep part." He held her arm stiffly until they reached more even ground, and then he walked to his Jeep alone, his heart as cold as the distant snowcapped peaks.

He hunched behind the steering wheel, waiting for Glen.

After she stopped for one more long look, she climbed into the Jeep, turned his way, and opened her mouth but closed it again. She sat near the window, her face against the glass.

Chad started his engine and silently negotiated each turn until they reached paved road. "Here we are, back in civilization."

"Forgive me for not knowing my mind more than that. That was lovely. I'm sorry to hurt you. You did nothing wrong."

"I'm a knucklehead," he said through clenched teeth. "Not good enough for you. It won't happen again."

"That's not it at all. I ruined things."

"I had it coming." His voice grated. "Where shall I drop you?"

"Let me think." As she gazed through the window, her phone pinged with a text.

He shook his head. "We're back in the real world for sure. They found you."

"Don't, Chad. That magic up there is the real world. I don't know what's wrong with me."

"You're in a transition with too many curve balls." He met her eyes. "If you stay and you're interested, I'd like to show you around more."

"Thank you. I'd like that." She tugged his sleeve. "Would you consider something now?"

"It depends. What?"

"That text said my shipped boxes reached Kalispell. If you have time to pick them up and take them to my duplex, I'd be grateful. I need to organize my stuff, whether I leave or stay."

He tried to read her face. "How will you decide?"

"Mostly from Monday's meeting with Higgins. I'm not ready to try a new church. Tomorrow I'll stay in, be quiet, and pray. I'll lose my lease deposit either way. I may as well use the place."

"That makes sense. I'll pray you get your answer. What about transportation? Are you ready to rent or buy a vehicle?"

"Not yet. But if you're still speaking to me and your schedule allows, I'd be grateful if you'd drive me to Monday's meeting."

He blew out his breath. "I'm speaking to you. If we go early, I can do that. Most of my work is remote this month."

"I think the office opens at eight. Does that work? I'd like to be there before people arrive."

"That's fine. I'm up early but have to start my evaluation trips later that day. Have you thought more about coming with me?"

She bit her lip. "It's a fabulous invitation, but there's so much confusion in my head. Can I tell you after meeting with Higgins?"

"Sure." He tented his hands. "Do you still want me to pray while you're in with him?"

"More than ever. That could be the game changer."

"I agree. Count on me. I'll park across the street, so he doesn't spot me and feel outnumbered, but I'll be praying."

She touched his hand. "I appreciate that so much."

"What do you have for groceries?"

"I'm so full of Bison Burger, I may never eat again, but there's a grocery on the corner. Just get me and my boxes to my place, and then come for me on Monday morning. That's more than kind."

"You could go to church with me."

"Thanks. Once I know I'm staying, I'd like that."

His lips lifted slightly. "This isn't how I hoped today would end, but I'll do whatever you need."

Eight

On Monday, Chad reached Glen's place, prayed up and ready. At first, he saw no signs of life inside, then the blinds rolled up, the door opened, and Glen rushed out with a bulging shopping bag. By the time he hopped out of his Jeep, she had already opened the tailgate and pushed her bag inside.

"Good morning." Her smile dazzled.

"It *is* a good morning." He breathed in the tantalizing aroma of whatever she had brought. "My mouth is watering. What's in that bag?"

"Hopefully a game changer so Higgins sees I'm a helpful team player—not a threat."

"That should do it." Chad slapped his flat abs. "It smells like my grandma's cinnamon rolls—only better."

"That's because I added Arkansas pecans to make these perfect." She opened the bag to show him.

He groaned. "Enter those in the Montana state fair, and you'll win top prize."

"Ha ha. If I stay in Montana, I just might."

He pointed to the bag. "You're taking those to Higgins?"

"And his staff. But the six wrapped separately are for you."

She handed him a Saran-wrapped package. "To thank you for praying and being so kind."

He accepted the package and grinned. "Hey, you're totally welcome. I pray for free, but might eat a roll or two to keep up my strength."

"By all means." She did a quick pirouette. "What do you think? Do I look like a Forest Service Education Officer?" She wore a tailored olive cotton shirt unbuttoned at the throat, creased brown gabardine slacks, and modest makeup.

"Impressive. Nothing showy or attention-getting. You're a capable, well-qualified woman anyone would be glad to work with. I would too."

"That's the look I'm after. Higgins must have had a really unpleasant workplace experience."

"It sounds like it. And earlier trauma may have prejudiced him. We may never know the cause, though we see the results."

"Definitely." She withdrew a smaller plastic container. "I also brought quality ground coffee just in case."

"Smart."

"My notebook's in the bag. I'll take notes while he shares his expectations and make it clear I'm a team player who supports my superiors well."

"That's the right strategy. Okay. I'll pray for you before you go in." He clasped her hands in his grip and prayed heartfelt words for favor and protection. "Bless her, Lord. Amen."

She sighed. "Thanks. That was perfect." Tears sparkled in her eyes. "I knew there were deep waters in you."

He eased his shoulders. "Praying feels so good."

Once they got inside, he put his Jeep in gear and drove through quiet streets. The ranger station yard and interior lights were on, though the place was empty.

Glen checked her watch. "Someone should arrive soon. I'd like to be at the door when they do. Here I go." Glen opened the Jeep door, lifted her bag, and crossed the street. One minute later,

Ranger Higgins pulled his U.S. Forest Service rig into the parking lot. He startled when he saw Glen.

"Good morning. No HR person?" Chad heard him ask.

She shook her head. "We can do this."

When they disappeared, Chad prayed as hard as he ever had in his life. "You're in charge, Lord. You alone."

Other employees entered. Finally, Glen exited, minus her bag but smiling.

She floated to his Jeep. "You won't believe this."

"Try me."

"It was a miracle. And the cinnamon rolls helped—they're his favorite. Plus, he loved the coffee and apologized about Saturday. The hotshot team emergency broadsided him, and I was a final shock. He had never heard of a girl being *Junior*. I explained that Eleonor Roosevelt's daughter, who shared her name, was called 'second,' while they called Eleonor 'Senior.'"

"Saturday was partly my fault," Chad said. "It wasn't smart to introduce you then."

"But how could you know? God allowed it. That was better than me walking into a buzzsaw on my first day of work."

"Maybe. You're a good sport. Is Higgins okay now?"

"He's better. They had a fiasco two years back with a female employee who made everything a crisis. Once she left, they didn't want a repeat. He has additional personal reasons but spared me the details."

"Be grateful for that. Is there any chance Supervisor Johnson will return early?"

"None, but Higgins has offered me a provisional hire for the first month to prove I'm a good fit. If that goes well, I'll be permanent in thirty days."

"Thirty days?" Chad jerked. "He wants you conditional for a month? That can't be legal."

"No, but I'll live with it. Since the school year's just starting, he asked me to suggest two programs I'd like to introduce. He liked my ideas." She chuckled. "It also helps that I make decent coffee. I think things will work out."

"Then so do I." Chad flashed a thumbs-up. "Now, for my question."

"What's that? You have my attention."

"Will you ride along on today's evaluation trip? Or shall I take you home?"

Glen rested her head against the seat but her eyes danced. "You caught me at a great time. After this success, I'm ready for anything."

"Just what I wanted to hear." He flashed a high five. "I'll pick up Peaches, and we'll be off."

Glen glanced at the empty back seat. "I meant to ask where she was."

"With my widowed neighbor. He had a dog for years and has an ideal setup. He keeps her any time she can't be with me."

As Chad started to climb out to reclaim Peaches, Glen's phone chirped. He heard her say, "Uncle Teddy. How are you?"

As soon as he returned with Peaches and opened the door, his dog slathered Glen with kisses.

She scratched his dog's head to keep her happy and filled Chad in. "I told Uncle Teddy things are fine here. He doesn't need to know about the difficulties."

"Good call. He'd just worry. I'm hopeful things will work out."

"Me too. His forest fire isn't contained yet, but they're gaining. He said to tell you he ran into someone you know."

"Who's that?"

"Do you remember Shorty Ross?"

"A massive Scot?"

"I think so."

"That guy wore a tartan kilt for military dress when we met with top Afghan leaders. They were shocked to meet a man wearing a skirt. And then he played his bagpipes for them, which sounded like their panpipes. They loved him."

Glen giggled. "He sounds like a character."

"For sure. Did Ted tell you what Shorty did on one parade inspection?"

"Not yet."

Chad doubled over his steering wheel and chortled. "It still cracks me up. He hid a spool of white thread in his dress uniform jacket pocket, with an inch of it dangling out. The Commanding Officer told him, "Ross, you've got a loose thread on your uniform."

"Shorty said, 'Please remove it, sir.'"

"When the CO pulled, yards of thread unspooled until everyone cracked up—even the CO." Chad laughed again. "Shorty's the best. Where did Ted see him?"

"On the fire line. He's leading a bulldozer crew clearing strips for back-burning. Shorty says you should visit there, and he wants to see Montana."

Chad slapped his steering wheel. "He should, and I'd like to." He used his turn signal to enter Highway 2 West. "Here today's schedule. Libby's eighty-eight miles west with terrific Fish, Wildlife & Parks areas. Besides my yearly evaluation categories, I'll check trapline and goldmining activity. I haven't forgotten our poacher friend either. We'll look for him."

"That's good, and today sounds wonderful." She opened her notebook. "What's my role?"

"Here's what I'm thinking."

Glen leaned forward, jotting notes between watching gorgeous scenery fly by.

"We'll also have fun," Chad said. "Have you ever panned for gold?"

"No, but I've watched reality shows and want to try."

"You'll have a chance. Twenty miles past Libby, Kootenai National Forest has an area where people can pan for gold and keep their findings."

"Seriously? Not all states have gold. Arkansas has hardly any, though we do have diamonds. You think I can try?"

"Yes, I'll show you."

Glen clicked more photos and checked a map. "I want to spend more time in this area. It's fabulous."

"Montana has amazing places. I've grown up here and haven't seen them all." An hour and a half later, he parked outside Libby's Fish, Wildlife & Parks local office and held open the door for Glen. "This manager, Sven Lindstrom, has fingers in many pies and knows most of the locals. He may help us find our poacher."

"Great." Glen smiled and stepped inside.

Chad had barely entered when a hearty voice roared, "Chad Kinkaid? Get yourself in here."

Chad and the Swede clasped hands. And then Sven gestured toward Glen. "Who's this breath of fresh air?"

Chad grinned. "Meet Glen Weldon, Kalispell's newest Forestry Education Officer and the niece of my best Army buddy in Afghanistan."

"Well done, Kinkaid. Welcome, Glen." He stretched out a hand, and they shook.

"Thank you."

Chad's face heated. "I'm showing her Montana, and she's improving my yearly evaluation reports."

"That's a win-win." Sven kicked two chairs into line near his desk. "Sit and rest yourselves. What do you need from me today?"

"Just the annual data."

"I knew you were coming, so it's ready."

"Terrific. I wish every manager were as helpful." He stuffed the brown accordion folder under his arm. "I plan to show Glen our fish hatchery and elk habitat, and also take her gold panning."

Sven laughed. "That sounds like more fun than work. I wish I could come along, but I'm chained to my desk for a while." He tapped the stack of paperwork in front of him. "Good luck, though."

"Thanks." Glen helped herself to some gold prospecting brochures in the rack on the wall. "These will help."

"They're good." Chad tilted his chair back. "Are there any promising gold claims for sale on that mountain west of town?"

Sven's forehead creased. "There's that one you and I thought about, but that guy recently found nuggets, so he doesn't want to sell anymore. I've seen several more advertised but haven't had time to investigate. Are you interested?"

"Yes, but not for the reason you think." Chad checked his watch. "I want to complete the easy part of my checklist today and get up into the hills tomorrow. That is, if you're free to come along, Glen."

She nodded. "Believe me, at this point you couldn't keep me away."

"Good." Chad sat his chair back on all four legs. "I have a question for you, Sven. When Glen's uncle was here, we camped in Glacier and had a great time. Except her uncle got caught in a snare that could have killed him."

"You're kidding." The manager gaped. "Where was this?"

"Near that camping site by the public boat dock. We found footprints and made plaster casts. Remember our friend Everest, who runs a ski lodge up there?"

"Sure do. We get together sometimes. Great guy."

Chad drummed his fingers on the desk. "He is. When we mentioned the poacher and said one boot print indicated a limp, Everest thought it could be a trapper prospector from up here that swings through his area from time to time. He couldn't recall the name. He thought you might remember."

"He means Brass Flannagan, and he's out of control." Sven rubbed the back of his neck. "He's our main suspect in a cabin break-in and in repeated gold-claim robberies, with someone stealing gold from a sluice box."

"No kidding? That's major." Chad grabbed his notebook and made notes. "Do you have enough evidence to nail him?"

"Not yet. We have a visual sighting, but he apparently deactivates the cameras on the claim. He only strikes when the owner's off-site, so he's observing from somewhere or has a camera of his own. We have two cast footprints that show the same limping indentation you mentioned."

"Interesting." Chad worked his phone. "Let me show you my photos, see if they match."

Sven studied the pictures. "We need to measure to be sure, but they look similar." He rose from his desk and retrieved his two plaster casts from an evidence cabinet. "See what I mean? Very close."

Chad snapped his fingers. "I'd say exact."

Glen wrote down details. "Chad, you didn't tell me your day trips were this exciting."

He grinned. "They're not usually, but awesome, right?"

"Right."

Sven returned his casts to the cabinet. "This miner is so riled, he's threatening vigilante action, but I don't think he can pull it off. I don't blame him, though. He's a fit, widowed, retired high school shop teacher. He and his wife put everything into this claim and don't deserve this. If Flannagan makes Paul and others mad enough, he should be glad for jail time instead of a lynch party."

Chad nodded. "What are your plans to end it?"

"A few ideas—nothing firm. I have to conquer this pile of paperwork first." He waved at the stack in front of him. "I need to finalize winter trapline leases and issue multiple use permits before our deadline."

"I hear you." Chad pulled his chair closer. "Do you mind if I get involved?"

Sven raised a hand. "Not at all. He has to be stopped."

"Good. Can you connect me with the claim owner? Maybe we can trap this guy."

"Sure will. Phone before you show up. Paul Wilson's a little trigger happy these days." Sven opened his desk drawer and pulled out a map with a flourish. "Here's his phone number and directions to his claim. I'll call him now and tell him you'll be in touch."

"Perfect." Chad beamed. "You're better than a three-armed paper hanger."

Glen laughed. "That's quite a compliment."

Sven sputtered. "Keep me informed and stay safe."

The three of them stood and shook hands.

After lunch and checking two other projects, Chad phoned the claim owner while Glen listened on speaker. She diagrammed their action plan in her notebook as an August sunset chased shadows down purple mountains.

"This sounds great." She tapped the page.

"There's a high chance it will work." Chad started his Jeep. "By this time tomorrow, I hope we have him. Do you carry?"

Glen wrinkled her nose. "Do you have to ask? I'm my uncle's niece. I'll bring my sidearm."

Nine

Headlights on, Chad left Peaches with his neighbor and picked up Glen at 5 a.m. They matched, dressed in camo, except she carried a pan of glazed doughnuts warm from the oven.

"Glen, you're killing me. How did you manage that so early this morning? The aroma alone will make Flannagan surrender to eat one."

She laughed. "That's my hope. Three are for you."

Chad groaned and accepted one in a napkin.

Ninety minutes later, he took a barely navigable dirt road west of Libby and followed sharp turns to Wilson's claim.

Glen clung to the door handle to stay upright. "He lives this far out?"

"Yep. This is where the gold starts. The problem is, Sven thinks Flannagan has a mountain cabin around here, but he doesn't know where. We might need a drone to find it."

"That's a good idea. I wish we had one." Glen surveyed the many tree-clad ravines barely distinguishable in the early light. "If we can't see him, he probably can't see us."

"We hope. That's why I'm going slow, and I'll complete the last stretch without headlights."

A sign was barely visible above the road labeled Brass Tacks Mine—a red arrow pointing uphill. "I'll bet Flannagan owns that." She tapped the window. "Wouldn't Wilson know if Brass was his neighbor?"

"Not especially. He may not know him by name, and people are scattered out here—not overly friendly."

Chad crept along for another mile and braked to a stop by a seismic line. "This must be where Wilson said to park."

"Yes, this screen of evergreen trees will keep your Jeep hidden. So, we walk from here?"

She checked her pockets to make sure she had everything.

"That's right. He said this leads to the creek and then his claim. Now, let's close our doors without a sound."

They both managed that with a soft click, and Glen moved forward with a relaxed gait.

"Wow, you move like a ninja." Chad shook out his limbs and caught up. They crept forward with swimming motions through the undergrowth paralleling the seismic cut.

"This reminds me of Sherlock Holmes and Watson," Glen said.

"Let's hope for their results."

She stopped. "Wait. Take a look at these slight footprints. The left sides indent deeper."

"So they do." His lips thinned. "It's gotta be him. I doubt many neighbors have a limp like that. We can cast them later if we need to, but I'd rather catch him red-handed."

They reached a metal gate crossing the seismic line. "This must be where Wilson's claim starts." Chad entered the passcode to swing open the gate and then quietly closed it behind them.

"We're close. This is when Wilson said to wait, so he should be nearby." Thick stands of spruce and pine bordered the stream, its bubbling flow silencing their footsteps. And then Chad and Wilson spotted each other at the same time.

"You said there'd be two of you." The fit, gray-haired man lowered his shotgun. "Good to meet you."

"I'm Chad. This is Glen." They shook hands.

"It's nice to welcome friends instead of trespassers. Maybe soon I won't be terrorized on my land."

Glen clucked her tongue. "Let's hope so. Nobody deserves that."

"Come this way. I'll show you my place and how my gold recovery room connects to the sluice box and riffles—as long as the perp's not around." He carefully looked all directions.

Chad worked a kink out of his neck as they entered the well-built room with dark curtains covering the windows. "Please tell us his usual pattern."

"Somehow, he knows every time I go to town. Whether he's got a camera or scope or trip wire—who knows? He enters this room, despite my double lock, and knows how to empty the sluice box and clean up the riffles. Losing one day's gold hurts, and he's done this five times."

"That's rough." Chad clenched his jaw. "We hope that ends today."

Glen paused. "Do you do any gold panning?"

"Some. Not much because it takes longer. Why?"

"I just wondered."

"The truth is," Chad said, "she wants to learn."

Wilson smiled. "Young lady, once we catch him, I'll put steaks on, and you can come pan all day and keep everything you find. Guaranteed."

Chad checked his watch. "Time to start. You'll drive out like an ordinary town trip but park and double back."

"Right." Wilson jingled his keys. "I'll take position above the creek and give a bird call when he moves down the hillside. I've found tracks, so I know his route."

Chad and Glen locked eyes.

"I'll show you the two best stakeout points. Thanks for your help." A smile creased Wilson's weathered face. "Be careful. He's dangerous."

"Will do. It's show time." Chad and Glen followed, faces grim.

* * *

Twenty-eight minutes after Paul rattled through his gate and relocked it, a black-clad figure eased down the hill, carrying a dark bag over one shoulder and something shiny in his hand.

Chad checked to be sure that Glen was safe behind a spruce. When she slid a gloved hand over her nose to stifle a sneeze, he breathed harder. *Good girl.*

The moving figure's hoodie slipped and revealed fiery red hair. It was Flannagan, all right. But instead of covering the distance to the creek or the recovery room, he dashed to the side and captured Wilson, who was inching down the hill.

Wilson yelped, but Flannagan smacked the widower's mouth and spun him in front of himself, hostage-style. He snatched his shotgun. "Thought you were smart, but I planted a tracker last time, and my mini-camera recorded your conversation. Tell your friends to come out." Flannagan jerked Wilson harder. "This time I want the gold in your safe, not just the riffles."

Wilson struggled. "You won't get away with this."

"Watch me."

Flannagan hadn't seen Chad. He barely breathed as he moved from tree to tree, getting closer, until a squirrel scolded overhead.

Flannagan froze. "Okay, I see ya. C'mon out, hands up." Flannagan pushed Wilson forward with his gun until he herded both men together. "Give me your weapon. I'll lock you two in the recovery room until I find the sassy girl."

Chad choked and surrendered his Glock. *Don't let Glen run out screaming.*

"Tell her to give up." Flannagan poked Chad with his gun. "Or her boyfriend might get hurt."

"Run, Glen!"

"Stupid." Flannagan cracked Chad over the head.

"Get help," Wilson shouted.

Flannagan slugged Wilson's jaw and stuffed a rag in his mouth.

"Run. Phone Sven," Chad shouted.

This time, Flannagan smashed his head. Pain radiated through his skull, ricocheting behind his eyes. He took a deep breath to maintain consciousness and turned to where he'd last glimpsed Glen. *Lord, keep her safe. Help her get away.*

"Leave them alone." She entered the clearing near the recovery room with her hands raised.

"Smart," Flannagan said. "You're too good for this guy."

With Flannagan distracted, Chad became Thunder again and launched a flying tackle that knocked Flannagan flat and wrestled for the gun.

"Get it," Glen shouted. But Flannagan slithered like a snake, and when the gun shot, fire blazed through Chad's thigh.

"Chad!" Glen shrieked. She whipped her sidearm from the back of her waistband and trained it on their attacker. "You're through, Flannagan. Chad? Can you handcuff him?"

Quick as a wink, Flannagan bent, grabbed Wilson's shotgun, and waved it in the men's faces. "What'll it be, Glen? Lay yours down, or I'll blast these guys."

Chad gave a karate kick to Flannagan's knee that dropped him, and the shotgun flew. Both men scrambled.

"You'll pay," Flannagan howled.

Glen held her Glock steady. "Stop or you're dead, Flannagan."

His fist froze midair, but he had the shotgun. "You expect me to fear a woman?"

"Maybe if she's a sharpshooter."

He swung the shotgun her way, but Chad snagged his foot and brought him down.

Glen's shot hit Flannagan's shoulder instead of center mass. Chad flipped him over and secured him. "Wilson, use these zip ties to secure his hands behind his back."

"Yes, sir. That was admirable, Glen."

Chad's voice shook. "Thank you, Lord. Remind me not to rile you, Glen. You're like Annie Oakley."

"Not quite, but close enough."

* * *

It took days to complete the police and administrative reports. One Saturday two weeks later, Chad drove Glen to Whitefish, where he'd reserved The Montana Grill's back room. The waitress seated them.

"It's good to be almost back to normal," Chad said. "My doctor is a bear."

"He's great. He's taking good care of you."

"How's your job going? Okay?"

"More than okay." She grinned. "Superintendent Johnson is back, but Ranger Higgins is championing me. Every day he asks how you are and wants to help with anything we need."

Chad's eyes warmed. "Will wonders never cease? It just goes to show relationships get easier when we know someone."

"Higgins acts like my new best friend."

Chad flinched. "Uh—next to me, of course."

"Of course." She grinned. "You're in first place. I'm glad I came to Montana and met you."

"Wait. I'm glad I met you."

The waitress returned. "Are you ready to order?"

"Chad, what do you suggest?" Glen tried to read his face. He seemed unusually serious.

"Let's try their best steaks. We're celebrating. And we'll order Peaches takeout."

"She'll love that. But no Rocky Mountain Oysters."

"Not today. Perhaps never." He laughed but coughed midway. "Laughing still hurts."

"Then don't."

"But there's this." When he extended his hand, she took it. "You collect stones. Sometimes I do too. My mom saved this

183

special stone for me." He slid his free hand up his shirt and slipped something wrapped in tissue paper out of his pocket.

"Glen, I've traveled many places on this earth in both war and peace, but I've never found a woman like you. I know this is fast, but you're a treasure. No one else can fit the special place in my heart the way you do. I want to spend the rest of my life with you —if you'll have me."

His eyes gleamed.

Hers pooled.

"There are better guys out there, but no one will love you more. I phoned Ted and have his permission." He fumbled to unwrap the tissue with one hand. "I inherited my grandmother's engagement ring. You're a keeper. Please stay. Say you'll marry me and make me the happiest man far past Montana."

Tears filled her eyes as her hands clasped his. "Chad, yes. Always."

He slid the diamond on her finger. "I'll have it reset if we need—"

"It's fine." She held out her hand, admiring the way the light reflected from the glittering stone. "A perfect fit."

Chad leaned over as his lips claimed hers. Their kiss deepened as she melted into him.

Their waitress bustled in. "Are you ready to ..."

When Chad surfaced long enough to wink, she smiled and tiptoed out.

For the next few minutes, Chad and Glen explored kisses that drew them closer than they'd been on the best life journey either of them had ever begun.

About Delores Topliff

Delores Topliff grew up in Washington state but married a Canadian, so she enjoys dual citizenship. She teaches online in a good Christian university, travels, takes mission trips, and has published four children's books and numerous non-fiction stories before finding her stride writing historical novels. *Books Afloat, Strong Currents, Christmas Tree Wars*, and *Wilderness Wife* have all been published since January 2021. *A Traveling Grandma's Guide to Israel: Adventures, Wit, and Wisdom*, released in 2023 and is half memoir and half insights into connections to Israel's land and people. Delores loves her two doctor sons and five grandchildren and divides her year between a central Minnesota farm and the gentle climate and people in Northeastern Mississippi.

Grace
and
Grit

Tonya B. Ashley

Scrivenings
PRESS
Quench your thirst for story.
www.ScriveningsPress.com

For the ones who show up,
even when it's hard.
Who carry what they cannot name,
but still keep walking.
Remember,
grace and grit go hand in hand.

One

The last thing McKenna Carter needed was one of her brother's Rally Point pep talks. Her heart drummed faster whenever he slipped into that circle-the-troops bravado of his. She didn't need more excitement. Or more nervousness. What she needed was a cup of comfort and Nash sitting on go, not drifting into his light-hearted, last-minute habits. After all, she still had to double-check the retreat supplies, run through the itinerary, and—thanks to a last-minute client crisis—pack her gear.

Stepping into Rally Point Roasters with her backpack strapped snugly and a second, brand-new pack looped over her arm, McKenna's shoulders loosened. Blues guitar poured from hidden speakers, each note edged with grit and aching vibrato. When her brother first pitched the concept, she pictured disaster. A coffee roaster that felt like a cabin, a field tent, and a quaint hardware store gave birth to a coffee-loving baby. Surely it was destined to collapse under its quirkiness.

Yet, it worked. Rich cedar beams framed sleek lines. Topographic maps shared wall space with black-and-white deployment photos and framed knots. Mason jar vases stuffed with slender tools and wildflowers stood on each table. Against her doubts, he'd crafted a grounded breathing space, masculine and soulful, warm and inviting, intimate and secure, yet not steeped in sentimentality.

A shelf beside the door, lined with field guides and survival books, displayed a brass sign. *Leave one, borrow one.* Across from it, a bulletin board overflowed with pinned notices for community hikes, veteran meetups, and wilderness survival courses. Under a flyer for the back-to-school backpack drive, a box sat half-filled with bright, kid-sized backpacks. McKenna slipped the new one from her arm and added it to the pile.

The real treasures on the community board were the handwritten quotes offering pocket-sized wisdom. She set down her backpack, dug out a sticky note, and pinned it in place.

In the midst of difficulty lies opportunity.
—Albert Einstein (or John Wheeler. You decide)

"K.K." The man behind the counter twirled a bottle of lavender syrup. "What's doing?"

"Boone Whitaker." McKenna slung her backpack over her shoulder as she approached the counter. She leaned in, plucking a green fleck from his beard. "Straight off the mountain, huh? You've still got moss in there."

"As the sign says, 'Brew bold. Return better.'" He chuckled. "Can't go wrong with a month off-trail, steeping pine needles for tea."

"And here you are with lavender." She arched a brow. "Wouldn't have guessed."

"You know my coffee rules. If it's not black, it's dessert." A grin broke through his curtain of auburn beard as he slid a cup toward her. "Custom brew. Special for you."

McKenna cradled the large mug and inhaled. "Lavender. Blackberry." She took a sip. "Is that rosemary in the background?"

"What do you think?"

"I think you've found your calling." She closed her eyes, the berry-bright, herbal aroma filling her lungs. "Now, where's my brother? What are you prepping me for?"

"Who says I'm prepping you for anything, K.K.?"

"Where is he?"

A crash in the kitchen answered for him. Nash limped out on crutches.

"Nash." Her backpack slid to the floor. "What happened?"

A roll of duct tape dangled from his pinky as his other fingers hooked around the crutch handle. With a tilt of his head, he directed her toward a couch by the wall. She scooped up her pack and followed, coffee in hand. Dropping onto the cushions, she folded one leg beneath her and took a long sip.

"I sprained my ankle." Nash patted his shin. "Can't be your survival skills guy for the retreat."

"Are you okay? How did it happen?"

"Breakfast rush. I took the trash out, and this crazy bird shot out of the dumpster—straight at my face."

"A bird? In the dumpster?" She set down her cup with a light thud. "Nash, if you didn't want to go, you should have said so up front. I wouldn't have been upset."

"Honestly, K.K. Ask Boone." Nash raised his hands, palms up.

She faced Boone with a grimace.

"Bird had a wingspan like a fighter jet," he reported in the same no-nonsense tone he used for wildfire protocol.

"What am I supposed to do now?" She massaged her temple, trying to ease the pressure behind her eyes. *Lord, if You're still in this, I could use a nudge.* "I've already postponed twice. This time, I'll have to cancel and refund the money."

"Not gonna happen, lil' sis." Nash wagged a finger. "I've got a guy."

Groaning, she pressed her palm to her forehead. "Not *I've got a guy.* That never goes well. Never."

"Come on. You don't need me out there, K.K. You've got instincts, heart, and a better compass than half the guys I served with. All you need is some duct tape, and you'll be fine." He passed her the roll.

"Hey, now." Boone slapped the counter, but Nash waved him off.

"I've got a backup with a jaw like a hatchet and the emotional range of a pocketknife." Nash smirked. "Should be fun."

She shoved the duct tape back at him. "You're killing me, Nash."

The corners of his eyes crinkled with mischief.

"What?" McKenna tilted her head.

Nash poked her knee. "You put up the Einstein quote today, didn't you?"

"Wheeler." She groaned.

"Eh. Einstein. Wheeler." Nash shrugged, shoving the duct tape toward her. "In the middle of difficulty lies opportunity."

"When do I meet him?"

"He'll be here any minute." He patted her knee. "You're gonna love him. He needs this."

"Needs it? Fantastic." She dragged her palms down her face. "I don't need a survival instructor who's there for a mental health retreat. That's not helpful."

"Not *needs* it." His head rocked side to side. "Just, you know, needs it."

The electronic door chime trilled, and McKenna turned. Her stomach did a little free fall the second her gaze landed on the muscular form coming through the door. Nash's hatchet-jawed backup, no doubt. Only time would tell whether he was good news or bad.

He stepped inside like the trail still clung to him. A sun-faded plaid shirt, sleeves rolled. Well-worn utility shorts, weathered like an old tent. Boots built for miles. Backpack locked and loaded. It didn't give. Neither did his expression. His hair needed a trim or a hand raked through it, or both. Not that she noticed. Had he spent the past month on the mountain with Boone?

She blew out a breath.

"Naturally," she whispered. "Tall, unreadable, probably allergic to eye contact."

He scanned the coffeehouse as if memorizing the exits. "Sticks." His voice carried like tumbling river rocks. He propped himself on the counter, drumming his fingers against the wood. "Where's Lucky?"

Boone raised a hand, pointing toward the couch with his eyes still on the grinder.

Nash grinned and waved the guy over.

The man nodded at Nash's crutches. "Your luck finally ran out, huh?"

"McKenna, meet Rough Scott."

Great. Rough. Not a name that screamed emotionally safe space. She shook his hand, torn between trusting him and issuing him a list of triggers and boundaries.

"Why is it you guys never use your real names?"

Nash smirked. "Real names are for emergencies and official paperwork."

"And therapy." Boone wiped the counter without glancing up.

"Five days on the trail with a man who doesn't even have a real name." McKenna shook her head. "What could go wrong?"

Two

Predawn solitude anchored Rough. He straddled a fallen log, feet planted wide, elbows resting on his knees, savoring the last moment of peace before the others arrived. Two squirrels rustled through dry leaves under trees scarred black from a spring prescribed burn. At the pullout's edge, where the road bent toward the creek, purple ironweed and goldenrod caught the first slant of sun. Pretty, yes, but also useful. The first could settle a sour stomach, the second might ease inflammation. He filed away the thought as a mockingbird flitted from branch to branch, thin rays of light trickling between the trees.

The frayed edges of the battered field notebook he held were bound together with duct tape—his go-to solution for most of life's challenges lately.

Inside, survival notes shared space with half-remembered Scripture and sketches of edible plants, makeshift shelters, and notable landscape features. A letter, worn soft as cloth from constant folding, rested inside the back cover. He didn't read it. His thumb traced the edge, but he didn't read it.

He checked his watch. Late. But they would come. Women. Emotions. The therapist, likely fueled by empathy and herbal tea.

This was the price of repairing his image. Damage control. However, he didn't plan on unpacking anything except his backpack. No way he would get pulled into the therapist's social-emotional experiment. He was here to keep them safe. Full stop.

A van rolled into the pullout and idled. This was it. Go time. He buried the notebook deep in his pack.

The side door creaked open, the sound setting his teeth on edge. Four women stepped out, each resembling a cover model from *Glitter Quarterly*, *Stonewater Outfitters*, *Missions Monthly*, and *Hoof & Paw*.

One started talking right away—about the drive, the playlist, the color of the leaves. One squinted at the sun as if it owed her money. One yawned, stretched, and lay across a log. The last one paused at the trailhead, glancing back at the van like she might bail.

He didn't require name tags. After leading enough groups, he could identify the archetypes. Chatterbox, Cynic, Hibernator, Runner.

Then she stepped out. The therapist.

She observed the others the way scouts read the wind—quiet, precise, and if he had to guess, a half-step ahead. Likely viewed list-making as a hobby and filed everyone's emotional baggage by color and carry-on size.

Rough folded his arms and let the silence linger. They would fill it soon enough. Emotions would rebound like an echo bouncing off a rock wall.

Sure enough, Glitter Quarterly dropped her pack beside him, muttered while digging, and handed him a mirror, followed by a headband bristling with animal print hair clips.

"Where's my lemon balm?" Her tight, dark curls bounced with every word, a riot of movement framing her small face. "I know I packed it."

"Lemon balm for what?" Stonewater Outfitters slung a camera strap around her neck.

"Everything. Bug bites. Anxiety. Insomnia."

Rough stood, cramming the items back into her pack. "So you didn't follow the packing list?" He didn't blink. "If you strayed from it, I hope you at least brought duct tape."

Four heads turned. Five, when the driver's door clicked shut.

The therapist raised an eyebrow. Her jaw set tight. He met her gaze without flinching.

"Name's Rough Scott." He slipped on his pack. "Your survival instructor. I don't do welcome speeches. Ten miles today. Five minutes to adjust your packs. Then we walk."

Glitter Quarterly whispered behind her hand. "Sounds more like severe weather than a name."

He leaned close to her. "And yes, Rough is the name, not the forecast." Straightening, his gaze cut back to the therapist, hard as flint.

"A moment?" The therapist pulled him aside. "What do you think you're doing?"

"Leading this little band on a five-day survival skills expedition." He clasped his hands. "No need to worry. Lucky briefed me on your expectations, Ms. Carter."

"It's McKenna, and you're failing to inspire confidence." She squared with him, locking eyes. "They've been here five minutes, and you've already hit them with commands and duct tape?"

He surveyed the group. Glitter Quarterly sprinkled lemon balm onto a pendant before handing it to Rip Van Winkle, who sat up and tugged her wide-brimmed canvas hat low on her brow, already two blinks from drifting to sleep. The other two cinched their pack straps.

"They're vertical, aren't they?" Rough scratched his stubbled cheek.

McKenna's mouth tightened. "That's not the point."

"Perhaps not." He shifted his stance. "But isn't it a start?"

McKenna crossed her arms. "They don't need coddling, but your tone could be less, well, rough. This isn't a forced march up Everest."

"This is the wild. If you want soft edges, grab a marshmallow."

"That's my point." Her gaze sharpened. "This is the Ozark-St. Francis National Forest, the Richland Creek Recreation Area. Some of the most beautiful landscapes in Arkansas—yes—but it can also be unforgiving. Elevation climbs of several hundred feet, creek crossings, slick limestone. They've had basic training for rugged, backcountry conditions, but ultimately, they'll be relying on us. What if someone freezes on a ledge or breaks down in tears?"

"I keep them from falling."

Her lips parted, teeth catching the bottom one. "You're serious?"

Rough met her stare with silence.

"You can't play the hero here." Her voice dropped to a whisper. "Coach them past obstacles and fears. The goal is to teach them to navigate their emotional ledges. It's our responsibility to prepare them to face challenges—step by step, one foot in front of the other. Understand?"

His eyebrow ticked upward. Arms loose at his sides, he tapped his thumb to his middle finger in a restless cadence. The last time he tried coaching, it had spiraled into a personality clash that nearly wrecked his business. And now here he was. He drew a steady breath. "I'll do what I can."

"Well." She hitched her pack a little higher. "This should be fun."

"Lucky said the same thing."

She closed her eyes, pinching the bridge of her nose. "I'm not asking for sing-alongs. But less grizzly, more guide."

His brow furrowed. "I'm not grizzly."

"You growled." She shrugged.

"I didn't."

She clicked her tongue and pivoted back to the group.

Rough grumbled and tugged his pack straps. Five long days ahead.

"Grizzly," he muttered.

The word bit harder than he expected—and stuck.

* * *

McKenna rocked on her heels. Rough stood at the tree line, arms folded, jaw set. If he possessed a soft side, it hid somewhere under a hundred miles of uncharted trail. And she had to hike ten of them with him today.

She hefted her pack and thumbed the compass dangling from her D-ring. Flicking it open, she traced the inscription inside the lid. *Steady on.*

Ten miles. Steady on. She would match Rough Scott step for step, physically and mentally. He wouldn't derail her retreat unless she let him. Compassion, grace, and boundaries. She would carry them as she had carried this pack. *Lord, help me hold to true north.*

Rough. Name or forecast? The question lingered. She stole another glance. Storm clouds brewing, no doubt.

Oh, Nash. What are you up to this time?

Her brother knew how much this pilot retreat mattered. Bird in the face. A flimsy excuse and a lousy cover. But why send this guy? Was he a therapy dodger and too obstinate to admit it? Or another one of Nash's ill-timed matchmaking schemes?

She turned back to the women. CeCe tucked the lemon balm inside a pouch labeled *Wedding Planner's Emergency Kit*. Blainey sat cross-legged on the ground, worrying the zipper on her pack. Naomi leafed through her journal, lips moving in prayer, while Jenna adjusted her camera settings, clearly more comfortable behind the lens.

McKenna took a sip of water, holstered the bottle, and drew a deep breath.

"Everyone, gather round." She beckoned them closer. "Give your packs a last once-over. Check boot laces. We're aiming for seven to ten miles today." She leveled a cautionary stare at Rough. "If you're not used to hiking with a full pack, it'll feel awkward at first. We'll pace ourselves. Survival skills with softer edges."

Nods and half-smiles.

She didn't glance Rough's way, but the weight of his presence pressed at the edge of her awareness. Her chest tightened at the sense of being sized up. No matter. She pulled her shoulders back, flexing her fingers around her pack straps. She hadn't built this retreat to win his approval.

McKenna straightened. If he doubted her ability to guide this group, he was mistaken. Five days could drag on. Break it down. Steady on for an hour. She set her jaw.

"All set?" She kept her voice warm but firm.

Jenna gave a thumbs-up while CeCe fussed with her gold-and-leopard-print hair clip. Blainey stood at the ready, waiting, while Naomi stowed her journal. McKenna hitched her pack and stepped toward the trail.

"Let's walk."

Humidity bore down, adding its weight to an already heavy pack. The sweet scent of pine and oak filled her lungs as her steps pressed into the worn trail. Nature had a unique way of stripping control—sometimes like a gentle creek, sometimes like a forceful river—laying bare wounds. Yet it always drew her nearer to God.

Ahead, moss clung to a weathered boulder, thriving where it had no business growing. She whispered a prayer for healing to take root the same way, on unyielding ground.

These women were stuck. They had reached a plateau that therapy alone couldn't budge. She could think of no better way to nurture their hearts than leading them here, letting God and the wilderness uncover what busyness had buried.

Boots scuffed behind her on the rugged trail.

"He seems like a prepper, don't you think?" CeCe whispered.

Had Rough overheard the comment? Of course he had. He'd probably hear a pine needle drop in this forest. His presence stretched like a long shadow, never close enough to confront, yet always there. A question mark on the trail. Would these women feel safe enough to open up with him looming? Would Rough leave the space needed for the process to unfold?

McKenna's toe snagged a root. She pitched forward, stumbling, until Naomi's hand caught her elbow. She winced as heat pricked her cheeks. *It's okay. We're all human.*

She peeked at her watch. Two minutes, forty seconds on trail. Steady on. Fifty-seven more minutes.

Three

After thirty minutes of hiking, McKenna stopped the group at the mouth of a box canyon. She slid off her pack and faced them with a sly grin. "It's early in our adventure, but I've got one serious question."

Rough leaned against a rock wall as the women traded wary glances.

She hitched her thumb over her shoulder. "Who can say 'Fuzzy Butt Falls' five times fast without laughing?"

CeCe snorted first. Blainey giggled, and Naomi hid a smile behind her hand.

"The winner earns bragging rights and immunity from the next awkward group question. Use it wisely." McKenna brushed her fingers across the compass dangling from her pack.

"Loser has to say it to Rough." CeCe snorted again.

"Hard pass." Jenna shook her head.

But they all tried.

When laughter ebbed, McKenna turned toward the canyon. "Don't expect much. Many Arkansas waterfalls dry up this late in the summer. Yesterday's rain might have left a trickle. Still, this spot is one of my favorites. It's like stepping into Narnia."

Each woman connected to the landscape in her unique way.

Jenna crouched to capture different angles of the falls with her camera. Blainey dipped her fingers into the shrinking blue-green pool. CeCe turned a slow circle, soaking it all in.

But Naomi. Where was Naomi?

McKenna's pulse quickened as she returned to the narrow entrance, half-expecting to see a retreating silhouette. Relief washed over her when she spotted Naomi sitting at the rim of the canyon. McKenna sighed and let her heartbeat settle.

A rough hand brushed McKenna's arm. "They're not ready to be cracked open yet. Let them hike."

She pressed her lips tight. Stepping past Rough, she removed her pack and lowered herself beside Naomi, choosing silence first. Rough hovered nearby, a shadow at the edge of her focus. Was he observing? Assessing her approach?

"Naomi."

"Mm?"

"Won't you join us?"

Naomi rubbed the webbing on her backpack. "I'm not sure the door to Narnia will open for me anymore."

McKenna let the pause linger. She followed Naomi's gaze to the thin ribbon of water, the moss-darkened ledge where it cascaded, and the fractured light glimmering at its edge.

"I don't think it has a door." McKenna rested her hand on her chin. "Not anymore."

Naomi's fingers stilled.

"I once believed it did." McKenna stared into the distance. "Like a threshold you could discover if you were worthy enough, still enough, believing enough. But now?" Her breath caught. "I think it appears at the most unexpected times when you're too weary to pursue it."

Naomi blinked, avoiding her gaze.

McKenna ran her fingers over a patch of moss nestled on layered rock. "Grace settles in hard places. Even when the wardrobe remains shut."

Naomi released a long breath, rose, brushed off her hands,

and drifted back to the others. No one called attention to her. Blainey shifted on her rock to make room. CeCe offered a smile. Jenna tipped her chin in acknowledgment before repositioning her lens toward the canyon's runoff.

McKenna hung back a moment. This—this was the work. Not always breakthroughs or tears. Sometimes, it was being invited to sit on a sun-warmed rock beside a trickle of water.

Light shifted overhead, dappling the canyon with a green-gold hue. A single leaf loosened and spiraled, a forerunner of the soon-to-change seasons, landing at Naomi's feet like a greeting—a bit of Narnia opening its arms. McKenna smiled, marveling at how nature spoke without a sound.

Closing her eyes, she exhaled a silent breath of prayer. She took her journal from her pack, jotted a few words, and returned it. Her skin tingled with an awareness of Rough's presence, and she glanced over her shoulder.

He stood back, arms folded as though the forest itself had posted him there. Challenging her? Protecting her? The line blurred. Was this irritation or intrigue niggling at her? Leaving her pack, she stepped toward the women. As she passed, she caught Rough's eye. Something unspoken tightened in the space between them.

The women began to gather. Jenna stayed behind her lens at the water's edge but moved close to Blainey. CeCe perched cross-legged next to them, followed by Naomi. McKenna paused at the edge, watching them settle like stones deposited downstream by the current.

Rough stood beyond the light, arms crossed. Not part of the circle, but not quite separate either. She didn't beckon him. Perhaps time would do the inviting.

McKenna sank onto the cool soil as the water whispered like a slow breath. A leaf drifted into the pool, sending a light ripple across the water. A reminder that even the slightest movement was mercy enough.

* * *

Rough aimed for ten miles. They were still four short. If they slept well, he could rouse them early and close the gap. Shade thickened as the sun eased behind the trees, shaving a few degrees off the heat. After dark, the temperature would drop ten to twenty degrees, making rest easier.

Ahead, McKenna unclipped her pack. His jaw tightened as he released a measured breath.

"Another break?" he muttered.

She didn't ask. Again.

"I thought we'd make camp here for the night." She dropped her pack against a log.

"Here? Now?" He sighed, scanning the area. "Not here. Move closer to that grouping of boulders and trees." He pivoted, shaking his head as he walked away. "Too early, if you ask me."

Stonewater Outfitters crouched low, her camera tilting at a sunbeam slanting across a rotted log. Glitter Quarterly shook her boot like a bridezilla had pushed her over the edge. Hibernator—no. She wasn't sleepy. Her shoulders drooped, fine lines edged her eyes, hinting at the strain of someone carrying loss.

He dropped his pack and busied himself, shifting its contents. He studied her quietly—a person, no longer a category.

Naomi sat cupping a small packet of trail mix. Her eyes half-closed, her lips moved. "Lord, bless this mess."

"You mean the snack or this trip?" Glitter Quarterly muttered, loud enough for him to catch.

He nudged Glitter Quarterly's shoulder. "Twenty minutes to find firewood, dry leaves, and two grubs. Bonus points if your critter wiggles."

Glitter Quarterly groaned and edged closer to Stonewater Outfitters. "Does Rough come with a soft setting?"

Hoof & Paw spoke for the first time. "I think he's watching out for us. In his way."

Rough stepped closer, meeting Glitter Quarterly's gaze. "No soft setting. Tumble dry only."

"You remind me of my brother," Hoof & Paw whispered, her smile faint and flickering.

Rough stiffened. Once, someone else had said that to him, light and teasing, moments before insurgents ripped through the village. "*You remind me of my brother.*" Last words. He heard them in quiet hours.

He shook it off. "Well—"

"Blainey."

"Blainey. Fire first. Shelter second. Sentiment doesn't block the sun or summer pop-up storms."

McKenna approached, touching his arm. "Naomi and I set stones for a fire ring. Want to check it?"

She asked? All day, she'd neglected to consult him about breaks, direction, even safety. Why bring him in now? She was capable enough. However, he knew too well that capability was where things could go wrong.

Rough followed her to the fire ring, giving the stone circle his nod of approval. Solid. Tight spacing, shielded, safe.

"It'll work."

"Glad it passes survivalist standards." Her words carried no edge—more truce than tease.

Rough cocked a brow. "What'd you use? Nash's handbook?"

"Used my gut." She tilted her head.

He rubbed his jaw. "Dangerous organ to trust."

"Yours or mine?" She smiled.

"Yes." His gaze slid back to the fire ring.

McKenna crouched to nudge a stone farther into place, one corner of her mouth tugging upward. "You know, you could give positive feedback without making it sound like a root canal."

"I'll work on that." Rough dragged a knuckle along his jaw, tamping down a grin. She was good. Too good. Unsettling, slipping past defenses he thought impenetrable. And he wanted more of it. "After everyone finds their bugs."

"We're actually doing that?" Her face pinched, and her shoulders drew up.

"They have to find them." He smirked, shaking his head. "They don't have to eat them."

"What a relief." Her shoulders relaxed, lips hinting at a smile. "Because nothing builds trust like protein with legs."

Behind them, Glitter Quarterly shrieked. "It moved. Rough, it moved."

"Bonus points," he called over his shoulder.

McKenna's laughter spilled out. Unexpected, bright, and unguarded, like sunlight through cloud cover. The warmth spreading through his chest caught him off guard. Her hazel eyes sparkled, the green flecks alive with mischief.

He stared a beat too long, pulse kicking harder than the moment warranted.

"What?" she asked, breathless.

"Nothing." His voice roughened. "Didn't know you had a laugh like that."

She rose. Brushing dirt from her palms, her gaze lingered a half second longer than necessary. "And I didn't know you had a sense of humor. Seems we're both full of surprises."

"Don't tell anyone." He winked. "It'll ruin my reputation."

McKenna's grin widened, playful and conspiratorial, like they had already forged a private pact. "Your secret's safe with me, Tumble Dry."

Blainey appeared at his side, holding her eyeglass case in one hand and a bandana knotted to form a pouch in the other. She held up the case. "Live crickets." Then the pouch. "Hickory nuts. Roast them?"

"You can. I'll show you how." He motioned her toward the fire ring. "You have a flint and steel?"

She nodded and knelt beside him. He demonstrated by striking steel against flint over a bit of dryer lint. She mimicked his actions repeatedly. Sparks leaped and fizzled until one caught. She coaxed the flame as it came to life, curling upward.

"You got it." He patted her shoulder. "Shell those nuts first, or they'll explode. Pass the crickets."

She opened the eyeglass case, and he plucked a cricket from it before the lid snapped shut. "Live or roasted?"

"Roasted."

He took the case from her, rolling it in his palm, thumb edging the worn lid open a crack. Five crickets hopped inside, their bodies bumping the velvet.

"Six?" He held up the one pinched between his fingers.

She nodded at the case. He eased it closed.

"Enough for the whole crew." Approval tugged at his mouth.

Blainey grinned as she crouched over the hickories.

"Glitter Girl, how you doing?" Rough moved toward Glitter Quarterly.

"Glitter Girl? It's CeCe. Short for Sicily." She jutted her chin. "And what's your story? Rough's not on your birth certificate."

He dodged with a grunt.

"I bet it involved a bar fight." Stonewater Outfitters snapped Blainey's picture.

"Nah." CeCe wagged a finger. "Bet it's military. My dad is in the military, and they all have nicknames."

"Did you find your dinner or not?" Rough arched a brow, not taking the bait.

"When I signed up for this retreat, I didn't know I was playing *Would You Rather*—glamping or gross."

"You've got five minutes to find a protein." Rough gave her a once-over. "Ever let a bridezilla run over you?"

"Never."

"Didn't think so. You're a woman with glitter and grit." He smiled. "Dinner is takeout. Bring it home."

CeCe inhaled with a little shiver. "I got this."

She turned and dug to the bottom of her pack, wrestling out a lint roller. Spotting a half-rotted tree log, she shoved it with her boot. She shut her eyes tight and squealed as she rolled the sticky paper over the disturbed area.

She thrust the roller out, one hand over her face. "Somebody else look. I can't."

"Ingenuity." Rough clapped her shoulder and took the wand. And a nice-sized centipede."

CeCe flew into a fit of disgust, stomping her boots and fluttering her hands. "I don't do bugs. Or firewood. Or silence." She stilled, a shiver crawling through her frame. Her voice dropped. "Especially not silence. It's too exposing."

Four

McKenna hugged her knees to her chest, chin balanced on top. The fire crackled in Naomi's stone ring, ribbons of gold flickering across worn boots and plaid sleeves. Firelight carved Rough's features as he demonstrated boiling water with a tin cup on a rock shelf. His deep voice carried like tumbling river rocks. The kind of voice a lost hiker would cling to, trusting it to lead them home.

He surprised McKenna. Instead of the barking drill sergeant she expected, he brought out the wise woodsman as he taught the women to build lean-tos. Blainey seemed to sense something familial in him, a glimpse of her brother. Rough hadn't leaned into the connection, but he hadn't discouraged it either. He showed signs of curiosity—and caution.

Same thing with Naomi. He crouched close as he coached her, like a son sharing a moment with his mother. McKenna sipped her cocoa, grateful for the sweetness of small blessings. Even with Jenna and CeCe, he hid a smile, swallowed a chuckle. Perhaps there were cracks in his walls after all.

The women eased near the fire one by one, the earlier tension thinning like the buzz of cicadas at dusk. Blainey shelled more hickory nuts. Naomi set a wide-brimmed canvas hat filled with blackberries on a nearby stone and scribbled in her journal. CeCe grumbled about smoke in her eyes, but didn't shift an inch. Jenna stowed her camera for once and pulled a small pouch from her belt loop, revealing a bright orange fungus called chicken of the woods, which Rough said was safe to eat.

Rough rationed roasted hickory nuts and crickets, keeping the centipede for himself. It was more than the others could stomach. Blainey popped a cricket in her mouth without hesitation, like it wasn't her first. Naomi prayed over hers and chased it with a big gulp of water.

McKenna pinched hers between two fingers, wrinkling her nose. "I can't ask you to do something I'm not willing to do myself."

She closed her eyes and chewed, the exoskeleton splintering between her teeth. Earthy bitterness spread across her tongue, and she forced it down, shuddering. "Tastes like"—she searched for the words—"burnt leaf and regret."

Laughter broke around the fire.

CeCe slipped a tiny bottle to Jenna. "Chocolate sauce. Emergency stash. Told you I was a planner."

Jenna eyed the cricket and grabbed the bottle. "This better not end up on your wedding planner blog."

"I make no promises."

Jenna drizzled the sauce and swallowed the insect in one gulp. She didn't speak, but the twitch at the corner of her mouth gave her away.

The laughter faded, and the fire settled. McKenna leaned forward. "If you want to write tonight, here's your prompt. You don't have to share, but you can." She scanned their faces. "What's something you've had to swallow, figuratively or literally, that you never thought you could?"

She paused.

"And what did it teach you?"

Uncomfortable silence snaked through the group. CeCe shifted. Naomi drew her journal to her chest. Jenna turned away from the fire. Blainey slipped away to her lean-to. Rough shook his head before leaving the circle and settling at his shelter, where he pulled a worn leather notebook from his pack.

McKenna resisted the urge to fill the silence. She let it breathe.

The fire crackled as a flurry of embers floated upward before vanishing. CeCe's usual wit was hidden behind pursed lips as she picked at a loose thread on her shirt hem. Naomi cradled her journal like a fragile child, staring at the blank page. Jenna moved into the shadows, lifting her camera from its case. Like a leaf slipping from a branch, Blainey's departure stirred the air, and McKenna let her go.

McKenna pressed a hand to her chest, letting the lingering warmth of her cocoa settle there. No one had to write or share tonight. The prompt had already done its work. Sometimes a question was enough to loosen tangled threads.

Across the fire, Rough sat on a rock by his lean-to, leather notebook in hand, thumb working the spine. Not shielding it. Not hiding it. Contemplating?

McKenna turned back to the flames, her journal resting on the log beside her. Perhaps they were all swallowing something tonight.

She breathed a prayer. *Let this be enough, Lord. For now.*

***

Rough stretched in his lean-to, pine boughs rustling under his weight. He propped his head on his pack, the notebook resting against his chest. He hadn't planned to write. He thumbed the page edges. Why had he even grabbed it? Force of habit, something to keep his hands from feeling idle.

That question of hers, though.

What's something you've had to swallow that you never thought you could? And what did it teach you?

He rolled onto his side, turning from the fire, from her.

Usually, he would've ignored a question like that. It reeked of a TED Talk. Or worse, therapy.

Yet she hadn't asked it that way.

No grand delivery. No pressure. Only a low-voiced invitation delivered on a cool evening breeze across a circle of cracked hearts and charred bug legs. The question carried grit. And grace.

Perhaps that's what got to him.

Not the words. But the way she gave them weight without demanding a response. He ran a finger along the notebook's edge, flipping it open.

There were things he had swallowed. Orders. Regret. Silence that still settled in his gut like a stone. No, he wouldn't write the answers. Not yet.

Instead, he propped himself up, pulled a pencil from his pack, and sketched. Moss clinging to rocks. A falling leaf. A dry creek bed. Her hands. Things that wouldn't stay.

The facing page stood blank. Fine. He wasn't here to unload feelings. He was here to make sure nobody died. He didn't need to write the words.

He thumped the page and sighed, keeping it ready for another time. Pulling a bit of twine from his pack, he marked the page, shut the notebook, shoved it back inside, and rolled out of his lean-to.

"Before you turn in"—he returned to the fire, gaze landing on McKenna still perched on a log—"a word about hogs."

Four heads turned, the rhythmic rasp and chirps of katydids and crickets filling the momentary silence between them.

"I saw a few signs earlier. Likely one or two in the area. Won't bother you unless they're cornered or spooked. You see ground torn up like it's been tilled, that's hog rooting. Fresh sign means they passed through recently. Best thing you can do is give 'em space. Don't run. Don't scream. Climb. Get at least six feet up if you can."

"Climb?" CeCe blinked as she licked peanut butter and chocolate sauce from a spoon. "Like a tree?"

"It's why we set camp this way." He motioned to the boulders and low-branched trees within reach. "Most hog attacks last about a minute. Whatever you do, don't fall. If you can't climb, stay on your feet and fight like mad."

"Encouraging." Jenna wiped sweat from her forehead.

"Don't overthink it." He pointed at the fire ring. "We've got scent, sound, light. If you brought food, hand it over. I'll secure it for the night. Tomorrow, if we see fresh rooting, we shift course."

Jenna and Naomi exchanged a glance. Blainey's eyes sharpened as she scanned the trees. CeCe handed the peanut butter jar to Rough and retrieved her lint roller, clutching it like a weapon. McKenna caught his gaze, appreciation flickering in the weariness of her eyes.

After leaving him a modest pile of food to stash, the women peeled off in pairs. Naomi and Blainey disappeared into their lean-to with soft, sisterly murmurs. Jenna slipped into hers without a word. CeCe straggled behind, pressing the lint roller into Jenna's hand before pulling out her wedding planner's emergency kit.

"I got you, girl." CeCe pulled tools from the kit. "I'll sleep with scissors and a nail file."

Rough closed his eyes, fighting back a smile. McKenna stayed a moment longer by the fire, stirring embers with a stick. She gave him a nod before retreating to her shelter.

His gaze followed her longer than it should have. Firelight brushed across her cheek, the softening angles drawing him in. Too long, too close. He forced his eyes back to the flames, his pulse unsteady.

He added a log to the fire, dragged a solid branch across his lap, and settled in as sentry. Arms folded, feet grounded, he kept watch. It wasn't the first time he had slept on the edge of alertness. Before long, his chin dipped toward his chest, eyes half-closed. He dozed in snatches, hands loosely around a thick tree limb, his only weapon. He couldn't leave anything to chance, not after spotting a couple of rooting patches.

A log burned through, shifting the fire with a loud crackle

and pop. Rough opened one eye. McKenna glanced over her shoulder. He gave a half-nod. She smiled and rolled away.

This crazy idea of hers. Therapy in the woods. Why not on a couch? Nash always joked real names were for emergencies and official paperwork. Boone added, "And therapy." They believed in its value. Insisted nature could quiet a man. Maybe. Or perhaps nature stripped a man bare until there was no ignoring what chipped away at him.

The fire snapped and hissed, sparks grazing the dark before vanishing. Five days, a few photos, a glowing testimonial. Would this gig scrape the mud off his reputation? What if it unraveled into bugs, blisters, and feelings he had no wish to confront? He rolled his shoulders, tension clinging as stiff and stubborn as tree bark.

Therapy.

Yeah, time to find out what the wilderness had to say about it.

Five

A faint vibration from McKenna's watch nudged her awake. She rubbed her eyes, silenced her alarm, and stretched. A barred owl called, "Who cooks for you? Who cooks for you all?" reminding her she had four more days until the hot, hearty breakfast Nash had promised to make up for his absence. The pine boughs beneath her were softer than expected. Journal in hand, she slipped from her lean-to and crossed to the fire ring.

Rough was already there. A shadow passed behind his eyes as she sat. He balanced his worn notebook on his knee. She handed him two tin cups. He poured the coffee and passed one back, a fragile offering across a divide where trust might yet take root. A glimmer of appreciation crossed his face when she sipped the morning brew straight. Lavender and blackberry were her usual flavorings, but Nash taught her drinking it black earned her points on the respect board with some people.

"Didn't figure you for a black coffee type."

McKenna opened her journal and angled sideways, her back toward Rough, so the firelight spilled across the page. She brushed his shoulder and froze, ready to shift away if he recoiled. Instead, he eased a fraction closer, his back steadying hers, lending support so she could write in the wavering light. The gesture was small, but it anchored her as she wrote a prayer of gratitude and observations about herself and the group.

Was it the firelight or the coffee that made him seem more human before sunrise? Less steel in his jaw. More space in his silence.

Her pen moved in gentle rhythms. The group was shifting. Naomi had begun to settle. CeCe was dialing back her sarcasm. And Blainey kept watching Rough, as though trying to solve a puzzle with her heart.

McKenna closed her journal and let the birdsong wash over her.

"Ready?" Rough arched a brow.

"To wake them?"

He nodded.

"I thought we'd let them wake to their own rhythms."

"Like you did?" His chin dipped. "If we wait, they might sleep all day. Camp won't tear itself down, and we've got miles to gain. Won't happen in their sleep."

"Slow down, cowboy." McKenna raised her cup.

"No time, unless you want to cut the adventure elements you and Nash had planned." He poured another serving of coffee and snapped shut the pot lid harder than necessary. "And after moving camp because of hog signs, I'd rather not let grass grow under us."

"Listen." McKenna tightened her grip around her tin cup. "With the change in instructors, I thought it better to ease off the adventure side. Stick to basics."

"You should've mentioned that at Rally Point." He dragged his hand through his hair. "I've got a lot riding on this." His voice edged with weariness. "I agreed to this because I owe Nash my life. But he also promised it would be worth my time."

His voice sagged like a pack carried too long. Right. Therapy, then. Nash must have twisted his arm into this whole healing experiment. Figures. What burden had Rough hauled into the woods with him? If only she could get a glimpse beyond his armor. Curiosity washed through her like a summer rain, unexpected but not unwelcome. If he bought into her theory of healing through wilderness challenge, the retreat might do him good.

McKenna sighed. "A compromise? Stick with the basics today —knots, signal fire, water filtration. Tomorrow, you'll get your adrenaline rush."

"Fine." His gaze drifted away. "We're still making up at least two of the four miles we lost yesterday."

"I'll get them moving." McKenna rose and crossed to the lean-tos.

Naomi, already stirring, shuffled to the fire, murmuring a prayer as she poured a splash of coffee into a tin cup holding instant oatmeal and peanut butter. Jenna slipped on her boots and polished her camera lens, though it already gleamed. Blainey woke with only a light touch on the shoulder. McKenna bent over CeCe, slipping the scissors and nail file from her hands before nudging her awake.

Rough barked orders to tear down camp. The predawn softness disappeared, replaced by a drill sergeant tone and clipped urgency, every move weighted with the coming miles.

CeCe groaned. "Eggs? Dry shampoo?"

McKenna blinked. Hopefully, two separate requests. Hopefully.

Blainey polished off her jerky before finishing her tasks and then helped the others without being asked. Naomi closed her journal, handing Rough a folded paper. His eyes scanned the page. Then he whispered in her ear, squeezing her in a side hug before delivering sharp instructions to the group.

"Twelve miles today." He circled a finger overhead, his voice tightening like a river around a bend. "Fifteen minutes. Don't dally."

Rough appeared to run on only two settings—still as stone or tumble dry, rocks included. McKenna exhaled, his drive crowding the air between them. She flipped open the compass her mentor had given her. *Steady on.* Again. One hour at a time.

She gathered the women for prayer before they dismantled the fire ring. Rough stilled, his head dipping almost imperceptibly. Something in her eased, the compass settling in her palm as she bowed her head. "Lord, guide our steps and soften our hearts. One breath, one mercy at a time."

* * *

Dry leaves crunched under their boots as Rough took the rear, ears tuned to breath rather than chatter. In front of him, Blainey moved light and quiet, as if she might startle the trees. CeCe muttered about needing a barista and a chiropractor. He didn't argue. He could go for both himself.

They weren't fast. But they were moving. Moving was enough. He didn't need them to love the pace, so long as they kept it.

Jenna stayed on the edge of the group, camera between her and the world. At first, he chalked it up to aloofness. Or was it more like armor? Some carved space with knives. She carved hers with a lens. When Blainey crouched beneath a bent cedar to help Naomi shake a rock from her shoe, Jenna angled for the shot.

Naomi pushed ahead and caught up to McKenna. Shifting her pack, Naomi leaned near and murmured to McKenna. Naomi had years on the others, but she kept his pace without complaint. Despite the quick miles and rugged terrain, no one had grumbled. No tears. No quit. No sharp words. The trail snaked on, doing its work in silence.

McKenna matched the group's rhythm without forcing it. Whispered encouragement to Naomi. Joked with CeCe. Pointed out every bug and lizard to Blainey. Held steady beside Jenna.

She didn't move like him. He drove. She guided. And somehow, it worked. Her way would have exhausted him by now, but she was on target.

How did she see him? Too harsh, muscling through everything?

He slowed his steps, letting the group stretch in his sightline —loose and uneven like dominoes nudged apart, but still standing. Not search-and-rescue team sharp but trying their best. McKenna passed Naomi a stick for balance. He wouldn't have thought of it. He didn't speak gently and didn't hand out metaphors. But perhaps the trail didn't always need grit. Maybe sometimes it needed grace that didn't announce itself.

After a few miles, he slowed to a stop. "Ten-minute break. Packs stay on. Show me a bowline, or I'll show you one."

The sun pressed down through the trees. Sweat slicked his palms. He wiped them on his cargo shorts and tossed CeCe a length of rope. He waited for her to crack wise. She only grumbled, fumbling at first before tightening a clean knot.

"Wedding planner, right?" He nodded at the rope. "Guess you've tied a few things."

"Knots don't scare me." She smirked. "Bugs and deep feelings do."

Jenna didn't reach for the rope. She lifted her camera instead, catching CeCe mid-pull.

McKenna joined Blainey. "That knot? It's called a rescue loop for a reason." Her voice was calm, soothing. "Even strong knots can be undone when you need to breathe."

Two different languages. Same message. He gave commands. She gave meaning. It worked. He wasn't sure what it meant for him yet. But his grip lingered on the rope longer than needed.

Back on the trail, Rough scouted ahead. A scar of earth stopped him cold. Dark, damp, torn as if a dull blade had gouged it. Small but fresh. He crouched and brushed clods with his fingers.

Rooting.

He rose, scanning the tree line. Quiet.

Too quiet.

The group bunched up behind him. He stepped in front of the scar, shoulders filling the space. No need to spook them. Not yet.

"We'll keep moving." His chin jerked toward the left trail. "This stretch narrows. Stay sharp."

The path funneled between limestone outcrops. Sun struck the rock face, bright as a signal flare. Rough paused. The terrain shifted. Jagged boulders, shallow crags, a dry scramble route he had used on advanced treks.

Perfect place for a hands-and-knees climb. Risky enough to feel like an accomplishment. It would test balance, focus, and fear.

CeCe squinted at the incline. "Tell me that's not the trail."

"Could be." His voice settled.

McKenna caught up, her breath steady, eyes searching the rocks. She didn't say a word, but her gaze met his. Not a warning, not a challenge, yet the question in her eyes was clear. Is this the right time?

Beyond her, Jenna rolled her shoulders, fighting stiffness. Naomi's stride shortened. Blainey worked her mouth side to side. CeCe still cracked jokes, but the silence stretched between zingers as she rubbed her knee.

They weren't ready. Not yet.

He exhaled through his nose and jerked his chin toward the alternate route. "Trail bypasses the scramble."

A few audible exhales followed. Blainey mouthed, "Thank you." Jenna lifted her camera, snapping a photo of the route they didn't take.

McKenna stepped close to Rough. "Good call."

He didn't answer, but his jaw unclenched.

By midday, they dropped their packs near a hollow creek bed. Tired but not defeated. That was the difference between pushing and breaking. Rough sat on a flat stone, his field notebook open across his knee.

He didn't write much but ran a thumb across the page.

Sketches took shape at the pace of unhurried thoughts. Blainey's hands firm on the rope, Jenna's lens catching the moment. Beneath the images in his rough block letters, one line.

Is this how rebuilding begins?

Six

They made camp mid-afternoon, gaining two of the four miles they had lost the previous day. McKenna was pleased by how they had tapped into their grit and resilience. The gain put them ahead of her distance goal for the two days. They were a tad shy of Rough's, but he offered encouragement marked with brevity.

The second night, the camp circled tighter. The shelters formed an uneven crescent around the new fire ring, tucked under a canopy of dogwood and oak. Rough pointed out a few dogwoods close enough to the oaks to serve as quick ladders to the higher limbs, should the need arise. Clusters of red berries hung in the dogwoods. Late-summer fruit the birds would strip clean come fall. McKenna almost wished schedules had worked out in the spring, as she imagined the trees in bloom. The closeness of the shelters was a sign something had shifted within the group.

Rough had demonstrated a second shelter option, an A-frame lean-to with better insulation and less exposure. He didn't bark orders. He only showed them how it was done and let them make the choice. It felt like a quiet test, not of skill, but of willingness.

Blainey stuck with the lean-to. "I like being able to see where everyone is."

McKenna made a note. A desire for connection or holding a safe space?

Naomi stayed with her. Their hands moved in rhythm as they built the new shelter with more agility and ease than the night before. With a few words between them, they added little luxuries like a place to hang a flashlight and tuck a book.

CeCe tried the A-frame, making jokes about being the meat in a forest taco. Once she got the hang of it, the shelter went up in short order with minimal help from Rough and not much fanfare. They were surprised when she pulled a section of battery-operated string lights from her backpack.

"What's the capacity of this pack?" Rough poked around the top of the bag. "And where is the duct tape?"

McKenna smiled at the progress.

Jenna positioned her shelter near the fire but a short distance from the group. She remained on the periphery. But she had asked Blainey to hold the support beams while she tied her knots. That, too, was something.

McKenna joined Rough as he stacked stones around the fire ring. He had been quiet since they set camp, watching the women work, eyes narrowed. It didn't read like judgment, though. Steeped in thought? Protectiveness? Perhaps even approval?

When the fire burned low, Rough slipped to the food stash. He drew a rugged perimeter line on the ground using a chunk of charred wood and what appeared to be cedar bark. McKenna tilted her head, curious, but didn't ask. She figured it was one of his survival habits, a system only he needed to understand.

Dinner was a reserve stash of trail-ready food from home and meager findings from the land. Blainey and Naomi had found some earthworms, and Rough had spotted a quail's nest. He promised an earthworm omelet for breakfast and laughed when their faces pinched.

A ghost of a smile lit Blainey's face. "If he makes an earthworm omelet, I'm leaving a Yelp review. Five stars—if he drowns it in ketchup."

Despite the warm days, cocoa was one luxury they had all agreed on during planning. McKenna sat near the fire, listening as the evening fell soft and quiet. Everyone dialed down. No banter. No complaining. Jenna's boots scuffing the ground beneath her feet accompanied the swift scrawl of Naomi's pen on the journal page.

They were tired.

But something deeper was stirring.

Rough joined the circle, sitting beside McKenna, and she handed him a cocoa.

"They did well today." He took a sip. "No coffee?"

"You did well. I know you wanted to do the scramble." She lifted her mug. "It's good to end the day with something sweet. It's a gentle reminder of the blessings."

"It wasn't the right time for the scramble." He tapped the tin cup. "A cup of blessings. I might add this to my wind-down routine."

She bumped her mug against his, a light clink of thanks, and pointed to his leather notebook. "Journal?"

"Field notes. Sketches. Verses of Scripture."

"And you brought it to the fire ring?" She sipped her cocoa. "You know I'm about to offer a prompt."

"Eh. It keeps my hands occupied. Reminds me what's important."

She smiled, then cleared her throat and pulled a small parcel wrapped in baking parchment from beside her. "I don't want you to think I'm bribing you to do these prompts, but tonight I thought a little comfort food might carry us through. Brownies?"

CeCe and Jenna leaped at the offer, followed closely by Naomi and Blainey. Rough pulled a plastic bag of pumpkin seeds from his pack. He pressed some into his brownie, like planting them in soft earth, then passed the bag around. McKenna's lips tugged upward. Trust him to turn even dessert into a lesson about endurance and new growth.

"Tonight's prompt, should you accept it"—she winked—"is

this. What have you chosen to let go of lately? And what won't let go of you?"

Long silence. Uneasy shifting. McKenna's gaze roved the circle, but no one left.

Naomi clutched her journal to her chest, as was her custom. Did she offer a prayer before writing? Blainey stared into the flames for a long moment. Jenna raised her camera and lowered it again, taking a beat to view her surroundings without the lens. CeCe poked at the dirt with a stick, quieter than usual, before pulling her journal from beneath her pink plaid overshirt.

"I'll tell you what I'm not letting go of. My lint roller," she muttered, but her pencil didn't stop moving.

Rough raked his thumb back and forth across the page edges. He didn't write. Not yet. But he didn't leave either.

McKenna didn't speak again. She let the question breathe, allowing the fire to carry it upward like a seed released to the wind and waiting. Whatever was shifting inside these women, she knew not to chase it. She held space, letting the moment rest.

* * *

Rough remained at the fire ring a bit longer, not ready to leave McKenna's side. Her questions had a way of shaking things up and settling them at the same time. It created an uneasy shift. Yet the way she held silence made him want to stay with her in it.

The firelight framed her face, and he found his gaze lingering too long. Again.

Clearing his throat, he nodded before getting up.

He moved beyond the circle, stretched his legs, then settled next to his lean-to, resting the notebook on one thigh. The fire burned low, casting slow-dancing shadows along the inner wall of the makeshift structure. He hadn't written anything. But he sat with the question.

What have you let go of? What won't let go of you?

He could think of a dozen things he'd let go of, most by force, not choice. But what wouldn't let go of him? It was a short list. And sharper.

Voices were few tonight. A tired quiet that came after steady miles and soul work. Even CeCe hadn't cracked a joke in twenty minutes. He glanced at her as she raised an oversized Razorback mug like she was about to toast the fire.

"This baby's a lifesaver. A cup of comfort, a cocoa tureen." She tapped the ceramic with one well-filed fingernail. "I bet it could take out a possum too. Or a man."

"You planning to do either?" Rough asked, his voice low.

CeCe grinned. "Not unless I must. But I've got range if I do."

She earned a chuckle from Blainey and a demure smile from Naomi. McKenna sipped her cocoa without comment, but her eyes were warm.

CeCe shifted, locking her gaze on Rough with the focus of someone who'd made up her mind. "Okay. I've waited. And watched. And now I gotta ask again."

Rough raised an eyebrow.

She leaned forward, cupping the mug like a campfire microphone. "What's with the name? Rough. I mean, it fits, but come on. Spill."

He didn't answer, only smiled.

CeCe squinted like she was solving a puzzle. "It's gotta be one of three things. Military nickname, bar fight, or you were raised by wolves, and Ruff was your foster dad."

Laughter. Even Jenna let out a quiet huff of air.

"Well, I don't care how tough it makes you sound. I've taken a shine to you." CeCe tilted her head. "Wait. You know what else shines? Diamonds. You could be a Diamond in the Rough. That's it, isn't it? You're one of those guys. All growl, soft center."

The fire popped. Rough didn't confirm it. But he didn't deny it either. He took a long sip from his cup, eyes on the fire.

"Wouldn't be the worst thing I've been called."

CeCe nudged Jenna with one elbow. "See? Marshmallow. Under all that gravel."

Jenna and Blainey giggled and lowered their eyes.

He should've shut them down. Deflected. Changed the subject. But something in the air said to let it land, even if it settled heavier than he wanted.

McKenna caught his eye across the flames. She didn't say anything. Didn't need to. The silence between them had started to feel like something steady, not jagged.

Later, after the others drifted to their shelters and the fire faded, he clicked on a small light and sat back against his pack, notebook open in his lap. He sketched the shape of CeCe's mug with the light catching the rim. Jenna's camera, resting on a rock like it needed a quiet moment too. Blainey's hands around a knot they had learned that morning.

At the bottom of the page, he scrawled in block letters.

What if letting go starts with staying still?

For tonight, the silence in the question didn't bother him. He closed the notebook and leaned back, eyes fixed on the dark canopy, when a rustle disturbed the stillness beyond the clearing. It wasn't leaves in the wind. He knew that sound.

A grunt. Low. Wet. Rooting.

He stiffened, tucking the notebook tight to his chest as he scanned the trees. Nothing stirred. No second sound followed. Still, he rose, crossed to the food cache, and adjusted the line he'd marked with charcoal and cedar bark. He placed another log on the fire and found a thick, solid branch. The tension in his jaw returned.

When he settled again, he didn't open the notebook. Didn't reach for the firewood. He sat with the sturdy branch across his lap. Watching. Listening.

And letting the silence rest.

Seven

༄

The gentle thrum of voices drifted from the fire ring as McKenna rubbed her eyes. She squinted at her watch. Seven o'clock. Her alarm hadn't gone off. She scrambled from her lean-to. Naomi and Blainey sat with their journals, each with one leg folded underneath them. Jenna sat near them, adjusting her camera settings, but not hiding behind it. CeCe hummed something peppy as she sipped coffee from her Razorback mug.

"Where's Rough?"

"Here." He held up three eggs.

"Oh, you're not—"

"I said I would." He grinned. "No one has to eat it. It's great protein, though. Any takers?"

"My husband and I served as missionaries in remote areas overseas." Naomi shrugged. "I'm not intimidated by unusual cuisine."

"My brother would have dared me to do it." Blainey tilted her head. "I'll try it in honor of him."

"I'm tired of hickory nuts." CeCe raised her mug. "But not that tired. It's nuts and granola with a side of dried fruit for me."

"Hard pass for me." Jenna raised her camera with a chuckle. "But you know I'll take pictures."

"It's down to you." Rough eyed McKenna, a mischievous twinkle in his eyes.

"Fine, but not a big bite. I don't want to deprive you of the extra protein."

After breakfast, McKenna asked Rough's thoughts regarding her plan to cover the two miles he believed were still owed, aiming to guide the group toward a more rhythmic day. Her thumb brushed over the compass attached to her pack before she retrieved the map. She outlined a route that would take them near the creek.

"I thought we could join the creek this morning for an exercise in letting go."

"Letting go?" Rough rubbed the scruff along his jaw. "Didn't they already do that last night with the journal thing?"

"The prompt? That was an open door. We can do something tangible to symbolize closure." She held up a baggie with dark chunks of debris. "I gathered bits of charred wood from the fire. They'll write a word or phrase on a leaf, release it into the water, and watch it drift away."

"Tangible symbolism. Isn't that like an oxymoron or something?" He kicked a root with the toe of his boot, then tapped a different section of the map. "I thought we would hike this area. The terrain is a bit more challenging, but it will cut time. We're almost guaranteed a fallen log crossing, which would make a great self-trust element."

She pressed her eyes shut, breathing deeply. Then she fixed her gaze on him. "You said we'd balance this. They're opening up, and you want to raise the stakes?"

"Listen, McKenna. You can sit with the hard stuff. Doesn't mean you have to pitch a tent in it." He stood, palms upturned. "Sometimes after the letting-go bit, you just move on."

Her stomach tightened. *Nash, what have you done?* She

should have canceled the trip. What was she thinking, trusting something this important to such an unpredictable variable?

Rough didn't push back right away. He stood, arms crossed, stance squared, scanning the horizon like he could will her to agree with him.

He hitched his thumb toward the trail. "We're burning daylight."

He turned to the group. "Boots on. We've got to push through to the mid-morning break."

McKenna didn't answer him. Not directly.

Instead, she turned toward the others, voice calm and clear. "You'll need your journals for a few lines. We'll stop by the creek before the next waypoint."

She didn't look at Rough again. She didn't need to. The line had been drawn.

They shifted packs into place, double-checked boot laces, and began moving. CeCe hummed her peppy tune. Jenna swung her camera over her shoulder, and Naomi gave a half-nod toward McKenna.

McKenna and Rough tried to shuffle to the lead as the trail narrowed. She shifted, inadvertently bumping him with her pack, and he stepped off the trail. Persistent moss muffled the steps behind her. She reached for the compass on her pack strap, fingers brushing the words etched inside the lid.

Steady on.

It sounded steadier than it felt.

By mid-morning, they reached the creek. The gentle shushing reached them first, sparking a flurry of excitement as a narrow ribbon of movement appeared, threading through the trees. Sunlight spilled across the water, creating a shimmer more refreshing than CeCe's twinkle lights. McKenna scanned the group. Shoulders sagged. They were warm, quiet, and worn.

"Take a breath. This is your moment."

The women set down their packs. Rough kept his distance. He didn't interrupt. Didn't instruct.

McKenna knelt near the bank, spreading a small pile of collected leaves on a rock with bits of fire-charred wood. "If you're willing, write a word or phrase. Something you've released. Or something still letting go of you."

She demonstrated, scratching the word *failure* across her leaf in careful strokes. Failure. It wasn't her whole story, but it whispered through the dark corners of her tale. She didn't say it aloud but held her leaf up for everyone to see before letting the water take it. The current caught it. It swayed, then drifted away.

One by one, the women followed. Naomi wrote as if she had known the word from the start. CeCe scoffed but crouched, writing with her hand covering the leaf. Blainey held her leaf the longest, her fingers lifting one by one as she released it to the stream. Jenna didn't write but raised her camera to capture the moment. The floating leaves, bent heads, and tiny ripples carried the weight away.

McKenna turned to Rough. He didn't speak, but gave the barest nod as if to say, "I see what this is."

She nodded back.

McKenna slid her backpack into place, buckling the chest strap. The women followed her lead. CeCe stretched before donning her pack, while Blainey and Naomi helped each other with theirs. Jenna untangled her camera and pack straps. The morning had taken a thoughtful turn, and McKenna wanted to protect it. She glanced around. Rough was gone.

But where? Not far, she hoped.

McKenna led the women back to the tree line, and Rough joined them shortly, offering no explanation. His tone sharpened as he gave a clipped nod in another direction. "We're going west." He was steady and firm as if he'd brook no argument. "Safer footing. Better tree cover."

She opened her mouth and closed it again. He had pushed for a different path that morning and was now rerouting without discussion? She pressed a hand to her ribs, steadying her breath. Something was building.

* * *

Rough didn't like rerouting at the last minute. It looked sloppy. Indecisive. But the hoof marks weren't there yesterday. Not so fresh. Not so close. He had told McKenna it was for tree cover and better footing, which was close enough to the truth. But the grunt he'd heard in the early dark, paired with the patch of rooting, didn't sit right. He didn't want them skirting risk for a leaf-floating exercise, no matter how *tangible* the symbolism. He could still see Blainey's fingers uncurl one by one as she let go of hers, like releasing a prayer into the rippling water. It struck a chord in him. He had once scoffed at the idea of tangible symbolism, but now he couldn't stop thinking about a floating leaf and a woman with steady eyes. He wouldn't say it out loud, though.

McKenna brought a stillness to the group, but Rough had never considered what might be happening inside. She seemed so self-assured and pulled together as she held her ground with him. Yet she'd raised her leaf displaying a surprising word. *FAILURE.* It stuck in his throat. Was that her word, or only an example?

Didn't matter. It had worked. Each woman made her mark and set something adrift in the creek. And they all carried themselves lighter afterward. Walked taller, moved with more freedom. He had never seen anything like it—an immediate but unspoken shift.

And here he was shifting them away from what? The hog, yes. But what was he carving away from McKenna's plan? Would she have an alternative activity to drop in? Something that could replace whatever he sidelined?

Of course she would. Her intuition was spot on. He found bits of his shield being stripped away, and they hadn't even dug into the adventure skills yet. It was her questions, the way she asked them. Her timing, knowing when to lead with humor, when to tread lightly, when to plunge deeper.

And the way McKenna challenged him. Flat-footed,

shoulders squared, but not barking like a drill instructor. It was like an invitation to lower his guard and show up differently. An offer to join forces in a work he had never been part of.

He didn't know what to do with that.

Now that she was picking up the new trail and keeping time, he slowed. The others shifted into formation, and he dropped back, waiting for the line to curve out of sight. The silence was thicker here, and he slipped away without announcing it.

He doubled back without telling McKenna.

Morning sun filtered through the trees in warm rays, dappling the ground with its light. Rough scanned the edge of their trail, eyes tracking for subtle signs. Disturbed moss, scraped bark at waist height, leaves turned the wrong side up.

Then he saw it. Again.

Rooting. Another small patch, but fresh. Damp soil clumped as though something had torn through. A few paces farther, scat. Old, but not that old. Beyond it, a thicket was broken where something short and broad had pushed through. Curious. And close.

Rough crouched, hand hovering over torn earth. He picked up a long stick, more as a weapon than a walking stick. Time for another route adjustment. McKenna wouldn't like it, but with any luck, she wouldn't question it. He didn't want to alarm the others. He needed them to stay calm and work together. How would they react if they knew?

He backtracked, adjusting his pace as he neared the others.

"Trail becomes more difficult ahead." He slid up next to McKenna. "Let's veer east."

He didn't offer more. McKenna's eyes narrowed and fixed on him. She outpaced the group with a glance indicating he should join her.

"What's going on?" She was smart. She knew there was something he wasn't saying.

He kept his shoulders square and jaw tight. "Listen, we don't need to incite fear right now. But we need momentum."

"Why?"

He mouthed, "Hog."

Her eyes widened. "How close?"

"Close enough."

She rubbed her collarbone, as though trying to smooth the worry down. "Why didn't you tell me earlier?"

"I needed to be sure."

She was silent for a long moment. Her lips pursed, eyes studying him as though weighing him. She finally spoke in a hushed voice. "You should've told me."

He nodded. "I know."

The air between them was tight, crammed with the things neither wanted to say. He should have trusted her more. He knew how lonely leadership could be, and he hadn't shared the burden the way he could have, the way he should have. But trust required vulnerability, and he had lost the last person he had fully trusted. He couldn't go through another loss like that.

As CeCe embraced her Razorback mug and the other women sipped from their water bottles, they exchanged concerned glances. McKenna took a deep breath and rejoined them as Rough fell in beside her, but not too close.

"We're going to make another course change, and as we do, I'm going to quiz you about what you've learned." She turned on her heel, and the women fell in behind her like ducklings. "First, tell me your favorite knot you've practiced."

McKenna seamlessly integrated the details of surviving a hog attack into her skills quiz while asking the women to point out their high-climb choices along the way. She mentioned a few signs had been spotted in the area without creating undue distress.

"Let's stay sharp and keep moving away from the signs." She folded her arms across her chest. "You have all the tools you need to do well, should we have a close encounter. Treat it like an emergency on a plane and take care of yourself before you help someone else."

Her voice was calm yet commanding, keeping the group

focused without rattling them. She took the lead and did it well. Her pace was steady, her eyes alert, and her posture was ready for action, yet not tense. If failure had been her word, she had learned how to carry it. Perhaps she could teach him a thing or two.

Rough dropped back with the walking staff in hand, eyes scanning the area. Maybe leadership wasn't about control, but collaboration. Listening. Yielding. Trusting someone to carry part of the weight. A breeze moved through the trees, and he drew the scent of moss and pine needles deep into his lungs. The importance of trust in their group dynamic was becoming increasingly clear, and it was a lesson Rough was beginning to understand.

Eight

McKenna glanced over her shoulder. Rough followed closely behind and to the side. He observed, without interruption, as she quizzed the women about the survival skills they had learned. She took a deep breath, steeling her stomach against the tightness. More than once, she had found herself in unexpected wilderness situations with Nash, but she knew her brother so well that she never questioned how either of them would react. She couldn't say the same about Rough Scott. The tension between them was palpable, a silent barrier that neither knew how to break.

Then there were the other women. Blainey and Naomi were no strangers to the wilderness. However, Jenna and CeCe had little experience in primitive environments. McKenna counted on their work experience dealing with unexpected twists and turns to help them remain calm if the group did encounter hogs.

If only Rough had told her about the signs sooner, they could have turned back. Why had he kept the information from her? Didn't he trust her? She was trying to build the relationship, but laying the foundation had been difficult. It's not like he'd left her an open door.

How many times had she had to reschedule this trip? What if

God was trying to tell her the wilderness was not the way to break barriers?

"I wish we had stayed closer to the creek." CeCe drummed bedazzled fingernails against her Razorback mug. "It was so beautiful there. Did you see those tall purple flowers? Even the babbling water made me feel cooler."

"Don't worry. We'll reconnect with the creek once we are clear of hog territory." McKenna reached back and patted CeCe's shoulder.

CeCe turned to Rough. "Why didn't you tell us about the hog signs? You don't think we can handle an encounter with them, do you?"

"Where is your climb point?" Rough paused, hooking his thumbs on his pack straps.

CeCe glanced around her before pointing to the tree about five feet from the trail. "There."

Rough shook his head. "Naomi gets there before you. Where are you going?"

"There." She pointed to another tree a short distance behind, on the opposite side.

"Blainey made the scramble."

"I suppose Jenna claims the large boulder?"

Rough grinned. "You might both fit, don't you think? But give me two more spots, for fun."

CeCe pointed out another boulder and two more trees. "More than two. Do I win a prize?"

"You're ready, CeCe. You mapped a path to safety for everyone on your team."

"You called me CeCe, not Glitter Girl."

"Well, it is your name." Rough began moving again, but he didn't outpace McKenna.

McKenna smiled to herself with a surge of contentment. Perhaps the foundation was more substantial than she realized, and growing.

He leaned forward. "There's a narrow section up ahead. With

any luck, we'll be out of hog territory once we get past it. After we're through, I'll do another check."

"I guess evading hogs is our extreme survival activity." She let out a shaky chuckle. "Let's pick up the pace and push through this narrow bit." She made a forward motion with her arm. "Okay, girls. A strong push here, and we can rest easy tonight. Stay sharp."

McKenna set her jaw, determined to ensure everyone's safety. There was no time to hold on to stubbornness. She turned to Rough. "You want to take the lead?"

"Together? There's enough room to walk in pairs for a while."

She nodded, and they continued side by side. No one spoke much, though McKenna tried to encourage conversation in hopes their voices might discourage any wild animals from approaching. The tension in the group was palpable, but so was the unity. A glance behind her revealed four sets of eyes scanning their surroundings, likely scoping routes upward.

"Jenna, any interesting pictures since our last stop?"

"I stowed my camera."

They all stopped.

"CeCe scoped out escape routes for the entire group earlier. I only picked one for me." She shrugged. "That's my problem, right? I hide behind a lens and miss what's important."

"You've been in uncertain situations before. What made you put the camera down this time?"

"I filmed a story once near Porter, Arkansas, about a woman who survived a hog attack. She was alone when the attack happened. Lucky, she survived. We couldn't air many of the details." She swallowed hard. "Too graphic." She tugged at her shoulder as though missing the camera strap. "I don't want this to be only CeCe's team. I want it to be mine too."

McKenna released a sigh. "All right. Make strong mental notes to jot down memories in your journals later. No photos for a while."

The group fell into a cautious silence as they pushed farther up the crude trail. They were flanked by a rock face and a thin strip of trees disguising a steep drop on the other side. The back of Rough's hand brushed McKenna's, and for a split second, he curled his pinky around hers. Her breath hitched as she tried to make space, but the trail was too narrow. Their hands kept making contact. With a subtle side glance, she tried to gauge his reaction. Eyes forward, shoulders relaxed, unfazed by it.

Jostling behind them drew McKenna's attention. She turned as Jenna lunged, catching Naomi under the arms and lessening the impact of her fall. The pair ended up on the ground. Rough rushed to kneel beside them, checking Naomi's ankle. She sucked air through clenched teeth.

"What happened?" McKenna took a step toward Naomi, but Rough held up a hand.

"Tree root." Naomi's voice went soft with embarrassment.

"Probably a minor sprain. Can you stand?"

A rustling caught McKenna's ear, and she angled toward the trail ahead. She scanned the area. Nothing unusual. She pivoted back to Rough and the women when she heard it again.

The rustle.

A slow, weighty sound in the distance, not the quick playfulness of a squirrel or bird. She swiveled, squinting ahead at the foliage-choked trail—still nothing in sight. The path appeared undisturbed, though every hair on the back of her neck lifted.

"Rough, I think something is out there. Something larger than a squirrel." Her whisper was sharp as she glanced his way. "Should we—"

Rough's head snapped up. He followed her gaze, eyes narrowing. Jenna and Blainey helped Naomi to her feet, supporting her between them as they moved to a nearby boulder.

"Can you pull yourself up if we help?" Jenna whispered, and Naomi responded with a nod.

CeCe stood a couple of steps behind McKenna, brandishing her Razorback mug. McKenna's breath caught.

A wild hog stepped onto the path several yards in the distance.

Medium-sized, thickly muscled, bristled under muddy, dark fur. It hadn't seen them yet. It sniffed the air, ears twitching.

McKenna's heart thumped in her chest as she stepped back, pressing into CeCe. "Up. Now."

"Not until Naomi is safe."

McKenna glanced over her shoulder again.

Rough had joined Jenna and Blainey. "You two get to a high point. I've got Naomi."

The two women scrambled up a pair of trees nearby.

"CeCe—" McKenna's whisper carried added punch.

"You don't have a weapon. I'm not leaving you." CeCe's knuckles blanched around the handle as she stood near McKenna, her body stiff with stubborn grit.

"Go. I've got this."

CeCe didn't budge. "You don't *got this* if you're empty-handed, honey."

The hog raised its head and spotted them. It squealed, high and sharp, then charged.

"Move!" Rough shouted as he gave Naomi a final shove farther up the boulder.

McKenna stood her ground. CeCe pushed past McKenna, rearing back with her ceramic mug. As the hog closed in, she flung the cup with all her might, the red Razorback hurling head over hoof. It struck the hog on the side of the head with a *crack,* and the beast veered. CeCe tugged at McKenna's elbow as she made for the nearest tree.

Before McKenna could move, the hog wheeled on her, fixed its gaze, and snorted.

There wasn't a tree or rock within reach that she could ascend before it reached her. She took a deep breath as her muscles tightened, preparing for impact. Rough barreled toward her, walking stick in hand. He shoved her out of the way as the hog charged, sending her crashing into a tangle of blackberry bramble. Her body twisted, thorns scraping her shoulder and tearing her tank top.

Rough swung the walking stick like a baseball bat, slamming it into the hog's snout. The animal squealed and stumbled. Shaking its head, it pawed the ground and charged again.

Another swing, aimed lower, struck its shoulder. It shrieked, staggered, and turned tail, vanishing into the woods in a crashing retreat.

A long silence settled among them.

"Anybody time that?" CeCe was the first to climb down. She walked the area, scanning the ground. "Felt like the longest and quickest minute of my life."

Blainey giggled. "What are you looking for?"

CeCe stopped, propping her hands on her hips. "If you think I'm sleeping without that mug tonight, you're crazy."

They all laughed.

McKenna gathered her breath before rising, wincing as she plucked thorns from her bare shoulder. Rough stood above her, chest heaving, stick still raised as he scanned the trail ahead.

He slumped beside her. "You okay?"

She nodded, breathless. "You?"

"I'm fine. Don't do that again."

"Do what?"

"Stand there like you're invincible."

"You tackled me into a thorn bush."

Rough deadpanned. "You're welcome."

Ahead, CeCe raised a hand in the air, her prize in hand. "Told you this mug was useful for more than cocoa."

McKenna chuckled, shaking her head. "Well, hang on to it because we still have to make camp somewhere—beyond that beast's territory."

Nine

Rough sat next to McKenna, catching his breath as they leaned against a rock wall. The walking stick hung limp in his hand, streaked with mud and something he didn't care to identify. He scanned the tree line once more. No sign of the hog. All quiet.

McKenna picked at her shoulder. Her tank top was torn, and her skin was scratched. She hadn't made a sound when he barreled into her like a linebacker on fire. He studied her with a side-eyed glance, but her expression was unreadable.

She should have moved. He should have said something sooner, should have insisted.

"Why didn't you move? Find a tree, a rock, something?"

She arched an eyebrow, her half-smile defiant. "I was trying to give CeCe time to get to safety."

Her grin slipped past the barriers he kept locked tight. He nodded toward the other women. "What about the instructions you gave them?"

"Which instructions?"

"Treat it like an airline emergency. Take care of yourself first." He tapped her hand. "Turn around here." He shrugged off his backpack and pulled out a medical kit.

"What are you doing? Shouldn't we get moving?" She brushed her hair from her face. "What if it comes back?"

"It won't be eager to tangle with us again so soon." Rough cleared his throat. "Let me see."

He took a pair of tweezers from the med kit and swept her hair aside. A warm sensation rippled through him as his fingers brushed her shoulder while removing thorns. He swallowed hard, his breath shallowing. He knew he was in trouble the moment he saw her in the coffee shop.

McKenna released a shaky breath.

"I think I got them all." Rough tucked the tweezers back into the kit and grabbed an alcohol wipe. "I hate to do this, but soap and water aren't an option. Ready?"

McKenna nodded. She sucked air through her teeth as the pad moved across her scratched skin. "Well, Nash promised it would be fun."

"I'll try to pad it since we've got quite a bit of hiking to do. Wearing a pack will be uncomfortable."

"We've got her pack." Naomi pointed to a small litter. "We'll take turns dragging it."

"I wondered what you were up to over there." Rough smiled. These women were more surprising than he expected. "Where did you learn that?"

"In Uganda, we drove an old Land Cruiser. Reliable, until it wasn't. We always carried water for the radiator and prayed the tires would hold." She shrugged. "Sometimes things still went wrong, and we'd find ourselves short of supplies, miles from a service station. And in Papua New Guinea, the rainy season made it easy to get stuck in the mud. Either way, we had to get creative about moving things across long distances."

Rough helped McKenna to her feet, then took the litter from Naomi. He leaned close and whispered, "God's not done with you, Mrs. Naomi. How's the ankle?"

"I made sure to wrap it while the girls were finding branches for the litter. I think I can manage all right."

He gave her a one-armed hug before turning to McKenna. "Lead the way."

McKenna shook her head. "I'll let you. I need time to regroup."

"Everybody ready?"

Nods ran through the group.

The remaining hike was quiet. Not solemn, but bone-deep tired with a side of shellshock.

They took a break at a bluff with good elevation, tree cover, and a few decent climbing points within easy reach. Rough dropped his pack and did a sweep—no rooting, tracks, or other warning signs.

When he circled back, he gave the go-ahead to set camp. Shelters sprang up, and CeCe had string lights hung in no time. Naomi sat on a flat stone, boot off, rubbing her ankle. Jenna helped Blainey build the shelter for Naomi and Blainey before building her own. Jenna's camera bag rested on a log nearby, but she let it be.

McKenna knelt by the fire ring, stacking stones with one hand. She paused, rolling her shoulder backward and forward. Rough crossed the camp before he could think better of it and crouched beside her with the med kit.

"Let me see."

"I'm fine." She shrugged him off.

"You're favoring it." His tone gentled. "You can be fine *and* in pain, you know."

That earned him a sigh, but she didn't argue when he peeled the torn fabric aside, exposing her shoulder blade. The tiny, serrated edges were red, a thin ridge forming like a welted seam. He squirted triple antibiotic ointment on a cotton tip and swiped it across her wounds.

"That's going to sting every time you move." He grimaced. "Take some pain reliever before we set out tomorrow."

McKenna's breath caught. "You could have warned me."

"You could have climbed a tree. CeCe was trying to buy you

time. Trying to provide cover." He sighed. "For a wedding planner, she's got great instincts."

Silence. Then her soft laugh rippled between them. "Mine were a little off. I should have seen it coming," she murmured. "The hog. The bush. You, throwing yourself at me."

"I didn't—"

"You did. You threw yourself at me like some backcountry superhero."

His thumb brushed the edge of the scratched area before he caught himself and pulled back. "Next time, I'll trust you and share what I know. And you'll trust me to safeguard the team while you climb. Deal?"

McKenna nodded, exhaustion shadowing her eyes, as she leaned against him.

CeCe plunked down on a log across from them, her eyes narrowed at Rough.

He stared back. "What?"

"You didn't clue us in about the hog signs."

"I'm sorry about that. I didn't know you all well enough to know how you'd react."

"It's not all you've withheld from us." CeCe leaned in, elbows on her knees.

Rough bristled, and McKenna straightened, fixing her eyes on him.

"I think you owe us the truth." CeCe's eyes narrowed as the other women gathered close. "A name, Tumble Dry. I think we've earned it."

Rough glanced from CeCe to McKenna.

"Don't look at me." McKenna giggled, though her smile softened. "You knew she wasn't going to let it go. You *could* tell her your name."

Of course it was CeCe. If anyone were going to rip the Band-Aid off, it would be the one who held her own with bridezillas and hogs alike.

"You did well today, Glitter Girl." Rough smiled. "Calm, cool, and collected." He ran his hand through his hair.

"I guess the bridezilla experience is good training for a feral hog attack." She smirked. "So, do I get a name?"

"You've earned it, but don't laugh." Rough rubbed his forehead. He hadn't said it out loud in ages. He learned long ago it would be met with laughter or pity. "Name's Darcy."

CeCe laughed. "Darcy. Like the girl's name?"

Rough shook his head. "Like Mr. Darcy. My mother is a big fan of Jane Austen. And I was an April Fool's baby."

"Darcy, hmm?" CeCe raised her coffee cup, faint cracks branching across the glaze. "That may be a better reward than my trophy mug. Darcy. I like it. He has a solid growth arc." She rubbed her tummy. "Now, what's for dinner? And don't say bacon. I'm done with pigs for a while."

Jenna and Blainey patted Rough on the back as they walked past to search for grubs. Naomi hugged his neck before retiring to the lean-to to prop up her foot. CeCe remained.

"Hey, Glitter Girl."

"Hmm?"

"Dinner is takeout. Again. Bring it home." Rough winked.

She smiled, shaking her head as she rose to leave. "Where's my lint roller?"

Together, Rough and McKenna got the fire going, and McKenna put water on for cocoa. She made him a cup, and their fingers brushed in the handoff. This time, he lingered in the moment.

"They did well today." McKenna took a sip.

Rough placed his hand on her knee. "They followed your lead."

The green sparked in her hazel eyes. "They followed *our* lead."

"It was a little bumpy."

"But we're figuring it out."

The firelight flickered across her face, softening the angles and catching her eyes. He wasn't sure if it was the adrenaline fade or something else, but the tension in his muscles gave way to a wet noodle limpness. His head grew a little fuzzy. Was it exhaustion? Or was it her nearness?

"I prayed on the trail today."

Her words struck a chord with him, but he didn't speak.

"Not out loud. It was short. 'Lord, keep him safe.'"

The heat from the fire wasn't the only thing warming his chest. "I don't talk to God as much as I once did. But when I shoved you into that bush, I said a prayer too."

A pause. Then her hand brushed his as she held his gaze. He didn't move away.

"You're becoming part of this. You've developed a closeness with Naomi and Blainey, a playfulness with CeCe, a quiet respect with Jenna." Her fingers curled into his. "Nash said you needed this. I'm not sure what he meant, but if you're carrying something heavy, I'll sit with you a while. No pressure."

"Yeah, I appreciate the offer." Rough cleared his throat and stood. "I'd better find a crutch and some goldenrod for Naomi. She was a trooper after the hog attack, but she'll need the crutch tomorrow, and goldenrod tea might ease the swelling. Then I'll handle dinner. It's not very gentlemanly to shove a lady into a bush and leave her hungry." He glanced at his toes. "I wish I'd thought to grab some of those blackberries after relieving you of the thorns. Might have eased the indignity of the injury a touch."

He hadn't come to unpack anything, only to keep them safe. He turned away, pressing an open palm to his chest, guarding the things he didn't want to surface. Then he disappeared into the brush.

Ten

The morning light streamed in hazy rays across the fire ring. Perhaps their fire had burned longer than she realized. McKenna poured a cup of coffee and settled next to Jenna. "Where's Rough?"

"He went to make another perimeter sweep. Hypervigilant since the hog attack." Jenna pulled her blonde hair to the side, working it into a braid. "I don't blame him."

"I guarantee he was as vigilant before the hog attack. But he didn't let on." McKenna pointed to the leather-bound book next to Jenna. "Isn't that Rough's?"

"Yes. He left it and said he wouldn't be gone long." Jenna secured the braid with an elastic. "Well, I'm going to do a quick search for creepy, crawly proteins—as Rough requested."

Jenna bumped Rough's field notebook as she was leaving. It teetered, steadied for a moment, then a breeze flipped it, and it landed open on the ground. McKenna reached to secure it, but her name scrawled on the exposed page stilled her hand.

McKenna seems competent. Passionate. They trust her. That helps.

Acting as lead co-facilitator may boost rebranding efforts.

This crew is soft and easy to guide. Potential for publicity opportunity if successful.

Her breath caught in her throat. The ache in her shoulder was nothing compared to the pressure forming behind her ribs. She traced her finger farther down the page.

Not sure how I feel yet, but a win here could relaunch everything. If I can pull this off, it might be enough to convince investors I can run the business without flaming out.

Without flaming out.

She closed the journal with slow precision, as though disarming a bomb. Her heart sank. All this time, his quiet steadiness, his protectiveness, the way he watched her through the firelight, she thought she'd seen something real. Guarded, sure. But authentic. The truth landed hard. She was a stepping stone. Her retreat, her heart, her work—just leverage for his business.

She snapped the book shut at the sound of footsteps behind her.

"Everything all right?" Naomi's brow furrowed as she hobbled to the fire ring on a makeshift crutch.

"Rough's field notes took a tumble." McKenna forced a smile, raising the journal. She dusted off the leather cover before returning it to the log. Standing, she tucked her wavy hair behind her ear.

"Mm." Naomi glanced from the book to McKenna as she sat. "Does it seem hazy to you this morning?"

Hazy was an understatement. The air felt thick, warped by the truth she had just uncovered. Rough hadn't come to help her or the women. He'd come to salvage his reputation. She was only part of the campaign. Even the brush of his pinky before the hog attack—had it been real? Or simply a tactic to ensure a glowing review?

She bit her lip. Had she been a fool to believe he was beginning to see the deeper work—the emotional strength born of challenge, the grace hidden in grit? She shoved the thought away, but his words echoed like a taunt. "Sometimes after the letting-go bit, you just move on."

"You might be right." McKenna glanced around as more than her perspective became increasingly fuzzy. "I thought it was smoke from our fire, but our morning fires haven't done this before."

Rough broke through the brush from the west. "I need everyone around the circle. Now."

"Hogs?" Naomi's eyes widened.

"Wildfire."

"Don't we need to pack up and go?" McKenna's brows furrowed in concern.

"Not until we know where we're going." He cupped his hand around his mouth. "Circle up, ladies. Now!"

CeCe, Blainey, and Jenna came rushing to the fire ring.

Blainey wiped her forehead with the back of her hand. "What's wrong?"

"Wildfire from the west. Slow-moving for now. My guess is a couple of miles per hour and roughly ten or so miles out." Rough rummaged through his pack.

CeCe rushed to her lean-to and pulled down the twinkle lights. "We gotta get out of here."

"It's moving slow enough that we have time to make a quick plan, a smart plan." Rough motioned her back to the circle. "I did some research before we left and marked prescribed burn areas on my map. The fire is moving northeast. If conditions don't change, it'll take eight to ten hours to reach this location." He tapped a spot on the map. "There's a prescribed burn area to the southeast —more than a thousand acres along the south side of a creek. It's our safe point."

"Can we make it? What about Naomi's ankle?" McKenna wrapped her arm around Naomi.

"Naomi, we'll carry your pack." Rough folded the map, tucking it inside his pack. "It'll be tough going, but you all proved what you're made of yesterday. You've got grit for miles. It will help us if you can manage on your crutch."

"I can do it." Naomi offered a determined nod.

"If it gets to be too much, let me know." He scraped his stubbled jaw. "We'll make a litter if need be. Now, let's get packed and smother this fire, but don't worry about the shelters. Leave no trace is abbreviated today." Rough patted Naomi's shoulder.

The women moved on instinct, tying bedrolls, stuffing packs, smothering the fire under a pile of dirt. CeCe, Jenna, and Blainey each stowed some of Naomi's things in their packs. They were ready to go in record time.

"We redistributed Naomi's things." Jenna nodded toward CeCe and Blainey.

Blainey shrugged. "Didn't know what to do with the pack, though."

"They wouldn't let me add to my pack." McKenna shrugged.

"You and Mr. Darcy are our way out." CeCe winked at Rough. "We need you fresh and unencumbered as much as possible. And you can't tell me your shoulder doesn't bother you."

"Great." He picked up her pack. "Smart redistribution. Naomi's going to need every ounce of energy for the miles ahead." Rough winked at Naomi as he situated both packs. "Everyone ready?"

There were nods all around the group, except for McKenna.

She picked up the field notebook and pressed it hard into Rough's chest. "Don't forget your journal."

* * *

"Field notes." Rough placed a hand over the leather-bound book.

"Right." McKenna's voice was cool and tight. "Field notes, sketches, verses of Scripture. Wouldn't want to lose it."

"No. I wouldn't." Rough's brows knit together. What had

cooled between them? Had she found the letter from so long ago? Or was it something else?

"Let's get going. Lead the way."

He brushed by her, and she stepped back. The muscles in his chest tensed as he swallowed past the knot in his throat, unsure of what he had done. She shuffled to the back of the group, and he overheard her tell Jenna it was for the group's safety. Practical, but he was sure there was more to it.

He couldn't worry about it now. Their lives depended on him staying alert and focused. He took a deep breath and set a quick, steady pace. He kept glancing back to check on Naomi. Her injury slowed them some, but she was keeping pace better than he had anticipated. He caught McKenna's eye, but she glanced away.

The trail narrowed and dropped into a shallow gorge, tangled with briar. Rough slowed the pace to make it easier for Naomi to navigate. The woman had grit for days and managed the trail like a pro. He should catch a quiet moment with her to hear more about her experience as a missionary.

"Naomi, I know you're tired." Rough paused as they approached a particularly rocky section. "We can take a break. We're making good time. Really."

"I want to keep going."

"We'll help her." Blainey slid an arm around Naomi's waist. "We can help take some weight off the injured foot."

"It's a tight fit through here." Rough shook his head.

Jenna stepped forward. "We're bushwhacking. It's as wide as we make it, right?"

"Well, within the restrictions of trees and rock features."

CeCe rubbed Naomi's shoulders. "If she wants to keep going, we'll make it happen. She's not alone."

A smile graced McKenna's lips, but it disappeared when he made eye contact. He couldn't figure her out. Everything had shifted this morning. Had he missed something?

"Okay, a little water for everyone before moving on." He wiped his brow.

By midday, the sky had dimmed to a dull pewter. Smoke from the west crawled across the sun like a curtain drawing shut, and Rough halted them at the edge of a bluff. Sweat trailed down his back.

"This is the fastest way down."

CeCe peered over the edge and whistled low. "Fastest or scariest?"

"Both." He uncoiled the rope from his pack. He motioned to McKenna. "I'll need your rope too. We'll get at least one Bear Grylls-style adventure element like you were hoping." He began to rig the gear. "It's about thirty feet. I'll take Naomi down first. She can't brace a descent alone. Then I'll ferry the gear up for the next descent. I hope you packed gloves." He winked at CeCe. "They were on the list."

"Whatever is needed, it's in here." She patted her pack and smiled. "I'm not letting you make gloves for me outta duct tape."

He chuckled. "McKenna, can you instruct them in descent?"

"Of course I can."

"I've rigged two lines for rappel and a thinner rope to send the harnesses back since we only have two." He helped Naomi get geared up. "I'm thinking Jenna and Blainey go together, and you and CeCe. What do you think?"

"Sound pairings." McKenna nodded.

"All right, Naomi. You ready?"

She nodded, and McKenna caught her arm. "I'll be praying for you."

"Oh, I'll be praying too." Naomi smiled.

As Rough edged over the bluff with Naomi, McKenna instructed Jenna and Blainey. Her eyes didn't meet his, and it unsettled him more than the fire.

Once he and Naomi were down, he coached the others as they descended. He kept his eyes on the bluff as the last pair descended. CeCe's boots hit the ground a beat before McKenna's, and CeCe gave a celebratory whoop as he steadied her.

"You all right?"

"Never been better," CeCe said, breathless. "If I ever get over my fear of dating and find a decent guy to marry, that's how I want to do the grand exit at my wedding."

"Why do you have a fear of dating?" Rough glanced at McKenna before returning his attention to CeCe.

"Wedding planner, man." CeCe shrugged. "I know twenty percent of marriages don't make it past year five. Fear of dating. It's easier to put up walls. But if I conquered that wall"—she hitched her thumb toward the bluff—"maybe I can bring down my relationship walls."

Rough half smiled and cleared his throat, turning away from the bluff. "Well, we have more ground to cover. This way."

The gentle babble of water grew louder as they followed a sloped path through thickening brush. When they reached the creek, Rough dropped both packs and scanned the far bank. Charred stumps and blackened scraggle painted the landscape across the water, a harsh contrast to the dense foliage they had pushed through.

"This is it." Rough bent over, hands on his knees. "The creek is a natural fire break, and the prescribed burn is our haven."

Jenna dipped her hand into the water. "What are we waiting for?"

Blainey was the first to shed her boots. She, Jenna, and CeCe crossed with Rough while McKenna and Naomi waited on the bank. The trio sloughed off their packs and returned to help. CeCe, Blainey, and Jenna assisted Naomi. When Rough offered his hand to McKenna, she hesitated but took it. Her grip was light. Distant.

Once across, they collapsed beneath a stand of skeletal trees.

"Rest for thirty. You've earned it." Rough wiped his forearm across his forehead. "Then we find higher ground to make camp. We're safe here. For now."

As he eased down beside Naomi, he caught McKenna watching him. Her expression was unreadable. And the blaze behind them felt easier to face than whatever smoldered between them.

Eleven

The creek water had been cold, chilling McKenna's toes, but it was nothing compared to this new distance between her and Rough. She dipped her water bottle into the stream and filled a spare collapsible bottle. Rough had circled the group, checking the expiration dates on everyone's filters before he would allow them to drink. He instructed anyone who had a spare to fill it in case the wind shifted, and they couldn't hike out tomorrow as planned.

McKenna splashed her face and neck, then dried off with a bandana. She had never felt so gritty. Perhaps ash from the wildfire was drifting in and settling on their skin. Was dragging these women into the wilderness the dumbest idea she had ever had? She splashed her face again and let the water drizzle down her neck—sweet relief from the heat.

Smudges of soot painted stump and stone, but moss and grasses were making a comeback. Wildflowers had room to grow. It wasn't as desolate as she first thought. She glanced at Rough. He was holding Naomi's hand and pointing, likely talking her through the next leg of their hike to safety. Could it be this was about more than business? How could she be sure?

"You okay?" CeCe flopped onto a log near the water.

"Because you don't seem yourself, and I'm about three marshmallows away from an emotional meltdown."

"I'll be fine. It's nothing I can't handle." McKenna patted her hand.

"I mean it." CeCe wrapped her arms around herself. "I'm this close to sobbing in my granola, and you're our emotional compass right now. No pressure."

McKenna smiled. "First, cry if you need to. Second, dig deep because you're stronger than you know."

"So we're resting here before moving higher?" Jenna stood, wiping her hands on her pants. She glanced at her watch. "I thought you said thirty minutes. Shouldn't we be going?"

"Take a breath, Jenna." Rough walked over, placing his hand on her shoulder. "Everyone needs a little extra time to catch their breath. How about McKenna and I find something to eat? We'll have a picnic by the creek and recharge. Fair?"

Jenna shrugged. "You're sure we've got time?"

"You know I'd change the plan if I thought we were in danger." He squeezed her shoulder. "I'm not keeping anything from you. We all have to work together to get through this, and you need all the information to do that. We'll be right back."

Rough motioned for McKenna to join him. They walked a few yards away, scanning the ground for anything edible. Rough knelt to pull up a dandelion by its roots.

"They're holding up well." He handed the plant to McKenna. "But they're showing signs of strain."

"Can you blame them?" She plucked the roots from the plant and dropped the leafy stem to the ground. "They fought off a hog and ran from a fire in less than twenty-four hours."

"I think that's only part of it."

"Oh?" She uprooted another dandelion.

"Something has shifted between us, and they sense it." He handed her a few more small plants. "And whatever it is, we need to work it out—before the next climb."

"Your field notebook fell open this morning, and I caught a

glimpse of your business plan." She locked eyes with him. "We were a tool to repair your image. *I* was a tool to fix what you had broken."

He blew out a long breath of air as he pushed his hand through his hair. "I'll admit I came into this trying to salvage my business. Nash knew I needed a successful trek to prove I'm not all bark and no grounding."

"So this"—McKenna waved her hands in a circle—"is a means to an end for you."

His voice rasped. "I didn't come into this without baggage."

"You're rebuilding. I get that." She folded her arms and toed the dirt.

"But I wasn't honest with you." He glanced toward the others. "You deserved that, and I didn't give it."

She stayed quiet.

He shifted, lacing his fingers behind his head. "I never expected you. I planned for a press release and a few testimonials. Not someone who knew what she was doing out here. Not someone who reminded me why this mattered in the first place."

Her throat tightened. "I'm still angry."

"I know."

"But I'm not walking away."

He faced her. "You're not."

"You showed up for them. For Naomi. For me. The hog, the bluff, the creek."

His shoulders loosened. "McKenna, why do you do this? And why here?"

"We get stuck sometimes. When we're working things out, we get stuck." She turned in a circle, her eyes tracing every shadow and sway of the wilderness. "We can't predict every moment in the wilderness. Stay out here long enough, and it will catch us off guard. And while our outer defenses are rising, our internal defenses are lowering. We can't manage both." Her gaze settled on him. "It creates room. Room to let others in. Room to let God in. That's why we're here."

She sat on a large stone at the edge of the creek. Scooting over, she patted the space next to her, and Rough sat beside her.

McKenna took a deep breath. "In high school, my defenses were so high that I missed the opportunity to let someone in. I was so worried that I wouldn't be accepted, I didn't speak to one young man at my lunch table. I ate lunch with him every day for nine months and never spoke to him."

"I'm sure that's common in high schools everywhere." Rough eyed her.

"One day, I showed up at the table and he didn't. He had taken his life the night before." She closed her eyes, listening to the water roll over the stones in the creek bed. "I don't know if things would have been different if I had let my defenses down and made room for him. But I can't go back." She cleared her throat. "So I do this. I make room for people. I help them make room for themselves."

They sat in silence a long while.

"Is there still room for me?" Rough curled his fingers around hers.

He pushed her. Cracked her open. Held space for what broke loose. From the moment they set foot on the trail together, he had challenged her in every way. But hadn't he also sustained her?

She slid her fingers from his and stood, walking to a nearby outcropping. Leaning against it, she ran her hand over the soft moss clinging to the rugged stone. Vibrant green, rich, earthy, full of life. Her fingers threaded through it, the moisture cooling them.

She closed her eyes. This was the way of it. Nature stripped everything else away. It was hard, wild, no respecter of persons. Then, when everything was laid bare, it offered up its gentle quiet, its soft embrace, its cool balm.

What kind of grace grows where nothing should?

She glanced at him washing his hands in the stream. Her heart softened.

She pursed her lips. "It's not fixed. But it's not broken beyond repair either."

"Good." He rubbed his hands together. "Because I don't want to lose the one real thing I didn't come looking for."

"Ditch the PR spin. I need *you*." She stepped toward him and squeezed his hand. "Life isn't a mission. It's a journey. And it's better when you let others join you. Got it?"

"Yes, ma'am." He grinned. "Mission aborted."

He stood and offered his hand, but screams pierced the air. They both took off running back to the group.

"Get it away from me!" CeCe was jumping and flailing her arms at Jenna, who was chasing CeCe with a wriggling button-up shirt.

"What's going on here?" Rough's eyes darted from one to the other.

Jenna turned, a broad grin on her face. "I used my shirt to make a net. I was playing around with the idea, but look."

Rough and McKenna leaned in as Jenna eased back the edges of the shirt, the damp fabric clinging before giving way to a glint of shimmering scales.

"A pair of sunfish—quite the payoff after such a hard day's work." Rough's blue eyes sparkled. "It'll spread thin, but everyone who makes it to camp gets a bite for dinner."

McKenna patted her on the back. "Welcome to the world on the other side of the camera, Jenna."

Twelve

T he last leg of the climb had scraped the bottom of their emotional reserves. The haze thickened around them as the wildfire moved across the terrain. The ridge they had descended that morning stood between them and the encroaching flames. If the wind didn't shift, it would move northeast, and they could continue south to their vehicles tomorrow morning.

Rough moved around the makeshift camp in silence, checking shelters, watching the sky, biding his time. Or dodging the truth.

His feelings for McKenna had taken a deeper hold than he imagined. He was surprised to discover he was holding his breath as he awaited her response when he asked her if there was still room for him. His eyes scanned the sky as the sun drooped toward the horizon, laying a gold-washed hush over everything.

Naomi rested near the fire ring with her ankle propped on a pack. Blainey sat nearby, her knees tucked to her chest, drawing with a stick in the dirt. CeCe was in her lean-to, rummaging through her backpack as Jenna cooked the prized sunfish.

McKenna walked over to offer Rough a handful of granola and a cup of cocoa. "A reminder of the blessings?"

"There's a lot to be thankful for, and I am." He inhaled the sweet aroma and sighed. "But there's a loss I can't shake."

"Is it the reason you do this?"

He stared into his mug, letting the silence settle between them like ash. He sat on a log at the edge of camp. McKenna joined him, brushing dirt from her pants as she sat.

"I'm here to listen." She tilted her head. "I know about the business plan, but it's not your why. Not really."

Rough stared into the distance. "Her name was Lacey. Young, sharp. Had a laugh clear as a bell. Said I reminded her of her brother. We were gathering intel, interviewing people in a small village. Different culture, different rules." He turned the mug in circles. "They wouldn't allow us to interview the women, only Lacey. She agreed to talk to them alone."

McKenna didn't say anything.

"I had a bad feeling. I knew something was off." Rough pressed his eyes shut. "There was an attack on the village, and I couldn't get to her. None of us could."

McKenna reached for his hand. He let her take it.

"When I returned stateside, I spent every moment I could in the wilderness. Limited contact with people." He sipped the cocoa, welcoming the comfort. "I had to earn a living, though. Oddly enough, the safety measures and survival techniques provided a framework of boundaries that allowed me to maintain a comfortable emotional distance from people. Couldn't fail anyone if I never got close again. And it worked—mostly."

"What put your business in trouble?"

"A client with too much money and not enough sense." Rough shrugged. "Guy was arrogant. Didn't follow protocols with food. Couldn't take a tackle as well as you." One corner of his mouth lifted. "Only once did I struggle to keep my barriers up behind all the survival tactics out here."

"Oh, yeah? When was that?"

"When an old military buddy asked me to help his little sister."

McKenna's cheeks pinked, and she stood, gazing skyward. "You didn't even like me at first."

"That's what I told myself."

A pause stretched between them. A breeze drifted through, as if exhaling for them both.

"I saw someone strong, capable, and stubborn. I told myself I was annoyed, but really, I was ... interrupted." He slipped his hand into hers.

McKenna looked down at their joined hands. "And now?"

"I realize I needed the interruption."

"Needed it?" She smiled as though she was on to something. "What is it?"

"Nash said you needed this. Not *needed*, but—" She wobbled her head to and fro. "Needed it."

"It feels like I've got all the time in the world to be here." He wrapped his arms around her waist. "And I'm not sure I want to go back to the way it was before."

She lifted her eyes to meet his. "Neither do I."

His heartbeat drummed, but his movements slowed. There was no rush as he closed the space between them, giving her time to back away. But she didn't. Her lips met his with a soft energy that reminded him of the first crackle of fire in the dark. Gentle, real, growing.

They parted like embers cooling in the night air, and she rested her head against his chest. "Thank you for telling me about Lacey."

A throat cleared nearby, and they both whirled to see CeCe with one eyebrow raised, holding a camp mug. "If you're done making up, Jenna's about to serve up fish flakes and optimism."

McKenna grinned and bumped her shoulder against Rough's. "Come on. Let's go celebrate the world's tiniest dinner."

They joined the others around the fire ring. Jenna served up a bite-sized meal of fish topped with a micro salad. Warmth spread through Rough's chest as he looked around the circle, making eye contact with each woman. This meal made him feel more blessed than any he had ever eaten.

He left the fire ring and returned with his field notebook.

McKenna raised an eyebrow. "What's this about?"

"Aren't you going to ask one of your annoyingly honest questions?" Rough winked.

"All right." She rubbed her hands together. "When you go home tomorrow, what is one thing you will leave in the wilderness? And what one thing will you carry home?"

CeCe left the circle.

"CeCe?" McKenna watched her. "What are you doing?"

"Getting my journal. I got this." She shook her finger in the air. "Leaving creepy, crawly dinners. Taking my Razorback mug and lint roller. Boom."

Thirteen

"Fire's holding a northeast path." Rough scanned the sky. "We're fine to hike out this morning. Our vehicles are well south of it. Everyone ready?"

A few grateful cheers followed.

They moved in a loose, straggling line as the morning sun painted everything in a hopeful light. The weight on their backs hadn't changed, but they carried it easier now. Something inside them had shifted.

The trail was steep in places, but the air grew sweeter with every mile. Smoky haze gave way to the sharp, resinous scent of pine, and they all breathed a little easier. Rough knew it wouldn't be long before the chatter kicked in.

"Naomi, are you sure you don't want a piggyback ride?" CeCe wiped her brow.

"I'm doing okay. Really." Naomi picked her way down the trail, testing each step with her makeshift crutch before committing her weight.

"Could you give me one?" Mischief sparked in CeCe's eyes, and everyone laughed. She wagged her finger. "If I ever agree to another retreat with six-legged food on the menu, someone stage an intervention. Tie me to a chair. Bribe me with carbs. Whatever it takes."

"You wanted a getaway off-grid where socialite brides-to-be couldn't find you." McKenna teased from a few paces ahead. "And you wanted to feel something again. Did you accomplish either goal on this trip?"

"Right, right. I said *feel*, not eat a worm or fall off a cliff." CeCe adjusted her pack and rolled her eyes. "I'm starting to think there might be a better route to feeling something. There's this guy at church I've been brushing off. Plays guitar and volunteers with the youth group. I wonder if he'd answer if I string two tin cans together. You know, go old school."

Jenna chuckled. "There's a healthy perspective."

"I've let fear drive my decisions far too long. If this week has taught me anything, it's that I'd rather be awkward than empty."

Naomi patted her crutch. "Rough got me thinking about God not being done with me."

Rough tilted his head at the mention of his name but kept quiet.

"I thought my years of serving were over when my Daniel passed. But I've had a little break now." She exhaled. "And I'm ready for more."

McKenna nodded, her eyes glistening.

Naomi continued, her voice stronger. "This weekend, we all stepped in when someone needed something, whether it was a physical or emotional need. I started thinking. I should try showing up where people are hurting. Women's shelters, hospital ministries, that sort of thing."

Rough glanced at McKenna, a lightness settling in his chest.

"I don't want to be behind the camera shooting footage of people's worst days anymore." Jenna opened a protein bar and offered Blainey half. "I want to tell stories of hope. It's time I documented new beginnings instead of devastation. I could offer photo shoots for new and expectant mothers. And I want a life away from the camera. This friend of mine has been after me to try something new—pickleball, of all things."

"You'd look fantastic in a visor." CeCe wiggled her eyebrows.

"I might try it."

They paused for a water and snack break, finding a spot for Naomi to rest. Naomi and McKenna sat together on a log. Jenna and CeCe propped themselves against a tree.

Rough settled beside Blainey on a boulder. "You've been quiet. Thinking about anything in particular?"

She didn't answer at first. Then, in her quiet way, she said, "I've been thinking a lot about my brother."

"Mm. Is this the brother I remind you of?"

"Yeah, he's two years older than me."

Rough gave her time. She bit the inside of her lip, probably searching for words.

"I was driving. He was reaching for a CD—so into retro things like that." A ghost of a smile crossed her countenance. "We were arguing about what song to play. I glanced away from the road for a second. Didn't see the deer until it was too late."

Rough propped a foot on the boulder, wrapping his arm around his knee. "You loved him."

"With everything I had. And I lost him because I was trying to win an argument." Blainey wiped a tear from her cheek.

"You didn't lose him because of an argument." Rough rubbed her back. "You lost him because life is fragile and very often beyond our control. But you're honoring his life by choosing to live yours."

"You think so?"

"Didn't you do some things these last few days that he would have done? Things you would have done together?"

"He would have loved this."

"Keep doing things you both enjoy and remember him."

"Could I come on another trek with you?" Blainey shrugged.

Rough stood and helped her up. He couldn't help Lacey, but he *could* sit with Blainey. "I'd like that."

They got back on the trail, and Rough fell in beside McKenna. They hiked in silence for a while. McKenna gave him a sidelong glance.

"So, what now? You go back to your business, and I go back to mine?" She shrugged. "We wave awkwardly across the coffee shop?"

"I was hoping for something a little less awkward. Something more—together?"

McKenna raised a brow. "Professionally? Or personally?"

"Both." He stopped walking. "We can build something new. Together. A new kind of adventure therapy where people can survive and cry. You bring the heart, and I bring the firewood."

"Ideas for a name?"

"You heard it. Survive & Cry."

"You cannot be serious." She bumped him with her shoulder, sending him off the trail for a step.

"Why not? It's honest." His lips curved into a slow grin. "Didn't you say you wanted honesty?"

"Not that kind of honesty. That name is emotional sabotage."

"Oh, come on. It's memorable."

"It's a train wreck with branding issues." She crossed her arms. "Try again."

He chuckled. "Fine. What's your pitch?"

"Resilient Retreats."

He whistled low. "It's got a little grit. A little grace too."

She smiled. "Like us."

"Sounds like something worth building."

Fourteen

~~~

cKenna glanced at the door when the electric chime
sounded for the fifth time in ten minutes. It had
been a week since she had ventured into the
unknown with four women, stuck yet curious, and a guide she
barely knew whose emotional range rivaled a Swiss Army Knife.
She was grateful to be back in her brother's coffee shop, enveloped
by the comforting aroma of espresso and lavender.

CeCe waved from across the room.

"I know you're not trekking mud across that floor again."
Nash grinned from behind the counter. "I swept for the third
time today."

"You mean you scooted dirt out the door with your foot?"
CeCe picked a pine needle from her hair as she made a beeline for
the couch along the far wall. "Where's my mug? The one with the
Razorback." She leaned over to McKenna. "It's my home-away-
from-home mug."

"It's in the dishwasher." Boone Whitaker stepped from the
back with a rag tossed over his shoulder. "And when it comes out,
remember it's not your backup weapon."

"I thought I saw a bug."

271

"It was a couple of chocolate-covered espresso beans you dropped." Nash's face pinched.

"Anyone besides me drinking black coffee?" Rough emerged from the back with a carafe. He stopped when he spotted CeCe. "They all came."

He sat in the couch corner next to McKenna and placed the carafe on the coffee table.

McKenna leaned close, grinning from ear to ear, and whispered, "They all came." Her gaze drifted from one woman to the next. "How have you all been?"

Naomi sat in a roomy chair across from them, a journal resting in her lap and a pen ready. "I'm happy my ankle is doing better. I'll be getting a lot of steps soon. I signed up for training with a hospital chaplaincy team."

"That sounds perfect for you." McKenna sipped her latte.

At the counter, Jenna held up her phone. "Guess who booked a newborn shoot for next week? It's a fresh start for me, putting hope in a frame."

"What about that visor?" CeCe called.

"I tried it on in the mirror. It was not a flattering look." Jenna flicked her braid. "But my first pickleball match is Saturday."

Boone wandered over with a caramel latte in a Razorback mug. He handed it to CeCe, then turned to Rough and McKenna. "Tell 'em about you two. Tell 'em what's next."

Rough glanced at McKenna. She raised her brow, daring him to say it.

"Are you referring to Survive & Cry?"

She elbowed him. "Resilient Retreats."

He laughed. "We've already started filling the Resilient Retreats calendar. Gonna be a little wild, a little heartfelt. We'll keep the menu light—only six legs, no centipedes."

CeCe rolled her eyes. "Have him put that in writing."

"Also, we're hiring Boone as our first assistant guide."

Boone smiled through his bushy beard. "I'm a pro at emotional icebreakers."

Nash dragged up a chair. "And if he's ever attacked by a bird in the dumpster, I know a guy."

McKenna grabbed Boone's towel, wadded it, and threw it at Nash. "No more *I know a guy.*"

Laughter filled the air, warm and full.

Blainey sat near the window, sketching something on a napkin. McKenna scooted closer. "What are you working on?"

"A logo." She turned the napkin so McKenna could see it. The drawing was rough, featuring two groups of pine trees arching over a winding trail.

McKenna rubbed the napkin with her thumb. "It's beautiful."

"Look closer." Blainey smiled.

"There's a couple in the distance holding hands."

Blainey shrugged. "It's not perfect."

"Neither are we." McKenna squeezed Rough's hand. "But look what we've started."

Rough looked over her shoulder at the napkin. "I've said it before, and I'll say it again. Looks like something worth building."

McKenna leaned in to kiss him. "And to think, it all started with a little bit of grace and grit."

About Tonya B. Ashley

Tonya B. Ashley writes stories of resilience wrapped in adventure, blending heart-deep faith with a quirky compass for navigating life's shadows. Her characters often face hard places with a little too much baggage and just enough courage to try again. When she's not writing, Tonya can be found hiking and exploring nature with family and friends, creating faith-infused junk journals, or experimenting with latte flavor combos that probably shouldn't work—but somehow do.

Anchor in a Whirlwind

Jenny Carlisle

Scrivenings
PRESS
Quench your thirst for story.
www.ScriveningsPress.com

For Jon and Gina

One

Tara's toe butted the edge of a cobblestone, and she created a new ballet move to save face. A recent shower made the pavement slick. Staying upright was a challenge. She didn't want to smash into the ground on her first day in Savannah. Cobblestones? This city took the preservation of its historic riverfront quite seriously.

Many of the businesses showed twenty-first-century improvements, but the brick structures and even the narrow streets were stuck somewhere before the Civil War. Back home in Arkansas, dirt roads progressed to gravel and then blacktop long before her generation was born. That must be the difference between towns founded in the eighteenth century as opposed to the nineteenth or twentieth.

Fat drops of rain pelted her face as she ducked under a protective awning. A painted signboard announced the River Street Marketplace. Inside, under the metal roof, her eyes adjusted to the dimness. Booths filled with homemade crafts, honey, jellies, and imported touristy items lined a narrow concrete walkway.

Gusty wind rattled the metal roof and freed a whirling cyclone of postcards and brochures from the table in front of her. Tara bent to collect pieces of paper from the wet concrete. A loud clap echoed as a wooden shutter on the outside of the structure slammed behind her. Tara dropped the postcards, her hands searching for anything nearby to grab as a bump from behind forced all her weight to her toes. Gentle pressure from an arm across her stomach kept her from losing her balance.

"What? Who?" Years of sitting in church pews kept any rougher words from popping from her mouth.

She straightened and turned. The strong arm continued to hold her against a wet jacket. She raised her eyes to focus on a rugged face with a black eye patch above a neatly trimmed red mustache and beard.

"Cap'n Mike to the rescue." The lady behind the T-shirt table applauded.

A twinkle in his eye accompanied his smile.

She forced her gaze away, his breath warming her forehead.

"My apologies, madam. Cap'n Mike at your service." He released his hold and stepped back far enough to execute an elaborate bow. "'Tis my hope you won't hold my clumsiness against me. The grand lady, Georgia Queen, and I would be honored to show you the sights of Savannah from the river's point of view while you're visitin'."

Tara wobbled a bit after he released her. She would have been okay with him holding her a moment longer. Still focused on his face, her mind erupted with questions. What kind of boat did he captain? Why an Irish accent in Georgia? She must admit that he resembled an overgrown leprechaun. An Irishman wasn't what she expected in Savannah, but she assumed no one would be fully prepared to meet this particular personality. Did other riverboat captains run around in jogging shorts and tennis shoes?

"Honored to meet you, Cap'n. I'm Tara. How do you know I'm a visitor?"

"Ah, I know me local neighbors as well as I know the showers that show up each afternoon in the summer. Battening down the market's shutters as needed is part of me daily exercise."

The lady behind the table handed him a steaming mug of coffee.

"Mayhap I might buy you a coffee?" His accent drooped a little. Could there be a real person under the bravado after all?

"No, thank you. But I do need to purchase an umbrella." Tara reached inside her soaked canvas bag for her billfold.

"Please, allow me." Cap'n Mike rummaged through a tall bucket next to him, selecting a blue model with a subtle ruffle around the edges. "Ms. Collier, please add this to my tab."

Tara took the umbrella from him as he backed away, bowing at the waist again. When he bolted back into the rain, her smile burst into a full-on guffaw.

* * *

Micah fastened the last button on his navy-blue captain's coat, perusing his appearance in the mirror in the first deck restroom. Stepping back out to the deck, gentle pressure on his leg reminded him of the sedate collie beside him.

"Ready, Nikki? Time for your transformation into Silver the Pirate Dog." He slipped an eye patch over her silken ear, pulling it into position. She tolerated more nonsense from him than any normal house pet.

Nikki was a magnet for college girls when he'd lived in an apartment a few blocks off campus. She'd accompanied him to class because everyone assumed she was some sort of guide dog. He'd never corrected the misconception. His lone functioning eye served him well for everything, including driving. His dog wasn't necessary for his success, but he couldn't imagine doing life without her.

"Carlos, me lad." Micah turned Nikki's leash over to a young man enjoying a break before his deckhand duties started. "Please allow Silver the Pirate Dog to remain with you while the Georgia Queen and I make ready to sail."

"Aye, aye, Cap'n." Carlos clicked his heels to accompany his salute.

Micah moved the chain blocking the "Staff Only" stairway and refastened it, then took the stairs to the pilot house two at a time. He paused to catch his breath before opening the gleaming white door. Daily runs were helping, but he might need to add some weight-bearing exercises somewhere in his crazy schedule.

"Evening, Cap'n." The ship's pilot stood at the wheel, checking the computer screen. "The rain clouds have moved on. We should enjoy a colorful sunset on our way back to dock."

"Give the people what they want, right?" Micah didn't bother with the accent. Jim's expertise enabled the boat to move. Travelogues and safety announcements were Micah's contribution to this job, and that suited him. Customer reviews complimented his attempts at humor, which didn't make him sad.

"Silver the Pirate Dog reporting for duty, Cap'n Mike." Carlos opened the door as the collie entered and took her accustomed spot under the ship's wheel to his right.

The long climb sent Nikki straight to her plush cushion. She'd rest and be ready for their customary stroll around the decks. Another highlight mentioned on the comment cards.

The iconic Savannah bridge formed the perfect backdrop for sunset photos as they came about and headed home. Monitors showed passengers standing near the rails and around the tables on the second deck. Too bad the blonde from the market wasn't among them. That flowery scent of hers would add the perfect ambiance for a sunset cruise. What? Could he quite literally be losing his mind?

"Welcome aboard the Georgia Queen." He held the microphone and nodded at Jim to begin the launching procedure. "I'm Cap'n Mike O'Flaherty, and 'tis my pleasure to show you a unique view of our beautiful Hostess City, Savannah, Georgia, USA."

* * *

"Our news this Sunday night is not all happy." The man on the television screen began his report as Tara enjoyed shrimp and grits inside a bar on the historic main street.

"This morning, as the sun rose in Savannah, police discovered a body in the park, the victim of an apparent gunshot wound." The anchor examined his notes. "The same park where police broke up a violent fight early Saturday morning."

Tara glanced around for reactions from the bar's patrons. Quiet conversation was punctuated by a few shouts while a football game played on another screen.

"We'll be live at the mayor's press conference addressing this tragedy tomorrow. Now, Chuck, what does the weather look like for Savannah's upcoming work week?"

"Can I get you anything else?" The bartender wiped the beer tap with a clean white rag. "Something stronger than tea?"

"No, no thanks." Tara waved him off.

Back home, a murder victim in the park would have consumed every report for several days. Until now, her most exciting interviews had featured the winner of a championship buckle at the rodeo or the coach of a small-fry soccer team. In a few days, she could be saying, "We move on from a murder investigation to the weather for the week." What a strange new world.

With one more glance at the river's flickering lights, she pulled her car away from the curb and began the dark drive to Tybee Island. The historic old streets were less than welcoming tonight. Hopefully, working in the city would allow more visits to the riverfront. Next time, she might bring her furry companion, who probably slept in her crate after their long journey. They might even run into the fascinating riverboat captain again. Whether it had been that hokey Irish accent or the way his only uncovered eye captured her gaze, something kept her hoping for more than an accidental encounter.

Her GPS guided her toward the comfort of Nina's house on the beach. Would this place feel like home soon?

Two

Tara released the squirming Corgi from her leash as they blazed a trail several yards away from the edge of the water. Jeannie bounded away, but soon slowed, testing the unfamiliar sandy footing.

Please, Lord, don't let her get lost out here.

Four tiny legs churned, and the dog picked up speed, stopping often to turn toward her mistress.

"Don't go too far." Moonlight cloaked Tara in comforting safety. The beach behind Nina's house hadn't changed in the years she'd been away. As a teenager, the lapping water's edge provided refuge from the hustle and bustle of a summer vacation. Mom and Nina watched with their coffee mugs from the deck. Her brother stayed inside, testing the local television reception to watch one of his favorite shows.

Back then, she'd been content to walk from one house's vapor-light ring to the next. The long, flat beach contained no visible dangers. No one waited on Nina's back deck tonight, the place where she'd been supervised during her childhood jaunts. Nina's friend Fannie still lived nearby in her modest home on the paved business strip.

"Jeannie, come!" The sea breeze caught her words, muffling

any urgency in her voice. The dog's pointed ears perked up. She changed direction, heading back toward Tara with typical excitement. Warnings about pets adjusting to new places did not apply here.

"Let's go home, girl." She fastened the leash on Jeannie's collar and trudged through the sand, the light in Nina's kitchen window guiding her. The wind sprayed her hair with a salty mist. Even at summer's end, the temperature didn't drop much at night, the oppressive humidity remaining from the daytime. She passed an Adirondack chair and fought the temptation to sit and allow the waves to lull her to sleep. Ridiculous. Tomorrow was her first day at a new job. Time to act like an adult.

Jeannie strained against the leash as they trotted across the timber walkover bridging a dune. Tara paused at the top of the structure to scan the property. A gust of wind disrupted her balance, and she used her free hand to steady herself. From here, she could see the back of a house on stilts that must be directly across from Fannie's home. How long would it take to lose this feeling of loneliness? She'd lived on her own in Arkansas and could certainly do the same in Nina's house.

"No use waiting until I'm gone." Nina's announcement of her generous gift still surprised Tara. "You always loved this place more than anyone else. I trust you will still welcome family when they want to visit?"

She'd be happy to host anyone who wanted to venture to the coast from the Arkansas mountains. Once she'd imagined this as a honeymoon spot. She shook her head to dispel the image of the handsome congressional candidate. Clay probably wouldn't show any interest in staying here. Much too tame for the exalted image he had of their future together. His image, not hers.

Jeannie barked from the last wooden plank on the walkover. Time to get settled in. No more vacation memories or romantic dreams. Time to make Nina's house her home.

* * *

Micah locked the front door and jogged down two flights of stairs to the roadway. Across the street, Fannie's wind machines reflected a glimmer of sunrise as they spun merrily in the breeze. A couple of quick steps later, a high-pitched bark startled him. Tiny legs churned along the fence line, matching Micah's pace as he jogged to the corner, each step punctuated by cheerful celebration. Like a miniature version of his Nikki, this pup was not aggressive, just happy to have someone to run with. Had Fannie added a new pet to her family? Undoubtedly, he would hear from his friend soon. Meanwhile, the barking subsided as he left the fenced yard behind.

He waved as he passed store owners performing their morning routines. T-shirt shops, museums, and cafes would soon welcome tourists. Locals passed in their cars, in no hurry to leave the quaint island for the city's hustle and bustle. A deep breath helped keep him centered as he left the busy "strip" for a side street, and the scenery transitioned from village to swamp.

Heading back toward the beach, he met a front license plate sporting a Razorback Hog. The red sports car it was attached to made a good fit for his eclectic hometown. A vaguely familiar blonde with oversized sunglasses smiled pleasantly from the driver's seat. Could this be the umbrella lady commuting to her new job from the island?

Yapping from the short version of Nikki accompanied him all the way down Fannie's fencerow again.

"It's okay, Jeannie." Fannie stood at her gate, scratching the wiggling dog's pointed ears.

"New pup?" Micah stopped next to her, jogging in place instead of stopping completely.

"Not mine. She belongs to our new-old neighbor. I'm running a doggie daycare while she works." The dog resumed yipping, her tiny legs churning back to the corner of the yard.

"She is determined to protect your yard." He laughed.

"I think she's trying to keep my wind machines under

control." Fannie waved as the dog attempted to catch the whirling colors above her head.

"So, is this a new neighbor or an old one? You're confusing me." Could there be a connection to the blonde at the wheel of the Hog-mobile?

"She's my friend Brenda's granddaughter. She spent summers here back in the day. Don't tell her brother or her cousins, but Tara was always my favorite." Fannie managed a quick scratch between the pointed ears as the Corgi ran past.

"I'll bring Nikki to visit before we head to the city." Micah turned toward his stairway. "Maybe that will help Miss Yip-Yap feel a little more at home."

"We're getting used to each other. Give her some time." Fannie picked up a stray paper cup from the street. "See ya later, Mikey."

He pushed the front door open at the top of his stairs. Nikki stood inside, her massive tail waving like the flag on the bow of the Georgia Queen.

"Mornin', glory." Micah rubbed both sides of the collie's neck with his hands. What a contrast with the bundle of energy in Fannie's front yard. Even when he and Nikki were young in college together, her movements exuded grace. None of the frantic action of the lively Corgi. The two dogs shared herding instincts, but their methods were much different, even considering the difference in their ages. If these two became friends, they might balance each other.

Nikki walked closer and nestled beside him on the tile floor underneath the breakfast table. He opened his tablet for the online version of the daily newspaper. More crime in the historic downtown area and alerts about a new tropical storm brewing in the Atlantic—this one christened Sally. Most years, the storm season didn't last long enough to reach names starting with *S*.

Other parts of the South would be wary of the slow and steady progress of this storm. Savannah banked on its unofficial nickname, Dodge City, and hoped for only refreshing rain.

"I'll jump in the shower and pack what we need for the evening. We'll go visit Miss Fannie before we head to town, okay?"

Nikki turned her head to watch as he walked toward the bedroom and bathroom. He slowed as he passed a canvas photo of Nikki surveying the beach, her silky hair rippling in the sea breeze. Brooke had presented him with this gift days before she left Savannah. The photo he'd taken of her that same day revealed a faraway look in her eyes.

Had she already applied for the job in New York City? Already given her notice at KSAV? Already arranged to move in with her new boyfriend in his high-rise apartment? At least Micah had never consented to her living here. No need to multiply the heartbreak of her leaving.

Bitterness filled his throat as he peeled off sweaty clothes on the way to the shower. Too much hot sauce in his eggs this morning? He turned on the water, filling the room with steam. The bad taste in his mouth that accompanied memories of Brooke did not depend on anything he'd eaten.

The yipping at Fannie's house carried through his bedroom window. How did the British royals put up with these short-legged furballs? The Corgi did have some charm. Her excited barking threatened no one. Fannie's little guest would calm down in time.

After finishing his shower and getting dressed, he followed Nikki across the artificial turf beneath his deck.

"Come on, missy. Let's go meet our new neighbor."

The Corgi's body quivered in anticipation of Nikki's regal approach.

"Here, let me open the gate." Fannie emerged from her ground-level front door.

"No, let's keep the fence between them for a minute." Micah held Nikki's leash loosely as the two noses met. "If they seem okay, I'll turn her loose in your yard for a minute. Then we've got to get to town."

"You won't have a cruise today with the hurricane approaching, right?" Fannie peered into the cloudless sky.

"My navigator checks the weather reports. I think the current storm is headed to the Gulf instead of up the coast." Micah steered Nikki inside the gate and removed the leash.

The Corgi took off, dashing from one end of the fence to the other, silent this time. Nikki's tail wagged in approval, but she wouldn't attempt to keep up.

"You might not have many passengers tonight." Fannie used a plastic bag on her hand to retrieve something left by the Corgi.

"Sure, and we'll oblige anyone who desires to come aboard." Micah trotted out his Cap'n Mike voice. "'Tis a grand view of our fair city from the water. You should come along. Don't be such a landlubber, Miss Fannie."

"Ha! I guess I am a stick-in-the-mud. Like a piece of driftwood marooned in the sand." Fannie laughed. "Me and Tara's pup will hang out here on the beach until our glamorous neighbors come home from their voyage."

"More's the pity. More's the pity." Micah laughed. He whistled for Nikki and smiled as she joined him. "See you tonight, Miss Fannie." His neighbor might not be too exciting, but her house commanded attention. Who else boasted so many colorful wind machines and chimes in their yard? Now a cute little yapping dog added to the busy ambiance. Tybee Island didn't need more commotion than this.

He opened the door of his black SUV and gave Nikki a boost into the front floorboard. Time to go give the tourists and regulars their daily riverfront show.

* * *

Graceful live oak branches swayed outside the news director's office window as Tara waited for his return. She'd been to the station for an interview more than a month ago, but the building still surprised her a bit. Instead of the modern office building situated on top of an Arkansas hill, the Savannah station nestled in a residential neighborhood. Southern charm and history were the bywords.

"How's your coffee?" The tall, slender man with a blue bowtie walked around his desk and sat.

"Perfect." Tara took another sip of her creamy latte.

"We can't afford to pay our people what they're worth." Mr. Landers tapped a pencil against a notepad. "So we try to make up for it with a few perks. I don't think it will take long for you to fit in here."

"That's my hope." Tara scooted to the edge of the upholstered chair. "Everyone has been very welcoming so far."

"We'll take a few days to help you get the lay of the land. You'll meet with producers and watch the newscasts this week to become familiar with things." He glanced out the window as the wind stirred the live oak branches more vigorously. "We'll also make promo spots to introduce you to our viewers."

"That sounds fine." Tara ran her tongue across her teeth. She'd need to be sure all this coffee didn't stain them too much.

"Brooke Baxter enjoyed tremendous popularity in Savannah. Our viewers are happy for her opportunity in New York, but we all miss her." His phone buzzed, and he picked up the receiver. "Okay ... great ... we'll be right down."

Tara fidgeted with the lid on her coffee cup. Her first few days as a reporter in Arkansas were much different. That first week included a stint on the side of the interstate, bundled up in a winter coat, gloves, and hat. Arkansas River Valley viewers learned about her grit and determination in a hurry as she shivered against the sleet and freezing rain. Promo spots? An anchor's job must be quite different.

"We have a remote interview with Brooke in a few minutes. With the two of you on screen together, folks can get to know you better. Does that sound okay?" He stood and walked toward the door.

Tara's eyes widened. A live interview with her beautiful

predecessor? Would she measure up? When she'd glanced in the mirror at home, she never anticipated she'd be on camera today. She'd met Brooke when she came for an interview, but how would she compare when they were side by side?

"I'll head down to the studio. You can run by makeup on the way if you want." He opened the door and led the way down the hall.

"This way." A young man with his hair in a bun waved from a doorway. "What's up?"

"Hi." Tara returned his smile. "I'm headed for a promo interview. What do you suggest?"

"First, introductions. I'm Julian. And you don't need much help." He waved at a salon chair in front of a mirrored wall.

"Thanks." Tara took a deep breath and settled into the vinyl chair. "I'm Tara Williams, the new anchor. Mr. Landers has a side-by-side interview set up with Brooke Baxter. There's no way I can measure up to her."

"Aw, take it easy." Julian stood behind her, massaging the tension from the back of her neck. "Don't compare yourself to Brooke. You are amazing. We'll give your hair a little zhuzh and brighten up your makeup. You be you, sweetie."

Tara smiled at her reflection. Why be intimidated by someone with a dream job in New York? She'd held her own as a reporter— she'd be fine as an anchor.

Julian sprayed her hair and applied lipstick two shades darker than she'd ever worn.

"Okay, honey. Knock 'em dead." Julian's face appeared next to hers.

Tara continued down the hallway, emerging into a studio with an impossibly high ceiling. Mr. Landers stood next to a chair upholstered in pale blue. She settled herself and faced the camera.

"Tara, Brooke will be on this monitor." Mr. Landers pointed to her right. "She'll talk for a few seconds and lead you through a brief conversation. Just the two of you talking. Easy, natural. We'll find the best bits and edit them into a promo. This is not live, so no pressure."

No pressure. Tara took a deep breath. The monitor to her right clicked on, and Brooke Baxter smiled at her from the screen.

"Hi, Tara. How's your day going?" Brooke showed no hint of nerves.

"Great. How about you?" Tara leaned back in the chair. If she'd made it through the job interview, she could do this.

Julian appeared in the doorway and used his hands to form Bullwinkle antlers on either side of his head. Whatever they paid this guy, he deserved more.

Somehow, she faked her way through the encounter with her predecessor and kept her smile intact.

"Don't forget. Wear something nautical tomorrow." Julian waved as Tara passed his makeup room after the promo interview concluded.

"Nautical?" Tara laughed.

"Yeah. You're cruising on the Georgia Queen with the evening crew, right?"

"Yes, at one." Tara glanced at the schedule on her phone.

"Think Americana—red, white, and blue. If you need help, we have a few items in our wardrobe closet." Julian started toward the next room.

"I'll see what I can come up with." Tara checked the monitor at the end of the hallway. She needed to be seated in her new office to watch the evening newscast before the supper break. "How about I come here before I go to the boat? You can tell me if I pass muster."

"You don't need my approval." Julian waved her off.

"But I want it. I appreciate your help so much." She caught his hand and squeezed it.

"Before long, our viewers will be saying, 'Brooke who?'" He hugged her shoulders.

Tara settled behind her desk, looking out her window at the same live oak tree that occupied Mr. Landers' view. A long, deep breath escaped her lips. Did she come off as a scared, inexperienced reporter from the hills when talking to Brooke? The former anchor excelled at interviews. If she'd been trying to put Tara at ease, the opposite happened. The smoother Brooke's delivery, the more Tara's nerves sparked.

Tomorrow should be easier. A trip on a paddlewheel boat through the heart of this beautiful city might be exactly what she needed to make her feel settled. Would she get a chance to watch the young captain of the ship at work? Or would he be busy in the cabin, or the bridge, or whatever they called the place with the steering wheel where they drove the boat? She had a lot to learn about Savannah and its river.

"What happened in your favorite city while you were working today?" The intro for the evening news played on the screen at the end of her office. "Here's our expert news crew with the latest updates."

Tara pulled out her iPad, preparing to take notes on the top stories. She'd need to remember to listen carefully for strange pronunciations. Nothing irritated locals more than an anchor who didn't sound like he or she was from the area.

* * *

Nikki pushed against the front door and whined, turning her head Micah's direction.

"Okay. Let me clean up the kitchen, and we'll go." He wiped the vintage laminate table with a paper towel and positioned his plate in the dishwasher. Not much cleanup involved with a takeout barbecue sandwich on the menu. Placing the sandwich and fries on one of Mom's china plates made eating alone more palatable.

Nikki barked impatiently.

"Let's go." He fastened the leash and pushed his shoulder against the pressure of the wind to open his front door. Jim's weather report during tonight's cruise assured him that Tropical

Storm Sally didn't threaten them yet. She wasn't even a full-fledged hurricane. The storm would probably fizzle somewhere in the Gulf.

The collie bounced down the stairs and headed to the street. The unsettled atmosphere must be agitating her.

Micah slowed to a comfortable walking pace as they continued down the paved road toward the beach. Sand washed across the road in front of them, and clouds created eerie shadows in the moonlight.

He stopped at the top of the dune before starting down another wooden stairway. Lights shone from the large house directly behind him. The new home of Fannie's friend?

"Come on, let's go down by the water." He left the dune without looking back and headed toward the edge of the beach. The wind picked up, moistening the sides of his legs and his face.

A familiar yapping filled the air, and the eager face of Nikki's new friend approached on those impossibly short legs.

"Jeannie!" The blonde from the Riverfront market ran behind the Corgi, stopping with a jolt when the dogs greeted each other nose to nose.

"Hi." He stepped back to avoid a collision.

"Looks like these two know each other." Her tanned arm reached down to pat the dog's back.

"Yes. They met at Fannie's this morning." Micah released Nikki's restraint. Little chance she would run far.

"I think we've met too. You bought me an umbrella?" Her smile outshone the cloud-shrouded moon above them.

"Yes. We were destined to crash into each other," Micah said. "But I don't think we exchanged names. I'm Micah Roland, and this is Nikki. Actually, her registered name is Picnic in the Park."

"What a lovely name." She scratched the collie's ears. "Didn't I hear someone call you Cap'n Mike? What happened to your Irish accent?"

"The tourists expect entertainment with their travelogue. And you are ..."

"Tara." She reached forward for a handshake. "Tara Williams. This furball is Petit Jean Princess, better known as Jeannie."

"Petty Gene?" Micah released her hand, soft as the scent that surrounded her.

"It's a mountain in Arkansas, where I'm from. French explorers named it after a young sailor on their riverboat. They confused him with a small boy, so they called him Petit Jean. Turned out to be a young lady instead. The local pronunciation lost its accent and became Petty Jean. It's a great local legend." She stopped talking.

He wished she would start again. He could listen to her all night.

The two dogs ran down the beach. Or rather, Jeannie ran, circling back often as Nikki loped along behind.

"I haven't seen her hurry that way in a long time." Micah picked up his pace. He didn't want Nikki to get out of sight.

"She's a few years older than Jeannie." Tara clapped her hands, prompting the Corgi to come back to her.

"Thirteen. A gift from my parents for my high school graduation. She was my best friend in college." No need going into the struggles the two of them faced when four years stretched into six. Gory details about eye surgeries would ruin the peaceful mood of a moonlit beach.

"Well, you have taken remarkable care of her." Tara scratched the collie's head as a wet nose touched her leg. "Your wife and kids must love her."

"It's just me and Nikki." Of course she would assume he was married. Wasn't everybody else at this stage of their life?

"Oh." She reached down and snapped a leash to her Corgi's collar.

He shared his relationship status. What kept her so quiet?

Tara took a step toward him, meeting his glance for a moment. He smiled and opened his mouth to say something. But what? His heart pounded. He pressed his lips together, waiting for her to speak, refusing to be the first to break eye contact.

Jeannie barked, knocking Tara off balance as the two dogs played hide and seek. His hand locked around her arm to keep her upright, and she leaned into him, her green eyes smiling.

He licked his lips. *No, too soon. You don't know this lady at all.*

"Well, I guess we'd better go. Work tomorrow after all." She tugged on the leash as Jeannie strained to get closer to Nikki.

"Yeah. Me too." He took a step toward the dune. "No kidding, you should take that cruise on the Georgia Queen. It's a great way to learn about the city."

"Oh, yeah?" Tara stopped a few yards away. "That's exactly what my boss has planned for me tomorrow. His suggestion. Our whole team will be on the afternoon cruise."

"Great. See you then." Should he offer to walk her home? He still didn't know if someone else waited in her beach house. For the first time in months, he regretted keeping his mouth shut.

Three

"**W**elcome aboard the beautiful Georgia Queen, ladies and gents."

Tara recognized Cap'n Mike's exaggerated Irish accent as the paddlewheel boat began its voyage down the Savannah River.

"I've lived here all my life, and this is my first time on this boat." Julian leaned against the railing. "The view of the city is crazy different from here."

"Yes. Mr. Landers must think you are extra special." Andy Porter stopped next to Tara. "When I came, he took the team to an afternoon baseball game. I didn't learn much about Savannah, other than their love for baseball."

"I don't know if I'm special." Tara laughed. "I guess Mr. Landers wanted an interesting introduction for the viewers."

"You'll be great on camera." Julian stood back, framing her face with his fingers.

"They pay you to say that." Tara waved to dismiss his comment.

"I hope by the end of our journey today you'll have a new appreciation for the Hostess City. You'll witness the business side of one of the busiest ports in the United States of America. Sure, and without the commerce on the Savannah River, this would be naught but a sleepy little southern town." Micah's spiel continued over the PA system.

Tara walked to the bow and allowed the wind to rummage through her hair as Micah talked about the historic locations they passed. To her left, a photographer captured candid shots before she faced him for a couple of poses.

"Hey, Micah." Julian waved as the captain approached with Nikki by his side.

"Cap'n Mike." Micah shook Julian's hand.

"Oh, yeah," Julian laughed. "I won't blow your cover."

"No cover needed for an old sea captain earning an honest day's pay." He stopped next to Andy, greeting him with another handshake.

"This is our new anchor, Tara Williams." Andy waved in her direction.

"Faith and begorrah." Micah's accent slipped, and he took a step backward.

"Good afternoon, sir." Tara accepted the hand he offered, and he shook it stiffly.

Nikki brushed against her leg and whined. "And how is Miss Nikki today?"

"You've mistaken Silver the Pirate Dog for a common collie." Micah patted the dog's head.

"Oh, yes, indeed. Excuse me." Why was Micah suddenly uncomfortable? She'd told him about the station's cruise. What changed?

"'Tis my pleasure to serve all of you today." Micah nodded at everyone while shuffling backward toward the other side of the deck. "Enjoy your voyage, and don't hesitate to call upon me if I may assist you."

"He's playing that Cap'n Mike schtick for all it's worth," Julian said as Micah greeted more passengers. "We all remember him as Micah Roland, associate producer. He left right before Brooke did. I'm surprised he didn't go work for another station."

"You're not serious, Julian." Andy watched Micah pacing the other side of the deck. "No one can blame him for being disillusioned with the television business right now."

"Well, there is that." Julian focused his attention on the river ahead.

Micah used to work at the same television station? What had caused his unhappiness with the business? What were Julian and Andy not saying?

"Andy, Tara." Mr. Landers appeared at the door leading to the on-deck ballroom. "We need the two of you for some indoor publicity shots. Julian, you come along too. They may need a quick touch-up after being out in this wind."

Tara caught Micah's eye as he greeted a small passenger. She smiled at him, but he retained his all-business persona, bowing to shake the young man's hand. Andy's comment rang in her head. Why did Micah leave the television business? Why should it matter?

"Come on. Your hair is fine." Julian took her elbow and whispered in her ear as they neared the ballroom door.

* * *

"Okay, Silver. You may retire to your accommodations for a few minutes." Micah stepped aside as Nikki snuggled into the plush pillow beneath the massive ship's wheel.

"How's the crowd today?" Jim turned the wheel over to Micah.

"Corporate types." Micah dropped the Irish accent. "They're here for photo ops."

"It takes all kinds. They paid for their passage, right?" Jim expanded the screen in front of him. "The stormy weather is gone for now. Unless Sally changes course."

"We can do without that." Micah reviewed the script he repeated twice a day. Though he'd memorized it long ago, today it might help to glance down from time to time. He couldn't believe the umbrella lady who smelled like fresh flowers had replaced Brooke at his old television station. Of all the rotten luck.

"Before we journey across the state line into South Carolina, you will glimpse historic Fort Jackson off the starboard bow." Micah's spiel took over again.

Rotten luck? He'd stopped believing in luck a long time ago. More like destiny. He'd been sentenced by some great power above to live a lonely life in an ancient town where everyone knew everyone else's history. Not what he expected when he graduated from broadcast school.

"Sure, and it was a dark and dangerous time for our great city ..." Some of his passengers enjoyed his tales of the past. He recited from memory, playing up the Irish brogue. Escaping from the present-day world would be the best course.

The huge boat drifted lazily past Fort Jackson.

"The fort is open to tourists, and you can learn about the brave men on both sides who fought and died there. We'll pause a moment to pay our respects as the colors are retired."

He scanned the monitors. Tara's hand covered her heart as the boat passed the fort's flagpole. Would Brooke have made that gesture without an audience? It might hint at a deeper, more sincere personality. Or maybe Tara was even better at hiding her true colors.

"And now, our promised excursion into the Palmetto State. In the middle of the Georgia Queen's turn to journey to the west, we briefly cross the border in the middle of the Savannah River. On the opposite coast, alligators may be lurking on the shore. They are forbidden by special ordinance to cross to the Georgia side."

He smiled. Cap'n Mike managed to get away with a lot of blarney. Many days, when there were young people aboard, he told some very tall tales or a few corny jokes. Getting paid to spout nonsense suited him fine.

"Okay if we come in?" Mr. Landers, his old boss, opened the door to the pilot house.

"Without a doubt, kind sir." Micah tipped his captain's hat

and gestured broadly. "Enter to witness the magic that is the Georgia Queen."

At the end of his exaggerated bow, his smile slipped as he stood face to face with Brooke's replacement.

* * *

"Great to see you again, Cap'n Mike." Mr. Landers patted Micah's shoulder before shaking his hand. Tara stood against one of the windows facing the South Carolina side of the river.

"'Tis a pleasure, sir." Micah retained his previous stiffness.

"Would you mind us taking a few pictures here? Could our anchors possibly stand at the wheel?" The news director motioned Tara and Andy forward.

"Are they trained pilots?" Micah glanced Jim's way, and the other man smiled and nodded. "The safety of our guests depends on them."

"We won't actually touch anything, Cap'n." Andy winked at Micah.

Tara followed directions for the next few minutes, aware of Micah's efforts to stay out of the camera's view.

"Can we get some audio?" A videographer squeezed into the crowded cabin.

"For a moment." Micah peered out the massive window ahead of them. "I'll be speaking to me passengers very soon."

Tara unclasped her hands. When had she assumed the nervous posture? Would it be recorded? Looking glamorous and confident grew more difficult by the minute.

The videographer nodded at Andy.

"Have you ever seen anything like this, Tara?" Her co-anchor was prepared for this off-the-cuff conversation.

"I've been on the Arkansas River quite often." She nodded. "But this one is so wide, and so busy. I don't think anyone could call it a lazy river."

Andy laughed. "There may be spots where it meanders. But

you're right. Here in the downtown area, there's always something happening. Can you tell our viewers what you think of our city so far?"

"It's beautiful. I'm looking forward to getting to know the city and her people better."

"They feel likewise. If I can steal a line from Cap'n Mike ..." Andy nodded, and the cameraman panned toward Micah. "Welcome aboard, Tara Williams."

"Thanks."

The videographer turned off his bright light and packed his camera in the case hanging from his shoulder.

Tara flinched as a cold nose touched her leg below her knee-length skirt.

"Silver." Micah patted Nikki's head. "A trifle forward, matey."

"She's fine." Tara scratched the silky ears, leaning down to whisper in one of them. "I'll see you later, sweetie."

She turned to speak to Micah. He picked up a portable microphone, never making eye contact with her.

"Ladies and gents, we're nearing the end of our glorious voyage on the Georgia Queen. Why not absorb the magic by taking a wee stroll on the deck? Allow the sights and sounds of the river to fill your heart, as they do mine. Savannah's skyline will make a wonderful backdrop for your photos. 'Twill feel so much like home, you might want to stay here forever. If leave you must, I will soon provide instructions to ensure your safety as we land. Thank you once again for joining us on the beautiful Georgia Queen."

Tara followed Andy and Mr. Landers as they joined Julian and the photographers on the narrow metal staircase leading down from the pilot house. Would she get a chance to ask Micah why he behaved so strangely? Should she follow his example and keep a separation between her true personality and her work persona? As a reporter back home, she'd been all Tara, all the time. Her co-workers said that's what made everyone love her so much.

Clay, on the other hand, resented her sincerity. He'd suggested on many occasions that she act more enthusiastic when covering his political rallies.

"Well, what did you think?" Julian stood next to her as the Georgia Queen brushed the dock bumpers.

"Awesome. Best orientation activity for a new job, hands down." Tara held the rail to avoid losing her balance as her head turned back toward the pilot house. What she wouldn't give to be reassured by Micah's presence, like on her first day.

"Yeah. Surprisingly fun." Julian followed her gaze. "The inside of the pilot house was more modern than I expected. I guess it takes a lot of state-of-the-art equipment to keep everything going, even on an old boat."

Ahead of them, Micah tossed an oversized loop of rope around a post next to the exit ramp. Balancing outside the gate blocking the passengers, he tugged the end of the massive coil to bring the boat to a stop in exactly the right place.

He probably enjoyed the physicality of his job as much as the public relations. Tara stood between Julian and Andy as Micah secured the rope, then lowered the gangplank before opening the gate.

"Have a lovely stay in Savannah." Cap'n Mike held the left hand of the first lady in line until she stood securely on the dock. He nodded at the man behind her.

"Wait. Are you smuggling contraband?" He reached behind a small boy's ear and handed him a piece of wrapped peppermint candy. The boy laughed and held tightly to Micah's hand while stepping off the boat.

Tara smiled as her turn to disembark arrived.

"Thank you, Cap'n Mike." Was his firm grip on her hand part of his captain duties or something more?

"The pleasure is all mine, my lady."

Once more, she tried to decipher the tone of his voice. The black patch hid his right eye, but his left one held a new, rather sorrowful expression. His tales of pirates and ghosts on the ship must have affected her. Had she imagined the connection between them last night on the beach?

"I hope you enjoyed this excursion." Mr. Landers spoke with her as the rest of the team made their way up the cobblestone incline.

"So wonderful." Tara nodded. "I have a whole list of places to visit after hearing Cap'n Mike's stories."

"He's a great storyteller. We miss the input he had when he produced for us." Mr. Landers steadied her with a touch on the elbow as they navigated the rough streets. "Listen, there's no need for you to come back to the studio today. Your car is parked nearby, right?"

"Yes, sir." She looked between the old buildings across from the River Street Marketplace. It would be quite a climb to the parking place she'd found on the street.

"You can watch the evening or nightside show on your own tonight. We'll see you at work tomorrow morning." Mr. Landers released her elbow and took a step away but turned to face her. "We're happy you're here, Tara."

"Thanks, sir." She smiled. "I'm excited to be here."

He waved as he jogged to catch up with Andy and Julian.

Did crossing old streetcar tracks to walk on cobblestones get easier, or did she need a different pair of shoes? Beads of sweat formed under her hairline. Were they in for another rainstorm? She stepped inside the market building, her eyes adjusting from the bright sunlight. She stowed her sunglasses in a patriotic-themed tote bag she'd found in Nina's closet. Today's cruise answered questions about her new hometown but added to her confusion about one of its residents.

* * *

Micah tugged Nikki's leash as the walk signal struggled for attention amid the blowing rain. Were these long days too much for his companion? He couldn't imagine an excursion without her, but he might need to make different arrangements soon.

The collie struggled to plant both back feet on the curb as she reached the other side of the street. His stride lengthened as he covered the last few steps to his car.

"Come on, girl, let's go home." Wind ruffled his unzipped coat and blew it open as his attention focused on opening the rear door. A wet plastic bag slapped his cheek under his eye patch, and he caught it as it drifted above his head.

He jogged to the trash can next to the red car parked in front of him. Streetlights reflected on the Arkansas license plate. He caught a familiar scent and turned to find Tara inches away.

"I should have brought my rain slicker tonight." She held her hand over her eyebrow, and the wind took her hair on a wild ride.

"Or that new umbrella?" Micah disposed of the errant plastic bag.

"I enjoyed that cruise today. Cap'n Mike is quite the tour guide." She winked at him.

Why did that raindrop hanging from the end of her nose capture his attention? He blinked, hoping it would be gone when he refocused. *Remember, Micah, this whole conversation may be part of her glamorous anchor act.*

"I found a great place to eat near here. Want to duck in for coffee?" Tara waved toward a nearby seafood dive.

She wasn't timid about making the next move. Did that surprise him? No. But could his heart afford taking another risk? Probably not.

"I need to get Nikki home. It was a long day." How pitiful, using the dog as an excuse.

"Oookay."

His obvious brush-off landed.

"I guess I'll see you back on Tybee sometime." She walked to the driver's side of her car.

"Most likely." This was not like him. He was bordering on rude. If only he could block out her occupation and be friendly.

Not happening. "Okay, Miss Nikki. Let's call it a night." He started his car and pulled onto the drizzly streets.

* * *

"Stay inside." Tara nudged Jeannie with her foot and closed the French doors on her balcony. Her hair whipped across her face, but at least the rain had stopped. Nina's voice rang in her head. "Always put the patio umbrella away, honey. Weather on the coast can change in a flash."

The wood-and-canvas contraption on top of Nina's glass table caught a gust and threatened to blow away. Tara ran toward the table as the umbrella lifted, popping the glass with a terrible crash. Her terrified scream cued Jeannie's frantic barking.

"What's happening?" Micah darted through the gap in the dune and bounded up the wooden stairway.

"There's glass everywhere." Tara touched a warm trickle of blood on her cheek.

"Glass?" Micah stood at the edge of the deck. "Stand still, I'll come to you. Ah, so this is the culprit." He picked up the umbrella and folded it, placing it under a chaise lounge.

Tara's hand shook as she touched her other cheek. What a crazy accident.

"Okay." His voice softened as he reached her side. "Let me take care of this."

She glanced down as he carefully removed a shard of glass from her right arm.

"I think that's the only one that posed a problem. You should sit down, but there's too much glass on these chairs."

Her left hand pressed against the cut on her cheek. His arm pulled her close, and he supported her as he opened the back door.

"Nope." Micah nudged the leaping Corgi farther into the kitchen as he escorted Tara to a bar stool and closed the door with his foot.

"Jeannie. Crate. Now." Tara surprised herself with the firmness of her voice. After a sorrowful glance, the dog padded to her sleeping spot.

"Dish rags?" Micah waved at the drawers beside the sink.

"Second drawer." She folded her hands, quelling the shaking for now.

Micah dampened a washcloth and pressed it to her cheek, his breath warming her forehead.

"So what is it with you and umbrellas?" His lips twisted in a mischievous grin.

"I don't know. I guess I have a lot to learn about life on the coast. I'm a little surprised Nina used a glass table out there." Tara's breath caught. They were talking about umbrellas while her heart pounded?

"I guess I'd better run out and sweep that up." Micah walked to a closet, hesitating before opening it. "Broom?"

"I think it's leaning against the fridge over there." Tara pointed. She held the washcloth against the spot on her arm where Micah had removed the glass. Did she need stitches? Where did Nina keep the Band-Aids?

The floodlight she'd switched on earlier provided enough light as Micah rounded up the glass on the deck and used the metal trash can lid as a dustpan. That task might have waited until tomorrow. He didn't seem the type to leave things unfinished. She spotted a first-aid kit on a shelf in the kitchen island and tended her arm as he re-entered through the French door.

"Quite the commotion during my simple run on the beach." He returned the broom and stepped toward her.

"I'm glad you happened by. That wind is wicked tonight. At least it stopped raining." Tara touched her cheek, searching for more blood.

"Here." Micah found a small Band-Aid and opened it. "I think you'll be fine."

Tara's hand shook as she accepted the plastic strip. She couldn't tell where to place it without a mirror.

"May I?" He leaned closer, taking it back and pressing it against her cheek. Her hand touched his, holding it against her face. His breath caught as their eyes met. She tilted her head back and closed her eyes. His lips pressed gently against hers for a moment, then brushed her cheek.

Tara's eyes opened to catch him shaking his head and stepping back. He held her hand, caressing her fingers.

Her heart fluttered as she found words. "Are you in a hurry, or can I get you some coffee?"

"I can stay for a bit." He sat on a barstool next to her, his fingers drumming idly on the counter. "You're lucky that glass missed your eye."

Tara turned toward him. This could be an opening for her question.

"Yes. I guess you know about eye injuries." Was that the proper way to bring it up? She found a mug in the cabinet and poured his coffee.

"Well, not so much. I underwent surgery to get rid of cancer." He stared at his hands. "Thankfully, after the radiation treatment, it's all gone."

"Wow. What an ordeal that must have been." She placed his coffee in front of him. "Do you need cream or sugar?"

He shook his head. "Complicated my college education for sure. But I managed to get my degree and a job as a producer down here. And the rest is history." He took a slow sip of coffee.

"My troubles with umbrellas and glass tables seem pretty minor." Tara laughed.

"Minor adventures are perfectly fine." He grinned at her.

His hand reached for hers as she joined him with her coffee. The gentle but strong grip reassured her.

So many more questions came to mind. His nearness satisfied her for now.

Jeannie broke the silence with a whimper punctuated by a short bark.

"Does she need attention?" Micah straightened, pulling away from Tara.

"She always thinks she does." Tara laughed. "She won't come out of the crate, even with the door open. Fannie said she wore herself out barking at the wind machines this afternoon." Why blather on about wind machines with this handsome man standing so close?

"Oops, there's another sliver of glass." He pointed at her shoulder. "May I?"

"Yeah. I guess I need to clean up a little better." Her shoulder tingled as he tenderly removed another remnant of her crazy adventure.

"Well." He stepped back. "I should finish my run and get back to make sure Nikki is settled for the night."

Tara moved closer to him. On tiptoes, she placed a kiss on his cheek, above that amazing reddish beard. "Thanks for coming by at just the right time."

His arms reached around her back, pressing her against him. This time, his kiss held more urgency. She yielded to the pressure of his lips.

"Yeah. Well." He released her, holding her at arm's length. "I need to go."

She stood with her arms at her side, already missing his touch.

He shuffled to the French doors, turning to wave.

Tara followed, waiting until he reached the bottom step to the dunes before turning off the floodlight.

Her phone rang from its spot on the kitchen island. She answered without identifying the caller.

"Hey." Clay's familiar voice didn't wait for her greeting.

"Hello."

He always assumed she wanted to talk to him.

"I'm in Savannah on my way to D.C. for a rally. Found a great bar. Want to join me for a nightcap?"

Join him? Tonight?

"Sorry, but I'm all settled at home for the evening." Not exactly, but he didn't need to know more.

"I'll be here until Monday. Meet me for supper tomorrow night?"

She should say no. She wanted nothing more to do with this man.

"Come on, sweetie. We have fences to mend. Can you give me directions to where you are? Your Nina's house, right? I think I have her address. She still sends me Christmas cards."

He assumed so much. If only she could use work as an excuse. He probably knew the weekend crew would handle things tomorrow.

"I'll meet you in town tomorrow night. Text me the address of the restaurant." Separate cars would be the best plan for this meeting.

"Have it your way, Princess Tara. See you at seven?"

"Sure." She disconnected, her heart pounding. What did Clay want from her? Would one last dinner convince him their relationship was over?

Four

T ara parked under a bright light in an empty parking lot across from the restaurant Clay selected. Small wonder ghost tours were so popular in Savannah. The city must pride itself on its lack of invasive streetlights.

"Hey." Clay greeted her with a kiss on the cheek as she approached the entry to the ancient building. "Your first time at Pirate's House?"

"Yes. Our family spent a lot of time on Tybee Island, but we didn't frequent the restaurants. Grabbing some groceries to take back to the beach was more our speed." She stayed a half-step ahead as they entered to avoid the inevitable arm around her waist.

"I've been here once before on a trip with some of my politico friends. The atmosphere is unbelievably cool. It's an adventure and a meal all in one." He handed the hostess a folded bill. "Your best table for two, please."

Would he peck the young lady on the cheek? Tara controlled the shudder that threatened to rock her shoulders.

"I read about this place. Word on the street is it's haunted." She allowed the gentle pressure at her lower back as they followed the hostess to a corner table beside rustic plank walls sporting gas-flame sconces.

"We shall see." Clay laughed. "Do you still like your steak medium rare?" He opened his menu.

Surely, he wouldn't order for her.

"I've heard about their honey pecan fried chicken. I've got to try that." She scanned the side dishes to find something light to add to her plate.

"Of course. Order whatever you like." His mouth wrinkled in the familiar show of displeasure.

Clay's arrogant attitude and condescending tone were on full display as they ordered. What had she ever seen in this guy? This ended here, tonight.

She gave the server a sweet smile and ordered her meal, nodding as she handed the menu back to the neatly dressed young lady.

Conversation lagged as Clay enjoyed the wine he ordered. Tara took another bite of her delicious entrée, savoring the mixture of flavors.

The lights dimmed. A shadow darkened the oil painting behind Clay's head.

"What was that?" Tara looked behind her. Other diners stopped mid-bite. A nervous twitter arose in the dining area.

"What was *what*?" Clay set down his glass.

"I thought I saw something or someone."

A man dressed as a pirate whirled through the room. Tara recognized the eye patch. The black hat, extra hair, and sword couldn't conceal Micah's sly smile. She covered her mouth with her napkin to stifle a giggle.

"I guess this place really is haunted." Clay picked up the large knife the server left for cutting their bread. "Never fear, darling. I will defend your honor."

"Not too scary." Tara smiled.

"Exciting, though, right?" Clay poured himself another glass of wine.

Micah the pirate sauntered near Tara. A glint of recognition crossed his face when he tipped his grand black hat in her direction. Her face warmed. No need to tell Clay they'd met. This should be the last dinner she shared with the would-be congressman. Would Clay pick up on the spark that had passed between her and Micah? Her cheeks warmed as she remembered Micah's tender kisses last night. Was he thinking of that moment too?

* * *

Micah pecked into the dining room from behind the large portrait on the wall. Tara folded her napkin and placed it next to her plate. The slightly stuffy young man who accompanied her slid his chair closer to her. Micah shouldn't be upset about Tara eating dinner with a man. What happened at her house after her accident must mean nothing to her. A television news anchor might have a different date every night of the week.

He sighed deeply, then darted his glance to the other side of the room. The painting he peered through sported an eye patch that matched his. The audience might not notice the left eye in this painting unless he kept it moving. His whole purpose tonight —to provide entertainment.

Tara rose from the table, obviously avoiding the advances of her date. Would this guy soon feel the sting of rejection as Savannah's newest TV anchor crushed his heart on her way up the career ladder? Why should Micah care?

He walked into the kitchen to prepare a plate of food and a to-go box for Nikki. Relaxation at home beckoned. He would do his best to avoid his new neighbor tomorrow.

* * *

The dark stretch of road between the Tybee bridge and the tourist strip prompted Tara to switch her headlights to bright. Back

316

home in Arkansas, she'd be watching for deer to cross in front of her. Should she watch for a stray gator instead?

Dimming her lights as she met an oncoming vehicle, Tara smiled. She never expected to see Micah as a pirate. Were all the ghost tours in Savannah as much fun?

What a contrast. Clay wasn't known as an entertainer. His public contact always seemed to have an underlying motive. Their last conversation before she stepped into her car replayed in her head.

"Hey, after I win this election, I'll be closer to the East Coast. A short commuter flight to D.C. for you. And if weekends aren't enough for us, you might even find a job there." He ran his finger up her arm to the cap sleeve of her dress.

"I'm not in a hurry to leave Savannah." She caught his hand and returned it to his side.

"Yeah, I get that. But think of the parties, the exposure you'd get if you're seen with a congressman." He raised her chin with his finger, teasing her with his eyes.

How to respond to that? She managed a nervous chuckle. "I wish you luck. Enjoy the rest of the campaign."

He leaned in for a kiss, but she skillfully offered him her cheek. With a jaunty wave in her direction, he and his sporty car left the parking lot.

A hint of salt air wafted through her open car window. Flickering neon heralded the businesses on the strip leading to the beach. As children, she and her brother learned which ice cream parlors stayed open late. The short walks from Nina's house on warm moonlit nights were a highlight of their summer. Tonight, all of them were shuttered until morning.

She'd never expected to feel at home so soon. When their three-person family retreated here after her parents' divorce, Mom met Tara's future stepdad. They all fell for him and were happy to relocate to his home in Arkansas. A moist breeze rippled her hair as her speed increased. Memories were easy to summon, regardless of the number of summers she'd been away.

She neared the end of the strip, just before Fannie's house. Above a covered parking area, on the opposite side of the street, soft light filled a window. Micah might be relaxing after his portrayal of Captain Flint's ghost. Or did he leave the light on for Nikki's benefit while he stayed out late? Tara would be comfortable in her place soon, but not without the usual loneliness.

Her car stopped in the driveway near the two-story deck that surrounded the house she'd always known as Nina's place. A sandy walkway nearby led to the ocean, not visible from the first floor of the house. Nina said the enormous dune behind it protected them from the threat of a surge. Should she worry about that? So much to learn as a homeowner.

Tara jogged up the steps and unlocked the door. A sleepy Jeannie wriggled in her crate.

"Did you have a restful evening?" She supplemented the night-lights in the kitchen with some brighter ones in the living room.

Happy barks greeted her, and she released her companion, crouching to receive the sloppy doggy kisses Jeannie offered.

"I missed you too." Tara laughed.

Clay never even inquired about Jeannie on their date. During the few times he'd encountered the Corgi, he barely concealed his irritation. Another reason to forget the man.

"Okay. Let's head out for a walk. Then it's back to bed for you." Tara attached the leash and opened the doors. Jeannie led the way down to the boardwalk and over the dune. Time to consider fencing a portion of the yard. The temptation of the long, open stretch of sand might be too much for her natural-born herder to resist.

"Okay, but only for a minute." Tara was glad she'd slipped out of her heels and into her beach shoes. Would Micah be enjoying the moonlight as well? She couldn't count on him accidentally showing up again. His tenderness after the umbrella debacle touched her, leaving her wanting something more. What about that sly tip of his hat tonight? Another part of the role he played?

Jeannie's bark prompted Tara to release her from the leash.

"Don't go too far." She took another deep breath. The salty night air and the lapping waves calmed her. If only she could retain this calmness at work, and in the presence of a certain ship's captain.

Back in their house, Jeannie headed straight for her crate. Running through the deep beach sand wore out those short legs, convincing the rest of the dog's top-heavy body to rest for the night.

Tara patted Jeannie's furry head, leaving the crate door open. She stopped in front of the calendar posted on her refrigerator door. Tomorrow was Sunday. A pang of loneliness pierced her chest as she thought of her church family's loving sendoff.

Didn't Fannie attend worship services nearby? She remembered Nina dragging Tara and her brother out of bed, insisting they wash their faces and eat a piece of toast before they dressed in something more suitable than their beach clothes. No one in Nina's old congregation would remember her, but she didn't want to start this new job on Monday without suitably worshiping the One who made it possible.

She found her cellphone on the kitchen counter and pressed Fannie's number.

"I hope I'm not calling too late." It didn't sound like she'd awakened her friend.

"Of course not. The night is still young," Fannie responded.

"Do you still go to church on Sundays?" The two didn't need a lot of preliminaries when they talked.

"Yes, ma'am. You're welcome to join us."

"How long does it take to get there?" Tara glanced up at the clock. Her mom would disapprove of her making a phone call at this hour, especially to someone older.

"For me, about thirty seconds. For you, a short walk." She could imagine the mischievous grin on Fannie's face.

"What?" Tara scratched her head.

"It's right here in my living room."

"You host a church service?" Tara was confused.

"My television does. Micah rigged up an online worship service back when we were six feet apart and wore masks. If you bring Jeannie, that will make three of us. I wear my pajamas most days, but you can wear whatever you like. We can see their crowd, but they can't see us." Excitement increased in her friend's voice.

"Micah won't be there to make it work?"

"No." Fannie's tone darkened. "He makes some sort of excuse every week. I've learned to push all the right buttons by myself. We normally have Bible study first, but it's canceled tomorrow. I'd love to see you for worship at ten."

Tara smiled. It would be comforting to spend some time with Nina's closest friend. Besides, God deserved all the praise she could send His way. The perfect way to start the week.

"Thanks so much for inviting me. See you in the morning, dear heart."

Tara caught a glimpse of her reflection in the mirror on her dining room wall. Worship would fill a missing place in her life. She'd try to tap into that feeling while streaming online.

* * *

Micah surfed past the end of the nightly news but found nothing worth watching. He walked to the front window, noticing Fannie's kitchen light glimmering at street level. Most likely she was creating something delicious to share with him in the morning.

Nikki snoozed peacefully on the huge cushion near his bedroom door. Too late for her to join him for a late-night jog. He settled into the sectional in front of the television and scanned available choices.

Why so restless? He loved acting at the Pirate's House and prided himself on making the ghost schtick more entertaining than terrifying. People endured plenty of scary things daily, particularly if they watched the nightly news.

Memories of the former brunette anchor at KSAV haunted him. Brooke had convinced him to accompany her to New York once. She loved being in the outdoor audience of a national morning broadcast. She spent the rest of the trip talking about that morning show, where she'd attracted a cameraman's attention without holding one of the creative signs other audience members carried. When Micah watched the replay, her smiling face appeared over and over behind the hosts and the special guests. The cameraman avoided Micah most of the time.

A few weeks later, back in Savannah, she made the big announcement. He'd never forget her half-hearted invitation to relocate with her to New York.

"We can live in one of those walkup apartments downtown," she explained.

"Walking up how many flights?"

"I don't know. Some of them have elevators. Why does that matter?"

"Nikki has enough trouble with the stairs at my place." He'd used the dog as an excuse. Shameless.

"Wouldn't she be happier with your parents out in the country?" Brooke floated this idea often. She never understood how much the collie meant to him.

"Would it matter what makes Nikki happy? Or even what makes me happy?" He knew the answer to both questions. It didn't matter at all.

The office grapevine reported that Brooke moved in with the cameraman from the morning show. How long before she found someone with a nicer apartment, fewer stairs, and no dog to worry about? He already felt sorry for this guy he'd never meet.

He opened his bedroom window, allowing the salty breeze to wash through the room. There must have been a real-life sea captain in his lineage somewhere. If not for leaving Nikki alone at night, he might rig up a hammock on the sand. The local homeowners would see him as a vagrant, but the peaceful sleep would be worth it.

He took one more deep breath, expanding his chest, feeling the air entering his diaphragm and letting it out again. Okay. This might work. Concentrate on breathing instead of remembering the new KSAV anchor with her Ken doll boyfriend.

Breathe, Cap'n Mike, breathe. No need for a two-legged female in his life. His loyal collie was the only companion he needed.

Five

J eannie ran her leash's full length and pulled Tara toward the blacktopped street, her toenails creating a staccato rhythm all the way to the back of Micah's house.

"What's your hurry?" Tara laughed. "Do you think Fannie is going to be happier to see you today than she usually is?"

The Corgi stopped, her tongue lolling as she waited for Tara to catch up or give her more leash.

"Good girl." Tara examined the bottom of Micah's wraparound deck. Once again, she wondered if raising a house off the ground would help. Nina never worried about hurricanes. Their summer vacations were full of only happy memories. No weather emergencies permitted. She extended Jeannie's leash and crossed the blacktop.

"Hi there." Fannie met her at the front gate, carrying a basket wrapped in a gingham towel. "I'll be right back. We're sharing fresh cinnamon rolls with Mr. Roland." She jogged across the street and set the basket on the steps leading to Micah's house. Her slender finger pressed the doorbell before she turned to follow Tara and Jeannie into her yard.

"Don't worry. I kept some cinnamon rolls for us too." Fannie opened her front door.

"How sweet. Are you running for Tybee Island's neighbor of the year?" Tara unclipped Jeannie's leash, patting her head to calm the hyper Corgi. "Settle down." She crouched to whisper into the pointy ears.

"She'll be fine," Fannie said. "She knows how to behave in Fannie's house."

Jeannie walked across the room and plopped next to a recliner. Tara smiled. "I assume that's where you sit?"

"She's my buddy." Fannie picked up the remote control that rested on the round table beside her chair. "Let's try to get our worship service tuned in. If I hold my mouth right, we can make this happen."

Tara settled on the sofa, tucking her legs under her.

"Eureka." Fannie raised her arms in celebration as the church's name appeared on the screen.

Tara closed her eyes, allowing the prayer on Fannie's television screen to wash through her. What a blessing to be here with her friend, worshiping. Her spirit needed this moment so much.

Fannie's telephone rang, causing them both to jump and Jeannie to bark.

"Oh, my." Fannie lowered the volume on the television and answered her phone. "Hello?"

The familiar smile lit up her wizened face.

"No, it just started ... It's okay ..."

Fannie nodded Tara's direction.

"You're more than welcome. I craved cinnamon rolls. You still have time to join us." She paused again.

"Us. Me, Tara, and Jeannie ... Sure. You know where I'll be at this time each Sunday ... Yes. Have a blessed day, neighbor."

"Micah?" Tara guessed.

"Yes. I'll turn my ringer off now." Fannie raised the volume again and sang along with the hymn filling her speakers.

For the next hour, Tara lost herself in worship, filling a piece of her heart. During the last few weeks before moving away, her church attendance had suffered. Avoiding Clay and his Sunday morning entourage had become too hard. How had she allowed him to steal her deepest source of joy?

She blinked back tears as she blended her alto with Fannie's thready soprano. How much more wonderful would it be to surround herself with a multitude of voices?

Where did this program originate? Could she possibly convince Fannie to visit the congregation in person next week?

* * *

Micah paced in front of the windows facing Fannie's house. He crossed the room and unfolded the gingham covering the delicious treat he'd retrieved from his steps. The role of poor, neglected bachelor shamed him. He wouldn't want to offend an elderly friend, though. Might as well play up the pitiful, lonely man routine, at least on Sunday mornings.

He pinched off a soft morsel and popped it into his mouth, relishing the sweetness on his tongue.

"Mmm." He squinted with pleasure as he cleaned his chin with a napkin.

Nikki barked from her post next to the front door.

"Okay, Miss Diva." He clipped a leash to her collar. "I'm coming. Let's go find out what's happening on your beach."

He tried not to get too far ahead of the collie, who slowly navigated the long stairway to street level.

A salty breeze licked his face. Fannie's in-home congregation had tripled today. When his mom clued him in about his home congregation's online services, he knew that making this connection for his elderly friend might be a literal lifesaver. He'd even occupied a vacant rocker in Fannie's living room on Sunday morning once.

The very thing that brought her such joy brought Micah nothing but pain.

Sundays had always included worship when he was a kid. Scheduling had been a problem when he worked for KSAV. Now that he captained the Georgia Queen, his Sundays were free, but he wasn't in the mood for praise. A little bit of peace on the beach came close to worship. Not communion with a higher power, but a closeness with creation. Good enough for now.

Nikki retraced her steps and returned to his side. Exercise helped her arthritis. Maybe they'd go into town and mingle with the tourists.

"Come on, girl, let's go spruce up a little bit. We need to socialize more." He rubbed her between her ears, prompting her to follow as he walked up the beach.

Excited yipping greeted them as they reached the top of the stairway over the dune. Nikki picked up her pace, running to rub noses with Tara's Corgi.

"Hey. How are y'all today?" Tara stepped next to him as the dogs focused on their happy reunion.

"Hello. We're fine. How are you?" He didn't try to change the formality of his tone. Nikki wiggled at the sight of her energetic friend, but Micah wished to avoid Jeannie's owner.

"I'm so glad you fixed Fannie up with that online church service." Tara stood facing him.

He took a step back. "Glad to do it. I never dreamed she'd continue watching after everything opened back up. That's my parents' congregation in peach orchard country. Fannie could go back to the church she used to attend here if she wanted."

"She said she feels a part of their family now." Tara laughed. "They even speak to the online attendees now and then. They're very welcoming."

"Yes, they're known for that." Micah wiped a bead of sweat off his forehead. "Well, Nikki and I should be going. I'm glad you enjoyed your visit with Fannie."

"I think worship was exactly what I needed after the stress of moving and adjusting to my new job." Tara opened her gate.

"Good." He'd never thought about needing to worship. More like an obligation, something he did to make his parents happy. To each their own. "Come, Nikki." He patted his collie's head when she reached his side. "Well, have a nice day." Would she catch on? How much more formal and dismissive could he get without being impolite?

"Yeah. You too." Tara's voice grew softer. "Come on, Jeannie." She patted her leg as the dog wriggled backward to stand beside her.

He jogged toward his stairway. Skipping daily news broadcasts might be easy, but avoiding the pretty new anchor was tougher. He'd have to find a new route to and from the beach.

Six

Tara glanced to either side as she crossed the bridge to Tybee Island. Was the wind creating larger waves in the dark water? Hard to tell without the moonlight that usually welcomed her home. The weather team held a special meeting today to update them on the path of Sally. Mr. Landers and the rest of the news team were matter-of-fact about the station's hurricane preparations. Tara's stomach churned like the water on each side of the bridge.

True to form, her new friend Julian reassured her.

"Honey, don't worry. You will be such a welcome face to the people who still have a way to watch our newscasts. They need something normal, a calm voice in the storm. And I'll be here to make sure you're as fresh and pretty as always."

Tara took a deep breath. She wished she could be as certain as her new work bestie. She stopped her car in front of Fannie's gate and jogged up the sidewalk.

"Hi, sweetie." Fannie opened her door, holding it firmly against a strong gust of wind. "Your Jeannie has been settled in her crate for a couple of hours now."

"Thanks." Tara controlled the trembling in her voice. "I didn't want to wait until the morning to talk to you."

"Come in, sit down." Fannie stepped back, then followed Tara to a chair in the living room. "I'm trying to find a movie to watch. I never could go straight to bed after the news."

"Did you watch the weather report?" Tara perched on the edge of a wooden rocker.

"Of course. It used to be the only reason I watched until my very pretty neighbor started reporting the news." Fannie brought Tara a tall glass of cola.

"The weather is all anyone is talking about tonight. That storm coming across Florida tomorrow might be bad by the time it gets here." Tara's heart pounded. Storm coverage happened in Arkansas, but the week-long tracking here threw her. How could Fannie be so calm?

"We've lived through storms before. Your Nina can tell you stories about some nasty ones when we were kids. Our folks knew what to do, and we always hunkered down and got through them. We went through one when you and your mom and Bubba lived here." Fannie found a photo album under the television and opened it to a picture showing past damage.

"I guess I feel differently now that I work at the station." Tara stood and walked to the window. Micah's lights were off. Apparently, he was asleep. Was she the only one concerned about the weather? "That's why I came over. Tomorrow I am moving into a special bunker at the station. I won't be coming back until the storm moves past Savannah."

"Mercy." Fannie laughed. "You won't be one of those poor souls wearing a raincoat and hanging on to a signpost while the wind whips you senseless, I hope."

Tara faced her friend. "No. Those are the people on the weather team. But I won't be allowed to come home. I'll have to be ready to go on air more often than usual. I need a place for Jeannie. If you are evacuating, I will find a safe place in the city ..."

"Honey." Fannie stepped forward and wrapped Tara in a hug. "Calm down. Let's all get some sleep, and we will form a plan tomorrow. I'd be glad to make sure that precious ball of fluff stays safe with me."

Tara took a deep, cleansing breath.

"Thank you, sweet friend." Her phone pinged and pinged again. "Uh-oh. My mom and Nina saw the weather reports tonight. I'll call them from my house."

"Goodnight." Fannie held open the front door. "I'll start praying right now. God has a plan. When He's ready, He'll reveal it to us. Now you go get some rest. You'll have to be your usual cheerful self on television tomorrow. All the folks in Savannah are depending on you."

Tears washed Tara's cheeks as she walked to her car. Obviously, praying was the best course of action. Her hair whipped in front of her face as she opened the driver's side door. *Lord, give me some of Fannie's confidence. I'm going to need it for the next several days.*

* * *

Micah paused at the bottom of his stairs as Nikki made her morning rounds, inspecting the edges of their property. A text from Jim popped up on his phone.

> Planning to stay on the island?

>> I think so. Pretty used to the boarding up process.

He walked to his shed, opening the door to find the needed supplies.

> You'll be stuck there. Bridge into the city will be closed soon. You're welcome to hunker down with me and the missus.

>> Thanks, Jim. I'll keep you in mind. I think Nikki and I will be fine.

Jim's concern warmed his insides. Living on the island had its drawbacks during bad weather.

"Morning, neighbor." Fannie's tiny voice was almost swept away by the wind.

"Hey." He waved and walked across the narrow street.

"We're in for a doozy this time." Fannie pointed at the sky behind Micah's house.

"Could be."

"Funny it's named Sally. Like Dirty Sally, who blew in and changed everything in Dodge City." Fannie pulled her windbreaker closer.

"There was a Sally on *Gunsmoke*?" Micah searched his memories of the classic television show.

"You're too young to remember. The later seasons weren't up to par. After Miss Kitty left town, no one cared. But Sally, now she was a corker."

"Oh, okay." Micah smiled. Savannah prided herself on avoiding major hurricane damage time after time. Thus the nickname *Dodge City*. But Fannie's memories of the classic show were much better than his.

"I'll be over to help you board up as soon as I get Nikki inside." The collie's silky hair ruffled in the wind.

"No rush. I'm more worried about Miss Tara. She said she's sheltering at work for the next few days. Her little dynamo will be helping me hold down the fort." Fannie pulled a wind machine out of the ground, placing it under her porch roof.

"Her grandmother has boarding up supplies at their house, right?" Micah turned to look behind his house toward Tara's two-story.

"Of course. Tara's Nina knows we'll batten down the hatches like always." Fannie pushed a stray lock of hair from her forehead.

Nikki stood at the back of his yard, barking into the increasing wind. Did she expect to find her new friend Jeannie back there?

"Okay. Well, we've got plenty to keep us busy this morning.

I'll be at your place in a few minutes." Micah whistled for Nikki, herded her up the stairway, and closed the front door behind her.

His phone jangled in his pocket.

"Dad? What's up?" Most days, his mom texted, resorting to phone calls now and then. But talking to Dad was rare.

"Son, Sally doesn't look like an ordinary hurricane, if there is such a thing." Straight to the point—Dad's middle name.

"That's what I'm hearing." Micah rubbed the back of his neck. "I think my place will be fine, though."

"The real danger may be flooding, especially on Tybee Island." Dad's voice lost all hint of teasing. "I know you're a grown man, and you've hunkered down there for other storms. But remember, we're only a few hours away. If you wait until the bridge is flooded, you won't have a choice."

Micah faced Fannie's house out his front window.

"Would you have room for my neighbor, Miss Fannie?" Time to swallow his stubborn pride.

"Of course. Bring her. Besides, going up and downstairs at your house with Nikki during the storm won't be fun."

"The older I get, the smarter you are." Micah laughed.

"Happened the same way with me and your grandpa." Dad chuckled. "Call when you're leaving, son, so your mom can start worrying."

Visions of a wiggly Corgi filled his brain.

"Oh, Dad." He wouldn't have hung up without their customary goodbyes. "We may have a stowaway. A neighbor's dog. The neighbor has to work through the storm, and she doesn't have a place for her Corgi. She's pretty lively ..." A severe understatement.

"Does Nikki like her?" Dad adored Nikki, and she loved him back.

"Yes."

"Any friend of Nikki's is a friend of ours."

Sometimes, even now, he wondered why he'd moved away from orchard country.

"Okay. See you soon. Love you, Dad." Micah disconnected. Now, if he could convince his favorite stay-at-home friend across the street to leave. Not an easy task.

* * *

Tara added one more pair of sweatpants to her suitcase. Mr. Landers had advised them to bring comfortable clothes to keep their on-air outfits fresh for as long as possible.

"A perk of being an anchor," Julian reminded her. "Ninety percent of the time you are only seen from the waist up."

Jeannie bumped her leg as she paced across the bedroom.

"I know. But it's raining. Let's put off going out as long as possible, shall we?"

Too late. The word *out* landed between those perky ears. Jeannie ran to the door, toenails clicking on the kitchen's luxury vinyl.

Tara grabbed her slicker from a peg near the back door. "Okay, but not for long. We're going to Fannie's in ten minutes."

Raindrops the size of quarters splashed against her cheeks. Blonde strands waved like Medusa's snakes when her slicker hood blew off.

"Don't waste any time, Princess." She held her hood with one hand and shoved the other into a pocket.

"Ahoy the house!" Micah's deep voice turned her head away from the beach. His laced-up work boots plodded through the deep sand on the east side of her home.

She caught a glimpse of Fannie's red hair as she opened her patio door and headed into the kitchen.

"Hi, honey. I'm going in to get your Nina's storage room key."

"What?" No use trying to form a complete question now. The wind would blow her words away.

"We need to get storm prep done on your house. Fannie and I have done it for your grandma quite a few times. Stand back and observe professionals in action." Micah pulled a hammer from his back pocket.

Tara's hand fisted and unfisted. She'd endured storms in Arkansas, but prep there involved listening for sirens and diving into the bathtub as tornado threats passed. According to the weatherman at her station, this storm circulated several miles offshore but was headed directly for Savannah.

"Sorry to be in such a rush, but Fannie wouldn't entertain any talk of leaving until we got your house boarded up."

Fannie opened the storage room under the carport, and Tara stood back as *Operation Hunker Down* played out in front of her. Micah hoisted plywood in place, and Fannie leaned against it while he nailed. In less than fifteen minutes, the lower windows were covered, and Micah scrambled up the outside stairs to the deck. Permanent shutters were pulled across the windows there, and a large bolt slid in place to secure them.

"Wait!" Tara stood at the bottom of the stairway, holding Jeannie firmly as Micah and Fannie descended. "Did you say you two are leaving?"

"Oh. I guess that should have been the lead story." Micah pushed back the bandana that covered his hair. "Yes, my mom and dad have agreed to find a spot for us at the family compound in the orchard country."

"Your sweet little Jeannie can come with us if that's okay with you." Fannie rubbed the Corgi between her ears.

"Well, I don't know." Tara's mind raced. Did she have a choice? "If it's okay with you, I guess that will work. She is a pretty good traveler."

Micah caught her nervous glance and smiled. "Sorry we blew in here with no warning."

"It's okay." Tara opened the door and dropped Jeannie inside the house. "I have two or three last-minute things to pack, and then I'll bring the princess to Fannie."

"See you soon." Fannie took off at a trot.

"I don't normally leave during these things." Micah's hand

rested near hers on the back door. "I'm worried about Fannie's house. I might be able to get her to stay at my place, but we'd have two dogs to chase up and downstairs. They might not be able to find a dry place to stand down there, which makes for a tough day. We'll try to rest tonight and leave early in the morning so we can get out of Dodge before the mass exodus starts."

"I'm not excited about this bunking party at the station. But I'll feel better knowing all of you are safe." Her hand tingled with the nearness of his. Had the coldness she felt from him earlier evaporated?

"Keep your fingers crossed that Savannah and Tybee live up to their reputations for missing the worst of the storms. This could be the grand adventure you need to get the proper attention at work." He patted her shoulder before following Fannie.

Keep your fingers crossed? What kind of advice was that? The last thing she wanted was more recognition at work. Did this man understand her at all?

* * *

Micah held the steering wheel tighter as the wind whipping across the bridge threatened to change their course.

"How long will it take to get to your folks' place?" Fannie pulled her skinny legs under her and turned toward him.

"Normally less than three hours." Micah checked the rearview mirror. Nikki slept peacefully, but Jeannie's tiny front feet were propped on the passenger side window. He should have figured out how to fit two crates in the back seat. The nervous little Corgi might feel more secure in hers.

"There are quite a few people out today." Fannie's expression held much of the same concern as Tara's dog.

"Yeah. Lots of Tybee residents are heading for higher ground." He stated the obvious. Fannie had agreed to evacuate mostly because of the dogs.

"First time I've ever wimped out." She faced forward.

"I know, and I appreciate it. My mom and dad weren't going to rest with me on the beach, and I needed some company." Micah cleared his throat to disguise the little white lie. He'd made this trip on multiple weekends all by himself. Today, though, he welcomed having Fannie, along with the two canines.

Fannie's phone jangled with an overly loud text notification.

"You might want to plug that into the charger." Micah handed her a cord.

"Thanks." She managed the connection before opening the text.

"It's Tara." She laughed. "As if she doesn't have enough to worry about at work."

"Tell her Jeannie is fine." He bounced off the end of the Tybee bridge onto the highway toward Savannah. A surprise gust forced a quick correction to keep them in their lane. This was no normal weekend visit to orchard country. Tara wasn't the only one nervous.

* * *

"Then I'll cue up the story about the National Guard rolling in." The on-duty producer nodded at Andy and Tara as he handed them their scripts for the next newscast.

The weather team huddled around their monitors on her left. Right now, the anchors were not as important to the viewers as the meteorologists. Once the storm started pounding the coast, their goal would be to keep smiling. Mr. Landers said that reporting on something other than the hurricane would be a welcome relief for everyone. Not an easy task, but doable.

Tara resisted the urge to check her cellphone for messages. Fannie sent a quick note when they arrived at Micah's family home. She'd learned to concentrate on her job years ago. Why was this any different?

"In five, four, three, two ..." The producer pointed at Andy.

She pasted on her smile and rechecked her notes. *Deep breath, Tara. Time to go.*

"Good afternoon, Savannah. Andy Porter here, along with our fantastic new anchor, Tara Williams."

Tara's monitor showed a pan outward, with both of them on screen.

"We know the weather is top of mind right now. What does the greatest team on the East Coast have to say?" Tara managed a tight smile as the screen shifted to the meteorologist to their right.

"You okay?" Andy lowered his mic and leaned toward her.

"Sure. Thanks for asking." Did she look as unsettled as she felt? Time to get her big-girl panties back in place.

Andy examined his notes, but Tara listened intently to the status of Hurricane Sally. The storm had reduced from a catastrophic category five to a four before making landfall in Florida.

"Reminiscent of Hurricane Irma in 2017." Tara needed more off-air studying. If she could find a familiar pattern to this, she might feel better about Savannah's prospects.

"The Hostess City is leaving nothing to chance during this lead-up." Andy's voice bumped her back to reality. "Today, National Guard troops from South Carolina, and even a group from Arkansas, arrived to mobilize and help where needed. Here's a spokesperson from this welcome entourage, Captain John K. Billings, with details about their mission."

John K.? The handsome husband of her friend, Faith, from their home town? Tara tried not to glue her eyes to the monitor as her friend's familiar voice resonated. Did he have experience with hurricanes? She'd try to get a contact number to message him tonight.

"Thanks for that, Andy. Now we go to a shop owner on Tybee Island, who is deep into storm prep. Before we hear from him, I want to repeat the advice from authorities tonight. If you are thinking of leaving the island to shelter on the mainland, now is the time. The only road in and out of the beachfront may become impassable soon. Check the KSAV website for real-time traffic updates. And now to the owner of *Wastin' Away*, a popular hangout near the beach ..."

"Not much more in this report," Andy whispered. "We'll go back to the weather team, then join the normal programming for a bit. Watching reruns of *Gunsmoke* should help everyone get their minds off this until it's time to take action."

Tara nodded. She didn't trust her voice. With any luck, Savannah would live up to her nickname of Dodge City once again. *Lord, stay with us. We're hanging on to You for dear life right now.*

* * *

"She looked terrific on air, don't you think?" Fannie walked across the family room toward Micah.

"Splendid." Micah smiled. Coming home meant giving up control of the television remote, and he understood his family's desire to stay abreast of the weather situation. Fannie, however, watched for one reason, to check on their new neighbor.

"Do you think this rain means the hurricane is here?" Dad stood at the back window.

"We watched the same weather report." Micah scratched between Nikki's ears as she stopped next to them. "The bands of rain rotate around the eye of the hurricane. It's still crossing Florida and may go back into the ocean before coming near Georgia."

"That Tara, she's your neighbor, Jeannie's owner, right?" Mom and Fannie must have completely ignored the weather portion of the show. "Will she be all right on the coast by herself?"

"Yes. Miss Williams is safe in her bunker at KSAV. Remember, I stayed there a time or two during a storm." Micah peered out the window. He'd grab an umbrella and take the dogs outside.

"Oh, she's texting again." Fannie held out her phone. "I understand that the dear girl is lonely, but I am terrible at typing.

Last time I tried to tell her about Jeannie, the phone said *jealous.* That makes no sense."

"I'm sure she can decipher it." Micah grabbed two leashes from a hook near the door. Corgi toenails scrambled across the wood floor, and the collie edged closer, waving her feathery flag behind her.

"Be a dear and give her a call while you're out there, please." Fannie thrust the phone into his free hand.

"Okay. But I'll use my phone." Two dogs, a phone, and an umbrella. With another glance, he left the unused rainy-day device next to the door. "Let's go ladies."

"I repaired that gap in the fence. They'll be fine to just run." Dad opened the door for a furry cannonball and a slightly more elegant duchess. "I'll have some towels handy when they come back in."

Problem solvers. Accepting the TV position in Savannah had proved his self-sufficiency, but now and then, he needed folks who truly tried to make his life easier.

He stepped outside to call Tara. She might be expecting a call from Fannie. Would she want to talk to him after he interrupted her date at the Pirate House?

"Hey." How to start this conversation?

"Is everything okay up there?" Her clipped words betrayed her tension.

"Great. If you like standing in the rain watching dogs do what dogs do." The contrast wasn't lost on him. Nikki would be perfectly happy in the bunker with Tara, but Jeannie loved making laps around his parents' yard. No time for the rain to soak through her thick fur.

"Thanks so much for taking care of my little nutcase. I know I'll be grateful for this shelter, but right now the waiting is driving me crazy." An office chair creaked. It must be as hard for Tara to sit still as it was for her Corgi. "And Fannie? Is she worried about her house?"

"Not so far." Micah backed under the protection of the porch roof. "I am, though. I think we have it boarded up well against wind damage, but the flooding ..."

"Yeah. Our meteorologist says the rain will be relentless, even after the initial storm surge. I wonder about Nina's house too."

Nina's house. Would she ever think of the house on the beach as her home? Or was Savannah only a stepping stone, like for her predecessor?

"I think the dunes will protect it." Micah ran his hand through his hair. Why hadn't he at least worn his slicker with a hood out here?

"Hey, thanks for calling. I may have to go on air in a minute. Our regular news schedule will change as the storm gets closer." The chair creaked harder.

"Take Fannie and Jeannie off your list of worries. They are being completely spoiled by the orchard branch of my family." Micah reached down with his free hand to pat Nikki's head. Jeannie bounded between his legs, shaking to soak his pant legs.

"Okay. Thanks again. And you and Nikki stay safe as well." Her voice softened.

"That's the goal. Oh, by the way, I can't be sure Fannie will remember to keep her phone charged. You can reach me at this number anytime." He waited to let the dogs inside since he'd need to locate those towels Dad promised.

"I may take you up on that, especially after lights out tonight. Good night, Cap'n Mike."

"Rest ye well, lovely lassie." Where did that come from? He lapsed into Riverboat Captain mode. *Best be careful, Micah. Remember, you are only a helpful neighbor.* The deeper his feelings, the harder the recovery when the winds of change inevitably took her away.

* * *

Tara walked down the hallway toward the dressing room, now being used as her private bedroom. Monitors and speakers echoed with the meteorologists' calm tones. By now, the citizens of Savannah were finished with storm prep. Time to hunker down and wait for whatever tomorrow would bring.

She opened the windowless door to her room, leaning against it as it closed behind her.

Lord, please be with the people in Florida who are dealing with damage from today's storm. Help them remember that You are with them now and throughout the recovery. Be with me as I prepare for another day of reassuring my new neighbors here in Georgia. I need You more than ever. Amen.

She sat on the side of the hide-a-bed. No doubt, her friend Julian was responsible for fitting it with sheets and blankets. She smiled when she found a chocolate mint on the pillow. Definitely Julian. What a treasure.

She scanned her text messages and formed a group text for Mom and Nina. She might want to hear their voices tomorrow, but with nothing beyond waiting to report tonight, a short message would do.

> Fannie and Jeannie are safe at the home of our friend Micah, in Fort Valley, GA. Settling down for the night. We will talk tomorrow.

Mom's heart response came in a matter of seconds. Nina was probably already in bed. She'd better mention the beach house to reassure them both.

Fannie and Micah knew what to do before we left Tybee. Micah thinks the house will be fine.

Faith, John K.'s wife, texted next.

> Here's John K.'s cell number.

> Thanks. I am so glad he is here. He may be the one to take me home after this storm.

Tara's hand shook as she replied. Facing the damage would be easier with a friendly face from Arkansas.

Sneak in a quick hug and tell him it's from me.

Faith's sweet personality shone through, even in a text.

Overwhelming loneliness crowded out the dread of seeing her new home. She wasn't tethered to a post in the windstorm, reporting on the coming catastrophe. That might not be as hard to endure as sitting in this windowless room alone. She scanned her music app, finding some hymns and connecting her earplugs. If she didn't calm her spirit somehow, she'd be worth nothing tomorrow when the real storm hit with all its fury. *Be near me, Lord Jesus.* The words from a childhood Christmas song provided the comfort she needed. *I ask Thee to stay.* God placed her in Savannah for a reason. She should trust that reason would become clearer soon.

Petit Jean Princess said to tell you goodnight.

Micah's text included a close-up of her sweet furry friend. She blinked back tears before responding.

Wanna talk for a minute?

Hearing a real voice would be much better than all this texting.

Her phone rang.

"You okay?" Even those two words pleased her lonely ears.

"Yes. No. I don't know. Let's talk about anything but the weather." She propped herself up on two pillows. "Here's your chance—what do you want to know about me?"

The long moment of silence unsettled her.

"Okay. Here's a question—why Savannah?" His soft voice held no trace of a fake accent.

"That's a fairly easy one." Tara cleared her throat. "You know that I lived here for a while."

"Summer vacations, right?"

Fannie had filled him in, at least a little bit. "Yes, but also for most of my fifth-grade year. We moved here from up north when my mom and dad got divorced. My mom met a man from Arkansas who helped rebuild the bridge. He swept all of us off our feet. They married, we moved to Arkansas, and the rest is history."

Tara smiled, remembering Mom's whirlwind romance.

"But why come back now?"

"I loved my job, but it was time for a change. I hoped this job would be like returning to my first comfort zone." Should she mention Clay? The pressure of behaving professionally while reporting on his campaign was a big part of her decision to leave. She didn't want to try to sort through those complicated feelings tonight. "Okay, my turn."

"Don't you need to get some rest before going on air again?" His teasing tone stretched across the miles.

"Not a chance. Speaking of job changes, how do you go from television news producer to captain of a paddlewheel riverboat?" She stood, stretching her legs for a moment.

"Hmm. Long story short? I needed a change too."

"And ..." Tara smiled. Maybe a little too short.

"Tybee and Savannah are my comfort zone. I wanted something that wasn't so much behind the scenes."

"Why not try for an on-air job, reporter or anchor at KSAV?"

"Not enough change." He paused.

She'd crossed the line. Too personal.

"I minored in drama in school. I enjoy acting. Cap'n Mike gives me a chance to show off a little, make people happy. Another eye-patch gig came open at the Pirate House. Also fun. Not many roles for a one-eyed man."

"But can't they replace your eye? With the right makeup, hardly anyone would ..." She googled *artificial eyes* while talking.

"It's not that simple. I'm the one living with this. Don't you think I've checked into the solutions?" His words were clipped and hurried.

"I'm sorry."

Was she trying to dictate Micah's future? Wasn't that exactly what she hated about Clay?

"Yeah. We'd both better get some sleep. See you on TV."

"Good night, Micah. All my love to Fannie and your family."

"Good night."

Tara switched off the overhead light and fumbled across the small room to her bed. Her eyes were wide open as she recalled how upset Micah sounded. Were all chances of getting to know him ruined?

Lord, forgive me. Help me make things right. Please continue to protect all of us from this storm. Amen.

* * *

"Micah. Come quick." Fannie ran into the breakfast nook from the living room. "Dirty Sally reached Savannah."

Micah placed both palms on the table as he stood. Sally had regained strength over the ocean. Outside his parents' back window, the awning over the patio whipped wildly.

"The wait is over." Tara spoke from the television over the fireplace.

"Hurricane Sally, now a category three storm, made landfall north of the outer islands." She swallowed and closed both eyes briefly.

Micah knew the on-air personalities tried to protect the locations of their homes. Viewers wouldn't detect the pain in her face when she talked of Tybee Island.

Fannie was glued to the screen as she stroked Nikki's soft fur.

"It goes without saying that residents are advised to stay in their shelters. High winds will be shattering unprotected windows, felling trees, and tossing unsecured debris everywhere. Be sure to charge your electronic devices for as long as possible. If power goes out, you will want to communicate and to hear our broadcasts via livestream. We will continue with our regular programming and break in when conditions warrant. Do you have anything to add, Andy?"

Tara's male counterpart repeated much of the same message but concluded with a promo.

"Tune in at the regular time for national news, and you might even spot a familiar face." He winked at Tara.

"Be safe, Savannah."

Micah detected a hint of fear and something else in Tara's eyes as they signed off. He knew the pasted-on smile from experience with Brooke. Real feelings were always broadcast through the eyes.

"There she is, Jeannie. See?" Fannie tried to turn a sniffing nose and pointy ears toward the television. The Corgi was not interested.

"So where is this new neighbor of yours from?" Mom lifted her coffee cup from the side table near her chair.

"Arkansas." Micah walked to the back door. Should they be boarding things up here?

"She's lovely." Mom turned toward Fannie.

"Isn't she? It's kind of hard to get used to someone besides Brooke on the screen, but Tara is a real peach." Fannie winked at Micah and headed toward her coffee cup on the kitchen counter.

The silence in the room was deafening. He could count on one hand the times Brooke's name had been mentioned within his hearing since the great move to New York.

"Yes." Mom walked by him and patted his arm.

The implied suggestion came loudly through his mom's familiar touch. Did no one understand why he couldn't give his heart to another television personality?

* * *

"We have watched your reporters in the driving rain, wind blowing metal roofs as if they were cardboard, beautiful historic trees shattered on the ground." The polished anchor on the

Washington, D.C., affiliate paused during Tara's interview. "What's the general feeling among Savannahians as this storm continues crashing in?"

Tara blinked to regain her composure.

"Cynthia, I've only been a part of this community for a short time, but I can already tell you they are among the most resilient folks I have ever met."

Julian nodded from his spot to the right of the camera, giving her a thumbs-up.

"Savannah's unofficial nickname has long been Dodge City because she is seldom hit head-on by hurricanes. This time, all the preparation, all the prayers, have been put to the test. The citizens of the Hostess City are holding tight, waiting for the opportunity to help each other. Sally has been rough, but our weather team reports she's weakening and may bounce off the coast before dissipating in the ocean. Then the real work will begin."

Her mind filled with the view from Nina's second-floor deck. Would she ever see it again?

"I hear the National Guard is mobilized to assist." Cynthia nodded.

"Yes. We are most concerned about the islands. Power is out, and there is only one way to reach the people there. I've requested permission to ride with the guardsmen when they're able to travel out to Tybee Island. The current plan is to go tomorrow." Tara folded her hands on the desk to keep them from trembling. What would she find when she arrived home? What about Micah's place? Or Fannie's?

"We'll look forward to that report tomorrow. The prayers of the Capitol City are with you, Tara. Oh, and one more thing."

Tara touched the headset that transmitted Cynthia's voice. Wasn't this interview over yet?

"A friend of yours from Arkansas happens to be here."

"Hey, beautiful."

Tara's eyes widened as she recognized Clay on the monitor.

"We are super proud of you. When I heard you were

representing your little station on the national news, I asked to say hello. Be careful out there on the disaster scene, okay?"

"Hi, Clay." Were they on national television right now? "Thanks, buddy. I will be careful."

The cameraman's right hand drew a line across his throat. Thankfully, the *cut* signal. She turned to her right, happy to see Andy was taking a break. She'd never hoped no one would watch the broadcast, but how should she react to that surprise? Removing her headset, she stepped down from the anchor desk. Leaving the brightly illuminated set, she headed down the hallway to her dressing room retreat. How much longer would she be required to stay here? She needed sleep if she planned to be on camera for an on-scene report from Tybee tomorrow.

Lord, prepare me for what happens in the morning.

* * *

Micah found his phone on the nightstand near the bed he'd slept in before leaving for college. He wasn't surprised by the power failure notification from the front porch camera at his house. He'd expected as much after high winds assaulted the power poles on the island.

He pulled up video of the last images recorded. Rain pelted the camera in huge sheets, then stopped as if someone had turned off a faucet. Was that Fannie's house? The view he saw every day looked wrong. A huge piece of chain-link fence was missing. Water lapped against the porch railings. The camera shook as high winds rocked it.

He stood from his bed as a scene from a disaster movie unfolded in front of him. A wave that would have challenged the most experienced surfer rolled up the walkway between the beach and his house. White caps rushed by, overwhelming the underpinning of Fannie's foundation. With a great shudder, the porch crashed to the ground. Then darkness.

Nikki settled on the bed next to him. Micah collapsed beside her and focused on the ceiling.

His hands shook as he plugged the phone into a charger. Old instincts kicked in. The television station needed this video. With the power off, emergency personnel must reach the residents of Tybee. He saved the last images he'd viewed. Sending this to Tara would be easy, but showing it to Fannie would be one of the toughest things he had ever done.

"Cap'n Mike." His sweet neighbor poked her curly graying head through his open bedroom door. "You missed it. Tara on television, with a cute congressional candidate from Arkansas. On the national news. Maybe she'll get a great network job after this."

Of course. Fannie was excited for their new friend's opportunity without realizing that Micah was reliving Brooke's betrayal. More importantly, Fannie was oblivious to the crushing news about her house. Roller coasters shouldn't be allowed to operate during a hurricane. Did Fannie say Tara was on television with her beau from Arkansas?

Seven

❦

"I'm sorry. The Guard will not allow civilians on this initial trip." Mr. Landers entered the open door of Tara's dressing room early Sunday morning. "They can only reach the islands by boat. Once they know the bridge is safe, we can send cameras and reporters. That could be later today, or tomorrow."

"Understood. My contact, Captain Billings, is waiting for approval from his higher-ups. He'll let me know when he hears something." She picked up her phone, locating the stream for Fannie's worship service. She'd find someone to help her cast the livestream onto a larger screen. Maybe worship would calm her nerves until a visit to the island could be arranged. She'd never enjoyed waiting.

A text from Micah appeared.

> Hey. What's up?

> > Still a lot of waiting.

She hadn't expected to hear from him after the way their last conversation ended.

> I have something you can share about Tybee if you want.

> Really?

Her heart fluttered.

> Brace yourself. It's the last video my front porch cam recorded before the power went out.

> Do I want to watch it?

> View it as a professional.

A rather strange comment.

> Okay.

Totally nonprofessional tears streamed down her cheeks as she watched a wave devastate Fannie's yard and front porch. What else happened after the camera stopped recording? Micah didn't have a camera that showed Tara's house. Would it still be standing?

She watched three times before responding. *Be professional.*

> Thanks. I'll pass this along.

Texting was so impersonal. Why hadn't Micah called her? Walking the line between her personal and professional life was not easy. She walked to the restroom near her dressing room. Time to compose her face before showing Mr. Landers this video.

Could she act like a professional when John K. escorted her to view her beloved Tybee tomorrow?

Be near me, Lord Jesus. It's all up to You now.

* * *

Micah followed the familiar scent of frying bacon to Mom's kitchen. Rain pelted the windows at the back of the house with a gentle but persistent swish.

"Is that what you're wearing to church?" Fannie greeted him from her perch on a stool next to the kitchen island.

"I don't ..." His feeble excuse died on his lips. Fannie had viewed complete devastation in his video less than thirty minutes earlier. Her response was to apply makeup and don the nicest outfit she'd brought from the island. How could he justify hiding here while the others ventured out in the storm? Fannie would label his reaction with one of her favorite "boomer" expressions. *Cop-out.*

He remembered the last time he'd attended church services with his parents. God had allowed him to survive cancer, arranged a new life in Savannah, but what good had it done? On that first visit after Brooke left, he'd felt abandoned. He was a disappointment to his old friends, his parents, and himself. Worship was hollow.

Tara's text arrived with a soft notification as he closed the bathroom door behind him.

> I want to go to Tybee so bad. I almost can't stand it. Mr. Landers says I can catch a ride with the National Guard this afternoon.

Micah stared at the phone for a solid thirty seconds. His video was one of many the station had received from the island. After watching the replay of last night's interview with the D.C. station, he assumed she was preoccupied with moving on to her next opportunity. Maybe even with the future congressman who surprised her on-air. Could she possibly be looking forward to the work of rebuilding after a hurricane, of staying in Savannah?

Be safe. Nothing you can do to change things right now.

His fingers typed the text almost before his brain engaged.

Suddenly, her safety was all that mattered. He needed to get himself together, and he needed help from the One who could calm the storm.

Lord, I have spent too long kicking at the pricks. Help me follow the path You've placed before me. Help me.

A glance in the mirror revealed a lone tear drifting down his cheek. Is this what he was wearing to church? Nope. Time to clean up and prepare for whatever was next.

* * *

"Wave at the camera." Fannie nudged Micah from his right and pointed to their left.

He gave a Cap'n Mike salute to the camera. The young man standing in the pulpit greeted their online viewers and said the next song was selected for those on the Savannah coast.

"Master, the billows are raging ..." The old hymn swept through him with all its accompanying drama. Micah willingly followed its rise and fall. Whoever wrote this song must have lived through an actual storm like the one the disciples faced before Jesus famously calmed the sea. "Peace, peace, be still."

"Why *do* bad things happen to good people?" The minister began his sermon. "Our text today includes the thoughts of Peter in his first letter, as well as the experience of the apostles in the book of Acts. Perhaps we can study this for a moment and realize that, like Job, we can begin seeing our misfortunes as an honor rather than a punishment."

Micah sat up, facing forward. If there was ever a message he needed, this was the one. *Okay, God. You got me. I'm listening.*

Scripture and song meant specifically for him continued. As the worshipers exited, Micah stopped Fannie before she left the sanctuary.

"Could you stay here with the pups for a few days while I go check things out at home?"

"Honestly? I may have a new home." Fannie turned away,

facing the front of the room. He followed her gaze to the huge cross displayed in the window behind the baptistry.

What would he find on the island he loved? Would he and Nikki have a place to return to? Time to find out if his new neighbor would come alongside him in his journey. Most of all, would they become more than neighbors, more than friends?

* * *

Tara pulled up the livestream of Fannie's worship service on her phone. No use trying to display it on a larger screen. She desperately needed this worship experience, but the events of the day hadn't permitted a quiet moment to truly engage. She scanned through the replay, stopping when the camera panned back to show the congregation waving.

This certainly was a friendly congregation, even greeting their online worshipers. There was a familiar smile attached to an elderly curly head. Amazing that Fannie's spirits were so high. Had Micah not shared the terrible video? Was that Micah sitting next to her?

There should be enough time to listen to a hymn.

"Master, the billows are raging." The voices of the congregation emphasized the drama in the old song. Tara fought back tears. Emotions ebbed and flowed as the words reminded her of Jesus's power over the storm. "Peace, peace, be still."

She closed the live stream and scanned her text messages from Mom and Nina. Their habit was to attend early worship service, followed by brunch at home. A phone call would be much better than texting.

"Hi, Mom." She craved the calming voice on the other end.

"Are you still okay, sweetheart?" Mom's words were quick.

"Is that Tara Denise?" Nina's voice carried from the background.

"Yes, I'm fine. Still safe in my bunker." What should she say about the condition of Nina's house? Nothing. Because that's what she knew at this point.

"Your smart brother figured out how we could watch your broadcasts," Mom said. "We are all so proud of you. The whole community is buzzing up here and lifting prayers for Savannah."

"Thanks, Mom. The community will have quite a bit of recovery work ahead, but so far, the damage in the city is not terrible." Again, don't mention the island.

A knock on her dressing room door was followed by her boss's head popping into the room.

"No rush," Mr. Landers whispered, waving his fingers.

"Mom, I don't have long," Tara said. "I needed to hear your voice."

"Honey, please know that we all love you, and God is with you. You are in Savannah for a reason. I am certain." Mom was always fond of Esther's story. "Remember, that's where Nina met your Gramps, and where I found the love of my life."

Tara knew her stepdad was in the room, and sly winks were exchanged.

"Yes. I feel at home here. The people are great." Tara swallowed the lump in her throat. There were changes ahead, but staying put was the best plan for now. "I hope to be back on Tybee soon. I'll let y'all know what the house looks like." Would she be all alone in a damaged house? Would Jeannie ever come home, or would she be better off staying with Micah's family in orchard country?

"Okay. Hugs and kisses." Mom's traditional sign-off made Tara smile.

"Bye." She walked to the hallway, finding Mr. Landers nearby.

"Your friend Captain Billings will meet you and a cameraman at the Tybee bridge in an hour. He reassured us he can have you back here before it gets too dark. Still no power out there. You ready?"

"Of course." Another hour? Couldn't she go now?

Julian waved at her from his makeup studio. "Come on, girl. You need to look like you mean business for this trip."

* * *

"You made excellent time, Cap'n Mike."

Micah's navigator from the Georgia Queen shook his hand as he prepared to board the much smaller boat docked between Savannah and the outer islands. Steady rain pelted them, sometimes directly in the face.

"I've made that trip before. Thanks for letting me tag along." He waited for his friend to board, then untied the rope holding them to the dock and jumped in, settling himself on a box filled with first aid supplies.

"The bridge should be fixed soon, but the Red Cross is unsure what might be needed out there. They can use any and all able-bodied help today."

Motor noise prevented further conversation as they headed across the debris-filled water. Micah was happy to volunteer, but his heart pounded as he considered what he might find as he neared the home he loved. Fannie had been more than glad to delay her first view of the damage. Her confident wave as he left his parents' house revealed what a trooper she really was.

His heart was not filled with the same peace. Not yet. He couldn't stand the way his last phone conversation with Tara had ended. Defensive, childish, even whiny were all descriptive of the way he'd responded to her suggestions for his eye condition. Quiet contemplation during worship convicted him. He was hiding behind this eye patch, using it as an excuse to cling to the status quo, abandoning all thoughts of pursuing the acting career he'd wanted. Could he make her understand his new resolve to follow God's plan for his life? Would she be willing to accompany him along the journey ahead?

Jim's boat bounced over a wave, spraying Micah's cheek. He'd never imagined being grateful for hurricane damage. Would this adversity be what he and Tara needed to come together? With God's help, his vision was now clearer than ever.

* * *

"Tara." John K. Billings jogged toward her as she closed the passenger door of the station's SUV.

"Hey, stranger. First time I've seen you in any kind of uniform in a while." She tied the hood on her rain jacket before accepting his strong hug, conscious of the videographer's hesitation as he approached.

"Yeah. My wife laughs at me. She thinks working as a firefighter should be enough excitement. But until she's finished with her nurse practitioner program, I'm spending a lot of time on my own, and you know I don't do well sitting still." He held her at arm's length. "You ready for this?"

"Of course." She waved at the young man standing a few feet away. Soft rain moistened her face. "John K. ... I mean Captain Billings, this is Boyd Jensen, photographer for KSAV. He will be telling the story of what's happening on Tybee."

"John K." The guardsman offered his hand.

"Boyd." The photographer jostled his equipment on his hip.

"Okay, you two can ride up here." John K. opened the large door and ushered Boyd into the back seat and Tara into the front of his oversized pickup truck, its enormous wheels towering beneath them. "The advance team says the bridge is secure, but we may have to splash through some massive puddles."

"I understand we'll be passing out supplies?" Tara turned to examine the cargo space behind them.

"Yeah. The Red Cross loaded us up with bottled water and other things. We'll do what we can." The truck started with a roar and lumbered toward the only access to the island.

Tara stopped worrying about her hair blowing all directions as the massive truck sped down the partially flooded road. Julian assured her that everything would fall back into place when the camera lights illuminated her face. Besides, looking rumpled would communicate her dedication to giving a real impression of the recovery effort on the island.

Her hand flew to cover her mouth as familiar sights emerged on either side of the road. So many trees were uprooted, pieces of roofing and other trash littered the roadside. As they approached the business district, people stood outside the boarded-up buildings, busily stacking debris in huge piles.

"Okay. Let's try to help a little." John K. stopped the truck, and the photographer seated behind Tara filmed as guardsmen handed bottled water to the people lined up outside a church building.

"Tara, do you want to interview one of these people?" The photographer turned off his camera and opened the back door, following her with an umbrella.

"Great idea." Time to put on her professional face. She stepped down and approached a man standing near the church doors. "Hello, sir. Could you spare a minute to talk to our viewers?"

"Nothing better to do, I guess." The man removed a baseball cap, running his hand through his hair. The videographer folded the umbrella and faced them from two feet away.

After the interview concluded, Tara peered down the street toward her favorite coffee spot, a few restaurants, and gift stores. They were not close enough to view the damage to Fannie's place. She wasn't too eager to get to that point, honestly.

At the next two stops, the photographer took the lead, pointing out places that would provide backdrops for on-the-spot messages from Tara. The first few were recorded, but as the time for the evening news drew near, she gave her live impressions to Andy, who manned the KSAV anchor desk. The live spot involved waiting on the perfect cue, which was picked up from her earphone connection with the director. She concentrated on the photographer, keeping her smile and encouraging attitude in place. No one wanted to hear desperation in her voice. This was all about highlighting the can-do spirit of the Tybee residents who didn't evacuate.

"Okay, missy." John K. helped her back into the passenger seat after the live interview. "We'd better get you back to town before it gets too dark. Only a few have generators out here, so it might get spooky in a bit."

Spooky? Tara bristled at her friend's assessment. This was her home, not a stop on Savannah's ghost tour.

"Actually, if you don't mind, I'd like to continue toward the beach. My house is down there, and I haven't returned since the storm." She caught the attention of the photographer, who nodded his approval. "It shouldn't take long."

"You got it." John K. used the truck's radio to relay the change in plans.

Without the prospect of another work-related report, Tara's eyes misted and leaked the closer she got to the turn toward the beach and Nina's house.

"Stop here. I'd like to walk for a bit, by myself." Her throat clogged with emotion as she searched for Fanny's missing fence and wind machines. Only piles of sand and mud stood between their truck and the front door. Metal roofing waved crazily in the breeze, and fallen palm trees blocked access to the living area.

To her left, Micah's house had weathered the storm better. Piles of sand rested against his stairway, but climbing to his door was doable.

She trudged through the muck toward the walkover leading to the beach. The stairway blended with the dune. In a few seconds, she found her footing and peered into her backyard.

Only the outlying shed was damaged. Extra sand and tree branches adorned the second-story deck. A huge sigh escaped through her lips.

"Thank you, God." She blinked back tears and stood a moment longer. If only Jeannie were here, she might sleep in her bed tonight. She could do without electricity. But staying in an empty house, all alone? She rested against the walkover railing. *How long will I have to do this by myself, Lord?*

Light raindrops moistened her eyelashes. Time to return to work.

"Need an umbrella?" A familiar deep voice warmed her ears. Strong arms surrounded her, holding the offered implement to her side.

Her heart pounded as she turned to gaze into Micah's face. "How? What? Where?"

"Typical journalist. So many questions. Let me speak for a minute." He pulled her close, gazing into her eyes. "You don't have to do this by yourself. Remember, I am an expert at storm recovery. Even if your latest exploits lead to a bigger and better opportunity, I'd like to come along for the voyage."

She waited, her pulse picking up by the second. His lips met hers tenderly, then more earnestly.

"I don't plan on going anywhere. I've found my home." She returned his kiss and melted into his arms.

"Tara," the photographer shouted from the end of the street. "Are you coming back to the station?"

A gentle sea breeze ruffled her hair and moistened her cheek.

"I'm about to miss my ride back to work. What about the dogs and Fannie?" As much as she wanted to stand here forever, reality was smacking her in the face.

"There will be a few more trips back and forth to my folks' place. I've got to get my Nikki and your Jeannie back home. Fannie may or may not want to come with me. Will you be here, or do you have someone waiting in D.C.?"

"What? Of course not." The laugh that escaped her lips lightened her heart even more. One more conversation about a certain congressional candidate from Arkansas might be required.

"Give me a minute." She stepped back and shouted to Boyd and John K. before leaning close to Micah. "I've got to go back to work tonight, but I'd love to spend tomorrow night in my house, with or without power. Can you help me get things shipshape?"

She searched that steady, sturdy face, enjoying the glimmer in his eye.

"Cap'n Mike at your service, my lady." Micah executed the ridiculous sweeping bow that had drawn her attention that first rainy day.

She barely waited for him to straighten before capturing his face in her hands.

"I'm ready if you are." She kissed him firmly, relishing the roughness of his beard against her cheek.

"Let the billows beware." He held her at arm's length. "The storms of life have no idea what they're facing."

"Amen, Cap'n Mike. Amen." Tara's bright smile was probably visible from the other side of the Atlantic.

Author's Note

"I can do all things, through Christ who gives me strength." (Philippians 4:13 NKJV)

When our son's job as a television news producer took him from Northwest Arkansas, to Orlando, Florida, he said he went from being a big fish in a small pond to being a goldfish in the ocean. We were thankful he found a home at the television station and then found love with a sweet young lady who was raised in Central Florida.

When my husband and I drove from our home in Arkansas, through Alabama and across Georgia, we were captivated by the beauty of the farms and orchards and then by the historic intrigue of Savannah. Rich in history and welcoming to visitors, a week-long visit was only enough to whet our appetite to spend enough time to learn more.

Tybee Island was not crowded when we visited during the hot, humid summer. We would love to go back to soak up the peace.

Jeannie is inspired by memories of our sweet Corgi, Sophie. Her herding instincts and short, always churning legs kept us constantly in awe of her energy, even as she grew older. Our home has not been the same since she left us.

"Away in a Manger" is a favorite old hymn of unknown origins. The third verse was first seen in 1892 in a collection by Charles H. Gabriel.

"Master, the Tempest is Raging" is a hymn written by Mary Ann Baker in 1874.

About Jenny Carlisle

Jenny McLeod Carlisle retired from a 35-year career in HR with the State of Arkansas to fulfill her dream of becoming an author of Christian fiction. Scrivenings Press published the three-book Crossroads series in 2022, 2023, and 2024. This novella, like the one included in the collection *A Gift for All Time,* features characters from that series.

She and her husband and traveling buddy love nothing more than adventuring with or without their three married children and eight grandchildren. A road trip through the orchard country of Georgia to historic Savannah and Tybee Island captivated her, and she can't wait to return to immerse herself in Southern culture and cuisine.

At home in Arkansas, they worship with a community-oriented congregation of the Church of Christ, where they are members of the JOY (Just Older Youth) group. Jenny's favorite volunteer role is as a Journey Partner for Women Equipped, Christian Job Corps.

Scrivenings
PRESS
Quench your thirst for story.
www.ScriveningsPress.com

Stay up-to-date on your favorite books and authors with our free e-newsletters.
ScriveningsPress.com